OF SKY & SEA

THE WINTER WARS
BOOK 1

K.M. MOHR

Cover Design by Bewitching Book Covers

Map Design by Luan Bittencourt

Winged Siren Logo Design by K.M. Mohr, created on Canva

Interior Designed with Canva

Formatted with Atticus

Editing by me myself, and I editing services

ISBN: 979-8-9994275-0-2

ISBN: 979-8-9994275-1-9

To the ones kept inside boxes,
the ones who've lost their way.
Whose voices have been stolen,
and made to feel smaller
and less than you are.

You are worth so much more than you know.

You are strong.

Never stop fighting.

For Stephanie

CONTENTS

CONTENT WARNING

<u>Proceed with caution.</u>
Before you enter the world of Lorralei, please be aware the themes contained in this book <u>are sensitive and intended for adults 18 years and older.</u> Please consult the full list of content warnings before reading further. Your mental health matters. You matter.

Sensitive themes within this book are as listed below:

Abasement
Adult language
Animal death (horses)
Attempted sexual assault
Bodily mutilation (including corpses)
Child brutality (including death, endangerment, and mutilation-*off page*)
Consensual sex
Dismemberment (including beheading)
Disturbing images
Excessive gore
Forced proximity
Gaslighting
Manipulation
Mental health issues (including panic attacks and thoughts of self-harm)
Mention of human trafficking
Mention of off-page sexual abuse
Mention of off-page pregnancy loss and maternal death
Off-page sexual assault resulting in death
Racism against a fictional race
Violence

PRONUNCIATION GUIDE

(listed in alphabetical order)

People

Faei – Fay (Faerie Queen, queen of Kaival)

Miran – Meer-an (Amasian spy sent to protect Seraph)

Nikolei – Nih-koe-lie (Amasian spy sent to protect Seraph)

Seraph – Sair-aff (the Child of Sky and Sea, under Aurorian's protection, ward of Amasius)

Venyx – Vee-nicks (deymon, hired protector of Seraph)

Wynnix – Win-nicks (the Winter Sprite, former lover of Queen Faei)

Part One

Ace – Ace (owner of Ace's tavern in the Northerlands, friend of Aurorian)

Aidra – Ai-druh (grandson of marauder chief, Cleya)

Cleya – Clay-uh (marauder chief)

Aurorian – Ah-roar-ee-an (unicorn, guardian of Seraph and ambassador to the mortal realm)

Sheila – Shee-luh (barmaid at Ace's tavern in the Northerlands)

Part Two

Delthia – Dell-thee-uh (an old friend of Venyx, owner of an inn in the Northerlands)

Lira – Leer-uh (an old friend of Venyx, works in the Braided Beard)

Layne – Lane (deymon, in the party that picks up Seraph)

Nyall – Nye-all (deymon, in the party that picks up Seraph)

Tollok – Tall-lock (dwarf, an old friend of Venyx's and owner of the Braided Beard in The City)

Part Three

Aluk – Ah-luke (Plains warrior escorting Seraph)

Atani – Ah-tah-nee (General of the Pensian army)

Calian – Kay-lee-ahn (Plains warrior escorting Seraph)

Geaith – Gay-ith (Queen of the Plains)

Kishil – Kih-shill (Plains warrior escorting Seraph)

Makya – Mah-kee-uh (Plains warrior escorting Seraph)

Mato – Mah-tow (Plains commander escorting Seraph)

Nibowin – Nih-bow-win (Chief of the final Plains village)

Nuka – Noo-kuh (Plains warrior escorting Seraph)

Patama – Puh-tah-muh (Prime Minister of Pensen)

Veyla – Vay-luh (deymoness, second Commander of the White Army)

Wiconi – Wih-cone-ee (Wife of the Plains village chief)

Places

Abaddon – Aa-buh-don (fallen kingdom where deymons are from, abandoned)

Amasius – Ah-mah-see-us (Northern country, known for their produce and armed forces, largest supplier of black-market information in the world)

The City – The Sih-tee (the largest settlement and only city in the Northerlands)

Denpendae – Den-fin-day (Northern country, home of the northern elves)

Dracon – Drah-cone (Northern country, historic homeland of dragons)

Kaival – Kye-vall (Northern island country, where Faei rules and Wynnix is kept)

The Northerlands – The Nore-thur-lands (stretch of ungoverned wintry land above the Northern countries, where Seraph is hidden)

Pensen – Pehn-sehn (legendary city-state in the northern hemisphere, lawmakers and upholders of the world)

The Plains – The Plains (Northern country, grasslands)

Siila – See-luh (capital city in the Plains)

Sirenia – Sir-in-ee-uh (Southern country, home of half-mer-people, Seraph's homeland)

Other

Amasian – Ah-mah-see-ahn (peoples from the country of Amasius)

Deymon – Dee-mon (ancient and powerful race of beings, formerly from Abaddon)

Lipfaseai – Liff-uh-see (western ocean bordering Kaival and Pensen)

Lorralei – Lore-uh-lee (the world in which the story takes place)

Pensian – Pehn-see-ahn (peoples from the city-state of Pensen)

Sirenian – Sir-in-ee-an (mer-folk, mostly refers to half-bloods)

Tabeto – Tah-bee-tow (a god believed to have abandoned Lorralei)

Vampyre – Vam-pie-er (cave-dwelling, blood-sucking creatures)

long ago, by Faire queen's hand
the lover Winter met his end.

he tried to flee to right his wrong,
she held him still within her bond.

on fields of war blood freely rained
until the bonds of love war claimed.

but on the wing of seraphim flew,
and from the depths of oceans blue,

did the promised Child bring
the song of hope the world would sing.

-prophecy of the child of sky and sea

Part One

Of the Lost

ONE CENTURY BEFORE

S TANDING IN A VALLEY laden with snow was a tree. Once green and thriving, long since petrified by frost, it remained a towering husk of its former self. Branches eaten by vengeful ice, leaving nothing behind but stumps and a memory.

Its massive trunk groaned and creaked beneath the furious howls of a cold, raging wind.

Through the many layers of the ghostly palace, a woman walked. Ignoring the pummeling winds outside, she climbed the stairs, jade gaze cast to the floor, fury upon her rigid shoulders. Salt from the roiling ocean clung to her skirts, her senses. Already, she missed it. But the war would not be won by walking a pretty beach.

At the top of the staircase hugging the belly of the tower was a hallway. Stationed at the opposite end stood a pair of guards in white, one hand on the shafts of their spears, the other on the grips of their swords. The Faerie Queen barely glanced at the men as she fumed past, bursting through the warped doors they stood sentry over, and stormed into the throne room beyond.

In its curiosity, the fuming winds died down. A wight-like creature peered between the columns on her right as Faei's furious steps clicked across the floor. As she passed through the illusion of a wall, the specter vanished in a whirling flurry of snow.

The Faerie Queen knew he followed. She did not care. Not today.

Inside her rooms, she glanced at the map laid across the desk, her snow-white curls bouncing with the movement, eyes lined in a spackling of tears. From her study she carried on, down the little corridor to the second door. Her private chambers.

She wanted for nothing but solitude. For none to bother her. For the warmth of the blazing fae fire to seep into her bones and banish the wintry touch she fought to keep. Even still, snowflakes tapped the windows. The swirling vortex of a face peered in at her. Wraith-like hands further frosted the glass as she finally opened the door to her bedchamber.

Faei stopped.

The hinges squeaked as the warped door tapped the wall behind it, swinging to a stop as the Faerie Queen stepped further into the room that *had* been her bedchamber. Wherever she was now, she did not know.

What she did know was it smelled of age. Of time. Of a deeper kind of magic than she was familiar with. Aside from, of course, that of unicorns. Vile things.

There were no windows. No glancing upon the miles and miles of pristine white valley. No mountains in the distance. No snow. No cold.

A wooden floor creaked beneath her steps as an unnatural warmth enveloped her, vastly different from the twinge of frost lingering just beneath the licks of flames that clung desperately to the corners of her room.

The wooden walls were lined with shelves. Bookcases towered on opposite sides of the room, standing sentry over the open space, creating an aisle down the middle toward a counter filled with curiosities. Before her, Faei found more curios staring back.

Perched on the wooden ledge was a globe holding a butterfly, fluttering as if alive. Sat next to it was a silver crown, molten, tinged with soot and ash. An embellished *R* engraved into the metal.

Lips pursed in curiosity, Faei reached out.

"Those are not for touching."

The Faerie Queen snatched her hand back, eyes darting around for the disembodied voice daring to order her about. It was human, older and feminine. Though for all her searching, the source evaded her. It seemed to come from all around, and nowhere.

"I am the Faerie Queen, Faei, of Kaival, and you have stolen me from my palace," Faei growled, gaze combing the little wooden shop, searching for the speaker, the root of the power skirting along her skin.

"You have not been stolen," the voice said, curling with a smile. "You are still here. And yet ... not."

"Wh—"

From behind the counter came a woman. Twined together were her delicate hands, time-eaten, riddled with wrinkles and age spots. Faei's gaze traveled up the woman, past her gray-laced golden hair, pooling down her shoulders, to the weathered face. A smile pulled at thinning lips. Her own jade eyes landed on pure white ones. Blind.

The woman stepped forward. Faei held her ground, chin tipped up.

Simply from looking at the woman she knew this aged thing was the source of the magic that tinged her flesh, made her own power feel so very inadequate.

"Who are you?" Faei demanded, calling forth her magic. When it did not come, she looked, surprised, down to her hands, screwed up her face, and called again, fingers forming claws as if she could tear it from her very being. Still, it did not answer.

"I believe you will find your gifts nullified here," the woman said. "This place exists outside the time you know, and so does not adhere to the laws of our world."

A furious scoff jumping from her lips, Faei's head snapped up. Something like fear flashed through her being, though she resisted its pull against her face.

"I do not come to harm you, Faei," the woman said, "but to bring you a gift."

7

"Damn your gift! I want nothing from you!" Faei roared. "Return me to my home!"

"Oh, but you will want this," the woman said. Faster than Faei could track, she latched onto the Faerie Queen's wrists, pulling the smaller woman toward her until the two were flush, her warm breath fanning Faei's face.

A shiver ran down Faei's spine, through her limbs, diving into the depths of her heart.

"Find the Child of Sky and Sea, Queen Faei, and your love shall again be yours," the woman whispered, her voice so soft the Faerie Queen was reticent to believe she had heard it. "When blood of the Child coats your hand, all this world shall be your land. Fail, dear queen, and pay the price, for on faith of love this Child flies."

With a furious roar, Faei reeled back, snatching her hands from the woman. She stumbled, catching herself, blinked, and was once again standing in the middle of her chambers. Her heart hammered as she looked about, chest rising and falling rapidly.

The fae fire in her hearth had been snuffed. The balcony doors open to allow a flurry of snow inside, coating the room.

Faei spun in a circle, but found herself alone.

Something akin to fear and hope filled her chest, the mingling amalgamation of emotions warring inside her.

It appeared she would be waiting for the next Descent.

ONE

G OLDEN SUNLIGHT CUT THROUGH thick clouds. It bathed my face in a semblance of warmth. Casting blinding blades off the unbroken surface of snow laid before me, forcing my already exhausted eyes closed against it. It only made me more tired, though I couldn't sleep. Regardless of how hard my body tried.

It was there, somewhere between awake and asleep, I relived that day on the beach, the last time I saw my home. The last I remembered of it.

To a five year old girl, cheeks ruddy and tear stained, feet covered in sand and her heart heavy with grief, the word *destiny* is too big. Somewhere just inside my dreams that little girl stood, waiting to be saved. I longed to go back, pluck her from the folds of time and plop her somewhere she could never be hurt again. But the destiny that came for her bound us both.

One life for all the world didn't seem fair. Then again, that one life was mine.

My horse snuffled, pulled me back to the present, and I realized I'd been dozing off again. I must have been teetering out of the saddle, because Miran's gaze warmed me, just like the sun's touch.

He held the reins of my horse along with his own. Remnants of the last time I'd fallen asleep. My horse had gotten too excited and tried to run off. I'm sure I would have fallen before she made it far, but it would have made little difference. She'd have her freedom.

My gaze slid sideways to Miran, to the halo of flaming curls beneath his hood, and his ice-speckled beard. Thin lines of worry etched between his brows.

"You gonna keep yourself awake, Seraph?" he asked as he pulled my horse closer. I nodded sleepily, even while my eyes drew closed with fatigue. He returned the nod, though it was half-hearted, as if he didn't quite believe me. *I* didn't believe me.

"Just tie her to the saddle already," Nik commented from the rear. The mound of lilac hair stuffed into my hood shielded him from view, but I knew the expression on his face. That stupid grin every time he made a joke. I rolled my eyes, only making them more tired. Which prompted a wide yawn. Increasing the worry on Miran's face.

I tossed a crude gesture over my shoulder. A pleased, rumbling chuckle was Nik's response.

Ahead, rising from the expansive white horizon, came the first signs of a building. Upon first sight it was a meager cabin jutting up from the snow, a thin tendril of inviting smoke curling from a singular chimney. But the closer we drew, I realized how wrong my initial view was.

The cabin wasn't meager by any definition. It sprawled across the snow with different wings and rooms branching off the center while a series of chimneys rose from the angled, slatted roofs. The whole thing stood five or six stories high.

My mouth fell open, taking in the sheer size. It was easily the biggest building I'd ever seen. Certainly larger than the Amasian safehouses I'd grown up in.

"Where are we?" Nik asked, voicing my thoughts. I glanced at Aurorian in front, leading from the saddle of her horse.

"An old friend's," was her reply. I knew at once that was the only answer we were going to get. Miran sighed in frustration, his shoulders sagging.

"Is your friend king of the Northerlands?" Nik asked. Aurorian didn't answer.

A stable sat attached to the main building by a single roof, almost as big. A few stable hands ran out as we rode up. One of them took Aurorian's reins as she slipped elegantly into the snow and shouldered her pack. Another took both Miran's and Nik's while a third waited for me.

Of course, I'd ridden horses before, but I'd be lying if I said I was the best at it. Not to mention it had been months since the last time I'd been on a horse, and I wasn't sure how long it had been since I'd ridden so long. Between all these things, I could already tell my legs were sore. It would be painful to drop down, and I'd likely end up ass-first in the snow for my trouble.

As carefully as possible, I swung one leg over, then dropped, a small amount of comfort filling me as Miran's hand pressed into my back, holding me up. Warmth spread across my face. The stable hand looked as if he'd seen any number of horrid dismounts, and mine was no different. Somehow, that didn't help.

Aurorian was already leading the way to the front of the place when Nik walked up beside me, chuckling. "Thought Miran would have given you plenty of *riding* practice already," he snickered.

"Go fuck yourself," I spat, eyeing Aurorian ahead, making sure she hadn't heard.

Nik huffed. "My hand *is* the best I've ever had." He grinned, raising one brow as he gazed sideways at me.

"From what I've heard, it's still disappointing," I shot back.

A hand flew to his chest, mouth falling open. "That hurts, Seraph."

"Keep your nose out of my business, then." Trudging through the snow, I caught up to Aurorian, leaving Nik and Miran behind. "What *are* we doing here? Are we not going to Amasius?"

She turned to me, stopping just before the door, her pale blue eyes sparkling like sapphires in the rising light of the new day. The gold and

11

silver hair tucked into her hood glittered, looking almost molten against her fair skin.

"We're here to get someone," she said. My brows pulled together and I glanced at the Amasians, slowing as they approached.

"Someone else? Why?" Nik asked, looking between us.

"Who?" Miran added.

Aurorian flicked her gaze toward them before it flitted to me. She said nothing before pulling open the door.

A wall of warmth and the smell of food barreled into me. I turned toward my escorts, the same blank confusion lining their faces.

A draft of cold air followed us in, though was quickly vanquished by the blazing hearth in the far-right corner. I blinked several times as the door closed behind me.

The room was large, though smaller than I expected, with a smattering of tables occupying the space. Most were empty. In the center sat a massive square bar, a wall of bottles every shape, size, and color behind it. From where I stood a single barkeep worked it, though it sounded as if another was on the other side. A small cluster of people sat at the far corner, wrapped in chatter amongst themselves. They didn't look up when we walked in.

Aurorian tossed a glance over her shoulder before she crossed to the bar and pressed into its edge, pulling the barkeep's attention to her. They exchanged hushed words and the woman swiftly left the room.

"Since we're here, I'm getting a drink," Nik said and walked away. Soft light from the hearth bounced along Aurorian's hair as I approached, wedging myself between her stool and Nik's. Miran's warm presence stood at my back.

Aurorian turned to us, her pale blue eyes flittering between Nik and Miran. "The man we're here to get," she started, drawing their attention. "Don't engage him. I don't care what he says, what he does. Do *not* engage him. Understand?"

They both muttered a shallow, "Yes."

It was another few moments before a man as tall as Nik walked around the bar. He had a thick, graying beard and a balding head. His middle was round while his arms were strong and hefty. Aurorian rose and strode toward him, and his wrinkled face broke into a grin as he threw his arms wide. A twinge of jealousy gnawed at my gut when Aurorian returned his smile and allowed the man to wrap her in an embrace.

"Auri!" he growled, pulling her close. She returned the embrace, her arms wrapping around his neck. "It's been too fuckin' long." He gently set her down and took a step back.

"Far too long," Aurorian replied, her smile persisting. "You've gotten old."

"While you ain't changed a fuckin' bit," he said, his belly jiggling as he laughed. "What the fuck brings ya all the way out here?"

Aurorian stepped aside, and his gaze slid to me. The first time people saw me, there was always a moment of hushed awe, as if they couldn't quite believe what they were seeing. He had that look on his face. His mouth went slack, green eyes wide. One hand rose to his head, stroking the sparse hair there before his gaze drifted back to Aurorian.

"I see," he said.

Aurorian drew a breath. "I'm here for him, Ace."

He took a long breath and slowly exhaled. The smile fled Aurorian's face all at once.

"Let's sit for a tick." He walked to a table nearest the hearth without waiting for an answer. Aurorian followed, the slightest lines creasing her delicate brows. Reluctantly, I trailed behind, my escorts in tow. Nik sat beside me while Miran remained at my back.

Ace dropped into a chair with a grunt and rubbed his knees. "These damn things ain't making life no easier," he grumbled. "Course, you don't have'ta worry 'bout that."

"I don't," Aurorian said. "Venyx?"

It sounded like a foreign word, a curse by how Ace flinched. It took a moment to realize it wasn't some exotic language—it was a name.

"He ain't right, Love," Ace said, shaking his head. His green eyes looked up forlornly, staring at Aurorian as if it were just the two of them. "He ain't been right since you was last here."

Aurorian drew a thick breath, held it, and heavily exhaled, tapping her fingers along the surface of the table. "What did he do?"

Ace opened his mouth, scratched his beard, as if debating whether to answer, before his large hand slapped the table and his gaze dropped.

"Some bloke come in, talking shite like they do. You know the type."

"I do."

Ace nodded. "Sayin' stupid shite, how deymons ain't good for nothin'. They's all for Kaival." He ran his hand along his balding scalp again. "He broke the man's jaw, Auri. He was drunk, couldn't barely stand. Couldn't talk worth shite, and he broke a man's jaw. Took six of us to get him off. He nearly killed one of us in the process."

"Seven hells," Nik muttered. He passed a look to Miran and slid from his chair.

"How long ago?" Aurorian asked.

"Couple months."

Aurorian nodded.

"I don't know what you want him for, Auri, but he ain't right. He can't stay here no more, though." Ace waved a hand around, his eyes dropping to the floor. "He's scarin' off all the customers. Ain't no one comin' here when there's a mad, drunk deymon runnin' round, breakin' men's jaws."

"Where is he now?"

Ace stabbed a thumb over his shoulder. "In Sheila's corner. Been there the last few weeks. She's the only one ain't terrified of him."

As I rose to follow Aurorian, I glanced at Miran and Nik, hissing words back and forth before the hearth.

"Aurorian," I called, her name rushing out. She stopped, turning toward me. The Amasians at my back fell silent. "What are we doing? Why are we here for ... for one of *them*?"

Her gaze bore into me, mouth forming a tight line.

"Does Amasius know of your little detour?" Miran spat. Her gaze flicked to the spy.

"We're under orders to-" Nik started, but a glare from Aurorian silenced him.

"Auri," Ace called. "You comin'?"

Aurorian took a breath, squaring her shoulders. "We're here because we need him," she began, gaze flickering between the three of us. "You may be under Amasian orders, but do not forget Amasius is governed by Pensen. And I do my business with them. Not your king."

"That's not good enough," Miran said. He stepped around me, coming nose to nose with Aurorian. "Why the fuck are we here?"

Without another word, Aurorian turned and joined Ace.

"This is bullshit," Miran snapped.

"What the fuck is she doing?" Nik asked.

Gnawing on my bottom lip, I pushed past them and followed Aurorian. With a growl and a sigh, my guardians followed.

TWO

THE ROOMS ALL BLURRED together before we came to a stop. Bright sunlight streamed through a series of windows on the far wall, muted from frosted glass. Behind the bar stood a short, plump woman, drearily polishing mugs and wiping down the countertop. We filed in and she looked up, the quick peek of hope dying at Ace heading our line. Then her eyes found Aurorian.

"You!" she shrieked, coming round the bar, stabbing an accusatory finger in Aurorian's direction.

"I tol' her, Sheila," Ace grumbled as he eased himself onto a stool. "She's come to take him."

The woman's brown face grew red with fury. "It's about fuckin' time! I've had it to here!"

"I'll send money for the damages and troubles once I'm able," Aurorian said.

"That ain't necessary, Love," Ace spoke.

In the same instant, Sheila shrieked, "Best make it double!"

Stepping to the side of the bar, I spotted a single figure slumped over a table, loosely gripping the handle of a mug. Any sign of the form's face was hidden behind a swath of dark hair and writhing shadows. He either didn't hear the screaming, or was unconcerned by it.

Deymons were rumored to be immortal. I'd been told they were hideous, with glaring red eyes and long fangs able to tear out throats. Their strength was supposed to be that of ten men, and they were said to have speed so great it was impossible to see them move. Claws sharp enough to slice through flesh and bone alike. At first glance, there were no claws to speak of.

"I already told Ace, either he goes, or I do!" Sheila screamed. "I ain't doin' this no more! He's been demanding dwarven whisky all week! You ever give a mean, drunk deymon dwarven whisky?" Her question was aimed at Nik, who, unfortunately, had taken a seat at the bar just as she walked behind it. He reeled back, clearly regretting his choice. I stifled a peal of laughter at his expression.

"Can't say I have," he mumbled.

"If I don't give it to him, he tears the place up. But if I do, I gotta clean his mess anyhow!" She threw down her rag and placed both hands on her full hips. "Thank the seven fuckin' hells he stopped fuckin' the barmaids! You know how tough it is to get new bedding all the way out here?"

"I understand," Aurorian said. "I'm sorry for the trouble he's caused, but I'm taking him with me."

"I want him gone now, Auri!"

"Just ... let me talk to him," Aurorian said, hands up defensively. She walked around the bar to the table with the single form, easing into the chair across from him. Nik slid from his stool and joined me and Miran as we walked around the other side, curiosity piqued.

Aurorian slipped the mug from the form's hand and set it upright, leaning forward. Soft snores emanated from the slumped figure.

"Venyx," she whispered. He stirred, something like a grunt rumbling from his throat. "Venyx." His hand, the one that had been holding the mug, lay flat on the table as he sat up and rubbed the other along his face, still cast mostly in shadows. He muttered something inaudible before slapping his palm on the tabletop.

"Sheila!" His voice was deep, riddled with sleep and spirits. "I asked for whisky, not this shit." He waved absently toward Aurorian.

"Nice to see you, too," Aurorian said. He grunted again and his head fell forward with a dull thunk. "Venyx," Aurorian said again. The deymon lifted his head.

"Aurorian," he mocked.

Sighing, Aurorian leaned back and crossed her arms over her chest.

Venyx leaned back, too, and rubbed his face again. "Sheila!"

"Sheila won't be serving you anymore."

"The fuck she won't. Sheila!" He rose shakily to his feet, stumbled over the chair and caught himself on the table, as if on the deck of a ship in a storm.

His gaze landed on the three of us, flickering silver in the dim light. Like those of a wolf I'd seen once between safehouses. I had looked into the beast's eyes, and it had simply stared back. I guess I had been too skinny to eat, for it had carried on without a second glance. That was the gaze peering at me now.

"What the fuck are you staring at?" he asked, stumbling closer.

"Venyx," Aurorian said, causing him to turn precariously to face her again. "I need you to come with me."

"*Need me.* Fuck you, Aurorian. I *needed* you," he snarled before turning away. The deymon stumbled toward the bar, toward us.

As one unit, Nik and Miran moved in front of me, pressing me into the bar, their solid bodies a wall between me and the deymon. Between their shoulders, the deymon's eyes flashed red, and I cringed backward. My heart thundered as the deymon took Nik by the scruff of his cloak, hauling him off the floor, despite Nik's towering height.

"Move," he growled before shoving Nik aside.

"Venyx, that's enough," Aurorian called, sounding far away through the blood pounding in my ears.

"Sheila!" the deymon called, leaning around Miran's tall, broad form. He reached toward me before Miran snatched his wrist and shoved him back. The deymon stumbled, unsteady on his feet, a low growl emanating from his throat.

"Miran," Aurorian warned.

My breath caught in my throat as I blinked and the deymon appeared before Miran, eyes blazing soft red. Nik jumped up and kicked a leg from beneath the deymon, one hand going toward the mop of black hair hanging about the deymon's angled face. He dodged backward, ducked beneath Nik's arm, and stood, throwing the Amasian into the bar, knocking the wind from me as our bodies collided.

I stumbled over Nik's feet as he turned, reaching up for his sword.

"Shit," someone spat. So focused on the unfolding scene, I didn't see who'd spoken.

Nik drew his sword, Miran following suit. "I don't want to hurt you," Nik said, sword loose at his side.

"Then you should have kept your blade sheathed," the deymon growled.

Nik and Miran sidestepped the deymon, corralling him between them.

Venyx turned his attention first toward Nik as the Amasian flipped his blade around his hand, readying his stance. The deymon reached underhand to his back, grasping at air.

"Nikolei, sheath your blade," Aurorian warned, voice low. "Miran, sheath. Now."

The deymon jumped forward as Nik swung up then down in a wide arch. A killing blow. Nearly too fast to see, the deymon snatched Nik's wrist from the air, yanked his arm down and thrust the blade back, wrenching it from Nik's grip in one fluid motion before he reared back and landed a boot square in Nik's gut, sending the spy sprawling to the far wall, head slumped to his chest.

With a roar, Miran swung his sword up and down in a sharp blow, the steel edge clanging against the deymon's stolen blade before the deymon spun the swords together, ripping Miran's from his hand, the thing falling to the floor with a clang. Venyx grabbed a handful of Miran's red curls and slammed his head into Miran's face, sending the Amasian to the floor.

Slowly, the deymon turned toward me, red eyes dropping to the blade at my feet. For a moment I was frozen, stuck like a deer in those eyes, torn between the desire to flee and the need to protect myself, before I jumped forward and grabbed the weapon. What chance I stood, I didn't know. He'd just disarmed and disabled both my Amasian guardians within moments.

"Seraph, don't you dare engage him," Aurorian said somewhere behind him. My gaze flicked from the shadows where Aurorian stood to the deymon, tightening my grip on the sword. It was heavy, already straining my arm.

The deymon stepped closer, his red eyes still glaring down at me; the sword he held perked up, as if eager for spilled blood.

"Venyx, leave her alone," Aurorian said, reaching toward the silver cylinders at her waist.

"Drop your sword," the deymon growled.

"You first," I breathed, straining to keep the fear from my voice.

He smirked, one fang pressing into his bottom lip, and jumped toward me, sword aloft. Mine rose of its own accord, vibrations rolling down my arm into my back and clear into my legs as our blades met. I uttered a squeak, from shock or pain I didn't know. He drew back, flipped the sword over his hand and moved to strike again.

Aurorian jumped between us, one cylinder in her fist, the blade shooting out to block his blow. She kicked one of the deymon's feet from beneath him and took a handful of hair on his way down, slamming his face into the bar. He slumped unconscious to the floor, the sword clanging beside him.

I blinked back my shock, a smattering of tears in my lashes catching the dim light of the fire. My chest heaved as I took in the deymon at my feet.

A groan pulled me from my thoughts. Aurorian spun around, casting a furious glare as Miran slowly sat up and shook his head, sending his curls flying.

"When I give you an order, I expect it to be followed," she spat, kicking the sword toward him. Aurorian walked toward me, snatched the sword away and pinned me with that same glare before she crossed the room to Nik and tossed the sword at his feet. Groggily, he looked up at her before succumbing to a coughing fit.

"Alright, folks, shows over," Ace cried, clapping his hands. It was then I noticed the crowds gathered in the doorways, peering in on the brawl.

I swiped the tears from my eyes, my cheeks, with the back of my hand and cast a look at the deymon again, at the hair splayed across his face.

"Get up," Aurorian growled, kicking at Miran's boot. With a groan, he pushed himself up and sheathed his sword.

Along the wall, Nik coughed again. He tipped his head back, brown curls falling from his face before he got unsteadily to his feet.

"His room the same?" Aurorian asked.

"Sure is," Ace said, sipping from a mug.

She pointed at both Miran and Nik. "It'll take both of you to carry him up."

"Can we have a moment?" Miran asked.

"Can you follow an order?" Aurorian countered, her gaze pressing him into the bar. He turned away from her, sapphire eyes cast to the floor. "Get him up. Now."

Nik lumbered across the room, sheathing his blade along the way.

Trembling, I watched them heft the deymon up, groaning beneath his weight.

"Seven hells, this fucker's heavier'n he looks!" Nik complained.

Miran grunted as if in agreement.

"That way," Aurorian said, pointing through the nearest doorway. As the two Amasians hauled the deymon away, Aurorian stalked back toward me.

"You are not a soldier, but you are still under my command and will do as I say," she said, her voice a mere whisper as she towered over me. "Do not engage him again. Do you understand?"

"Yes," I breathed, my blue gaze flicking across hers.

She turned on her heel and stormed after the Amasians. I spared a glance to Ace and Sheila, huddled together behind the bar, whispering amongst themselves, before hurrying after Aurorian.

A small shelf stacked with books sat against one wall. Most were tucked in neatly, more still piled atop the others. I ran a finger over the spines of some of them, marveling at all the different languages I didn't know. Some I'd never even seen.

Miran and Nik groaned, heaving under the deymon's weight as they dropped him onto the bed. For a moment they stood, talking with Aurorian. Or rather, while Aurorian scolded them again. My attention drifted back to the bookcase.

I pulled one of the tomes from its spot and let the pages fall open in my hand, running a finger along the elegant script. It looked elven. I snapped it closed, slipped it back into its spot and picked another, this one in the common tongue. A book of legends from a place called Abaddon.

The book fell open in my hands, and I skimmed the page. It was toward the end, where one of the corners had been folded over, though it was riddled with similar markings. The first sentence that caught my eye mentioned something called *the Last Princess of Abaddon.*

"Seraph." I started at Miran's voice and snapped the book closed. "Are you coming?"

I looked between him and Nik, then to Aurorian and, finally, to the unconscious deymon.

"We're going to get something to eat," Nik added. I slid the book back and went to the desk in the corner. Atop it sat a stack of clean parchment alongside a quill with a stoppered inkwell.

On the floor, leaning against the wall, was a strange holster, the sheaths hung upside down. Slightly curved toward the tips, the twin blades ran straight into the hilts, flush to the grips and up to the rounded pommels. Elven swords. I longed to draw them, to see the blades, feel the leather gripping. Like the clothes he wore, along with the ones scattered across the floor and hung over the chair, the swords were black.

"Seraph," Miran repeated. I looked back over my shoulder where he and Nik hovered by the door, their large bodies filling the small space.

"I'll be down shortly," I said, giving no room for argument. Miran's brows creased, his lips pursing in the midst of his reddish-brown beard.

My gaze flicked to Aurorian before she turned to the deymon on the bed.

"We can't just let you wander around alone," Miran said.

"I'll be fine."

He grumbled, but conceded and he and Nik filed out, closing the door on their way.

Aurorian sighed, easing herself in the chair along the wall, her gaze pointedly facing away from me. In that moment, all the timelessness of her face, the unnaturally smooth planes and ethereal beauty, faded, leaving behind a woman far older than any living creature should ever be.

She pulled the long, straight locks of gold and silver hair over her shoulder, running her long fingers through it, appearing, for a moment, very mortal. She could have been any woman my age, a meager twenty-five years old. Not the thousands upon thousands of years I knew her to be. Not a unicorn. Not one of the greatest warriors I'd ever known. Not the only mother-figure I'd had outside my childhood. Just a woman.

"You said we came to get him," I blurted. "Why?"

"Why what?" she asked, still turned away.

Ah, yes. Her gift for evading answers by pretending she didn't understand the question. An old tactic. Once upon a time, it had worked. When I'd been a child.

"Why are we here, Aurorian?" I pressed. "Why, of all the people you must know, are we here for a deymon? Why the sudden move to Pensen? Why any of it?" My voice rose steadily as I spoke, the lump in the back of my throat surprising me. Still, I forced my words up around it, beating back the emotions welling in my chest.

"There are things in this world you are better off not knowing, Little One," Aurorian whispered, dropping her gaze to the floor as she uttered an endearing name she hadn't used in over ten years.

"Maybe not, but this is my life," I spat. "Perhaps it is promised to others, and perhaps it was never really mine. But it is still my life, and I still have a right to know what is happening with it." I took a breath, hoping she would answer. Instead, she set about picking at her trousers, at some invisible thing caught in the fabric. "Decades, you'd said. Decades before I would need to uphold this damned prophecy. Before I would be required to go to Pensen. Before I would have to sacrifice my—" I stopped and took a breath. "Why now?"

She took a breath, opened her mouth, and exhaled in silence, her delicate brows pulling together. "It has come to my attention there may be a leak in the Amasian court."

All at once, the ground dropped from beneath me, sending me into a spiral as the room tilted. My breath came in great, heaving gasps as I stared at her.

"I do-don't understand," I stammered, moisture filling my eyes.

"There's little else I can give you, because I have nothing else to give," Aurorian said, facing me.

"Kaival found me?"

"No." She stopped, took a breath. "But they might know where we were."

My mouth gaped, opening and closing like a fish as I fought for composure, for air. Spots swam before my eyes as the room spun. I reached out, steadying myself on the wall and sank into the chair before the desk.

"How do you know there's a leak?" I forced out, afraid she wouldn't hear the whispered words.

"I know nothing for certain," she said. "Only that it is highly possible."

Licking my lips, I forced my gaze up to her, taking in the smooth planes of her face as the timeless mask slipped back up. "How are we going to get to Pensen if Kaival knows where we are?"

She nodded toward the sleeping deymon and I couldn't help the peal of laughter that ricocheted from my throat, filling the room.

"I know he doesn't look like much now, but given a few days—"

"And how long has he been like this?" I asked, unable to stop the anger from curling my words.

She looked down, leaned forward and laced her fingers together.

"Right," I whispered, following her line of sight to the polished wooden floor. "So you mean to march me across the whole of the Northerlands with naught but two Amasians, yourself, and a single drunken deymon." It wasn't a question, and she didn't answer. "Knowing we could be attacked by the White Army." I pushed up to my feet, staring at her as I crossed the small space.

She looked up beneath her lashes before turning away. Pulling my bottom lip between my teeth, I nodded and left the room, fighting the urge to slam the door.

For a long moment I stood there, staring down the darkened hallway. At shifting light, I looked up. A series of skylights lined the ceiling, open to the milling, gray clouds and the snow as it fell. The glass was crystalized from years of cold, giving the appearance of being underwater. Fitting, since I suddenly found myself drowning.

THREE

COLD PERMEATED THE ROOM when I woke the next morning. It clung to the swath of blankets I huddled beneath, to the polished wooden floor, sending shivers through my being as my feet touched down. I hurriedly stood, shoved my boots on and bundled into my warmest coats, teeth chattering through the motions.

Aurorian lay in bed, completely still. The only sign she slept was the gentle rising and falling of her chest. I'd once heard an Amasian use the phrase 'sleep like the dead' and had immediately thought of Aurorian, wondering if all unicorns slept so eerily peaceful.

Though I knew she wouldn't wake through all my rumblings, I still tiptoed about the room, tying my hair into a braid. The lilac locks had never truly been fond of cold. They seemed less so here, where the frigid air turned the long tresses frozen and brittle.

Outside our room, the hallway was empty. A strange stillness hung about that hadn't been there the previous night. Before, people had milled about, laughter and chatter filling the halls and rooms, voices hanging over my head like the cold now lingering about my feet and hands. This early in the morning, there was nothing.

I felt like a wraith descending the steps, every boot print lumbering and loud, haunting in the thick silence. It wasn't until I ventured further into the emptiness that I found sounds of life, of workers setting up for the day. Stuffing my icy hands in my pockets, I approached the bar as the women worked, idly chatting as they went about their duties, oblivious of my existence, at least until I cleared my throat.

Mustering my softest smile, squinting my eyes to hide the ocean lurking in their depths, it was still disappointing when they both stopped, their voices falling to the floor as their jaws went slack. The person I'd nearly felt like the previous day was gone in their awed stares.

"Good morning," I said, hating the softness of my voice, the timidness balled up in my chest. "I was hoping to get some food."

"This way, darl," Sheila's voice rang out. I turned toward the sound, stretching my smile across my lips at the women before following the older woman.

She waddled through the doorway into the adjoining room and I trod behind, the stares burning into my back until long after the threshold swallowed me.

Sheila quickly took her place behind the bar, setting a tea plate before me and clutched a teapot in her hands. "Cook's already got going for the day, so it shouldn't take but a moment," she said. "Bacon, eggs, and spiced potatoes if ya care to know what's fer breakfast this mornin'."

"Thank you," I squeaked out.

"Be right back." She walked from behind the bar, disappearing around the corner before her footsteps vanished into the great silence of the giant tavern.

Running a finger around the rim of the plate, my gaze drifted up and roved the room. Like the ones the previous day, the walls were hung with weapons—maces and swords and axes and bows—some large enough to question what kind of being hefted them. Turning on the barstool, my eyes followed the deadly decor until they landed on a pit of shadows in the farthest corner, and I jumped at a flicker of silver hidden there. The longer I looked, the clearer he became.

Licking my lips, I rose and took the tea setup, tiptoeing across the room like approaching a beast, the plate held close to my chest as if it might protect me.

I pulled out the chair across from the deymon and sat down, the plate and all its things rattling as I placed it on the table. The deymon raised a forkful of food to his mouth, his movement slow, methodical, as he took a bite and lowered his arm. Aside from a flicker of silver in my direction, he didn't acknowledge me.

Somehow, the silence felt thicker, more ethereal, sitting across from him as he silently ate, ignoring me. It made me question my own existence, so used to the stares and gawks and questions. Even the Amasians took a couple days for the shock to wear off, for my presence to become normal. For them to realize I was just a girl.

The deymon across from me was unfazed. Or he simply didn't care. It was equal parts humbling and refreshing.

"Oh, hun!" My head snapped up at Sheila's voice as she shuffled across the floor toward me, one hand grasping a plate laden with food, the other holding a pot of steaming water. "You ain't wantin' to be sittin' there. Let's get you another table, yeah?"

I smiled up at her, adjusting in the chair, making a show of staying where I was. Regardless of our rough start, I was going to be traveling a long way with the man—deymon—across from me. Best to get acquainted now.

"I'm fine," I said. Her brows pulled together before she sighed in resignation and placed the heaping plate of food before me.

"He gives you any trouble, let me know and I'll toss him out," she whispered.

"She sat at my table, and you want to throw *me* out?" rumbled the deymon.

Sheila's gaze snapped up. "You could pretend you don't hear so good," she spat before waddling away.

The smell of hot, fresh food filled my nose as I turned from the barmaid to the plate, my mouth watering at the sight. For a solid moment, I considered that I was dreaming. The plate before me would vanish with the next blink and I would wake in the safehouse to cold, thin sheets and a bowl of barely warm porridge. But as I placed the first bite on my tongue, the potatoes melted in my mouth, sending shivers of pleasure through me. My eyes closed and I sighed in contentment.

Another few bites and I remembered the hot water.

I looked up as I fixed a cup of tea, my eyes adjusted to the shallow pit of darkness. The deymon's plate was still half full. He took his time, waiting several moments between each bite. Then again, with as long as deymons were said to live, he could take as much time as he wanted.

The deymon blended seamlessly into the cool embrace of thick, writhing shadows, aside from the silver flickering in his eyes. And the sharp outline of his face. Dark hair hung past his shoulders in desperate need of combing.

"It's not polite to stare," he muttered between bites, sending a swath of heat to my cheeks. I dropped my gaze to my plate and shoveled in another bite.

"I'm sorry," I finally said. "I just ... I've never seen a deymon before." How I hated my soft, meekness as I spoke.

In his own, deep, grumbling tone, he replied, "I've never seen a prophecy before. Suppose we're even."

The heat in my face vanished, migrating to my gut. I dropped my brows, a sneer curling my mouth at the flickering silver as he eyed another bite.

"I am a person," I spat.

He stopped, fork halfway to his mouth, those strange eyes meeting mine. "And I'm not?" And carried on eating.

The color drained from my face as I buried my gaze in my plate, pushing the food around, pretending to search for a suitable bite. But as I stared, my own judgement stared back. I'd done to him the same thing everyone I'd ever met had done to me—treated him as less than a person.

"I'm sorry," I squeaked out, though he gave no reply. No indication he'd heard me at all. After a moment, I returned to eating, sipping my tea already tinged with cold. An uncomfortable silence settled between us, though the awkwardness must have been mine alone. He'd sat himself in shadows, in silence, for a reason. Chose to ignore my presence for a reason. *I* had invaded *his* breakfast.

I cleaned my plate far sooner than I liked, only stilling myself from licking the remnants of yolk because of the deymon sitting across from me. Still, he wasn't done. It looked as if he'd only eaten half of what had been there when I first sat down. Had only touched his own teacup twice. The liquid inside must have been nearly frozen, but he sipped from it regardless. Unbothered.

It seemed rude to seat myself at his table uninvited and then leave and so I lingered, scanning the walls above, taking in every detail of the weapons adorning them. The grain of the table before me. It was worn in places, cracked in others, made me think the wood was older than I was.

After growing bored, I plucked my fork from the plate and gazed upon the smooth silver finish, the embellished engravings on the handle. The three tines showing their age in the slight dents, the scrapes and scratches along the metal's surface. Over and over I turned the thing, examining every inch of it. Ran a finger along the edges.

Another moment and the deymon's hand shot toward me without warning and snatched the fork from my grip, slamming it on the wood beside his plate, silver eyes glinting red in the dark.

"That's mine," I snapped.

"Then don't be so loud," he growled.

"Don—?" I stopped, the word falling halfway formed from my mouth, before realization struck. He'd heard my fingers on the fork, my skin running along the metal as I'd turned it over in my hand. My mouth fell open in awe as he daintily placed another forkful of potatoes on his tongue. "Is that one of the gifts deymons have? Keen hearing?"

He sighed, shoulders rising and falling with the sound, and his eyes slowly lifted to meet mine again.

"I just want to eat in peace."

I gulped. "I'm sorry."

"Don't be sorry. Just ... be quiet." He licked his lips and returned to his food.

I leaned back in the chair and crossed my arms over my chest as he chewed, as his jaw worked. Had he ever bitten his tongue with his fangs?

"Thought we established staring is rude," he grunted.

I took a gulp of air, stopped the words from spilling out of my mouth, before barreling onward anyway. "What did Aurorian promise you?" I asked. His hand stilled. "To get you to agree to come? You seemed adamant yesterday about not going."

He sighed again, dropped his fork, and looked up. "This is likely to be among the last hot meals I have for a while," he growled. My brows pulled together. "I want to enjoy it in silence."

"I ju—"

"Let's get something straight, yeah?" He pushed the plate away and sat up, the broadness of his shoulders standing out against the darkness enveloping him, as if he chose when the shadows surrounded him. "We are not friends. I am not like your Amasians. I was hired to take you to Pensen. This is business, nothing more. Let's keep it that way."

For a moment, I simply stared at him, at the rigidity of his body, the stiffness of his shoulders. And those silver eyes. "Okay," I finally said, my voice weak.

He nodded and returned to his meal, or the remnants of it, and I was forgotten. Dismissed.

Sucking in a stiff breath, I pushed up from the chair and walked away, not bothering to look back at the deymon, or at Sheila, regardless of her gaze burning into my side as I left the room.

Wandering the empty halls and rooms, not a soul in sight aside from those few setting up for the day, I was reminded of my own isolation. The juxtaposition of having never truly been alone. In the safehouses, there were always two Amasians. Always two bodies milling about, their voices filling the tiny space. The clang of their swords or thwack of their arrows as they kept their hard-earned skills sharp as their blades.

Sometimes, Aurorian was there. Hovering over me, teaching me politics and histories. Piling book after book into my lap. Why, I didn't know. My life would only go on as long as my blood was needed. Then I'd be dust. A means to an end. Nothing more. My sole purpose fulfilled. The training she'd given me, instructed the Amasians to give me, seemed useless in the face of such a fate.

The weight of that destiny settled over me like a mound of fresh powder—heavy, cold, unshakeable, and smothering.

Walking through the halls of the tavern was the closest inkling of freedom I'd ever had. No one lingering at my heels. Telling me what to read, what to eat. What to do or where to go. And so I wandered. And wandered. Gazing at all the weapons and artifacts, the stuffed skins, the tapestries on the walls. The cases filled with things from eras long gone. How long had it taken to acquire all these things?

At a case filled with bone weapons, I stopped, placed a hand on the glass, and wondered at the people who'd made them.

Four hundred years ago the Faerie Queen stole the winter, trapping the very essence of the Winter Sprite in Kaival.

Four hundred years seemed like such a long time, and yet, no time at all.

In that time, the human kingdoms had risen, taken power. Pensen was founded and became the Land of Law, the governing country of the world.

Kaival had become a force to reckon with, had stolen the nomadic deymons from the world, convinced them to lay their allegiances with its queen. Three wars had been fought against Kaival. Three times the world had called stalemate.

In four hundred years, Pensen had erected the Boundary, the thing separating the Northern countries from the South—an attempt to stop the Winter Wars from further ravaging the world, Aurorian said. So far, it had worked. But to what end?

The weapons in the case appeared far older than four hundred years. They looked one fingerprint away from melting into the dust from which they'd come. Time had warped them, yellowed the bone, cracked and splintered it. Much like Kaival had done the world. Sapping water from across the globe until it limped along, all except the Northerlands. I supposed that's why the population had boomed in the last few decades, or so Aurorian said.

But what was four hundred years to a being as old as her? Timeless. Probably as old as the world itself. I often wondered if even Aurorian knew her age. Or had that, too, been lost to time?

Gazing at those aged weapons, the danger from them long passed, I pondered my own mortality. Would I have grown to be Aurorian's infinite age? Mermaids, the mothers of Sirenians, lived notoriously long lives. And angels, well, they were angels. They didn't die. I wasn't even sure if they were truly born, or if, like unicorns, they merely existed.

My focus shifted from the weapons to my reflection, to the bright, sapphiric blue staring back at me, and the ocean roiling within. Would lines have ever graced my skin? Or would my face have remained smooth like Aurorian's? Despite the many ages.

Thick emotions boiled in the pit of my stomach, rising to my throat as I pushed away from the case and continued wandering. After a while, the rooms blurred together in a collage of wood and weapons and bars. But most of all, emptiness.

When my feet finally stopped, I turned to the doorway at my right, taking in the sight with bated breath.

The room beyond the threshold was nearly as big as the others. Inside, there was no bar standing center. No staff setting up for the day. There was simply a small gathering of well-worn furniture, a little table in the center, and a series of walls made entirely of glass.

Even the ceiling shown through, gazing upon the gray, pregnant clouds as they delivered more snow upon the open landscape. Unhindered by the frost that clung to everything else. Each sloping pane framed in a gathering of powder.

I'd never seen such a room, such beauty.

Slowly releasing my breath, I looked up and around, taking in the warmth from the burning hearth at my back, and crossed to the far wall. The glass was chill to the touch, my fingers clouding it on contact.

Sick as I was of the snow, of nothing but white, I could gaze upon this image all day. And so I sat, curled up in the corner of the largest sofa, pulled the blanket off the back and around my shoulders, and settled in, watching the world fall around me safely behind a wall of glass.

FOUR

S OMETIME IN THE SILENCE of that room, chilly beyond the blanket hugging me, I'd fallen asleep. I'd spent the previous night tossing and turning, watching shadows dance across the ceiling as if lulling me to slumber. Waiting to attack. But in this open room, where I was completely exposed, I'd slept.

A whisper of something across my face hauled me from the depths of a dreamless sleep and it took a moment to realize it was my hair being brushed behind my ear. I jolted up, everything in me screaming to protect myself, but the bright blue eyes staring down gave me pause. The smile hidden behind a reddish-brown beard stopped my panic. The tumble of fiery curls around Miran's tanned face a halo bathed in dull sunlight.

"Hey," I said, sucking in a breath as I pushed myself up to sit.

"Hey," he responded, still wearing that smile. The one that made me crumble. "How'd you end up here?"

A glance at my surroundings, at the snow falling against the glass walls, and wonderment stirred in me all over again.

"I don't know." I met Miran's eyes, studied him as he rose from his haunches and settled beside me, one muscled arm wrapping around my shoulder, pulling me into his warm side. "I just ... found it." I nestled into him, breathed in his scent. He smelled like the forest.

"I thought we talked about you wandering around on your own," he whispered into my hair before planting a kiss on my crown.

"No one was awake."

He chuckled at my lame attempt at humor.

"It's still not safe to wander alone," he said on an exhale, leaning further into me. His weight pressed against my body, smothering me with comfort and warmth, with the corded muscles lining his form.

"I can protect myself," I mumbled into his shoulder.

"Then what's the point of me and Nik?"

I drew in a deep breath, knowing he was right. Of course, he was. Miran spent a lot of time proving he was right. He was, after all, one of the most experienced Amasian spies in the field. Fourteen years and counting. There was much I could learn from him, should learn from him.

Miran brushed another lock of hair from my face before hooking a finger under my chin and pulled me toward him. I closed my eyes as his breath fanned my skin, sending shivers up and down my spine just before his lips found mine.

Roiling heat settled in my stomach as Miran pressed into me, pushing me against the sofa. His hand cupped my jaw while my fingers dug into the wild curls of his hair. My thighs fell to either side of him, savoring his weight as he settled there, his desire already pressing against me.

It'd been weeks since the last time I'd held Miran, been held by him. Had him inside me. Aurorian's presence had stoppered any stolen moments. I knew what she would say, and I didn't want to hear it. There was so little joy in my life, so little happiness, I siphoned it from wherever I could. After all, happy moments to a dead girl were more precious than gems.

At my own moan smothered under Miran's lips, I pulled away from him, shoving backward until cool air swamped the space between us and the heat between my thighs died. By the expression Miran wore, he would have gone further. Much further. But I couldn't risk it. I wouldn't let Aurorian rip this from me.

I smoothed my hair back, shoving aside the longing in his eyes. It might not seem like much to see us together—one of the spies went everywhere with me—but still.

"If Aurorian came looking for me…" I started.

He sighed, shoulders slumping, the disappointment ringing across his handsome face. He nodded. "I just don't understand why we have to keep this from her." He glanced up at me, his blue eyes dancing back and forth, as if tracing the wild waves in my own.

"She wouldn't approve. She might send you away."

He clicked his tongue. "She approves of nothing you do." Closing the distance between us, Miran wrapped an arm around me and hugged me to him, placing a delicate kiss on my lips before speaking against them. "Why don't we take our horses and go. I can keep us safe. You know that."

With an exasperated sigh, I dropped my chin, pressing my forehead to his mouth. "You'd be killed if they caught us."

"It's a big world, Seraph. They'd have to find us first."

I tipped my head back, gazing into his face, his eyes.

His thumb ran along my jaw, up into my hair, before he brushed his lips against mine. "I want to take you away from here. From this. You don't want any of it."

I wrapped my arms around his waist and hugged him, absorbing the thrum of his heartbeat. Swallowed the swell of emotions in my throat and the stinging tears in the backs of my eyes. I would never admit it to Aurorian, but he was right. I wanted to live. And it didn't seem fair I'd been born, destined to die for all the world.

The *yes* rose into my mouth, danced along the tip of my tongue. "I want to," I whispered. "I really do."

"But," he started, disappointment hanging off his voice like icicles. "Aurorian."

He sighed, pulling away from me.

"She raised me, Miran," I pleaded. "She's protected me all these years. Kept me alive, kept me safe. I can't just—"

"Can't just what?" he bit. "You're not a child anymore. And she shouldn't treat you like one."

I bit my bottom lip, staring at him. "She's the only reason I'm still alive."

He stood, shoving his hands into his pockets. "Amasius is the reason you're still alive."

"Miran, please."

He sighed, deflating all at once. "I just miss holding you. I don't want to give you up."

"I don't want to give you up, either," I confessed, curling back against the sofa.

"I know." He dropped to his haunches, took my hands and kissed each knuckle in turn. Trailed his lips up and around my wrist. I smiled knowingly as a mischievous grin curled his mouth. "Meet me back here. Tonight. After Aurorian goes to sleep."

"Here?" I peered around at all the glass.

"No one will be awake."

I chewed the inside of my cheek, biting back my smile as he used my logic against me. "Ok."

"Ok." With one final kiss, he stood and offered me a hand. "Care to go see what trouble Nik is getting into?" Smiling, I let him pull me up. The moment we passed through the threshold, my lover was left behind while my bodyguard trailed in my wake.

When we found Nik, he was at a table with Ace playing some kind of card game, the inn around us thriving. At least, as much as it was the previous day. Ace beamed and invited us to join. While I opted to merely sit and watch, Miran jumped at the chance, much to my chagrin. After losing all the money he had to both Nik and Miran, Ace threw down his cards and shoved his chair away, grumbling as he left the room.

"Not very nice of you to hustle him," I said as they counted their loot. Nik shrugged and dropped his share in his purse.

"Never been one to pass up a good opportunity," he said, a stupid grin on his face.

"And you?" I asked, turning to Miran.

"Just keeping my skills sharp," he said, pocketing his own winnings.

"You're both awful."

"That's the job," Nik said as he raised his mug.

I sighed, shaking my head. "Have either of you ever been hustled?"

Miran smirked. "I'd be terrible at my job if I told you that." His brows furrowed as he spoke, leaning sideways in his chair. Fingers playing in his beard. Biting back my smile, I playfully swatted his arm. He flinched back, laughing.

Nik flicked a glance at me over his drink as he kicked his feet up, leaning back in his chair. "I've never met anyone who can out-hustle me," he boasted.

"What makes you so confident?" I asked, one brow raising.

"I've earned it." One corner of his lips tipped up before he took another swig.

"Keep yer fuckin' shit-clad boots off my table, or I'll take all that *earned* confidence and mop my floors with it," Sheila barked, shoving his feet down as she walked by. Nik's chair tipped back, face falling as he struggled to regain himself and ended up wearing his ale. I swatted a hand over my mouth, biting back the worst of the laughter when the chair's front legs slammed into the floor, rocking Nik nose-first into his tankard.

The rest of the day dragged by. Aurorian flitted in and out of the tavern room, a constant scowl on her face. I could only imagine it was due to our recent addition, his poor attitude clearly transferring to my guardian.

Around midday, I convinced Nik to explore the tavern with me, since going off on my own wasn't likely to happen again. Round and round the labyrinthine building we went until we found a small library. As my gaze roved the titles, covered in an array of brilliant colors, Pensen again crossed my mind. Over the years, the Amasians had told tales of their adventures, including in Pensen. They'd spoken of buildings taller than the eye could see, with domed glass ceilings and books from hundreds, thousands, of years ago. The Great Library was said to be the most magnificent of them all.

It was silly, but when Aurorian came back, proclaiming we were leaving for Pensen, a bit of me dared to hope. Hope that I might visit one of those massive libraries. Hope for warmth and sunshine. For comfort and safety and people. More than just three.

I even hoped to meet another like me. People born from the sea. Though I was unlikely to find another soul with the same Divine blood I was told I carried.

Nik leaned against the shelf I examined, ripping me from my reverie. Just beyond the windows, night enveloped the world, and it was time to get back.

On the way, the spy effortlessly glided through rooms as if he'd been there for years, pointing out little things here and there he'd latched onto, guiding us back to where we'd started.

At dinner, we sat in silence near the hearth, sipping on warm ale and spiced soup. Afterward, Ace pulled out an old, discolored map of the Northerlands, and stretched it across the table. Aurorian, Miran, and Nik poured over it, discussing different routes and paths we might take on our journey.

After a little longer of sitting, as they discuss routes and trails and roads, I feigned a yawn, stretched, and headed upstairs, knowing Aurorian wouldn't question it. We'd already planned on leaving the next day, regardless of whether our newest member was ready.

Beneath the blankets, I was still in my trousers and sweater. For a moment, I worried I would doze off. My anticipation would fade and I'd fall asleep and miss the only chance I'd have with Miran for ... I wasn't sure. There might not be another time for us to be alone. Ever.

But as I lay in bed, silvery moons' light drifting across the floor, peeking through fat, fluffy clouds as they birthed more and more snow, I found sleep evasive. Between the journey ahead, the deymon we had acquired, and the whirlwind of thoughts ravaging my mind, the danger of missing my rendezvous with Miran dissipated.

It was a while longer before the door opened, bringing Aurorian's whispered steps. She made hardly a sound as she undressed and slipped into bed. Though she was the only unicorn I'd ever known, and probably ever would, I couldn't imagine the others being any less delicate, any less graceful. Even in sleep.

When I rose, tiptoeing to the door, I spied a line of light cast along her elegant face, freezing to make sure she was enthralled in slumber.

Slipping into the hallway, I crept down the stairs and into the silent common room, noting how much more eerie it was in the dead of night. In many of the rooms, the only light was cast by the dying hearths. In others, the fires had already gone out, and so the only source of light, albeit broken, faded, and weak, was that of the moons streaming through the frosted windows.

The glass room was empty when I found it. I'd been hoping Miran was already there, lounging on the sofa so I might crawl into his arms and savor every stolen moment. My heart thrummed with aching disappointment as I plopped down.

My wait was short-lived as footprints rang down the hall before Miran was there, leaning against the doorway, hands in his pockets. That mischievous grin on his face. A soft smile prickled the corners of my lips as I took in his towering form, red curls ruffled, as if he'd just run a hand through them.

"Been here long?" he asked.

"No," I responded as he crossed to me. He braced his hands on the back of the sofa and leaned down.

I couldn't stop the smile tugging at my lips as I slid my arms around his neck, pulling him closer. Our mouths moved together, my center throbbing as he settled between my thighs, one hand snaking along my waist, beneath my layers. His touch was cold, ripples of chilly pleasure racing through me. We came up for air long enough for him to rip away my sweater and the shirt beneath, leaving nothing but my thin bra. Miran made quick work of the lacings, tossing the thing away before our lips crashed together again, the kiss deepening, becoming frantic as our need grew.

Running my hands from his shoulders, I slipped them beneath his layers, over the rippling muscles of his stomach to his chiseled chest. While I fumbled with his shirts, Miran loosened the strings of my trousers and shoved them down my hips, followed by my underwear and tore them away, the cold nipping at my most intimate parts.

I fisted his hair, pulling him down, needing to taste him. Miran grabbed my chin, tilted my face up to his and crushed our mouths together. A gasp wrenched itself from me as he slid his fingers inside me, already slick with wanting, moaning as he moved his hand, my hips rolling in time. I fumbled over the lacings of his breeches before tearing the things open and releasing his hardened member. Easily the largest Amasian I'd been with, it had hurt the first time. But oh so sweetly.

He trailed his lips from mine, down my jaw and to my neck as his pace increased, my pleasure mounting, clawing its way to the surface. Tipping my head, I arched my back. Raked my fingers down his arms in time with my desperate moans. His free hand grabbed my wrist, then the other, pinning them to the sofa as his ministrations continued. On the cusp of release, I whimpered as Miran tore his fingers away and thrust himself into me. I arched against him, taking every inch, and still craved more. My moans filled the room, Miran's joining the chorus.

A guttural cry flooded my mouth as his thrusts became harder, deeper, the closer he came to release. I called his name as pleasure burst through my pelvis, my entire body relaxing and tensing all at once, tingling from my shoulders to my feet, my toes curling.

"Miran," I whimpered. He released my hands and they jumped up, dove into his hair, and pulled him down. He cried into my mouth, kissing me with a foreign passion.

42

"Fuck, Seraph," he whispered into my ear, and finally relaxed atop me.

My heart hammering, I slumped against the sofa, gasping for air.

A soft whimper fell from my lips as he pulled away. When I faced him, he was righting his trousers before running a hand through those flame-colored curls. He traced his fingertips along my leg as he settled beside me, releasing a great gust of breath, head lolling backward.

As the heat from our coupling dissipated, the chill of the room nipped at my skin, my breasts still exposed. I shivered as Miran ran a finger around one nipple, then the other, moaning as he pulled one into his mouth. His free hand trailed down, skirting along my stomach. My breath hitched as his fingers reached the apex of my thighs, still pulsing. My hips rocked up as he rubbed circles around it with his thumb, sliding his fingers back inside me.

I grabbed his hair, whimpering as he brought me to the edge of release again, thumb and fingers stroking and circling, while his mouth jumped from one nipple to the other. As I dove off the wave of pleasure, I cried his name, the sound muffled by his mouth. And as the ebbs faded, as he pulled back, I ran one hand from those rabid curls down his cheek into his beard. Gazed into the endless depths of his sapphire eyes.

"Did you want to go back to your room?" he asked, voice husky from pleasure. I shook my head.

"No." I dragged him down. Kissed him again. "I want you a little longer."

"Okay," he whispered against me. He righted my trousers and pulled the blanket over us both, tucking me against him. I rolled over and breathed in his scent, my fingers playing in the soft smattering of hair in the center of his chest. Warmth filled me as Miran pressed a kiss to my forehead, wrapping his arms tighter around me. His fingers playing in my lilac locks.

It was to the sound of his heartbeat that I drifted off.

Perhaps it was ice crystals tapping the glass. Or Miran's snoring. Maybe my dream, that same, bloody beach, woke me.

Whatever it was, I drifted up from sleep, slow at first, then all at once. I blinked the darkness away, the flames in the hearth having already died to a ghostly glimmer, indicating how long I'd slept.

However enchanting the glass room was in the day, it was tenfold at night. For just a moment the thick clouds swept apart, offering a rare glimpse of the stars. Dancing within their embrace were the twin moons, bathing the world in ethereal light. Why had it taken so long to realize the beauty of this place?

I sat up, gazing around in awe, and carefully slipped from Miran's arms. Shrugging on my shirt and sweater, I padded across the chilly floor. My breath fogged the walls as I neared.

The clouds rolled back over the moons, once again hiding their cache of gems, returning the world to shadows.

It was then something moved.

Starting, I peered into the darkness, not realizing how hard I breathed until my vision was blocked by steam. Wiping the glass, I strained against the pitch, desperately searching for the movement that, by all accounts, shouldn't have been there.

Licking my lips, I looked again as the darkness split open, spilling a cascade of silvery light from the twin moons. And, as before, there was nothing.

No sign of movement.

Not so much as a breath.

I must have imagined it.

We were due to leave tomorrow. I was simply tired, jittery from the prospect of the long journey ahead.

The clouds slowly rolled back over the snowy landscape, a thick, inky darkness filling my vision. And there was nothing.

But then...

There.

In the distance, two silvery gems stared out from that inky void, blinked, and were gone.

My heart skipped a beat, frantically pounding against my ribs as everything in me screamed something was wrong.

"M-Mir-Miran," I stuttered, his name more like a prayer as I stumbled toward the sofa, and plunged my hand onto his firm shoulder. "Miran."

"What?" His voice was filled with sleep, eyes still closed, as he responded. He shrugged deeper into the blanket, soft snores filling the room within moments.

"Th-there's something outside," I said, forcing the words past my lips. One sapphire eye popped open, peering at me from beyond a tendril of flaming curl. I glanced toward the walls, brows furrowing as only the night stared back.

Grunting, Miran pitched himself forward and stood, padding across the room. His hulking frame flexed as he rolled his shoulders. He leaned against the glass, his reflection staring into the expansive black before he turned to me. He rubbed a hand over his eyes and scratched his beard.

"Let me go wake Nik," he offered. "We'll check it out."

I turned back toward the glass, then to Miran, licked my lips as he crossed to the threshold. Bags hung under his eyes, shoulders slumped as he walked. Clearly, he was exhausted.

I suddenly felt ridiculous asking him to go out, in the frigid cold. In the dead of night. "Miran, wait," I called, stopping him in the doorway. "It was probably nothing."

Miran stopped, turned to face me.

Maybe it had been a play of shadows as the clouds covered the moons.

"You sure?"

I wasn't, but didn't want him to freeze to death. "Yes."

He yawned, stretched his arms up and overhead before he leaned to snatch his shirt off the floor. "We should check anyway. Just to be safe."

As Miran shrugged his shirt on, sharp crackling burst through the air. I turned, hair flying as I sought the source, before a wave of furious, flaming light filled the night. My eyes widened as my heart grew frantic. The wall of glass exploded, drowning Miran's scream as I was thrown back. My body collided with something solid, my head slamming back. And the world blinked out.

FIVE

"**S**ERAPH!"

The voice screamed from some far-off place; the woman it was attached to did not exist. Not when such a precious little crab scurried along the sand, begging to be plucked up.

Child laughter filled my ears and it took a moment to register whose it was. So very much time had passed since I'd dreamt this. The last good part.

"Seraph!"

No longer able to ignore the voice, the girl stood and turned, but not to the woman running down the beach. To the fleet of ships just offshore. To the little boats rowing furiously across the waters. The child didn't know why the boats were there, but the woman did. She knew this was all a dream, and I begged the child to move. To turn and run. To keep running. But she didn't. Because I hadn't. And, no matter what I did, this part would never change.

"Seraph!"

Finally, I faced the woman. Briahna. Her foam-green hair flew about her frantic, tanned face. Brilliant purple eyes roiling with an ocean that mirrored my own as she dropped to her knees and scooped me into her arms.

Too soon, the happy part, the good part, was over. I longed to go back, to exist in that space just a little longer. To chase the crabs and the birds. The surf tickling my toes. Just once more.

But we were running now, up the beach, to the village just beyond, as screams burst behind us.

Briahna covered my face with her hand, blocking my view. It didn't matter. I knew what was happening. Perhaps the child hadn't known, but the woman did.

Time shifted around us, and the beach, the sand, the surf and waves, fell away, replaced by huts, homes, buildings, as we ran.

No, please not this part, *I begged. But it would happen all the same.*

A strong hand ripped Briahna back, throwing us to the ground as if we weighed nothing, spilling me from her arms. Briahna scurried on hands and knees toward me, throwing herself between me and the woman. The woman with flaming red eyes.

I clambered to my feet, sticky tears rolling down my cheeks, as the woman moved faster than I could see, hefting Briahna off the ground.

With her last breath, Briahna turned to me, whispering one word. "Run."

I jolted awake, dragging in a smoke and dust filled breath. And cold. So much cold. Eyes still shut, my lungs rejected the air, heaving up a hacking cough, my body racking with it.

Trembling, I wiped my eyes, something sticky and thick along my face now coating my hands. I blinked. Coughed again. Glass and wood clattered around me as I pushed myself up, my gaze sweeping the area. Somehow, I'd ended up in the hallway. Where the room had once stood was now a gaping hole, flurries of snow ripping through the tendrils of smoke as it rose from debris.

As the dream slowly faded, pain set in. My arms, legs. My back and stomach and chest. Every bit of me was alight with fury, though I was so covered in debris I could scarcely find my own injury.

Another moment and the initial shock faded. Terror ripped through me as I realized the one thing not there.

"Miran." My voice was a harsh whisper as I called his name. "Miran!" I cried again, little more than a wheeze. Panic set upon my chest like an iron ball.

Slowly, I stood on shaking legs, one arm reaching to brace myself against the remnants of the wall at my side. "Miran," I said again, turning in a careful circle.

One foot before the other, I picked my way through shards of glass and lengths of splintered wood, down the hall spilling with snow. Smoke made the way hazy. The ground beneath each step crackled and snapped, grinding under my weight. In the distance, someone screamed.

My chest hammered, blood pulsing through my ears.

One of the rooms opened before me, the wall to my left missing. Tables were upturned, the floor blown away in places, leaving behind a gaping void.

More hot sticky mess rolled down my face and I wiped it away with my sleeve, refusing to acknowledge what it was.

Somewhere to my right came another scream, footsteps pounding against the floor. Icy fear shot through my veins as I neared the doorway, toward the sounds.

Boots crunched behind me and my heart leapt. I spun around, the word jumping from my mouth before I saw who approached. "Miran!" I cried, horror filling me as a man in white armor stopped, eyes widening.

The world around me tipped on its side, the edges of my vision fading.

"You can make this easy on yourself," the man in white said, "or we can do it the hard way." From his side, he drew a length of rope, coiling it slowly around his fist. My gaze stayed trained on those hands, as if they held a venomous snake instead, and spied the sword on his hip.

My hesitancy must have come across as compliance, for he stepped toward me, relief flooding his face as he pulled the rope taut. "Good girl," he said, inching closer.

Pulse drumming in my throat, in my hands, I held out my wrists, even as my feet begged to run. The soldier's mouth opened, as if about to speak.

Muscle memory took over and I struck, snatching the rope as I kicked one leg from beneath him, sending him to the floor. Diving behind him, I snapped the cord around his throat, his hands clawing as I cut off his air. Gasping, he scrambled to his feet and rammed us back, slamming me into the wall. I gasped as my head knocked backward. Shaking the dizziness away, I refused to loosen my hold, burning my palms as he fought my grip.

The soldier threw himself into my chest, knocking the air from me. Gritting my teeth, I tightened the rope further, the muscles in my arms straining against the pressure, against his strength. We slid to the floor, my feet slipping on wood and glass and snow, my hands slick with sweat, with blood. I wrapped my legs around him and pulled harder, driving into my shoulders, blinking back tears. The swell of emotion in my throat. A roar tore through me as I squeezed.

He gurgled, his hands trembling. He shook beneath me, gasping for air. When his body finally went slack, I released a gust and slumped against the wall, my arms and back and legs screaming before I kicked the body away. From the corner of my eyes, he stared up blindly.

My first kill.

Refusing to allow myself to sink into guilt, I pushed off the floor and slid the sword free. My hard-earned prize. My palms ached from the rope, from the cuts, each wound stinging with sweat against the weapon's grip.

Wiping my tears, I slipped against the still existing wall and slid to the doorway. One steadying gulp of air and I peered around the corner into pitch black. Adjusting my grip on the sword, I stepped into the dark, terrified of what I might find. Or, more importantly, what would find me.

My steps creaked along the floor, the wood groaning. Taking a breath, I stepped further into the room, aware of all I couldn't see. Behind me, the wind whistled through the gaping remnants of the wall. Frigid air played along my spine, sending shivers racing along my skin. My bare foot made contact with something solid—a chair—and I sucked in a curse, letting it fly in a strained whisper as the blade of my stolen sword clanged on another piece of overturned furniture.

Any moment I expected a deymon, or another White soldier, to jump from the shadows, to strike me down. I waited for those piercing red eyes to alight in the dark. Anxiety gnawed on my gut as, the further I went, I remained alone.

Behind me, silvery ribbons of light filtered through the threshold before being swallowed by clouds, casting me in living, thriving shadows. Somewhere outside, both far away and far too near, a beast roared. The air around me crackled. Followed by a battle cry, and the roar sounded again. The ground trembled, threatening to send me to my knees.

I took another step into the sickening darkness, and my entire body stilled as a bright ball of pinkish light ignited the writhing shadows. Behind that spark was an impish face. Smiling.

Shit.

The faerie threw the ball at my chest with the force of a solid kick that sent me hurtling into a weakened wall. I found myself sprawled on the floor on the other side, tendrils of snow tickling my nose as I fought to regain my breath.

A cough expelled itself from my lungs, followed by a blossom of pain. Sucking in breath after breath, desperate for air, I rolled to my side and wiped the sudden spring of tears from my eyes. My hand grappled in the dark for the sword, my fingers skimming it before the pink light returned, my heart sinking into my gut.

"Pretty little mermaid, lost and all alone," the faerie sang, strutting into the room, her long legs skipping over debris. She didn't wear the heavy white leather of her comrades. In fact, she wore little more than trousers and a loose blouse, long tendrils of pink hair falling elegantly about her slender, pretty face. And her eyes—bright red—shown with mirth as she raised her hand, calling forth another ball. "A fine prize for my queen," she continued in her sing-song voice.

My breath hitched as I scrambled up, grasping the sword. I raised it the instant the faerie jumped forward, closing the space between us in a single bound, the ball of light slamming down. On pure instinct, I hoisted my blade, gasping when steel hit something solid, and realized it was the glittery light the faerie held. Shoving my sword away, she reared back and kicked my chest, sending me again to the floor.

Stars danced before my eyes as the floor reached up to catch me. I blinked, staring dazedly at the ceiling as the faerie's face hovered above me. She leaned down and grabbed the collar of my sweater, hauling me to my feet as if I weighed nothing, red eyes glowing as her smile grew. A ball of pink light in her free hand. My hazy gaze flicked between her and the magic within her grasp, my limbs too heavy to move.

Suddenly, the faerie dropped me and whipped around, sending the ball to the doorway as another form rushed forward. I pushed myself up on trembling arms, shaking my head to clear my vision, and watched with bated breath as Aurorian jumped through the air, twin swords crashing down with a clang against another handful of pink magic.

I scrambled backward, frantic to get out of the way as the faerie shoved Aurorian back and jumped out of range of the silver swords before she threw a handful of light forward. Aurorian dodged the glittering ball, spun and brought one sword down, swinging directly into the faerie's aloft right hand, cleaving through flesh and bone.

A sickening scream pierced my ears as the faerie dropped to her knees, holding the stump of her wrist. Blood gushed down her white clothes to the floor where she knelt. Swift as the first strike, Aurorian brought her second blade down, sinking the silver through the faerie's neck. With a wet thump, the body dropped. The severed head smacked in the pool spreading beside it.

Aurorian's swords collapsed into the little silver cylinders with a flick of her wrists, and she replaced them on her waist. Without a backward glance, she crossed to me and extended a hand, hoisting me up.

It took a moment to regain my composure, to not topple to the floor. Once I was steady, my gaze was drawn to the dead faerie mere feet from where we stood, her sightless eyes staring up, faded to a dull red.

"Are you hurt?" Aurorian asked, her melodic voice pulling me from my thoughts, from the sight. Dumbly licking my lips, I glanced up at her, then back down, before forcing myself to find her pale blue eyes and focus on them. To see nothing else.

"I-I'm fine," I stammered. She nodded once and turned, heading in the direction I'd come from. "How'd they find us?" The words spilled out before I had a chance to stop them.

Aurorian stopped, though didn't turn to face me as she said, "I'm going to find out," and continued on her way.

A bubbling cauldron of emotions swelled in my throat at her words, my feet refusing to move. Until something wet, cold, and sticky touched my toes, sending me back to that day on the beach. When it had been Briahna's blood I'd stood in.

Battling tears, I traced my scarlet tracks before peeling my eyes away and followed Aurorian to where I'd last seen Miran.

SIX

MY VISION NO LONGER fuzzy, I took in the remnants of the hallway for signs of Miran as I followed Aurorian to the glass room. She picked her way inside, ordering me to stay in the corridor as she investigated.

"What exactly were you and Miran doing here in the first place?" she asked, her back to me.

From what I'd learned of unicorns, they didn't reproduce. They didn't crave the same intimacy I did, that I shared with Miran, with the spies before him. And so I'd never had to explain myself. As far as I could tell, it never occurred to her what happened in the safehouses when she was gone.

And so, for a long moment, I stood there, mouth gaping as I thought of an excuse. Some reason that would make sense why Miran and I would have been down here, alone, in the dead of night. Nothing came to mind before she turned around, those piercing eyes finding me and the lie poised on my tongue.

"I see," she said simply. The disappointment in her voice drove like a hot knife through my chest. "Had it never occurred to you the dangers of becoming so close to the men in whose hands your life rests?"

I swallowed thick, syrupy guilt, blinking away the mist forming in my eyes. "I just..."

She closed the space between us, her towering height staring me down. The weight of her gaze shoving me to the floor. "I raised you better than that," she said before shoving past me into the demolished hallway. I stared at her back as she walked away before trailing after her, head down, picking my way through the debris.

Near the front of the inn, another roar filled the air, startling me. Aurorian didn't so much as look up. She did, however, slow her gait, hands going to the cylinders on her waist. Following suit, I adjusted my grip on my sword, thankful I hadn't lost it.

Her back rigid, Aurorian turned just enough to raise a single finger to her lips before she crept forward, pulling one cylinder, then the other, from the holders on her hips. She flicked her wrists, and they again became swords, glistening from within.

I'd never been so thankful for the blinding light casted off the snow as it illuminated the gutted tavern. It made the shadows plunge into the corners, even while a stubborn chill hung in the air.

The next room was poised like a yawning mouth as another roar shook the ground, threatening to drop me. If I hadn't known better, I would have thought the beast was dead. Though who would have killed it was beyond my imaginings.

I rounded a corner and found a gaping hole where the front wall of the inn had stood, the corpse of a dragon laying in the snow just beyond. It was a great purple, the scales a rich gem-like color, its breast coated in thick, scarlet blood. Scorch marks lined the floor of the inn, the snow outside melted and refrozen into twisted shapes and patterns, beautiful in the growing morning sun.

The wings of the beast lay to either side, one of them in tatters. Its maw stretched open, the bones broken, angled strangely.

"What did this?" I asked, my voice little more than a whisper.

Bodies littered the floor, as if most of the battle had taken place here. Some were in white. Others not. Some of those not wearing armor I recognized from wandering the inn. One had worked here. Sickening guilt curdled my stomach.

Blood was splattered about, washing the floor. Tables were over-turned, chairs broken. Several limbs lay scattered, my stomach souring at the sight. Across the room was a head behind an overturned table. I told myself the body was lying behind it. I didn't believe myself.

A bright green light surged into the room as a faerie lunged forward, wielding two small balls of glitter. I fell back as Aurorian jumped toward the fae, swinging her blades with quick precision, one after the other, in perfect synch with the faerie's hands. As the two clashed, it sounded for all the world like a match between two sets of swords.

Whatever time I'd had to observe the fight was cut off as a solid form was thrown into me, knocking me to the floor. A mop of brown curls hung down in sweaty clumps. Nik groaned. Blood ran down the side of his face, one eye swollen. A thick blossom of bruises already lined his cheek down to his neck, punctuated by long, deep scratches.

I blinked away a stab of dizziness as I slid from beneath his uncon-scious form, reaching for my sword before finding a pair of glowing red eyes piercing the dark. I'd almost wished it was another faerie as the deymon reached down and hefted me up, throwing me back to the floor.

My teeth rattled, the bones in my back cracking, straining against the abuse. Shaking away the dizziness, I turned onto my belly and crawled for the sword, all too aware of the battle happening on the other side of the room.

A firm hand gripped my ankle, pulling me away from the blade. I rolled over and lashed out with my free foot, kicking once, twice, three times, until the deymon roared in fury, his dimly glowing eyes intensifying. While the deymon drew his sword, I turned to Aurorian, her name on the tip of my tongue, knowing she was locked in her own battle.

A roar tore from the deymon's throat as his sword flew down before Miran threw himself into the soldier, the two falling to the floor in a flurry of limbs. Clambering to my feet, I snatched up my sword and looked around as if he'd materialized from nowhere, a million questions swirling in my brain.

The deymon kicked Miran, the spy tumbling to his back before the former jumped up and swung his sword down, my Amasian protector just barely catching the blow with his own, grunting as their blades sang.

Adjusting my grip on my sword, I rushed the deymon, swinging up, pulling his attention from Miran. It wasn't for long, but long enough for Miran to kick the deymon back and pounce, straddling the deymon before he buried his blade in his throat.

As Miran stumbled back, breathless, I found Aurorian battling a deymon of her own, the faerie dead, slumped against the far wall. Within moments, that, too, was over, and Aurorian stood before another corpse, blood sliding off the edge of her silver swords before they again collapsed to their harmless cylindrical forms.

The unicorn stepped back, chest heaving.

"Where were you?" she asked, charging Miran, fury lighting the backs of her eyes. Miran stared up at her, fear blanketing his face, mouth falling open. "You just left her!"

"Aurorian!" I cried, jumping between them.

"I was sent through the fucking wall." Grunting, he shoved to his feet, meeting Aurorian's gaze head on. "By the time I came to, she was gone. I've been looking for her. So don't fucking question me."

"Time and place, people," Nik grunted as he sat up, swiping blood from his face.

Aurorian huffed, but said nothing else before she stormed out.

A clang of blades made me jolt to a stop, gripping my sword tighter as Miran shoved me behind him. Before I was able to react, a white blur rushed toward us, knocking both me and Miran to the floor, his heavy body pressing into me as a deymon sat atop him, snarling, all eight fangs on display.

I could scarcely breathe for Miran's weight as he fought the deymoness, a handful of claws driving toward him. With a snarl of his own, he grabbed her wrist and twisted before delivering a punch to her jaw, further crushing me before he kneed her and kicked her away.

Scrambling backward, I barely kept hold of my sword as Miran jumped up, drawing his blade before the deymoness was on him again. Heart pounding wildly, I dove onto the deymoness' back and drove my sword into her spine. Instead of killing her, the deymoness reared back with a wild roar, the sword ripped from her flesh as she jumped up. It clattered uselessly to the floor as she turned toward me, eyes glaring bright red.

She jumped the distance between us, driving me to the floor. A scream tore from my throat as she grabbed a fistful of my hair and pulled me to my feet, my hands clawing at her, tears spackling my eyes. The deymoness was suddenly ripped from me and I dropped, gasping for air.

With hazy eyes, I glanced up as the deymoness feinted back, dodging a blow from Nik as the Amasian cried out. Bolting to my feet, I ran toward him, though skid to a stop as another faerie, bright purple hair and green eyes, popped into the air before me.

He landed nimbly, both hands raised and filled with glittering purple light. Ducking the balls of magic, I grabbed my sword and reared back, blocking his hands with the weapon. With the balls of light, he caught the blade and spun it, ripping it from my hands, pulling me toward him.

The magic seared like fire the closer it got to my skin, burning and itching, before the fae was ripped away and thrown to the floor. I stumbled back, just catching myself, as Nik hefted a sword toward the faerie.

The fae climbed to his feet, fury lining his beautiful, impish face. "Mind your own battles, *human*," he spat. He raised one hand, a ball of glowing purple light forming. Jumping back, Nik shoved me behind him. My gaze was torn between him and the faerie, entranced as the ball shrunk, concentrated, the glitter growing brighter until it became a solid, wet-dry thing lying serenely in his palm.

Faerie dust.

The fae raised his hand, pointing it at both me and Nik, and, smiling, breathed into his palm, scattering the dust on the chilly breeze.

Nik's body went rigid, his shoulders going taut, moments before the dust hit me in the face. It knocked me back like a physical blow, sending me to the floor as I coughed and sputtered, swatting the air, trying desperately to rid the stuff from my airways. It stung my tongue, burned my nostrils and lungs, made my eyes water.

Another moment and it faded, leaving me strangely unscathed, gasping for breath. I blinked away the remnants and looked up at the faerie, at the confusion he wore before he turned to Nik, still standing rigid where he'd been. The fae's full lips curled into a malicious smile as Nik turned toward me. The dust had dissipated from his face, his hair. His eyes, however, held a purple glow as he raised his sword.

SEVEN

I GULPED A BREATH while scooting backward, my limbs sluggish and heavy. My throat went dry as Nik stalked toward me, his gray eyes unseeing. Before I knew it, the wall rushed up, pinning me there, my Amasian protector now the one who might end me.

Across the room, Miran was thrown into the far wall, the structure collapsing at his weight.

Nik kept coming. Each step slow and steady, those purple glowing eyes never leaving mine. He flipped his sword over his hand, adjusting his grip, before raising it higher, aiming for a killing blow.

I spat a curse and scrambled up, fighting to gain purchase on the floor, for control of my limbs, before falling face first, arms beneath me, legs splayed uselessly. With a frustrated growl, I pushed up with the same result before deciding to crawl.

Hot tears burned my eyes. I blinked them away, reaching for my sword, knowing it would do little good until I regained control of my body.

I growled as my fingers refused to grasp the handle while Nik stalked closer. The faerie watched with rapt attention, that smile still curling his face. Spittle flew from my lips as I finally shoved my knees beneath me, forced my hand to grab the sword, rolled over and thrust the blade up just as Nik swung down. The blow reverberated down my arms into my back as he raised his sword again.

"Nik, listen to me!" I screamed. "It's Seraph!"

Mere feet away, the faerie chuckled, as if amused by the irony of my situation.

I blocked another blow and kicked one of Nik's feet from beneath him, sending him to his knees, before landing a foot in his gut. He jutted backward, the blade falling from his hand as his head smacked against the floor. I rolled over and shoved to my feet, catching myself on the wall before my legs again collapsed.

One step, then another, and my legs were mine again. They weren't capable of running—there wasn't enough energy in them—but they were mine. I staggered away as Nik picked up the sword and clambered to his feet, putting as much distance between us as possible.

The air before me popped and the fae sprung from nowhere, a ball of purple light clutched in his fist. He hurtled it into my chest, sending me back into Nik's solid form, the both of us tumbling down in a flurry of arms and legs.

Chest heaving, I scrambled from beneath him, but Nik reached out, dragging me back by my ankle. I fought the urge to kick his face, to cause more damage than was already done. Instead, I clawed at the floor, grappling for anything useful. But there was nothing.

Tears streaming down my cheeks, I flipped over and drew my leg up, aiming for Nik's face. A silver arrow suddenly plunged into the faerie's neck, spurting blood like a fountain. Aurorian emerged from the adjacent room, one sword now a bow, the other clutched in her fist. Her gait was calm as she nocked a fresh arrow from the fisted cylinder, drew, and aimed, striking the fae in the other eye before another sank into his throat, vanishing upon impact. His fingers clawed at the wound, failing to stop the flow of life pouring from him as he dropped to his knees.

Gasping, I whipped around to Aurorian before my vision landed on Nik, the purple fading from his eyes. He blinked, and his body slumped forward. Groaning, Nik grabbed his head before letting it hang to the ground. I scrambled away, unsure of him. Of myself. Of the faerie.

"He's dead," Aurorian said. "Once a faerie has been killed, any person afflicted by their dust is released. Nikolei will be fine in a while."

I swiped the tears from my cheeks and looked around. It seemed impossible it was over. Aurorian sighed as she reattached the silver cylinders to her waist.

Glancing from her to Nik, I forced myself to my feet and ran to where Miran had disappeared through the wall, dropping to his side as he sat up. His gaze hazy as our eyes met.

"I'd like to leave now," he wheezed. Despite our circumstance, I smiled, a chuckle rising in my throat as a hand rose to my face.

"We'd have to talk to Aurorian," I said, stabbing a thumb over my shoulder.

Miran opened his mouth to respond, but the words died on his tongue as a deymoness stalked into the room, dragging a body behind her. Scarlet streaked the floor, trailing her before she dropped the carcass and glanced up, pinning me with her red glare.

"There you are," she seethed, drawing her sword from her back.

Miran clambered to his feet, sword in hand, as he placed himself before me. The deymoness appeared before Miran and tossed him aside, despite his towering, bulky size.

"Do you know how many fucking men I've lost because of you?" she growled, displaying all eight fangs, her red eyes glowing. Fury dripping from every word.

My breath hitched in my throat. I tried forcing myself to step back, to move, to do anything, but my body refused, trapping me in her sight as if I were shackled to the floor.

I fought against the useless bubbling tears as she stormed toward me, dragging the tip of her sword across the wooden floor.

"One fucking girl! One girl and two fucking Amasians!" Her eyes shown bright as she hefted her sword. My gaze caught along the sharpened edge, following the glimmer of dawn on steel. "Preferably alive, she'd said. I've just decided for her!"

For a moment, I was held captive by that sword, an arch aiming directly toward me. I waited for my death, for an explosion of pain that never came.

A flash of red streaked through the room as Miran barreled into the deymoness, knocking her to the floor. He pulled a knife from his boot and thrust it down, but the deymoness was faster. She flipped them over, grabbed a handful of red curls, and, roaring, slammed his head into the floor. Miran's body went limp, blade falling from his fist.

The deymoness' gaze rose to mine, rage curling her features.

Finally, my feet moved, stepping back. As she stood, she didn't swing at me, but picked me up with her free hand, lifting me off the floor. Her hand a vise around my throat. I kicked at her, clawed at her hand, her fingers, though her grip remained like steel.

She hoisted me higher and slammed me to the floor.

Blinding pain shot through me, stars blinking and flashing. My stomach turned, threatening to spill whatever food remained as I fought to see. Struggled to move. I vomited across the floor, over my hands, in my hair. I coughed and sputtered, my vision swimming as the world spun. Tears filled my eyes, blinding me.

All aside from the glint of metal beside Miran.

Wrapping the knife in my vomit-covered hand, I pulled it to my chest and slammed my eyes shut, sipping cool air as I begged my head to stop spinning, my stomach to still. I was lifted again before it had the chance.

Vision still spinning, I roared and hoisted the knife above my head, plunging it into the nearest flesh. The deymoness shrieked, her cry splitting my ears. Suddenly, I was falling, the floor reaching up to catch me.

A hazy river of blood ran down her face, between her fingers and across the pristine white of her leather armor. She snatched her hand away and roared, one eye glaring red. The other a glistening flood of it.

Forcing my knees beneath me, I reached for my sword, the grip slick in my hand, and gingerly climbed to my feet, swaying before the deymoness' pure rage. Before my very eyes, the wound in her face healed, all save her eye—a patch of puckered, mottled flesh left in its place.

I gulped down the sour taste in my mouth, stupidly standing before her as she threw a fist into my gut, igniting a bolt of pain through my back and into my spine. Gasping, I sank to the floor, holding my stomach as I fought the urge to retch again.

A hand curled into my hair, hoisting me off my knees until I hung before her. My breath came in heaving gasps as I fought blinding pain while shoving down a scream. I clawed her hands. Tears streamed down my face, my legs weakly kicking out. Fire burned along my scalp where she gripped me, my back stretching against my weight.

My vision was hazy, bespeckled, as a sickening smile curled the deymoness' mouth. She brought me closer before again slamming me to the floor in a burst of color, sound, pain. Vomit spilled forth, the stench of bile curdling my nose, making me want to retch again.

Boots stepped closer, filling my spotty vision, as the deymoness dropped to her haunches. She took my chin in her hands, stretching my neck at a painful, awkward angle, making it difficult to breathe. All eight fangs on display as she hissed at me.

"For the loss of my eye, your friends will die slow," she whispered, forcing me to strain against my drumming pulse to hear. "And you will watch their deaths before I take my time enjoying yours."

I panted against my strained neck, eyes watering, throat raw. Parts of my body tingled with numbness. Pain throbbed just beneath, strumming the deepest folds of my brain. Spots burst before my eyes as I stared at the deymoness, fighting the urge to beg her to spare them.

Finally she stood, her movements slow and controlled as she took up her fallen sword. The tang of steel bit against the wooden floor as she turned to a form in the doorway farthest from me. Pockets of sunlight leaked through the windows and gaps in the walls, drenching the form in a golden silhouette.

Grunting at the effort, I rolled over and pulled myself toward the wall, braced against it, and tried pushing myself to my feet, only to end up back where I started, chest heaving. Stuck, my gaze drifted back to the deymoness and the form she faced before she hoisted her blade and jumped.

I desperately rubbed my eyes, opening them as the dark figure drew a pair of swords, catching the deymoness' single blade in the cross before kicking her back.

Swords flashed in the growing sunlight. Blows were exchanged, clangs echoing about the demolished room. At times, their movements were so fast they became mere flashes of black and white, glinting steel, and sprayed blood.

The deymoness roared as she kicked the form's middle, sending him shuddering into the wall. For a moment, his head lolled to his chest, appearing defeated. Then he glanced up, eyes flickering silver before glowing bright red as he jumped up and sped toward her. Wielding both swords, he caught her blade between his two and twisted, disarming her. The sword skittered across the floor and the deymoness stepped back, stunned.

With one blade, he sliced so swiftly through her neck he seemed to not leave a scratch. The second, he plunged into her gut, lifting her off the floor before slamming her body down, her head rolling free.

Shakily, the deymon stood. He cleaned both blades on the dead deymoness' white armor before sheathing them and turned around. His eyes found me as the red faded, returning to pits of shadows.

He approached with an uneven gait, collapsing to one knee, chest heaving.

I took in the fuzzy sight of him.

Twin rivers of blood ran from his nostrils, which he wiped away with a sleeve. Dawn cast a golden aura around him, rending his face in thick shadows. Silver flickered about as he looked me over. Amongst the movements of his eyes, buried in the dark, lay their true color.

Brown. A rich, soft velvet begging me to fall into them.

He turned my chin this way and that, one soft thumb running across my jaw. His face stoic, all sharp angles and smooth planes. His sharp eyes ran over me, brows furrowed in concentration.

His tongue worked in his mouth before he turned away and spat, coughed, and turned back to me, inhaling sharply as more blood ran from his nose.

I could barely lift an arm as he picked up the edge of my sweater, poking my sides. The cold stung, though it was a long moment before I registered its prickly touch. By then, the deymon had dropped my sweater and was pulling me into his arms.

All at once, a thick, heavy feeling swamped me, pulling me under. Fatigue washed over me like a tidal wave, and I was powerless against it. The last thing I heard was his deep, velvety voice, though the words were lost in an ocean of slumber.

EIGHT

WARMTH SURROUNDED ME, EMBRACING where I lay. Taking a deep breath, I inhaled the scent of a burning hearth. My fingers splayed out, brushing something soft, both above and beneath. A mattress and a blanket.

My head was fuzzy. My body heavy as if buried under rocks. The closer I drifted to consciousness, the more pain crashed over me in waves. It spread from my neck to my shoulders, down to my hands and all the way to my toes, lingering around my left side. Every breath burned, my lungs screaming with each inhale.

I forced my eyes open, but they immediately closed in protest against the brightness. When I tried to change position, to lessen the burning in my side, my entire back shrieked. Every muscle, every tendon, cried out, and so I settled back down, breathing ragged, before again attempting to take in my surroundings.

My eyes fluttered against the wavering light as humming caressed my ears, in tune with the crackling fire. The room shuddered into focus and I found Sheila, back facing me, busied with a task at a counter stretching the length of one wall.

Sucking in a breath, I turned to the window at my left. Overlooking the expanse of white landscape beyond. For a moment, I'd hoped it had all been a dream. Or a nightmare.

Next, I turned right, my heart sinking into my stomach. Hot tears prickled my eyes.

Miran sat slumped against the wall, half his face covered by a swath of mottling bruises and cuts. The other by fiery tendrils hanging like drapes. His tall, corded form spilled over the sides of his chair at awkward angles, long legs stretched before him as his hands nearly scraped the wooden floor. His chest rose and fell softly in sleep.

Spotting signs of battle strewn across his hands and face, hidden by hair and shadows, it came back, bit by bit. The demolished inn. All the dead scattered about. How Miran and Nik and Aurorian had fought so hard to protect me. And what had I done? Gotten in the way. Nearly got myself killed. If not for the deymon...

The deymon. Venyx.

The deymoness and his fight against her.

I gulped and tried to sit again, a bolt of lightning jolting down my side. A gasp flew from my lips.

Sheila spun around, her long, graying braid flying with the motion. In the same instant Miran's sapphire eyes popped open. Groaning, he eased himself from the chair and limped to my side while Sheila dropped her work and scurried from the room.

"Seven fucking hells," Miran cursed under his breath, shoving hair from my face as he sank onto the bed beside me. "I was terrified you wouldn't wake."

"Where am I?" I groaned.

Miran licked his lips and looked around. "Sheila said it's a storeroom." He chuckled. "I don't know many storerooms with beds in them."

His face dropped as his gaze found mine. He took my hands, calloused thumbs running circles around my palms. Pressed his lips to my knuckles, one at a time. Thick, prickly emotion filled my throat at the dire expression on his face. Try as he might, the guilt couldn't hide behind his curls, his beard. It was there, hanging off his lashes like tears.

"How many are dead?" I asked, forcing the words out. Biting back the sour taste of them.

He ran his tongue along his lips, chewed the inside of his cheek. "A lot," he finally said, those two words carrying so much more weight than they had right to.

Firelight glistened along the tears gathering in my eyes, casting him in a hazy, otherworldly glow.

"I shouldn't have fallen asleep," he said, filling the silence. He peered up, eyes misting over, on the verge of spilling. "I should have moved faster. Woke Aurorian, Nik, while we still had a chance. If I—"

"Miran." I squeezed his hands. "This isn't your fault. You couldn't have known. None of us did."

Sniffling, he kissed my hands, one at a time, before placing his lips on my cheek. Taking the opportunity, I breathed in his scent, the warmth of his body. During the battle, I thought I'd never see him again. I thought he'd never be so close to me again.

A pair of footsteps echoed down the hall and Aurorian's tall, lithe form appeared, her face rigid, arms across her chest. "Miran." She needed no other words.

Placing a chaste kiss on my forehead, Miran rose and left, closing the door on his way. After the echo of his boots faded, Aurorian threw the lock and crossed the room, sitting gingerly on the edge of the bed. Gritting my teeth, I braced myself, shifting against her added weight.

"How are you feeling?" Her question was one of concern. The tone she used, however, revealed nothing. It wasn't with affection she asked, but the need for tactile knowledge. Was I well enough to travel?

In all honesty, I had no clue.

"Like shit," I said, letting the words drop between us. Aurorian nodded, her mouth set grimly as her pale blue gaze wandered over me. "What aren't you telling me?" The words blurted out before I could stop them. Instead of the harshness I'd expected, Aurorian's face softened, albeit only just.

She sighed, her shoulders dropping, back curving, as she took one of my hands and stroked my palm, turning it over to gaze at the lines upon it.

As a girl, Briahna had told tales of Seers who could divine a person's entire life simply by gazing at their hand. The lifeline ran down the center, telling the length of a person's life. Aurorian's fingernail traced that line and I recalled when I'd first told her of it.

"Do you remember when I first came for you?" she finally said, though gave no room for reply. "I told you of your destiny. Of what awaited you once you grew up." There was no illusion of control as she spoke. No authority. Only the woman who'd raised me. My surrogate mother. Her eyes lifted to mine, holding my gaze as she carried on. "I told you I would protect you so long as fate allowed it."

My brows furrowed as I stared at her, wondering what she was getting at. Dread filled my chest, rising like the tide. Like a swelling of water, waiting to drown me.

"It..." She stopped, the word hanging off her lips like a bauble before she continued. "It's possible we were followed from the safehouse."

"No." I shook my head. "There are precautions." I forced the words out, forced them to sound stronger than they were. "That's not supposed to happen," I breathed.

"No, it's not."

"How?" My heart thundered as that one word dropped between us. My pulse thrummed in the edges of my eyes as I waited for her response, vision darkening with the beat.

"I'm going to find out."

Biting back a surging rage, I snatched my hands away.

"Twenty years, Aurorian," I spat, venom thick in my voice. She nodded. "Twenty years and we've never b- I have *never* been attacked. What has been the *point* of keeping me so fucking isolated?" I shot, spittle flying from my mouth. Tears blinded me, catching the firelight. "If I was going to end up being attacked anyway, what's been the *point*?"

She swallowed, her throat and jaw working, the wheels in her head turning. But she didn't face me. Didn't turn those pale blue eyes back on me. Instead, she focused on the blanket beneath my hands, fingers toying with a loose thread. Finally, she stood, brushing off invisible dust, lint, whatever it was, from her lap, running her long fingers through the fine tendrils of gold and silver hair cascading over her shoulders.

"I have to go to Amasius," she suddenly said.

My heart dropped into my stomach, all the pain in my body fleeing at once. "I'm not going with you, am I?"

"No." Her eyes jumped up, meeting mine, and the question must have been plain on my face, for she said, "I need to go alert them."

"About what?" I asked, my voice strained, still filled with shock at her sudden revelation. "Didn't you learn of the leak from them?"

Her face remained a placid mask, and I knew nothing had changed. She still wouldn't tell me anything. I sank back into the pillow, fuming, fighting the tears threatening to fall.

"Dragons were with the White Army. There could be an alliance between Dracon and Kaival. Amasius needs to know," she said. "Dracon may no longer be our ally."

I swiped at a stray tear. Licked the salt from my lips. "And what about the plan?" I asked, carefully folding my arms over my chest. "What about the ship?"

"You'll be going through the Plains now," she said, forcing my gaze up.

An involuntary chuckle spewed from my chest, igniting a line of fire down my back and side, making me wince. Taking gentle sips of air, I licked my lips and focused on her through the throbbing. "We don't even know if the way is safe. And now we have to contend with faeries *and* dragons? Aurorian-" I stared at her, mouth gaping.

Aurorian took a breath, held it for a long moment. "Venyx just needs a few days and he will be-" She stopped, started again. "You can trust him with your life."

Our gazes held for a long moment, Aurorian's form again going rigid the longer she stared at me. Finally, she took a step back. And the moment of vulnerability between us was gone, replaced again by the ambassador. The huntress. The warden of my life.

"I'll stay until you and the others are well enough to travel. A few days," she said. "You'll need to move quickly. Avoid small towns and villages.

71

Go to The City. It's large enough, you might go unnoticed. There's a safehouse. From there, go to the Plains. Their queen is expecting you in a few months. An Amasian diplomat will meet you. Geaith will have her own people escort you to Pensen, but make sure your escorts remain with you."

She took another breath, as if wishing to say more. A part of me wished she would.

Wished she would apologize for leaving me.

Offer some kind of comfort, however thin.

That she would stay.

But I knew she wouldn't.

NINE

N OTHING WAS BROKEN. THAT I could say with confidence. The expression Sheila wore as she pulled up my shirt suggested the bruising up and down my left flank hadn't improved.

Breathing hurt. Moving hurt more. Staying still hurt most, because eventually I'd have to move, and that hurt like a bitch. Little could be done, but Sheila did everything possible to ease my pain.

The tea she gave me was bitter, scalding on the way down—it worked best piping hot, she said—but within moments, most of the pain melted away and I was literally able to breathe easier. Which was fantastic since, over the last few days, the men had been preparing, and today we were setting off south.

Bitterness hung in my throat as Sheila helped me pull on my boots. Aurorian left before I'd woken. She hadn't said goodbye, or when I would see her again. If she would meet me in Pensen. She'd just vanished. As was her way.

I would have felt safer with her by my side, with her blades protecting me. That had, after all, been the plan. But those plans had changed. And it was clear I had no say in them.

Whatever survivors remained after the attack fled in the days following, leaving only a handful of people offering to help rebuild. As I hobbled through the remnants of the inn, great portions of it ripped from existence, I tried to ignore the glances, the whispers and sneers, as I leaned my weight on Sheila, using her for support.

I hadn't expected anyone to give a shit whether I'd died; the world hung in the balance of my life and death. But I was the reason this place had been attacked. And the guilt wrapped around my throat was heavy. Moreso upon learning one of the casualties had been Ace. Whether Sheila resented me for that was unknown—she'd been so kind. Her compassion, along with the flaming cut taking her right eye, only stoked my guilt further.

Gusts of icy wind buffeted us as we stepped into the cold morning. Venyx tightened the tack on the horses, mumbling to the beasts. He barely spared us a glance as he worked. Or rather, he barely spared *me* a glance. Ace, after all, hadn't just been Aurorian's friend. And now, he was dead.

I was thankful as Sheila led me to my horse, already saddled and bridled. Any words I'd wanted to speak died on my lips as she shrugged from my touch and trudged to Venyx. The words they spoke were ripped away by the frigid winds, but the hug they exchanged was unmistakable. I thought they'd hated each other. Without a backward glance, Sheila limped back inside.

I chewed my bottom lip, biting back a fresh wave of tears I had no right to. If I hadn't been here, this wouldn't have happened. Ace would still be alive. Sheila would have both her eyes. An inn that had stood for over three hundred years would still be whole.

Venyx's silvery eyes gleamed from the shadows of his thick hood as he glanced up before turning to his horse. I wanted to say I was sorry, but the words died on the wind, stolen from my lips. Just as well. Some things *sorry* couldn't fix.

The prospect of journeying to Pensen had been terrifying. Even more so when we'd started. And now, all I wanted was to get there. Put as much distance between me and the people whose lives I'd destroyed as possible.

Gritting my teeth, I lifted my foot and shoved it in the stirrup. Bit back searing stabs of pain as I stretched, gripped the saddle, and pulled myself up. I was halfway there when the throbbing became too great and I fell backward, helpless to stop myself.

"Seven hells, Seraph!" Concern ran rampant in Miran's voice as he caught me and held me to his chest. Growling, I elbowed him out of the way, chewing on my bottom lip to keep from crying. I wanted to do this. One simple thing. Just get myself in the fucking saddle. "Seraph." A warning rest in that word. Still, I ignored him. Finally, he stepped around to face me, one finger tucked beneath my chin. "You're going to hurt yourself more trying to do that on your own."

Furious rage bubbled inside me. It curled my features, steeling my brows, settling around my mouth. Until Miran sighed and stroked my jaw, leaning down to press a gentle kiss to my lips. A hiccupping sob tore through me and I leaned into him, into his warm, waiting arms. He hugged me, swaying back and forth as his hands stroked my back.

"And you didn't stop her because..."

The deymon turned away, ignoring us as he continued mumbling to his horse.

"Wonderful," Miran grumbled. I blinked away the tears and pulled my hood up, burying my face in shadows. Miran turned to face me, catching my gaze. That same, blinding smile curling his mouth. "If you try to make our jobs a little easier, I'd appreciate it," he cooed. I couldn't help but smile in return. He pressed a kiss to my forehead.

Words bubbled up, but I refused to utter them. The moment I opened my mouth, a flood of tears would follow, and I had neither the energy nor the time for a breakdown. I did allow Miran to help me into the saddle and pulled my hood down further, blocking out the stiff buffets of wind while shielding my face from his prying blue eyes.

"Nik!" Miran called.

A few moments later, Nik limped out, shouldering his pack. His brown curls hung around his face, still swollen and bruised. Though it looked like he could see out of both eyes as he trudged through the snow to his own horse.

Miran grumbled before he swung up behind me and turned the horse to face the deymon, who had yet to mount up. Instead, he was feeding the beast an apple.

"We're leaving, with or without you," Miran said. Venyx tossed a glance over his shoulder, brown eyes glinting from the depths of his hood.

"Don't tempt me," he grumbled.

Miran scoffed. "We were here to get your sorry ass," he snapped. "Don't make all this in vain." He nodded toward the tavern.

Venyx adjusted the reins a final time, shifting the bit in his horse's mouth. "We all know they weren't here for me. I didn't want to go in the first place."

"Get on the fucking horse," Nik said, guiding his mount next to mine and Miran's.

Venyx turned, piercing Nik with those glaring silver eyes. "Make me."

Nik swallowed, gaze shifting nervously.

"Thought so," the deymon grumbled.

"You'll get your payment once we get to Pensen," I said, dragging the deymon's attention to me. "Please, just … let's go."

Shadows bathed his face, only the glimmer of his eyes visible. Sighing, he grumbled under his breath before finally mounting his horse and snapped the reins, trotting out in front.

"This is going to be a very long journey," Miran mumbled before urging our horse to follow. Nik murmured an agreement, trailing behind.

The day went slow. Miran and Nik chatted occasionally, filling the void of silence around us. Mostly, I leaned into Miran's chest, too sore and tired to keep myself upright.

Flurries of snow danced through the air as we went, coating my cloak, our horse, Miran's arms, in a dusting of powder. In the distance, a thick congealing formation of clouds promised an incoming storm, so it became a race to find somewhere to make camp, lest we all froze to death.

For the most part, Venyx lingered ahead. Often times, he was little more than a dark spot on the edge of my vision, leading the way. On rare occasions, he trotted back to let us know when the snow deepened. Otherwise, he stayed silent, out of the way.

The first night, the sun set in a backdrop of biting cold, no shelter in sight save for a copse of evergreens, swaying and groaning in the wind. The few supplies we'd wrangled from the ruins of the inn included a tent barely big enough for the four of us. Miran and Nik quickly erected it, and the former helped me settle inside. True to his charming personality, Venyx perched in the branches overhead.

Unable to light a fire, I was forced to reconcile the pain shooting down my side without Sheila's tea to ease it. Determined, Miran gathered a handful of snow and compressed it. The compacted snow stung as it pressed against my skin. But the chill relieved the feverish heat, allowing me a minute rest.

Between the creaking branches and howling winds thrashing against our meager shelter, I slept little. Several times, the clouds parted to reveal the twin moons, casting a bright silvery light upon us. The tree trunks became jutting ghosts, dancing back and forth along the walls of the tent, Venyx's form among them. Splayed along the limbs like a cat.

Shoving aside the flaming discomfort of my left side, I shifted to my right and snuggled into Miran, using his body for heat. His arms wrapped tighter around me, pulling me closer. Nik lay behind me, his back to mine. Both snored, though I couldn't say that's what kept me awake.

Every time I drifted off, I dreamt of the beach. Or the inn. Of Ace's body being dragged along the floor, blood trailing behind. The dey-moness glaring with those ruby eyes, fangs dripping with saliva.

The following morning, if Miran noticed the exhaustion written across my face, he said nothing. We simply packed our little camp and carried on.

In the distance, the mounting storm clouds drew closer, and it be-came more urgent to find a proper shelter. Near dusk, a cropping of rocks came into view, a cavern hidden within their depths. Nik and Miran climbed from their saddles, stretching their legs, while Venyx went inside. After a short while he called down, letting us know it was safe.

The space was small, tight, just big enough for us and our horses. Whether it would be enough space if we were snowed in remained to be seen. I hoped we didn't find out. The tension between the men was thick enough without being trapped inside a cave.

Nik set up his sleeping roll in the corner farthest from the cave's mouth, immediately setting to work on a fire. Miran laid our beds nearest the heat, where I could sit against the cavern wall, the cool stone at my back keeping the swelling at bay.

He pulled out the kettle Sheila had given us, filled it with snow, and handed it to Nik for boiling, then set about gathering another handful for my compress. I took a big gulping breath, eyes slammed shut, and braced as he pressed the ice to my skin.

My winces echoed off the cavern walls as Miran's gaze flickered from his hands to my face. I tried to not move, to keep my focus on him, as he wrapped a bit of cloth around me, securing the compress.

"Let me know when it melts," he said, before turning to the kettle to ready my tea.

Rivulets of frozen water ran down my side, soaking the waistband of my trousers into the seat of them. Cold bit into my skin, making me shiver. Still, it was either bear the pain of the ice and let it bring down the swelling, or suffer further damage.

Keeping my thoughts from the melting ice, I watched Venyx pace back and forth, so much like a caged predator. He gazed into the endless ceiling, to where the smoke curled out, and, in a single motion, jumped, vanishing into the pooling shadows above. Only the occasional shifting rocks indicated he was there. If I tipped my head just right, I could make out his silver eyes as they flickered before disappearing again.

He remained there the rest of the night.

Sometime during the night I woke to shuffling stone, my eyes shooting open. Miran crouched in the wavering firelight, a fresh ball of ice in one hand. With his other, he lifted my shirt. I hissed as he placed the compress against me, whimpering, wanting with everything in me to scurry away.

"I'm sorry," he whispered as he lashed the new ice to me, "but if we don't do this, it could fuck up how you heal. I've seen people die from lesser injuries."

And so I bit back the tears and let him work, let him take care of me.

Instead of the pain, the ice biting into my skin, I focused on his hair. How each strand was a different red. His eyes and the varying shades of blue. The gentle swoop of his brows and the curve of his full lips. The laugh lines around his eyes. How, if I looked close enough, the reddish-brown of his beard was spackled with gray.

How utterly human he was.

How utterly beautiful.

"Miran?"

He looked up, brows raised, bottom lip between his teeth in concentration. A soft noise vibrating in his throat.

"Tell me something about yourself." The words tumbled from my lips without thought.

Only after they echoed throughout the cavern I realized what I was asking. The very nature of his job prevented him from revealing anything personal about himself. Where he came from. His family. If he even had one.

Smiling, he dropped his chin to his chest, focused on tending my wound. "What prompted that question?" he asked, tucking my shirt back around me, making sure no part of my skin was exposed. He peered through his lashes before running a hand through his scarlet crown.

"Just trying to find a way to distract myself," I breathed, shifting against the ice, the stone at my back.

Groaning, Miran sank to the cave floor at my right and I leaned against his shoulder. Slipped my fingers between his as he took my hand and brought it to his lips.

"What'd you want to know?"

Pursing my lips, I stared into the flames as they flickered and danced, casting seductive shadows on the walls. "Something from when you were a boy."

He chuckled, sucked in a breath. Kissed my hand again. "When I was a boy," he said wistfully. I looked up at him as he licked his lips before drawing another breath. "I grew up on the southern coast of Amasius. Overlooking the Interland Channel."

I glanced down at our intertwined hands as he spoke, how his thumb stroked mine.

"I liked to take my father's spyglass and spot the ships sailing from the Plains to the Amasian capital," he continued. "One day, a hot one—then again, I suppose they're all hot in Amasius," he paused, chuckled, and continued, "I spotted this outcropping of rock I'd never seen before. So I borrowed a fishing boat and rowed out to it."

"You stole a boat," I said, glancing back up at him. He chuckled again, tipped his head onto mine.

"Borrowed. I brought it back." Miran kissed my hair. "It must have spent years underwater. The floor was covered in algae and moss. It smelled awful. It was so dark I had to take a piece of oar and use it as a torch. But the ceiling of the cave," he gestured up with his hand, the one not grasping mine, and I followed his movements as if seeing what he saw, "was full of ... stars." I smiled, eyes drifting closed at his words, his voice. "In the back of the cavern were these little cubbies carved into the walls. I used to hide things in them. It was my own little place."

A bittersweet tang clutched my chest at his words. At the idea of having something all to himself. "When was the last time you saw it?" I asked.

He paused in thought, tongue clicking. "Before I went on my first assignment."

"Where were you sent?"

His thumb stroked the center of my palm, easing warmth into my belly, a soft chuckle filling my ears. "That, I'm afraid, is Amasian business." Smiling, I pulled my bottom lip between my teeth.

I drew a deep breath, snuggling further against him. Carefully, he wrapped his arm around me and pulled me closer, his free hand wrapping around mine. I breathed in his scent, relishing his warmth. "What kinds of things did you put in the cubbies? When you were a boy?" I tipped my head up, and he met my gaze with a mischievous grin.

"I stole wine from my father's stores," he snickered. "I think some of it might still be there."

"Such an awful boy," I chuckled. He shrugged nonchalantly, a faraway look glazing over his eyes.

"Maybe one day I'll get to go back," he said, entwining our fingers. I glanced down at our hands. "I'd like to see home one last time."

He drew a breath, as if to say more, but stopped, and silence filled the space between our words. He kissed my forehead, fingers still dancing with each other's. His hand fell from mine and he tipped my chin back, brushing my lips with his.

"Aurorian went to Amasius," I whispered before opening my mouth, allowing his tongue to slip inside. His hand ran up from my chin to my cheek, fingers playing in my hair as his lips moved against mine. "She thinks Dracon made an alliance with Kaival."

He stopped, pulling back. Sapphire eyes going dark.

Another moment passed, the only sounds breathed by the crackling fire. "She thinks there's a leak in Amasius."

He sighed, sat back, and dug both hands in his hair, nodding. Scrubbed his face. "What have I been telling you?"

Leaning against him, lips pursed, I nodded. My gaze dropped to the blanket and I started picking off wool pearls, flicking them aside.

"What made you decide to tell me?" he asked, taking my hand again.

I shrugged. Mouth gaping. "I just ... I wasn't sure what she told you. And I think you should have all the information. If we're going to make it to Pensen."

Miran nodded against me. "Thank you," he said, raising my hand to kiss it.

"You did almost die for me."

"I'll try not to make a habit of it," he snickered.

Biting back a smile, I elbowed him in the gut. He chuckled before pulling me closer still. As we settled back into a warm, comfortable silence, my eyes drifted closed. Until I fell asleep. Wrapped in Miran's arms.

TEN

I WOKE TO THE clink of steel striking rock. A sharp *ting-ting-ting* dug its way into my ears like a tick, burrowing between my brows. Sitting, I found Miran hunched beside me, a steaming cup of tea in his hands. Pushing past the bitterness, I gulped it down and waited for my soreness to dissipate. Within moments, I was able to stand, albeit gingerly.

After assuring him I was steady, I limped behind Miran as he followed the sound, my mouth gaping helplessly at the glistening wall of ice capped like a cork at the cave's entrance. Struck with disbelief, I shuffled between the Amasians and raised a hand to it, convincing myself it was there. Keeping us prisoner.

Slick wetness came away.

Nik stood in the center of the wall, knife in hand. A thin sheen of sweat coated his brow, his floppy brown curls damp, clinging to his face. At his feet lay a pile of ice. He wiped his forehead with a sleeve, glanced over me, and carried on. *Ting-ting-ting.*

"How did this happen?" I asked. "How long was I asleep?"

"Snow, Seraph," Nik teased, stopping to glance at me. "We got snowed in."

"Eat a dick," I snapped.

"I've already had breakfast, thanks," he grunted between strikes.

83

Miran sighed. "We had to keep the fire burning all night." He waved absently at the cavern mouth.

"Oh." I flicked my gaze from him to the wall.

"We've been taking turns trying to crack through, but the fucking thing's thick," Miran said.

Snickering, Nik opened his mouth.

"Shut it," I spat. A grin split his face, but he remained quiet. Another moment and I noticed we were short one person, little as I'd seen him since finding our makeshift shelter. "Where's Venyx?"

Nik scoffed and glanced at Miran, who said, "We don't know."

"He fucking took off," Nik spat. "Left his horse here."

A silent question perched on my lips as I gazed between them. "No," I mumbled, more to myself, and hobbled into the belly of the cavern. Tipping my head back, I peered into the shadowy pits of darkness above, searching for those pinpoints of silver. Nothing.

"Of course his horse is here," Miran said, his voice reverberating around me. "How would he have gotten her out?"

"I don't fucking know," Nik spat.

"Shut up," I seethed, tapping my fingers against my forehead. This couldn't be happening. Not so soon.

Aurorian told me, had sworn, I could trust him. She'd risked our lives taking us to the tavern for him. She wouldn't have done so if she thought he'd leave at the first opportunity.

"Venyx?" I called. The only response was my own echo, worry etched into the crevices of the cavern as it ricocheted back. Miran shuffled to my side.

"He didn't want to come in the first fucking place," Nik grunted from the wall.

"Aurorian swore—"

"She swore a lot of things, Seraph," Miran said, cutting me off. "We should consider that Aurorian's pet deymon isn't on as tight a leash as she'd like to believe." Tears burned the backs of my eyes as Miran

84

crossed the small space to our little bundle of blankets. He began picking them up, folding them with quick, neat precision.

Turning back toward the icy wall, I licked my lips and buried my face in my hands. Miran was suddenly there, pulling me into his chest. I bit back the tears as he swayed back and forth, my fingers digging into his sweater.

Miran couldn't be right.

If he was, he might have been right about other things.

"I know you want to believe the best in Aurorian," he whispered against my hair, "but you're still seeing her like that little girl did. You're not a child anymore."

Behind us, the clinking of Nik's knife continued, chipping away little by little. Pecking at my ears. "Not that she'd ever treat you like an adult, anyway," he huffed between strikes.

"You're walking well enough you might be able to ride on your own," Miran said, pulling away to continue packing. "May as well take his horse if he's gone."

Wiping my tears, I nodded. Forced myself to recall how the deymon had been at the tavern. He hadn't seemed pleased to see Aurorian, so maybe he'd only agreed to appease her. If that was the case, we were better off without him.

A sudden, sharp crack filled the cavern, stinging my ears. I met Miran's eyes. We both turned to the entrance as Nik jumped back, a curse flying from his lips. Miran rushed forward, reaching for his sword.

For a moment, it seemed we'd all hallucinated the same noise.

Then it came again.

Something sharp struck the ice. Hard. Then again. Gasping at my side, I shuffled to the cave's entrance and shoved between Nik and Miran, who pushed me behind them, relegating me to stare between the seam of their shoulders.

The mounds of snow burying our icy prison tumbled away. I reared back, a hand covering my face. Bright golden sunlight pierced the wall, illuminating a single figure on the other side.

An arm came down, striking the ice, pulled back, and struck again. The wall cracked open, sending forth a great puff of frigid air and dust. I blinked against it, wiped debris from my face, and opened my eyes.

Standing in the cave's mouth was Venyx, sheathing a knife at his back. He glanced between the three of us and pushed through without a word.

I exchanged a confused glance with Miran before we both turned as Venyx stormed to the rear of the cave, where the horses were.

"We thought you left," Miran said.

"How the fuck did you get out?" Nik asked.

Venyx took his horse's reins and led her out, barely sparing us a glance. I stepped from his path, pulling Miran with me. After a moment, I followed.

"Hey!" I shouted, feet crunching through the snow. His step halted, and I collided with his solid chest. I glanced up and met a pair of red-tinged eyes glaring at me. Heat spread throughout my cheeks as I stepped back, gathering my courage. "You don't have to tell us everything you're doing, but a bit of communication w—"

Venyx dropped the reins and stepped closer, the heat radiating from him sweltering. "Don't assume just because I'm not your fucking lapdog I've abandoned you," he snarled. "I was hired for a fucking job and I will do that job. My not wanting to come, not wanting to deal with the bullshit that's been dropped onto my fucking shoulders is irrelevant. I said I would get you to Pensen and that's what I intend to fucking do. If you have a problem with my methods, you can take your little Amasians and go your own fucking way. Are we clear?"

I blinked rapidly, staring up at him, seeing him clearly for the first time. A breeze played in the strands of his straight, black hair, turning it golden red in places. His brows were drawn together, casting heavy shadows over his eyes, giving them a silver glimmer.

"Y-yes," I stammered, stepping back.

Without another word, he turned and swung himself into his saddle, snapped the reins and set off.

"Miran, Nik!" I called, rushing back into the cave.

The storm had dropped several inches of snow overnight. Our horses trudged through, carving trenches as we went. At several intervals, Miran dropped from the saddle to relieve our mount of the extra weight. Ahead, Venyx did the same, the dark outline of his cloak swaying back and forth with each step.

Sitting upright all day irritated my side, leaving my back and legs writhing in agony. So it was a great relief when the deepest sloughs fell behind and Miran remounted our saddle, allowing me to lean against him. Sensing my discomfort, he rubbed circles in the small of my back and up my sides. I moaned in relief, my head falling back on his shoulder.

"Should we have stayed in the cave another night?" Nik asked as he rode beside us, a grin peeking from his sparse beard.

"Fuck off," I snapped. Miran chuckled.

"Just trying to be helpful," Nik snickered.

That night, we unloaded our supplies and set up a small camp beneath a cropping of snow-covered rocks, using each other and the horses for warmth. All save Venyx, who roosted outside. Again.

The following morning was bright. Rays of golden sunlight glistened off miles and miles of unmarred snow, allowing us a perfect glimpse of a forest on the horizon, the trees capped in diamond dust. From the silhouette, it was vast, extending in either direction.

In the distance, Venyx pulled up and trotted back, guiding his mount alongside mine and Miran's.

"We should find a way around," he said. Nik scoffed. Venyx's gaze flicked to the other Amasian, and Nik's chuckle died in his throat.

Miran sighed. "That'll take miles, days if not weeks. We don't even know if there is a way around. Our supplies won't sustain us that long."

"Yes, but a forest is a great place for the White Army to hide," Venyx growled.

"If they can hide in the forest, so can we," Nik said. "Far easier than an entire army."

"You're applying human senses to non-human beings," Venyx countered, glaring. "Most of them will be in the trees. We prefer to attack from above."

"And you know they're already there because..." Miran started, his voice trailing off. I glimpsed him over my shoulder, an annoyed look splayed on his face.

Venyx grumbled deep in his throat, grip tightening on his reins, turning his knuckles white. "I can sense them."

"How long has it been since you've sensed anything aside from a tankard?" Nik scoffed.

"Don't start," I warned. Nik threw up his hands defensively.

"I refuse to trust the instincts of a *man* who spent the last few decades living in a tavern, harassing customers and drinking through each and every day," Miran spat. "We don't have time to *find a way around*, and staying out in the open discussing this isn't safe."

"I'm not risking my life—"

"You're not risking anything," Miran said. "She is. We are. Since Aurorian came to you, I'm assuming you're an older deymon. Which makes you nigh invincible, while us mere mortals are far more damageable. You don't get a say."

"Don't fucking tell me how to run my miss—"

"Your mission?" Nik scoffed.

"Who put you in charge, deymon?" Miran asked.

From the depths of his hood, Venyx's eyes glimmered silvery red. The reins groaned in his fists.

"Amasius is charged with her protection, and I'm the senior agent," Miran continued. "You're a hired sword. Nothing more. Don't over-inflate your worth."

"Stop," I said, forcing firmness into my voice. "Arguing about this isn't getting us anywhere."

"Why don't we ask Seraph what she would like to do?" Nik asked, nodding toward me.

My stomach bottomed out as I regarded Venyx and Nik, aware of Miran's presence at my back. The weight of their stares barreled into me. "How much longer would it take to go around?" I finally asked.

Venyx took a breath, exhaled sharply, frustration seeping from his shoulders. "The time shouldn't matter. Getting around sh—"

"You're not answering her question," Miran snapped.

Venyx growled. "Another week, perhaps more. Depends on how many miles south it stretches."

Miran and Nik both laughed. Even the horses seemed to agree, stamping back and forth along the snow.

"Another week?" Nik asked. "Another storm could hit us at any moment."

"Nik's right," Miran said. "We'd be exposed."

I licked my lips, glancing between Nik and Venyx to the forest in the distance. It spread so far east and west, the silhouette vanished into the horizon.

Pressing my lips into a thin line, I blinked away a snowflake clinging to my lashes before blowing out my cheeks. "I think we should go through."

"There are caches where we can get supplies and rations," Venyx said, pointing. "If we cut that way, through those hills—"

"Those are Amasian caches," Nik grumbled. "How the fuck do *you* know about them?"

My brows furrowed, mouth opening around the question forming on my tongue.

"They aren't substantial enough to support us, anyway," Miran said. "She made her choice. We're going through."

Venyx nodded once, not another argument falling from his hood before he turned his horse and trotted off, retaking the lead at the front of our procession.

As the words faded and the weight of my decision pressed into me, I wondered if I'd made the right one. I wasn't a soldier. My experience was relegated to going between safehouses, nothing more. The men around me were warriors. They knew how to travel, how to survive. It seemed wrong to leave such a vital choice in my hands.

But it was done.

Snow began falling as we neared, adding a chill to the already frigid air, making me curl further into Miran's body. Shivering against me, he wrapped his cloak around us both, pulling me closer to him. Nik glanced over, a twinge of jealousy lingering in his eyes as he wrapped his cloak tighter about himself.

"Maybe ask the deymon if he'd like to cuddle," Miran snickered. I laughed at the sneer curling Nik's face.

"I doubt he's the snuggling type," Nik bit. "Besides, I rather prefer my intestines *inside*."

The sun rose high in the gray, pregnant sky, casting a gloomy, ghostly light upon us as the forest loomed ahead. A layer of frost encrusting the trees glittered as if the trunks themselves were carved from ice. Mere decorations instead of living things.

Evergreen boughs stretched above as the wood embraced us. A light speckling of green seemed strange in so much white, but it was a welcome reprieve. The limbs hung low, weighed down by so much powder, the trees themselves swaying and creaking with every breath of wind.

Every groan of a trunk, snap of a twig, every falling pat had me on edge, peering around the trees, through shadows. Into them. And a sudden thought occurred—what if there were faeries? An even more frightening realization followed. I had no idea whether Venyx was immune to them.

After a while, a quietness settled over me. Over the forest. It was eerie, how silent it was. The only sound for miles was the chuffing of our horses, their hooves crunching along.

Nik seemed to share my thoughts, for he said, "It's so quiet, we shouldn't have a problem hearing anyone approach."

Miran grumbled in agreement.

Venyx threw over his shoulder, "If they don't want you to hear them, you won't," before he fell back into silence.

I met Nik's gaze, his face blanching. His throat working through the nerves plain in his eyes. "Always so fucking cheerful, that one," he mumbled. I didn't have the heart to tell him Venyx had likely heard.

With Venyx's disturbing comment fresh on our minds, it was decided that Nik would ride behind us, placing me and Miran in the center. Venyx continued to head our procession. Both Miran and Nik kept their hands on the grips of their swords, the tension clear in Miran's body. Even our horse seemed anxious.

Afternoon faded quickly. The chill hung between trees deepened as dusk descended. Glimpses of the stars and twin moons danced shyly overhead, hiding between the canopy and the clouds. I longed to see more of them. Then reminded myself that, eventually, I would. Once we reached the Plains.

For the second time that day, Venyx slowed his mount to allow us to catch up, riding on mine and Miran's right. Tree trunks marched between us, casting his face in shadows, all but pinpricks of silver.

"I understand you'll want to make camp soon, but we should keep moving," he said. "It'll keep us warm, get us through faster."

Miran growled deep in his throat, arms tightening on either side of me. "You're right, I do want to make camp. And we're going to."

Venyx turned away, shoulders tensing. "Just because we can't see anything do—"

"We don't even know if they've made it this far," Miran reasoned. "We've seen no sign of them since the tavern."

I sighed, let my head roll forward.

"They could still be here."

"I am *not* relying on your *senses* to keep Seraph safe," Miran spat.

"If we break now, you won't be keeping her safe."

"You're both acting like children," I snapped.

91

"I think we should at least consider it," Nik offered, his horse crunching along the ground behind us.

Growling, Venyx shoved his hood back, casting beams of spackled moonlight across his face. "You two cannot possibly think this is a good idea."

"We all need a break," Nik said. "Even the horses."

"Not everyone can exist on so little rest," Miran added.

Venyx's brown eyes flicked to me, and the decision again became mine. I swallowed a breath, glimpsed over my shoulder at Miran, then at Nik, before finding Venyx's gaze again.

"We need to rest," Miran said softly. "We'll set up a watch, take turns until dawn."

"I cannot protect you if you do not let me," Venyx growled.

I bit my bottom lip, considering them all.

"It's a bad idea to break here." The deymon's gaze flicked over me as he spoke.

"And a worse one to fall asleep in the saddle," Miran said. "What if we wait until the other side of the forest and there's nothing? Or it goes on for days? You expect us to carry on all that time without rest?"

"I understand the risks," Venyx said, "but stopping so soon w—"

"Stop, both of you," I spat. I rubbed my face with my hands and leaned forward, my head pounding from their arguing. From the decision placed upon my shoulders.

After a moment of burying myself in the darkness of my palms, I dropped them into my lap and looked up, meeting Venyx's gaze.

"What if we keep going," I started, Miran already tensing to interrupt me, "*just* until we find some kind of shelter?"

"That could take hours," Miran said.

"It's better than resting in the open," Venyx said with a nod. "I'll agree to that."

I turned to Nik. He sighed, but begrudgingly nodded. Finally, I turned in the saddle, peered at Miran over my shoulder.

He scratched his beard, but finally assented. "Okay."

"Good." I sucked in a breath, turning back around. "Now all of you can shut the fuck up."

Venyx flicked his hood back up, once again burying himself in shadows, before he retook his place at the front of our parade. Nik fell behind, and we carried on.

Before long, the forest was cast in long-legged shadows as a thin fog twined between trunks. Even the pats of snow seemed to stop, leaving only the ghostly creaking of trees to guide us.

Sleep tugged at my brain. Several times, I found myself leaning back on Miran, chin to my chest, fighting the embrace of slumber. Not yet, I told myself. Soon, hopefully. I wasn't sure I would be able to stay upright much longer. And if Miran went after me, we'd lose our horse, our supplies, and possibly our escort.

I told myself Venyx wouldn't just leave us, but I wasn't so sure. I wanted to think that, eventually, he would find a way to co-exist with Nik and Miran, since so much road lay ahead. Just a few days in, and I wasn't so sure they wouldn't kill each other before we reached the Plains.

A little while later, a gentle tap on my arm woke me. Starting at the silver gaze from within Venyx's hood, I realized I'd fallen asleep. Miran jumped behind me, rubbing his face to wake himself.

"I found something," Venyx said, pointing in the distance. "Not far."

Miran cleared the sleep from his throat and guided our horse in the direction Venyx indicated. I glanced back, making sure Nik still trailed behind.

True to Venyx's word, it wasn't far. A rock jutted up from the earth at an angle, balancing across several boulders. A fallen tree hid the whole thing from view. All of it dusted in snow, rendering it nearly invisible.

Venyx gracefully dropped from the saddle, striding across the snowy ground and vanished inside the rock shelter. Nik followed, a hand covering his yawning mouth.

Grumbling, Miran slipped to the ground and stretched his arms up. I grit my teeth as he pulled me down beside him. The cold did nothing for my side, achy and stinging again. But there would be no fire, no tea. It was a risk we couldn't afford.

The shelter was small, much smaller than the cave. A stiff cold permeated the surface of the rocks, curling against my body. The ground was frozen solid. My teeth chattered as all three men set to work, laying out bedrolls and blankets, warming the space as much as possible.

Rubbing his hands up and down my arms, Miran kissed my forehead and tucked me into his chest. Boots and all, we settled onto our nest of blankets and bedrolls. All save for Venyx. Tonight, though, I paid no heed as the deymon chose to segregate himself.

Despite the throbs playing along my ribs, and the cold biting into my skin through all my many layers—regardless of the warmth of the men on either side—it took no time at all to slip into slumber.

Set on Aurorian's lap, my small form bundled into her many cloaks and jackets, I yawned and glanced up, starting when a single white fleck landed on my cheek, a shiver running through me. My eyes widened as I tipped my head back, gazing into the sky boiling with clouds birthing endless amounts of snow.

"Where are we?" I asked, my childlike voice startling me.

"We're in the Northerlands, Little One," Aurorian said, her pale blue eyes flicking over me. Face wide in awe, I looked to the left, then the right, at the Amasian spies flanking us as we trotted along.

"The where?" I asked, meeting her gaze again. A flicker of a smile passed along her thin lips.

"The Northerlands. We will be living here for a time."

"How long? It's too cold." I snuggled closer to her, shivering against the chill permeating my layers.

"Long enough for you to grow up," Aurorian said. "For you to become strong enough to go to the Faerie Queen and liberate the Winter. It is your duty, and yours alone, to free this world."

Another snowflake kissed my nose. I shook the chill away.

"Why?" I asked.

"Because you are the Child of Sky and Sea, the sole being in this world with Divine blood and that of Sirenia." I peered up at Aurorian again. "Because it was foretold long ago. With your life, your blood, our world will be free."

"Do I have to die?" I asked, not quite understanding the words as I uttered them.

"Yes. But," Aurorian said, that smile pulling at her mouth again, "you will be united with your mother and your father. And all those who have given their lives to free us. And all the world will look to you as their savior. Stories will be told of you for generations. Eons."

"But why?" I pressed.

Aurorian sighed. "Because, Little One, the Faerie Queen stole the Winter Sprite, and she doesn't want to give it back. So you must go and take it."

"What's a Sprite? What does it look like?"

Her responding chuckle tickled my ears.

"What if I don't want to die?" I asked.

No, I didn't remember this part. This never happened.

The softness in Aurorian's face, the smile pulling at her mouth, vanished. Replaced with a grave expression cold as the earth around us, beneath us. Beneath me. "What you want does not matter, Little One. It is for all of us you give your life."

I was jolted awake by a chill, though not from the air.

Frozen tears burned my cheeks as I peered into the dark, Miran's face hovering over me. He cursed under his breath, held his hand to my cheeks, my forehead.

"Are you okay?" he asked.

"What? Why?"

"You wouldn't wake."

I wiped the icy remnants from my face and gazed around. Nik was gone. So was Venyx.

"What happened?"

Miran turned away, his eyes catching a glimmer of moonlight. "The deymon heard something. He went to check it out."

My heart skipped a beat, diving to the base of my throat and into the pit of my stomach all at once.

"Where's Nik?" I asked, swallowing my rising panic. Miran helped me to my feet and began gathering our bedding, folding and rolling and packing.

"Getting ready to leave. We have to go. Now." He gathered our supplies and we stepped out of our makeshift shelter, cold air pummeling into me without its protection. Snow crunched underfoot as we hurried to Nik, hastily fastening the last of the supplies onto the rump of his horse.

"What the fuck took so long?" Nik seethed.

"Just hurry up," Miran said, strapping our things to our mount.

I rubbed my arms as I took in the forest, hoping, praying, whatever Venyx had heard was nothing. It had just been a trick of sound, a play of light and the eerie, I told myself. Nothing would be there and we would carry on.

"It's nothing," I whispered, the words barely audible. But I needed them to be true.

"Alright," Miran said, the only warning he gave before hoisting me into the saddle.

Both men suddenly stopped, Nik's hand flying to the grip of his sword, drawing it in one fluid motion. My gaze snapped up, flicking around the shifting shadows cast by the trees.

In the distance, clashing swords echoed through the forest, making me start. I whipped my head in that direction, the same instant a blood-curdling scream ripped through the night.

"Shit," Miran seethed.

My heart danced wildly in my chest.

I was wrong.

I'd been wrong.

We should have gone around.

ELEVEN

M IRAN JUMPED INTO THE saddle behind me, snapped the reins, and launched us into the forest. The icy wind broke along my face, tore into my eyes. Another scream ripped through the silence, followed by clashing swords. Miran yanked the reins to the right, in the opposite direction.

Nik galloped on our tail, sword clutched to his side.

Overhead, a branch snapped. Snow plopped to the ground. A white form hurtled toward us; a scream wrenched from my throat at the sight. Miran cried out and pulled back on the reins. A body slammed into me before solid earth reached up, pounding into my back, knocking the wind from my chest and lungs, reigniting my side.

Stars danced before my eyes, spinning overhead in the form of glittering ice droplets and pine needles. Slowly, I rolled over, biting back the urge to vomit. My hair hung in snow-covered tresses, scattered about, blinding me to all but a flurry of feet.

Something hot and sticky spilled into my mouth and I spat, gazing for a moment at the bright crimson staring back.

I shook the daze from my head and sat up, shoving my hair back as Miran traded blows with a deymon, the beast's blade a mere silver blur. Miran dropped to the ground as the blade sank into the tree behind him, his eyes shooting open as the trunk was bit deep by the blow, the whole thing trembling to the roots.

Miran jumped to his feet and shot toward me, hoisting me up. I barely registered as he pushed me toward the horse, our mount picking himself up from the snow, shaking it from his mane. In a blink, the deymon was swinging his sword in a wide arch, the blade digging into the horse's throat. The animal screamed before a fountain of blood spilled along the ground, splattering the deymon's uniform.

Turning toward us, the deymon jumped the distance, sword aloft. Miran shoved me behind him, spilling me backward into the snow.

Somewhere behind me, someone screamed. Swords clashed. Snow crunched underfoot. Another horse screamed its own bloody death.

Above, the trees swayed, creaking in protest as another deymon in white launched himself from the branches.

Breath hitching in my throat, I forced myself up, ignoring the jolt in my side as the deymon drew his sword, lunging toward me. Sobering from the fall, I kept my gaze on the deymon's body as he swung.

I lunged sideways, narrowly avoiding a strike to the head, then jumped backward, hands to either side, terrified every step of losing my balance. The deymon lunged forward. Relying purely on muscle memory, I reached out, grabbed his wrist, and shoved up, dislodging the sword from his grasp, and caught it, burying the blade in the deymon's throat.

Just in time to be tackled to the snow.

Explosions of pain rippled up and down my side as I hurtled to the ground, my ribs striking something hard and sharp. Breathless, I clawed at the snow, sparks darting before my vision as I curled in on myself.

I barely registered the hands gripping me, flipping me over.

A pair of red eyes pierced the night while a handful of claws dove toward me. From nowhere, an arrow struck the deymon's temple, spraying blood. I gasped, hands shooting up to protect my face. Still, iron coated my tongue. The deymon collapsed to the snow, half-burying me beneath his immense weight.

I scooted back with one arm. The other clutched my side, my chest heaving for air. Every part of me burned, screaming in agony. I started upon colliding with a tree and let my head fall backward. Waited for the dancing stars to dissipate, for my lungs to recover and the pain to fade.

There was no time for any of it.

A woman in white dropped from the trees, drew a sword, and charged. I screamed at my body to move, my legs to push me out of the way, but they refused. Moisture stung my eyes as I grit my teeth, pulling myself along the snow with one arm.

A dark form hurtled through the air, tackling the deymoness to the ground. It took several blinks to clear my vision enough to see Nik as he rolled atop the deymoness and slammed a dagger into her throat over and over again.

Nik shoved himself to his feet. Beside him lay a bow. He didn't bother retrieving it. Chest heaving, he crunched along the snow toward me, wiping blood from his face.

"I-I'm sorry," I gasped. "I made the wrong choice." Tears rolled down my face, cutting through the blood splatter.

"The only one who didn't is Venyx," Nik said. "Let's find Miran and get the fuck out of here."

"Our horse is dead."

"Mine's not," he said. "Or it wasn't."

Nik leaned down, threw an arm around my waist, and hauled me to my feet. The moment I stood, searing pain shot down my leg as moisture prickled my skin through my layers.

"Wait!" I shouted. "Stop." Nik did as I asked, bracing me against the tree with one shoulder to keep me upright. With his free hand, he peeled back my layers of cloaks and jackets to reveal the spreading scarlet along my left side.

"Mother fucker," he spat, tearing up my shirts.

My hand shook as it came away slick with blood. Panic blinded me, even while Nik's cold fingers prodded my side, his probing accentuated by throbbing bolts. Not even Sheila's tea would fix this.

"Nik?" Hot tears spilled down my cheeks, slicing through the air's icy touch. He hissed, one hand gingerly wiping away the blood.

Somewhere above, the trees groaned and creaked. Branches snapped as plods of snow dropped. Nik's head shot up, curls flying around his face.

"Time to go." He hauled me into his arms, my body melting in his embrace, as he hastened through the trees. A flash of white pulled my gaze up as a set of glowing red eyes, skipping from branch to branch, launched itself at us, claws illuminated by moonlight.

Nik dropped my feet to the ground. I grit my teeth with the impact and launched myself toward the nearest tree as he drew his sword. He blocked the deymoness's attack, a deafening scream filling the forest as a lump of flesh dropped to the snowy floor—a hand. The deymoness's gaze shot up, turning pure white, before she launched at Nik. At an unnatural angle, the Amasian swung up, catching the deymoness on the chin, throwing her off just enough for Nik to swing again, slicing through the deymoness's throat.

He stepped back, chest heaving, and turned to me, wiping blood from his face.

With a cry, I forced myself up and limped to him as he rushed to meet me, every step eliciting a line of fire through my body. Warmth spread along my side with each movement. I glanced the spreading wetness in the light of the moons as it seeped down my leg and along my hip.

"Fuck," I spat, meeting Nik's worried eyes.

"Those fuckers really do like using trees, don't they," Nik said as he hoisted me back into his arms.

"Kind of makes me terrified what Venyx looks like when he's not..." I trailed off.

"Hungover?" Nik finished. "Yeah." He chuckled, the sound filled with a twinge of fear.

"Seraph!" Miran's voice preceded him as he darted through the trees, punctuated by snow crunching underfoot. He skid to a stop before us, eyes wild as he took me in. "Shit! What the fuck happened?" Gaping, he reached up, pausing before he touched me, as if afraid he'd do further damage.

"We don't know," Nik said.

With a frustrated sound, Miran hunched in front of me, prodding around my wound. I sucked in a breath at his fingers and he pulled back, face contorted with a myriad of raging emotions. As he stood, he stopped before running his hands through his hair, still soaked in my blood.

"Well, Seraph," Miran said, "I think I owe you an apology. We should have listened to the fucking deymon."

"Yes, hindsight and all that," Nik said.

"You can apologize once we get out," I grimaced.

"First we gotta find him," Nik said.

"Pretty sure he's either dead," Miran began, "or he can handle himself. He'll find us."

Miran looked over me in Nik's arms, as if assuring himself I would be okay, before he put his back to us and drew his sword. Nik adjusted me in his grip and I wound my right arm around his shoulders, burying my face in his neck, peeking between his brown curls. As a single unit, my guardians edged forward, each step placed with care, Miran leading the way. Whatever light we'd had vanished as the moons again became obscured by heavy clouds. Within moments, fresh snow began falling.

"My horse ran that way," Nik said, nodding left.

We adjusted our direction.

In the distance, another clash of steel split the night, followed by another scream.

"See," Miran offered, "he's fine."

I couldn't help the peal of laughter that bubbled up my throat, hissing as it tore through my side.

The trees above shuddered, boughs and needles trickling down, joining the fresh snow. Our tracks stopped as all three of us looked up, eyes trained on the sky, knowing what would follow.

Miran stepped forward as Nik set me down and drew his sword.

But it wasn't a single deymon that jumped down. In moments, we were surrounded by them, no time to consider what we might do before several lunged at once. Miran growled as he was tackled to the ground. I slid away from Nik, ignoring the bolts of fire running rampant down my side.

My gaze grazed the snow, looking for some way to defend myself, but there was nothing. No weapon. Nothing I could do. As if hearing that thought, one of the deymons lunged toward me, barreling me into the ground. My own scream tore through me at the explosion in my left flank, blinding me. A pair of hands hoisted me up, throwing me across something solid. Forcing my eyes open, I found myself upside down, hung over a shoulder.

Mustering as much breath as I could, I screamed, calling to Miran, to Nik, anyone, for help. But the sounds of battle, of clashing swords echoing between the trees drowned out my weak and breathless cries.

Suddenly, we were in the trees, branches tearing at my hair, at my back and arms, snagging my cloak. I reached up, stifling a cry, and gripped a passing branch, desperate to catch myself, to stop the deymon from carrying me away. It ripped off in my hands.

Hissing through my teeth, I braced myself against the deymon's back and tried shoving myself up. Reaching for his raven hair. But it was too far. The echoes of pain ravaging me too great. With a desperate, animal growl, I snapped off another passing branch and stabbed the deymon's back over and over. Screeching, he fell backward out of the tree.

The breath was knocked from my chest. Lights flashed before my eyes as warmth spread against my layers, the cloth sticking to my skin. Holding my side, I shoved my feet beneath me. After several failed starts, I forced myself up and limped away from the deymon, screaming Miran's name.

A solid force tackled me from behind, shoving me face-first to the snow. Blinding lights flashed along my vision as pangs ricocheted through me, rending me breathless. The deymon curled a fist in my hair, dragging me to my feet. Vision blurred by tears, I reached up, scratching and clawing at the deymon's hand, ripping skin as my fingernails dug into his flesh. Crying out, the deymon snatched his hands away and shoved me back.

"You can go to Kaival alive, or in pieces," he seethed, fangs catching the rolling light above.

"Go fuck yourself," I spat. I sat up, braced against a tree, one hand to my side as blood trickled between my fingers. Seething, head tipped back, I prepared to jump up, to claw the thing's eyes out as he stalked toward me, sword in hand, when he suddenly stopped. His gaze flicked up, toward the sky.

No, to the trees.

The deymon whipped around and began running, but not fast enough. A dark shape launched from the tree onto the deymon's back, a pair of swords slicing through the air. I gulped, cringing, at the sound of tearing flesh, of a gurgling scream.

Shoulders rising and falling with each heaving breath, Venyx faced me. The tips of his swords dragged through the snow as he approached and dropped to my side, head hanging to his chest. Twin rivers of blood ran from his nose. After a moment, he tipped his head toward the sky, taking one slow, deep breath after another and wiped his face on his sleeve. He cleaned his blades on the edge of his cloak and sheathed them before turning to me.

The deymon licked his lips as he examined my side, carefully peeling back the layers of soaked cloth. I winced as his fingers prodded the sensitive skin.

"It's not deep," he said, "but we need to stop the bleeding."

"I figured that," I said, teeth clenched.

"Can you stand?" he asked, ignoring my quip.

"Does it look like I can fucking stand?" I spat.

The ghost of a grin pulled at one corner of his mouth. Blowing out his cheeks, he shoved himself up and leaned down, wrapped an arm around me and hoisted me into his arms. I whined against him, my fingers digging into the shoulder of his cloak, face tucked into his neck.

"Where are the pups?" he asked.

"What?" I barely mustered the energy to look at him.

"The Amasians."

I winced with his every step, trying to find the strength to answer. "I don't know," I finally said.

At a bright light, I forced my eyes open as the tree line fell behind and the blank landscape stretched before us. The twin moons shimmered down on all the miles of snow like a mine of precious gems.

Venyx suddenly stopped, glancing over his shoulder, his hair falling about his face. It was strenuous to even follow his gaze.

One arm fell from around me and he gently set me on my feet, drawing his swords. Placed himself between me and the trees. Cursing under my breath, it was all I could do to not drop to the ground, exhausted. From blood loss, from fatigue, from running. My shoulders sagged, a great gust of breath rushing from my chest as a group of deymons emerged from the forest, some dropping from the branches, to surround us.

Venyx flipped his swords over his hands, casting a long glance at the deymons surrounding us. His stance relaxed—far too casual for being moments from death.

The ground began rumbling, nearly dropping me to my knees. The deymons traded glances, a spackling of silver darting behind us. Venyx's gaze followed, and I faced the same direction.

A hopeless gurgle spilled from my mouth as a horde of horses thundered along the snow, battle cries churning the air, weapons glinting in the night.

Venyx stepped around me, placing himself between me and the horde, the deymons forgotten as they fled back into the forest.

Within moments, we were surrounded. The riders wore thick furs and leathers, faces masked, shielded from the cold. A pack of them peeled off into the forest, on the heels of the White Army.

"Marauders," Venyx said over his shoulder.

"Of course they are," I scoffed, rolling my eyes.

The first row of riders dropped to the snow, brandishing their weapons. Venyx adjusted his grip on his swords. Grimacing, I stepped back, allowing him room to move. How much he would need I didn't know, only that I wanted to be nowhere near those blades while he wielded them.

Somewhere in the forest, a scream rent the night and my heart dropped. I strained to hear. To know if it had been Nik or Miran. Still, it could just as easily have been a soldier, though, at this point, it hardly seemed to matter. My journey had come to an end, and I'd only just started.

The nearest marauder raised a battle axe, seemingly unintimidated by the deymon before him. I glimpsed around Venyx as the man stalked closer, gaze intent. At movement behind me, I turned to the men surrounding us. They all appeared eager, weapons held at their sides. As if waiting their turn.

Grimacing with each slight movement, I turned back to Venyx as he rolled his wrists, his shoulders.

The marauder raised the axe and swung down. In the same instant Venyx swung up, the force of his blow slicing through the haft of the axe, the head diving harmlessly into the snow as its wielder watched, helpless, before his gaze snapped up. Just in time for Venyx to whip both blades through the man's neck, severing his head completely.

Two more jumped forward at once—one with a curved blade, the other wielding a short sword—the pair working in tandem. Venyx batted away both blades with precision, the battle seeming more like a dance, a work of art, than a fight for our lives.

Another swipe and the man with the curved sword had his throat opened, hot blood spraying across the snow. He spilled forward, sword dropping beside his corpse. I glanced at it, then back to Venyx as he finished the second marauder.

I licked my lips, eyes darting back and forth, a sick feeling boiling in my stomach at allowing Venyx to fight for me. Alone. But the burning in my abdomen, the wet heat sticking to my skin, held me in check.

Venyx stepped back, pressing himself into me, both swords held aloft as we shuffled in a slow circle, waiting for the next attack. One of the marauders nearest the tree line nodded, and three more men jumped forward, weapons ready.

"Eventually they'll find the number of men it takes to kill you," I seethed over my shoulder.

Venyx huffed. "I've got a while."

Biting back the stab in my side, I lunged forward, grabbed the curved sword, and stood up, slamming into Venyx's solid back.

"You pick up a sword, you better know how to use it," he spat.

Another marauder sauntered into the circle, hefting a pair of axes. Eyes trained on me.

The man before me lunged, swinging both axes at once. Gasping at my side, I threw my blade up, hissing at the vibrations on impact. The marauder seemed unfazed. Beneath his mask, it appeared he was smiling.

He stepped back, rolled his wrists, and attacked again, the axes raining down in a flurry, one after another, clanging and slamming against my blade. Each blow wrenched more tears from my eyes, searing pain mounting along my flank. Though it was too late to back out, regardless how bad the idea had been.

Behind me, one of the men attacking Venyx screamed a bloody, gurgling cry before snow crunched underfoot. I forced myself to focus on the battle before me, ignoring the spreading wetness prickled by cold.

Another body hit the snow.

The marauder before me swung down.

My side tingled, going numb. Panic flooded me as my arm refused to raise, resisting the need to cooperate, even as the marauder's blades performed a slow arch through the frozen air.

I blinked and Venyx stood before me. He caught the twin axes between his blades and kicked the man, sending him sprawling to the ground before pouncing on him, driving both swords through his gut. I cringed at the sound.

A solid arm suddenly wrapped around my waist as the sharp edge of a blade bit my neck, pulling me into a chest piled with furs. I went stock still, the sword dropping from my hand.

"Deymon!" the man who held me shouted. A rush of thoughts swirled through my head, blood pounding in my ears. Venyx turned, his expression darkening as our eyes locked. My captor pressed his chin to my forehead, smiling.

Venyx sheathed his blades and dropped to his knees, hands going to the back of his head.

"Good," my captor said. "You been initiated in how we handle deymons." He turned to the men circling us. "Dragon irons. Make 'em tight. Don't want the fucker gettin' out."

Several of them trudged through the gathered crowd toward their horses, lingering only a moment before rattling filled the night. Through the snow they dragged chains, scarcely able to lift them.

The men beside Venyx hefted one of the longer chains, wrapped it around the deymon's waist, and shackled it while another bound Venyx's hands behind his head. The chains on his wrists linked to the one around his waist. Another of the men tested it, the iron clanging together as they checked the tension. Yet another brought forth a strange muzzle. It was wrapped around Venyx's mouth and fastened at the back of his head so tight it cut into his angled cheeks.

"What are you doing?" I asked.

"Gotta be careful of deymons, darling," the man holding me said. "Thems is dangerous creatures."

The blade finally fell from my throat, thankfully without having bitten my skin, before a hand gripped my hair at my scalp, holding me aloft.

The enclosure of men and horses parted and my heart dropped to the pit of my stomach, to the very soles of my feet. More marauders filed into the center, accompanied by a pair of bodies. Like Venyx, Miran's hands were lashed behind his head, sapphire eyes blazing with fury. He looked tired, breathless, sporting a reddened, swollen eye.

Nik was dragged through the snow, brown curls hanging limp around his face, before he was thrown unceremoniously to the ground. His bottom lip was split open, oozing blood.

A tear-filled gasp fled my lips as Miran was forced to his knees beside Nik's prone form.

"You're gonna behave," the marauder said, walking me forward, "or I'm gonna start takin' pieces off your gents here, yeah?"

"Yes," I seethed, fighting the urge to lash out.

"You okay?" Miran mouthed, meeting my gaze.

My vision went blurry as moisture flooded my eyes, heart drumming at the base of my throat. I nodded, several tears falling free.

The marauder holding me led me to where Venyx knelt in the snow. His brown eyes flicked up, flashing red, and fluttered over mine before shifting to the man holding me.

"Now, deymon, we're gonna lash you to one of these nice horses, and you're gonna go behind it nice and gentle, ain't you? No pulling, or tugging, or ripping it in half. Nothing nasty. Or little miss here gets whatever punishment I see fit."

Fighting the urge to squirm against his hold, I dropped my gaze to my feet, swallowing my flailing pulse.

"If you put one fucking finger on her," Miran roared, "I fucking swear I—"

"You ain't in no position to be giving demands, mate," the marauder said, dragging me around to face Miran. He pointed his knife in the spy's direction, flicking it between Miran and Nik. "And since you two's easier to kill than the deymon here, I would suggest you keep that tongue in your fucking mouth before I find it in me to cut it out."

Miran's breath erupted in a ragged, foggy stream, rage seething from him. But he said nothing else.

Beside him, one of the marauders tied Nik's wrists together, then his feet.

"Tie that one to that saddle." He gestured to Miran. "An' throw that one over it," he said, pointing to Nik. "Lash the deymon to that one. Round it up, boys! Let's head back!"

The marauders burst into a flurry of activity as the spies and deymon were dragged and tossed around like goods rather than people.

To me, the leader whispered, "And you get to ride with me."

TWELVE

THE MARAUDER LEADER KEPT me close, his body warm against my back. Though his hands stayed around my middle, they still sent shivers up and down my spine as a quiet, tearful fury boiled inside me.

His breath fanned the side of my face. A constant reminder I was at his mercy, fueling my rage all the more.

My side ached and burned at my stature, forcing me upright so I could breathe. My captor was either oblivious or uncaring at the blood painting me, rivulets oozing down my leg. Its frozen touch bit into my skin, only making the whole ordeal that much more uncomfortable.

From the corner of my eye, I spotted the horse carrying Nik. The same one Miran trudged behind, lashed to its saddle. The marauder occasionally glanced back, chuckling, as if my guardians' plight brought him joy.

Nik's hair flopped and bounced with the horse's every step, his head swaying along. He was so tall, his hands nearly skimmed the snow. Occasionally, the marauders chuckled at him. It made me want to rage against them. But, begrudgingly, I kept my mouth shut. It would do no good to lash out.

The marauders seemed to take joy in throwing slurs at Miran, tossing snowballs at him, pelting his fiery curls. Nik was not exempt from their bullying, even in his unconscious state. But Venyx...

The last I'd seen the deymon, three marauders on horseback had taken position behind him, bows trained on him. As if he could hurt any of them with his hands bound behind his head.

Sometime after we'd been taken captive, I asked the marauder, "Why don't you just kill us? We don't have anything." I bit back the fear lacing my voice, despised the smile in his when he answered.

"I ain't so sure you don't got nothing useful," he purred.

I stifled a sob, disguising it as a disgusted growl, curling away from him as much as I could. The marauder only chuckled, the whole interaction seeming to please him.

The day passed before the silhouette of a large campsite appeared against the darkening horizon, the blurry image of a bonfire igniting the air above. My heart pounded louder, harder, the closer we drew. Would they kill us when we reached the camp? Or would our deaths be dragged out for their amusement? Their treatment of me, of the Amasians, seemed to suggest the latter.

As we rode through the camp, crowds of people approached. A myriad of faces peered at us, all wearing heavy furs and leathers, same as our captors.

I wasn't sure what I'd been expecting, but a village had not been it.

Standing between the adults, men and women and elderly, were tiny faces, eyes wide in wonderment. My mind flashed back to my dreams. The little girl on the beach. The children I'd played with all those years ago. I returned their awe at the realization—the last time I'd seen a child, I'd been one.

Some of the children pointed to their own hair upon seeing mine, delight curling their faces. "A real mermaid!" one cried, a smile pressing into her chubby cheeks. A field of smiles spread before me. They did not reach the adults.

There was an audible gasp. Turning my head, I strained to see what the fuss was about. Between the marauder's form behind me, and the stinging reigniting in my side, I saw nothing. But I heard all the same.

Those gathered took a step back, mutterings of *deymon* passed about. Their faces full of awe, of fear. Some even painted with disgust.

"Told ya," my captor said, pulling my attention back to him. "Deymons is dangerous creatures."

I swallowed, having no argument. Just that morning, he'd slaughtered a handful of men single-handedly. I couldn't blame them for fearing him. Even other deymons were terrified of him.

Most of the procession fell off as we marched through the village. The spectators dissipated as we went, though a few lingered, following in our wake. They muttered as they trailed us, curious gazes shifting over our party.

At the very center stood a tent far larger than the rest. The leather sides were painted with images of horses and dragons, groups of people riding into battle.

My captor dropped to the snow and pulled me with him, my side reigniting at the movement. He'd left my hands unbound, though I didn't suppose there was a reason to bind them. I wouldn't get far on foot.

One of the marauders ventured into the largest tent, disappearing for several long moments. While he was gone, Miran and Nik were brought forward and forced to their knees in the snow beside me. Swallowing the thick sludge of emotions welling in my throat, I glanced at Miran, at the fear glimmering in his bright blue eyes. Then to Nik, his breath ragged. He looked disoriented, haggard, and within moments of vomiting.

Finally, the marauder exited the tent, standing off to the side as an old woman hobbled behind him, leaning heavily on a walking stick. She, too, was swathed in fur and leather, her hair indistinguishable from her fluffy white coat. Her face was leathery, riddled with wrinkles. Deep set eyes so blue they looked transparent alongside the paleness of her skin.

Those eyes ignored me completely, going instead to my captor at my left. She looked over him, something akin to a snarl falling from her lips. One hand jolted up, a bony, wrinkled finger pointing at him. "What have you got, Boy?" she asked, her voice as weathered as her face.

The man beside me cleared his throat, his tanned skin reddening as he stepped forward. He bowed his head. "Quarry of the White Army. They been huntin' 'em for days. Figured they'd be worth something. Specially this one."

He shoved me forward and the old woman reached out, gripping my wrist faster than seemed possible for her age. She pulled me down, peering into my eyes and, grunting, released me with a wave of her hand. I hobbled back.

"She certainly is," she said, adjusting her walking stick. "And what, my grandson, do you think this prize truly worth?" Her pale eyes shifted back to her grandson, gazing at him with an intensity I didn't envy.

The marauder stammered, eyes shifting back and forth. Finally, he licked his lips and nodded. "Only Sirenian woman I know hunted by the White Army is the Child o' Sky and Sea," he said. "Figured we could sell her to the Queen Faerie."

The old woman snorted. She took a step forward, waving for him to approach. He nervously complied.

"And you know what Kaival would answer with," she asked, "if you told their queen we have in our possession the Child of Sky and Sea?" He blinked, licked his lips again as if searching for the correct answer. "It certainly wouldn't be coin! Stupid boy! They'd wash over us like an avalanche in the night. Rape our women, slaughter our children, and decimate our people. And take her anyway." She scoffed again. "Thank the gods I been wise enough not to drop dead yet! You'd drive our people to extinction."

He stepped back, feet shifting nervously.

I swallowed thickly, my gaze fixed on the snow before me.

"Besides all that," the old woman continued, "we don't deal in flesh peddling." Her gaze slid back over me like a physical touch. "We're thieves and killers, Boy. Not monsters."

The old woman motioned to Miran and Nik beside me before waving a hand in my direction. I stepped aside. "And these two?"

"We heard on the wind the Child was bein' escorted by Amasian spies. So..." His voice trailed off, filled with nerves.

She stopped and regarded him before bursting out laughing. It was a cold, cruel sound, broken by worn-out lungs. The woman turned to face me. "I told his mother his father wasn't a good match. Didn't have two thoughts in his pretty head to rub together. But he was good with a sword and had a big cock, so what did I know?"

The man's cheeks reddened further. She faced the marauder before pointing her walking stick first at Nik, then at Miran.

"What in the name of the gods do you intend to do with a couple Amasian spies?" she shouted. "Sell them back to Amasius?"

"We—"

"Dear, idiot boy, they'd faster send someone to slit their throats than pay for their return. Wouldn't they?" she asked, facing the Amasians. Miran assented, his curls bouncing. Nik nodded in agreement. "The only thing more useless than a captured Amasian spy is a limp dick," she said, turning back to her grandson. "And we got two of 'em. Did they at least have anything worth their capture?"

"Uh—"

"No," I interjected. "We were attacked in the middle of the night, in the forest. All our supplies were lost."

She scoffed, shaking her head as she said, "You fucking idiot boy. Did you bring anything more worthless than these three?"

"We captured a deymon," he said. Her face fell.

"A deymon." She pulled in a deep, shuddering, breath. "You captured a deymon and brought it back here? To our campsite?"

"Yes...?" he stammered, looking as if he wished to melt into the snow.

"Was it part of the White Army?"

"No."

The old woman scoffed again. "Should have removed its head and left it to the wolves. Well, let's see it, then."

I looked on helplessly as the woman motioned for Venyx to be brought forward. My gaze shifted to Miran, his concern mirroring mine.

If we got out of this, how were we supposed to get to Pensen without him?

I very nearly stepped toward the old woman, biting back the plea on my tongue for Venyx's life. But what could I tell her? He was protecting me? She'd already made it perfectly clear my life was worthless to them.

Rattling chains filled the empty air as the crowd parted. Venyx was led forward by one marauder, three bowmen trailing behind, arrows nocked and trained on him as he was forced to his knees in the snow on Nik's right. He still wore the muzzle, his arms still chained behind his head.

The old woman approached him, hobbling across the frozen ground, her weight pressing into the walking stick with every step.

Nik licked his lips, as if about to say something, then thought better of it. Miran remained silent, motionless, as the old woman regarded the deymon.

I wanted to speak up, but I wasn't sure how to address her, or even what to say. Still, my mouth fell open, silent words poised on my tongue, when she began chuckling, her furs shaking with the motion.

"I'll be gods damned," she said. The woman turned, facing her grandson. "Three deymons in the world older than the Fall, and you found one of 'em. How in the seven hells you're still breathing is beyond me."

Breath hitching, I exchanged a glance with both Miran and Nik before turning to the marauder leader. His face grew more red, if such a thing were possible, as confusion marred his brow.

The old woman took a step back, shoulders still trembling from laughter. She carefully lowered herself to her haunches, meeting Venyx eye to eye. "Once upon a time I'd given anything to have you chained up like this. Maybe not the muzzle bit." She rose and returned to stand before the large tent. "Release them."

There was an audible gasp, my own among them.

"Grandmother, wh—"

"Are you deaf, boy, or just incompetent?" the woman barked. "Release them, now! Start with him. Get that fuckin' muzzle off him. He ain't a damned dog." She pointed her walking stick toward Venyx. "Now!" she shouted, stamping the stick.

One of the marauders rushed forward with a key while another fumbled at the back of the muzzle. A third unlocked the shackles binding Miran's wrists before moving on to Nik.

"I thought you were going to abolish that practice," Venyx said once the muzzle fell away. The old woman shrugged.

"Lots of deymons in the White Army now, and the Northerlands playing host to 'em. Can't be too careful," she said.

"What the fuck is going on, Cleya?" one of the onlookers asked.

"Yes, do tell," my captor grumbled.

"Venyx and I go back a ways," Cleya said.

Venyx's face screwed up as his arms were unchained, then his wrists. He brought them down, rolling his shoulders back and forth before standing.

"You ain't aged a single day," Cleya remarked.

"Wish I could say the same," he grumbled. She laughed. This time, it almost sounded warm.

"Apologies for my dim-witted grandson," Cleya said. "Aidra's set to take over, since his mother and father passed. He's still learnin' what it takes. Still young."

Venyx crossed the open space to Aidra, coming to a stop before the shorter man.

"You can't kill him," Cleya said. "I ain't got another heir."

Aidra stared up at Venyx, panic filling his face at the deymon's glare. Venyx suddenly threw his forehead into Aidra's, dropping the man to the ground in a heap. Cleya chuckled. Two other marauders ran toward him.

"Leave him!" Cleya ordered. The men stopped in their tracks. "Maybe he'll learn something." The old woman gestured to me, her gaze sliding to Venyx. "She yours?"

Simply the way she'd spoken made my face erupt in blush, and I crossed my arms over my chest.

"She's under my protection," Venyx said. Cleya nodded.

"Where you headin'?"

"We're taking her to Pensen."

Cleya made a noise, nodding again. "Pensen's a long way off. Plenty of miles between here and there. We'll take you far as The City. Then, I want my debt considered good as paid."

"Done," Venyx said. I looked between him and the marauder woman, then to Nik and Miran, my mouth hanging open. Moments ago they'd threatened to kill us, and he was making deals with them?

"We'll leave in the mornin'," Cleya said. "You, take 'em to a tent. Get 'em somethin' to eat. I can hear the girl's stomach rumbling, even with my old ears. And give 'em something to patch her. Gonna let her bleed all over the fuckin' place."

The marauder she'd pointed to nodded and cut a path through the throng of people. Nik peered around, confused, before following the man. Miran met my gaze, brows furrowed, and trailed behind, Venyx on their heels.

For a moment, I stood, staring at the woman before her gaze met mine. She stepped toward me, wobbling with every movement. That penetrating gaze piercing my soul.

"Why are you helping us?" I asked.

"I ain't helping *you*. I'm helping *him*." She pointed with her walking stick. "Best get along. Don't wanna get lost."

THIRTEEN

MIRAN BRACED ME AS we walked, one arm clasped around my middle. By the time we reached the tent, my side was burning from my armpit to my knee, even with his support, as if seared by flames. I grit my teeth with every limping step, eyes brimming with stinging tears. But I didn't stop. Not with Cleya's words ringing in my head.

Our guide pointed at the entrance, and Nik filed in without preamble, his damp brown curls flopping around his face as he ducked inside. Venyx stopped, assessing me and Miran. Whether it was with concern or annoyance, I couldn't tell. He only seemed to have one mood.

The deymon nodded toward the entryway, brown eyes flicking over us as he held the flap open. Stifling a whimper, weight pressed into Miran, I went in. Any energy I'd had to argue was currently being used to not fall apart at the pain splitting me open. Thankfully, Miran didn't argue either.

Nik stood in the center, gazing around the small space. It was big enough for one person to stretch out. Certainly too small for four. Still, I wasn't going to complain. Even if I'd had the strength.

Two cots sat along the tent's stiff canvas walls, running beside each other, enough room between them we could move around, but little else. Nik looked up, face expectant. Grimacing, I gestured to the one on the left and Miran eased me down. I gasped at the relief flooding me as my weight left my feet, a hand going to my side.

"It belonged to brothers in the party that captured you," our guide said, stepping inside. The vitriol in his voice was unmistakable. I swallowed my guilt and shoved it down. "For the Child," he said, handing Venyx a small leather pouch.

He began shuffling around, gathering personal items. Quickly, he packed the scattered things in a small trunk, all that was needed for the sparse belongings, and left without another word.

The moment the young man was gone, Venyx stepped before the entrance. Though smaller than Miran, shorter by mere inches and not nearly as broad, he seemed to take up more space than he should as he shuffled around, sorting out blankets on the floor to, I assumed, make a nest for himself.

"Are they expecting us to stay confined in this thing?" Miran asked, easing down next to me. With a sharp breath, I leaned into him, resting my head on his shoulder, stifling a moan as the pressure fled my abdomen.

"No," Venyx grumbled. "Tents are for sleeping, not living. Marauders spend most of their time in saddles. It'll spend its days in a wagon, like everything else."

Miran licked his lips and leaned forward, weaving his fingers together. "How is it that of all the marauder tribes roaming the Northerlands, we got caught by the one whose chief you're friends with?"

Venyx ignored him.

"I was wondering that myself," Nik added, tousling his curls. "Then there's the White Army."

"Yes," Miran said. "What were you doing with them all that time?"

Venyx stopped. His silvery gaze glimmered in the dim light of the tent. "Don't imply it. Say what you mean."

"Fine," Miran snapped. "I think you were plotting with the White Army. Or, at the very least the marauders. It's awful convenient they showed up when they did."

A heavy, tension-fueled silence settled in the miniscule space as the men glared at each other.

"If I wanted the two of you dead, you'd have never left Ace's," Venyx finally grumbled.

Miran's back straightened, his mouth opening to retort.

"Alright, that's enough," I winced. "You're acting like children. If not for Cleya, we'd all be dead. We owe her our lives."

"On that, I agree," Nik said. "Even if her grandson is a fucking prick."

Miran sighed and rubbed his face, remaining silent. With a groan, he leaned into me.

I closed my eyes to the tent, to the dimness filling it, the bodies around me, and tried to push past the throbbing. The drying blood's stickiness. The harsh, crustiness of my frozen clothes, scraping my skin with every movement. Every breath.

"Do you want me to take a look?" Miran asked into my hair. The idea of someone poking around, prodding at skin sensitive to the touch, sent ripples of pain up and down my side. But if left alone, there was no telling what would happen to it. So I nodded, even that small action tugging and pulling at the wounded flesh.

Miran slid off the cot and dropped to his knees before me. I straightened as best I could, tears springing to my eyes at the movement. Nik lit an oil lamp hanging from the tent's peaked roof, casting us in dull, fiery light as Miran slowly pulled up my shirt layers. I whimpered as the cloth pulled away, some of it stuck to me. He hissed through his teeth.

"That great?" I asked, leaning on my arms.

"Nik," Miran said over his shoulder, "go get some snow to wash the blood away." Nik nodded and did as he was asked.

Without a word, Venyx handed over the small leather pouch before he followed the Amasian. And, for the first time since the glass room, Miran and I were alone.

I gazed at his fiery hair, glowing ruby red in the lantern light. At the thick fringe of lashes hanging over his sapphire eyes. He sighed, grimaced, and looked up as Nik came back, tin cup in hand.

"It's not much, but—"

"It's fine," Miran said, taking the offered mug. For a moment, Nik hovered over Miran, eyes on my side, as Miran directed me to sit up. Whining, I let Nik raise my hands as Miran removed my sweater, and instantly melted back into position, resting on my arms. The fibers of the tattered thing tore and snapped as Miran ripped the remnants into strips, dunking a piece in the water.

Miran hunkered down and began peeling the soaked fabric from my skin as Nik again raised my arms, my whimpers and cries filling the space as the latter slowly removed my shirts. I knew most of them would need a thorough cleaning, soaked in blood as they were. Some were beyond help. But they were all that stood between me and the cold, nipping my skin the moment the clothing was gone. Goosebumps raced down my arms, my back and stomach, making the soreness and stiffness in my side all the more uncomfortable.

Miran sat back on his haunches, expression intense as he examined me. Nik sat beside me, holding my hand. In curiosity, I glanced down, and wished I hadn't. My entire side from breast to hip was covered in a mottling of black and blue bruises, the worst hovering above my ribs. Just below was a furious gash, blood oozing from the broken skin. More shivers rippled through me at the sight.

"Seven fucking hells," Nik whispered.

Miran sighed, wiped his eyes and beard, as if preparing himself for the work ahead. "It won't scar neatly," he said. "Looks like a rock or something."

"The stitching will be difficult, won't it?" I asked, preparing myself for the pain ahead. Nik squeezed my hand. Miran's gaze jumped up, locked with mine, and he nodded. I drew in a shaky breath and slowly released it.

Miran's hand dipped to the mug on the floor, splashing the water inside before he squeezed out the makeshift rag. I took a deep breath and leaned further back. Tipped my head to the ceiling, closed my eyes, and forced myself to not flinch when the cloth touched my skin. As if to hold me still, maybe as a form of comfort, Miran's free hand rested along my right side, rubbing gentle circles along my belly as he worked, slowly freeing the stiffened blood from my wound. As he did, Nik continued stroking the back of my palm.

Against my will, a sob flew from my lips, tears eking from the corners of my eyes. Miran sucked in a breath. I wanted to see his face, to glean even a small amount of comfort, but didn't dare look down. Not again.

"Do you need a break?" Miran asked.

I shook my head, lip between my teeth. "I just want it over with."

"We can still run," Nik quipped. Despite the pain, I chuckled, and immediately sucked in a breath.

"I know you want to rely on him, because Aurorian said you could," Miran said, voice just above a whisper, "but Nik is right."

"Do we have to have this conversation right now?" I gasped.

Miran chuckled. "Just trying to distract you."

"I think it's working," Nik said.

"Shut up," I spat.

Nik laughed.

I looked down then, at the subtle smile pulling on Miran's mouth, the ghostly dimple in his right cheek, begging to be set free. He bit his lower lip in concentration, gaze flicking up to meet mine.

"Ok," I said, giving in. "Why?"

He drew a sharp breath, dunked the rag again and continued his ministrations. I fought the urge to squirm out of his reach, knowing it would just hurt more. Nik's grip tightened.

"You already know I dislike how Aurorian treats you."

"We both do," Nik added.

Miran nodded. Whether to himself, to Nik, or to me, I didn't know. Didn't care. "She's never had your best interest at heart. Even if Amasius does. She's the one pulling the strings, and we all know it. Her deymon friend is just an extension of that. And the timing of it all..." He shook his head. "Of all the marauder tribes, and there are probably hundreds, *this* is the one that finds us?"

123

"He saved my life."

"So have I," Nik added.

"As have I," Miran reasoned, dunking the rag a third time. By now, I was sure the water was as red as the blood in my veins. "And not because we were hired to do so."

"It's still your job," I countered. He nodded, bit his lip again.

"It is, I won't argue."

"You can't."

"No, I can't." He put the rag aside and picked up the pouch. "Here comes the painful part," he said, setting the contents on the cot. I took a breath, settled into my arms, into Nik's side, and tried with everything in me to relax. "But I swore an oath, Seraph. We both did." His gaze jumped to Nik. "To serve and protect you. To lay down our lives if need be. His loyalties lie with whatever payment awaits him in Pensen. Nothing more."

He threaded the needle as if knowing how to stitch a person. He probably did. A few of his own scars had probably been mended by his own hand.

In that moment, as he placed the sharp tip against my skin, I wondered if he was right. Again.

Then again, the reasons I had for trusting Aurorian were innumerable. After all, she had raised me. She'd taken me in, hidden me. Protected me. Kept me from a world intent on using my blood as a bargaining chip.

But for what?

For all the same reasons the world wanted to use me. For my life. My blood. I was, she'd told me, meant to die. Meant to free the world from the clutches of the Queen Faerie by sacrificing myself. That was my purpose.

At least I could say she'd never hidden it from me.

I flinched as Miran tugged the thread through my skin, leaning into the warmth of his hand as Nik's arm wrapped around me, squeezing me against him. Miran bit harder on his lip, as if his actions caused him pain, as well.

How long had she known there was a leak in Amasius? Had she known about Dracon before stepping foot in the tavern? She had, after all, taken us there to get her deymon friend. As if she'd known beforehand she'd have to leave.

But even with all that, there was still the White Army to contend with.

"I don't want to leave." The words fell from my lips before I registered them.

Miran gazed up between stitches, saying not a word before digging the needle back in. I stifled a cry as his left hand tightened around me, holding me in place. Holding me together. Nik pulled me closer, lips pressed into my hair.

"I think..." I blinked away the tears, my words lost in the flurry of emotions mingling with the pain, nearly blinding me to both. "I think it would be easier to move through the Northerlands in a marauder tribe than on foot by ourselves. We don't have to trust Aurorian, or Venyx, to recognize that."

"No, we don't," Nik added. "Though he's already proven himself useful."

For a long moment, Miran was silent as he finished his work. With the final stitch, thankfully, in place, he cut the remaining thread and washed his hands and the needle before placing the kit back in its pouch. A sigh of relief tore from my mouth.

"That he has," Miran finally mumbled. He slipped off his cloak, removed his own torn, bloody sweater, and eased it over me, enveloping me in his warmth, the scent of him. Nik situated it around my middle as Miran sat on my other side and pressed a kiss to my temple.

"Ok," he said. "We'll stay." He sighed, leaning into me. "For now."

He reached up, thumbing stray tears from my cheeks before he kissed me.

"Thank you," I whispered against his lips.

FOURTEEN

S AT IN THE CENTER of camp was the largest bonfire I'd ever seen, flames licking the darkening sky. I hissed through my teeth with every limping step, Miran and Nik bracing me on either side. Both their gazes constantly swayed toward me.

Though it was spotted in blood and dirt, Miran's sweater protected me from the worst of the cold. Still, a chill slid along my skin, snaking beneath the sweater's thick knit. No amount of clothing would stop the icy caress of the biting air. That was life in the Northerlands.

As we settled in among the marauders, a myriad of faces glared at me from the depths of their hoods—elven, dwarven, and human alike. There seemed to be no one race amongst them. Every single one, however, stared us down as if knowing the blood we wore belonged to their own, splattered beside that of the White Army. I couldn't shake the sensation as I eased onto the makeshift seat between my guardians.

Just after we sat, Venyx appeared from nowhere and swatted Nik's head. The Amasian jumped, eyes wide, as he turned to face the deymon. "What the fuck!" Nik shrieked. "Wear a fucking bell!"

Venyx nodded in the direction opposite the fire.

"Suppose I'm going with him," Nik grumbled before shoving to his feet.

Beside me, Miran sighed and rubbed his face. Exhaustion hung off him, heavy in the slump of his shoulders. As his hands fell from his eyes, our gazes locked and he smiled, a thin, weak thing, and pulled me into him, kissing my temple. I melted into his embrace.

Venyx and Nik returned a few moments later, hands full of bowls. I silently accepted mine from Venyx as Nik handed one to Miran before retaking his seat. Gazing into it, I wasn't sure what it was aside from food. It looked like a sort of porridge, which only made my stomach turn. I'd had enough of the stuff to last a few lifetimes. But the smell elicited a grumble in my gut, so I forced the first bite down. Only to be pleasantly surprised. Moments later, the dish was clean and my stomach full.

After our bowls were collected and returned, I gazed around as the camp came alive. Despite the descending night, lively chatter and songs filled the air. Children ran around the fire, chasing one another. Played with hand-carved toys. A group sat in front of an elder, listening to a story full of hand puppets and noise effects.

Sensing a pair of eyes on me, I turned to Miran, a soft smile pulling on his full lips.

"What?" I asked, unable to help my own smile. He shook his head, curls flying, and sighed.

"Nothing," he breathed. "Just ... watching you watch them." He nodded toward the children.

I scoffed, and immediately regretted it, a hand flying to my side. "Happy to be of service." I flicked my gaze away before finding his again, my lips tipping up in response.

His smile deepened and he plucked my hand off my knee, kissed the back of it, and threaded his fingers between mine. So we sat, absorbing the warmth of each other's touch. At least until a girl, little more than six or seven, slinked to us, brown eyes wide with wonder. She bit her bottom lip, swaying back and forth.

"Hi," I said, unable to help my growing smile.

The girl tucked her hands into the pockets of her coat before she finally spoke, as if mustering the courage. "Are you a real mermaid?" she asked, her voice little more than a strained whisper.

My heart warmed at the innocence on her face, in her eyes.

"I am," I whispered. The girl's face lit from within, brighter than the bonfire at her back. Teeth on full display, save for the missing front one. She giggled and stepped closer, reaching toward my hair. I leaned carefully forward to meet her.

In that instant, a woman stormed toward us, something like rage and fear mingling on her features as she grabbed the girl's hand and ripped her back, scolding her in another language. The woman's furious gaze speared me, flicking across the Amasians to either side, before she tugged the protesting girl away.

A heaviness settled in my heart as they left. Shrugging into myself, I tucked my body against Miran and stared into the snow before finding the writhing flames.

The darkened ceiling of the tent loomed above. Beside me, Miran's soft snores rumbled, though that was hardly what kept me awake. He slept on his side, allowing me room to lay on my back. The writhing, throbbing pain, however, didn't seem to care which position I lay in.

Somewhere in the forest lay all our supplies, scattered about for animals to pick through. Strewn amongst the rubble was the tea Sheila had given me. What I would have given for it in that moment.

Sighing, I rolled onto my side for the thousandth time, facing Miran as he slept. The cascade of curls draping his face made him appear younger. Almost boyish. A snore tore from his throat and I groaned and rolled back over. The flash of heat along my side stopped me, made me lay on my back again, though it did little to ease the pain.

"There's plenty of room down here." Venyx's deep voice rumbled in the dark. My body stilled at his words, wondering if I'd groaned too loudly. If I'd spoken without meaning to.

Then I realized he probably heard me shifting as I tried to sleep, and wondered if my moving kept him awake. So I lay as still as possible. Eventually the pain would fade.

When it didn't, I groaned and eased off the cot, tiptoed across the small space and sat beside the deymon. His silvery gaze flicked to me as I settled, though he said nothing.

Swallowing, I scooted over, putting as much space between us as possible.

"I won't hurt you," he said from where he lay. I wanted to cringe back from those words, crawl into the floor and never come out. He'd already saved my life multiple times, and I was still terrified of him.

The deymon pulled a pillow from beneath him and handed it to me.

"Place it under your side," he said. "It'll help with the pressure." Hesitantly, I took the pillow and laid it down, easing myself atop it, sighing at the sudden relief. "Here," he said, offering me his blanket.

I took it and threw it across myself, looking up as he turned and faced the opposite direction. Between the pillow beneath me, the blanket atop me, and the cold seeping through the thick canvas floor, I was the most comfortable I'd been all day. With a sigh, I let my eyes slide closed and slipped into sleep.

The first week with the marauders was the hardest. Though my wounds healed, I still writhed in aching pain. Hating every movement. The long stints in the saddle.

We broke for camp at dusk. Learning how the tent fit together, how everything worked, was an arduous task I would have hated in the best of health. But the leaning, bending, kneeling, standing, had me gasping, sweating, and grimacing, one hand clutching my side. All while Miran growled in my ear about needing to rest, to be easy on myself.

Within the first few days, the tribe began to accept us. Or rather, they no longer scowled every time we passed them at the bonfire.

True to his ways, Nik found a group to spend time with, even in the saddle. He rode alongside them, laughing and joking, sharing his adventures around the world—those he could—and spent his evenings with them, as well. At night, they broke into knife-throwing contests, which Nik always happened to start horribly, and ended up besting everyone.

"He hustled us!" one of the men cried, stabbing an accusing finger at the spy.

Nik looked affronted, hand on his heart, as he pocketed his treasures. "I would never."

"Yer a damn spy!" the man yelled. "Course you would!"

"A spy, yes. Not a thief," Nik countered.

A cluster of men stood to the side, chuckling and laughing as the accuser's face grew more red. Hissing through his teeth, the man waved a dismissive hand and stormed away.

"A cheat, Seraph," Nik gaped. "He called me a cheat! Can you believe that?" He eased himself onto the seat beside me.

"You? A cheat?" I asked. "The nerve of him." He huffed in agreement.

Miran bit back his chuckle.

Venyx tended to wander back and forth, remaining close to me and Miran as we rode. At the bonfire, he lingered nearby, though never seemed to pay much attention to either of us.

Near the end of our first week, the deymon rode before us, tailing a wagon carrying the tribe's children. They poked their heads out of the canvas flaps and stuck their tongues out. Some of them would make faces, screwing up their little features so I couldn't suppress my chuckles. Behind me, Miran laughed, making faces in return.

Inside the wagon, the children laughed and giggled. They whispered, though not very quietly, while deciding who would stick their head out next. As they deliberated, Venyx leant down from his saddle, flexing in an impossible angle to scoop up a handful of snow. He balled it up and hid it behind his back, waiting for the next child to pop out. The moment one did, a little girl with blonde curls, she was met face first with a snowball.

She ducked back inside, squealing, "No fair!" while the other children burst into uproarious laughter.

At the bonfire that night, I observed how the strongest warriors assisted the eldest among them. They helped them move about, fed them, wiping their mouths with care, displaying a softness I hadn't expected among a people who embraced such a harsh, cruel existence.

"Seems like the eldest would slow them down," Miran said between bites of food. His expression showed no malice, only practicality.

Venyx's voice cut through the chatter, startling me. I hadn't been aware he'd been listening. "They value the elderly among them. They've braved the harshest battles, the coldest winters. Faced every enemy head on and survived. The only enemy left is death itself."

FIFTEEN

A FEW NIGHTS LATER, after camp was set up, the whole tribe gathered around the bonfire. Miran rose and tapped my shoulder, motioning toward our tent. I glanced at Venyx, then at Nik, neither paying us any attention, and followed.

Inside the tent, I slipped off my shirt layers, gifted to me from the tribe's women, and sat on our cot, blinking away the light of the lantern as it swung overhead. Miran placed a cup of water on the floor, a clean rag in hand.

I couldn't help examining my side, how the bruises turned pink and purple as they faded. Bright, sickly yellow in places. Every day Miran cleaned it for me. Every day he commented on how well it was healing.

"I guess we can say your healing ability is far greater than humans," he said with a smile, the bruising around his eye still dark.

"I suppose so," I agreed, head tipped back. It barely hurt anymore as Miran cleaned it, his ministrations soft and gentle, aware of every flinch, every movement of my face. And always with one hand on my right side, rubbing soothing circles against my stomach. The less I hurt, the more that pain drifted down into my belly. Between my thighs. Burning inside me.

I hated sharing a tent with Venyx and Nik.

Silence stretched between us as he cleaned, making sure the stitches were still tight. Restitching what needed it. As he worked, my thoughts drifted to the camp outside our tiny, borrowed world.

"What if I chose to stay?" I asked absently. Miran's hands stilled. I risked a glance, noting his raised brows, the firmness of his mouth.

"Stay?" he asked, that simple word laced with so much. Heat rose to my face, burning down my neck and into my chest.

"I mean." I stopped, licked my lips, and started again. "I ... I like it here. With the ... the tribe."

"Seraph..." he grumbled, voice trailing off as he dunked the rag into his cup of water.

I sighed in exasperation. "I just—"

"They tried to kill us," he reasoned.

"You're getting along with them," I countered. He chuckled, wiped his nose, and looked up at me.

"What are my options? The deymon made a deal with one of them without consulting us first. Left us stuck in this camp. With these people." He huffed, closed his eyes, and pinched the bridge of his nose. His mouth opened again, working for words that wouldn't come.

It struck me how correct he was and I deflated all at once. I folded into myself, relaxing now that it no longer caused bolts of fire to parade down my side. "I just..." I picked at my breeches, at some imaginary stain there. "Everyone has a purpose here. They all belong. They all *mean* something," I said, my voice drifting off as I spoke. The last words I wasn't entirely sure he'd even heard.

He grabbed my hands, kissed my knuckles, and ran a thumb along my cheek, my gaze rising to meet his. "You mean something to me."

I smiled despite myself. Despite the tears prickling the backs of my eyes. A heavy feeling of worthlessness sat like a stone in my gut. The only meaning I carried was the one my blood provided.

And yet, in his eyes, in his smile, reverberated every word he spoke. They lingered on my lips as he leaned up and kissed me.

"I know," I said. My vision faded around the edges as moisture gathered in my eyes and I blinked it away. "It was just a silly idea. I'm sorry I brought it up."

"Don't be," he said, hunching back down. "It's not silly to want to belong, Seraph. It's human."

I scoffed. "I'm not human."

"You're more human than most of the people I know," he said, eyes dropping to my side as he continued his work.

Day turned to night on the endless, open tundra. Cold became colder. Snow fell. I woke constantly to frost nipping my toes, kissing my cheeks.

One morning, we woke to a fresh mound of powder just outside our tent, leaving us to crawl out of it. Even this did not deter the tribe from our pace. We simply dug around the fluff, packed up as normal, and carried on.

As night fell nearing what had to be our second week with the tribe, I huddled even closer to the bonfire, desperately warming my freezing hands.

Nik finally talked Miran into joining his knife-throwing hustle, and, between the two of them, they relieved the crowd of every bit of valuables they had. As good as Nik was, Miran was better. It was all I could do to suppress my laughter as the marauders walked away confused.

Venyx lounged by the fire, one leg folded up, the other splayed before him. He bowed over his work, the tang of a knife biting into it.

A small group of children approached him, tiptoeing as if sneaking around a sleeping wolf. His gaze jumped up, making the children fall back in a fit of laughter. A smile tugged at my lips at the scene.

One of the children held out a small bit of wood—a broken toy. As it fell into the deymon's outstretched hand, the boy asked, "Can you fix it?"

Venyx sheathed his knife and set his work aside, twisting and turning the toy, examining it. "I'm sorry, but I can't," he said. Though he didn't return the thing. Instead, he plucked up what he'd been working on, the end pinched between his fingers. The whittling of a horse. "You can have this one."

The boy's face lit up and he squealed in delight, the children around him gathering to see. As one, they ran off, giggling.

The hint of a grin curled his lips, making mine wider. His brown gaze drifted up and met mine, whatever ghostly smile I thought I'd seen long gone. I faced the flames, watching from the corner of my eyes as he picked up the broken toy and continued whittling.

A shard of light from the dwindling bonfire burst through the tent flap, and I peered over my shoulder as Venyx walked in, the entrance falling closed behind him. He groaned as he sat, taking his place on the floor at the foot of the cots. After two weeks, he seemed on sentry duty in the middle of a war camp.

For a long moment I lay watching the faint shadows play on the canvas walls. Finally, I turned over and faced the deymon, his silhouette slicing the dark.

"That was very kind of you," I whispered.

A flicker of silver jumped up. I picked at the blanket, snuggling into it further, convinced that was the only reaction I would get.

"I whittle to pass the time," he said, his velvety voice cutting the silence. "While everyone else sleeps." He shifted amongst his blankets, the silver of his eyes jumping around before flickering out. "My kind don't need much sleep, so I keep myself busy."

"Oh." I licked my lips, rolling a wool pearl between my fingers before flicking it away. "Is that the only thing you do? I think I would have seen more toys if you did."

Some grumble, reminiscent of an actual chuckle, fluttered through the tent. "No," he said, rustling on his blankets. "I ... read, too." He sighed, settled back down. His hands ran over something, a cover. Then the rough pages of what sounded like a book.

"What is it?"

"It's um..." He cleared his throat, as if embarrassed. "Poetry."

I bit back the smile pulling at the corners of my mouth. "Will you read something to me?"

He grumbled, rustled on his blankets. The pages slid beneath his fingers as a glimmer of silver flicked up. "I suppose I set myself up for that."

"You did."

He cleared his throat again, rustled on the blankets. Flipped through the pages, back and forth, as if deciding what to read.

"Which is your favorite?"

He blew out a breath, flipped the pages again, and began to read.

On one frigid fate-kissed night,
In wretched odyssey,
Neath the gaze of dual lune light
She cried out for me.

At her side I fend and fought
As timeless city fell.
With my blade, I rent and wrought
Haven shorn from hell.

Sheltered by a hope-bricked wall

OF SKY AND SEA

Of secret pass, we fled.
With forbidden lovers' call
Silent vows we shed.

And in her arms my final bed,
Gentle as the sea,
On her breast I lay my head
For brief eternity.

But with the fiery dawn so bright
If the fates they deem
Lost my love, my life, my fight
On field of shattered dream.

A long moment rest between us as the cadence of his voice faded.

"That was beautiful," I whispered.

"That's all you're getting," he said, snapping the book closed.

"Thank you," I said, biting my bottom lip.

"Go to sleep."

Smiling, I rolled over and snuggled into Miran's chest, relishing his arms tightening around me as I finally drifted off to sleep, Venyx's poem echoing in the back of my mind.

SIXTEEN

T HE NORTHERLANDS TRUDGED BENEATH us, bringing us ever closer to The City. Days passed, all similar to the previous. It was in that growing familiarity I found a sense of belonging, making me regret that, eventually, it would end.

As if some unseen force heard me, I woke on my own. No rustling and bustling about the tent. No packing up, telling me we had to go or be left behind. No milling about in the snow just outside. Nothing except a dull *thump-thump-thump* somewhere to my left.

My eyes slid open and I rolled over, rubbing the sleep from them as Nik came into focus, slouched on his cot. I groaned, pushed myself up, and sat. He ignored me as he tossed his knife into a square of wood on the floor at the tent's entrance.

"Nik," I said, my voice husky with sleep. He sighed, scratched at his scraggly beard, and loosed another knife. *Thump.* Running a hand through his floppy brown curls, he groaned and pushed himself up to fetch his knives. "Nik," I repeated.

Finally, he glanced my way. "Good morning, sunshine," he mocked, smiling.

"What happened?"

A great gust of air fled him as he plopped down, reclined back, and loosed another knife. "I've been put on babysitting duty," he grumbled.

I scoffed, quirking my brows. "What does *that* mean?"

"I get to watch the Child," he cooed, a wide grin taking over his face. Jumping up, I lunged across the small space and threw my fist into his arm as he fell into riotous laughter, hands up to defend himself.

"I hate that fucking name!" I yelled.

"I know! Ow! I'm sorry! Stop!" he cried. "Stop hitting me!"

With a frustrated huff, I plopped beside him and fell back. Relaxed against him. Nik rest his head against mine, the fuzz from his beard tickling my cheek.

"Where are the other two?" I asked, looking at him from the corner of my eyes.

"Scouts spotted a contingent of White Army soldiers east of here."

I went rigid against him. My mouth fluttered. Images flashed before my eyes of our last battle with them. All the blood. The screaming.

"Are you alright?" he asked.

I nodded, forcing a smile to my face.

Nik sighed, rubbed his face. "Aidra took some of his warriors to check it out. Miran and Venyx went with him."

Moisture sprang to my eyes. We barely survived our last encounter with the White Army, and only because Aidra and his men had shown up.

Worry gnawed at me. That they hadn't taken enough men. That Venyx wouldn't come back. That Miran wouldn't.

"Seraph." Nik's voice pulled me back to the present, back to him. To the freckles along his nose, the red streaked through his brown beard. "It'll be okay. They'll probably be gone most of the day, though, so we get to relax."

I nodded again. "Okay."

Groaning, Nik rolled over and pulled me into his arms. Clutching his shirts, I sank my face into him and inhaled his scent.

"Now that you're awake, wanna go do something?"

"Like what?" I mumbled into his chest.

"Wanna learn to throw knives?"

I scoffed and tipped my head back, finding his gray eyes. "You're not bored of it already?"

He shrugged. "Come on. It'll keep us distracted."

Begrudgingly, I hauled myself from his cot and dressed, meeting him just outside the tent.

Much like our first day in camp, the tribe members milled about, going through tasks they couldn't do while traveling. They beat rugs and washed clothes. Melted fresh snow to put in the bathing tubs near the bonfire, still burning from the previous night.

As Nik and I trudged through the snow, heading toward the fire, people waved at us. They smiled and tossed us pleasantries. As if we'd been with them months. Years, even.

"Nik," someone called. A stocky dwarven man held out his hand, brusquely shaking Nik's as we stopped beside the fire. "Joining us today?" he asked, turning to me.

"I suppose," I answered.

"I'm teaching her how," Nik said.

"Shit," someone else chuckled, shaking his head. "Not too long, she'll be shakin' us down, too."

Nik's mouth fell open, hand to his chest. He certainly put on a good show. "I would never teach her such things."

The marauders laughed and meandered off.

For the rest of the morning and into the afternoon, Nik went through stances and hand motions. Proper techniques of how to make the knife do what he wanted. How to make it sink into the target, dead center, every time.

Between my constant motion and the blaze at my back, I worked up a thin sheen of sweat. Just enough for the chill to latch onto when I stopped moving. Enough for my hair to stick to my skin.

I studied Nik as he went through the motions, his arm lining up perfectly with his shoulder. The firm, straight lines of his body. How he managed to move so gracefully for someone so tall was a mystery.

"Did you learn knife throwing in the Program?" I asked. His gaze flicked to me just before he loosed another knife. A resounding *twang* rang out as it sank into the target and he faced me, one hand running through his wild curls. He unbelted the next knife, flipped it and caught it, throwing it underhanded in a single motion. It bit into the target with ease.

"No, actually. I was chosen for special projects and missions during training because I already had this skill." Another knife into the target.

"Assassinations?" I asked, a wicked smile curling my mouth. Nik flicked his gaze at me.

"That's Amasian business," he said, grinning. "My father taught me. He was a butcher by trade. Probably the last gift he gave me."

My brows pulled together. "What happened? Why was it the last gift?"

"He died." He released a grunted breath before tossing another knife and went to retrieve them.

"I'm sorry," I mumbled. He shrugged as he retook his position.

"It was a long time ago. It's why I went in. My mother died having me. I didn't have siblings, or family. Nowhere to go." He sniffled. Shrugged again. "So I decided to go into the Program. Become something. Not much else for a thirteen year old boy to do in Amasius."

Blinking away falling snow, I trudged the short distance and threw my arms around him, pulling him close. Nik sighed and draped himself around me. For a moment, we stood there. Wrapped up in each other. Listening to each other's breath.

After the moment passed, I stepped back, took one of his knives, and threw it, sinking it square in the target. Nik's mouth fell open.

"What the fuck?" he asked, arms falling to his sides.

I shrugged. "You never asked if I already knew how."

He chuckled. "You've been around spies too long."

I sighed, swiped the hair from my brow. "I'm gonna go take a nap." Nik sheathed his knives, going to fetch the ones in the target.

"Hold on, let me—"

"It's okay. It's just that way."

His brows pulled together, one ticking up.

"I'll be fine," I chuckled. "Stay here and work on getting better."

"Haha," he spat. He rolled his head, then his shoulders, spun around and threw another knife, the *twang* resounding through the air.

I meandered back through the sprawling village. Once my feet landed before the tent's entrance, I realized I didn't want to be there. Alone. Then scoffed at my absurdity. But I kept moving.

At some point, I wasn't sure when, my feet stopped. It took only a moment to recognize where I was, what tent I stood before. The largest in camp. My head tipped back, taking in the towering peak and I wondered how they even got the damn thing to stand every single day.

"Girl."

The voice made me start at its suddenness and my gaze dropped to Cleya, leaning on her walking stick in the tent's entrance, grizzled eyes trained on me. Heat swarmed my face. I wanted to turn, to go back. To peel myself from beneath that glare, but it held me transfixed.

"Come inside," she grumbled, nodding behind her.

I bit my lower lip, fighting the nervous smile tugging at my face. "I-I'm sorry. I didn't mean to end up here. I just ... I got lost."

"Hmm." The old woman's shoulders rose and fell with that sound, her leathery cheeks pulling into the semblance of a smile. "So it was your feet wantin' to talk to me."

My mouth fell open, but nothing came out.

"Come on."

This time, I followed.

Inside, the tent was larger than I imagined. Canvas walls divided the sprawling space into sections. Many of those were filled with children, laughing and playing, running around. My brows drew together in a question that Cleya had, apparently, foreseen.

"After raids, parents don't always come back," she explained, pointing with a trembling hand to the room we passed. "They need someplace to stay."

It suddenly made sense why hers was the largest tent. Why every corner seemed to be filled with warriors, hands stationed on their weapons. They weren't protecting Cleya.

And my sense of longing to stay only intensified.

She led me into a small section of the tent, a fire burning in the center, surrounded by seats of all kinds draped in furs and leathers. Cleya eased herself into one of the more worn ones, groaning as she did, as if her bones were speaking. The old woman motioned for me to sit across from her.

For a long while, she silently regarded me, making me squirm under her penetrating gaze. Another moment slid by and a young woman entered, carrying a tray laden with a steaming teapot, tea leaves beside it. The woman left and Cleya leaned forward, assembling her cup with quick precision.

"Well?" Cleya asked sharply, leaning back with her mug. I started, eyes wide, mouth gaping as I struggled to latch on to her meaning. "You gonna spit out whatever you got to say?"

"I don—"

"Yes you do." She sipped her tea. "Things got a way of leaking out whether you want 'em to or not." She pointed up. Same as the outside, the walls, the ceiling, every bit of canvas was covered in paintings. "My thoughts leak out my hands. Prolly why they shake so damn much."

I gazed around in awe.

Cleya cleared her throat, bringing me back.

"I don't have a um..."

"Everyone does, girl. Just gotta find it."

My gaze flicked down to my hands. Then to my thighs. A soft tingle rose between them, reminding me of my own tendencies. I supposed I did have my own way. Heat rose to my cheeks, deepening when Cleya chuckled.

"Well, what is it already?"

My gaze flicked up, brows creasing. Tears prickling the backs of my eyes, I took a breath, and let loose the longing I'd shoved down. Regardless of Miran. Of my destiny. Of Aurorian. "Can I stay?"

For all the reaction I received, it seemed as if I'd asked for a cup of tea.

"I don't want to go to Pensen," I choked out, uttering those words for the first time in my life. "I don't want to go to The City. I don't want to face my destiny. I don't want any of it." My throat grew thick, heart hammering loud against my chest. Before I realized it, tears streamed unabashedly down my face, splattering along the backs of my hands. And still, Cleya didn't move save to raise and lower her tea mug.

Finally, she placed the cup in the flat of her palm and chuckled. Dread filled me, poured into my every fiber at that sound. Cleya leaned forward, set her mug aside and began fixing another. She handed it to me and I took it, lacking the courage to deny her.

The old woman leaned back, taking her mug with her. "The funny thing about destiny? It don't need permission. It does what it will, and we're powerless to stop it."

Hot tears filled my eyes, rolled down my face and dove into my tea. I wrapped my hands around the mug, willing myself to absorb its heat. It seemed to be the only warmth around me, the cold hand of rejection flat along my back.

"It does flatter the Child of Sky and Sea wants to join my tribe," she said with a chuckle. "She said you might ask." My gaze snapped up. Hers softened, her smile loosening around the edges. "But I can't allow it."

I swallowed the lump in my throat as icy betrayal slapped my face. And I understood. Her tribe finding us hadn't been coincidence.

Cleya continued, "Yer sweet. My people come to adore you. An' you keep them airhead men in line, 'specially the ginger. But you's dangerous." She shook her head, eyes never leaving mine. "The Faerie Queen ain't care you don't want your destiny. She'd come roaring in here to take your head anyway. An' I can't endanger my people."

Bottom lip quivering, I gazed into my cup, at the reflection staring back at me. Another tear fell.

"It's risk enough havin' you here so long, 'specially with them fucking White soldiers roaming round."

I nodded absently, shoving the sting into my gut.

"We still heading to The City. You be leaving us then. As planned. As *agreed.*"

Licking my lips, I met Cleya's rheumy eyes and nodded. Without a word, I placed the cup on the table between us, rose, and left. In a rejection-fueled haze, I made my way back to the tent, through the entrance, and onto my cot. It smelled of Miran as I lay down. Bundling the blanket as tight as I could, I shoved my face into it and cried.

SEVENTEEN

"**H**OW BIG A PARTY you think it was?" Nik asked beside me, licking his spoon clean. I made a disgusted noise, turning away from him. He ate like such an animal.

"Small enough to not need two hundred men," I grumbled, reaching over and snatching the spoon from him.

"Hey," he whined, snatching it back. Thankfully, he popped it in his mouth.

His gaze jumped up first, prompting mine to follow, as Miran trudged into the light cast by the fire. He plopped beside me with an exaggerated sigh, head falling back on his shoulders.

"Well?" Nik asked. Miran didn't answer for a long moment. When he finally did, Venyx came into view and sat beside Nik, silent as usual.

"Group of fifty," Miran said on a deep breath, rubbing his eyes. "Looks like they'd been tracking us since the forest."

"That was weeks ago," I said. Miran glimpsed me through the slit of one eye and nodded.

"They are persistent," Nik said.

"Yes, well, now they're dead," Miran said, closing his eyes again.

"You brought one back," I said. Not asked. Miran sighed. I turned to Venyx, spearing him with a glare. He returned it before averting his gaze. "We've been hearing chatter."

Venyx sighed, pinched the bridge of his nose. "Why does it matter?" he asked.

"I want to see him."

Miran and Venyx snapped to attention. "No," they both said, the only thing they'd ever agreed on.

"It's *me* they're hunting. I think I have the right to—"

"Which is precisely why you won't go anywhere near him," Miran said, nodding in thanks to the woman bringing him and Venyx each a bowl of food.

"Mir—"

"If he's allowed to see you," Venyx said, my attention swinging to the deymon, "he could send word to others you're here. It would compromise the entire village."

I faced Nik, who only shrugged, raising his hands in surrender. "I'm not getting into this," he spat, gazing into the bowl in his lap.

"Seraph," Miran said. "We can't do our jobs if you won't let us. Please. Listen."

Sighing, I slumped back into my seat and nodded.

At the crunch of boots on snow, I rolled over on the cot, careful to not jostle Miran. The tent entrance parted and Venyx's silhouetted form filled the space before falling closed again. Silver eyes flicked about, avoiding mine. He sniffled and wiped his nose. The deymon groaned as he sat down, loosing a long, heavy breath as he lay against his nest of blankets.

"You went to see the prisoner," I said. Not a question.

He inhaled, sniffled again, but said nothing. It was all the confirmation I needed.

"What did you do to him?"

"It's best you don't know," he grumbled. "Go to sleep."

I rested my chin on my arm, playing with the blanket. "Did you find out anything useful?"

Venyx scoffed, as if enraged at the very question. "He was a low-level foot soldier. We weren't *going* to get anything useful from him, which is what I said when we captured him." He groaned and rubbed his face with both hands. "There's nothing to tell. Go to sleep." He rolled over and buried himself in his blanket.

I turned back over and snuggled into Miran. My heart thrummed in the base of my throat, curiosity digging into my brain, playing images of all the ways a deymon might hurt someone. Shuddering, I closed my eyes and shoved the thoughts away, forcing myself to sleep.

But when sleep finally came, I found myself again at the beach. Staring into those red eyes as the deymon ripped out Briahna's throat, that fanged smile pinning me where I stood.

Regardless of the sun blazing overhead, a thick, leaching cold hung about as we trekked through the Northerlands the next day. So very slowly, the flat tundra gave way to soft hills.

I found myself fidgeting with my hood, stuck somewhere between being too hot and too cold—the sun too bright in my eyes, yet not hot enough to warm my freezing hands.

While riding behind the wagon full of children, a group of marauders alongside me, Venyx's horse fell back, trotting near mine. As if sensing my gaze, he tossed a glance over his shoulder, allowing me a glimpse of twin scarlet streaks running from his nose. He turned away and wiped his face.

"Are you okay?" I asked, edging my horse closer to his.

"I'm fine," he grumbled.

"Just that you're bl—"

He turned and glowered at me before snapping his reins, riding further up the caravan.

Beside me, one of the marauders scoffed. "He barely did nothin'. We hadta kill the man ourselves." At that, I whipped around, facing him. Another slowly drew a finger across his throat, sending a shiver down my spine. "Deymons is able to dig into people's minds, to 'milk' thoughts from 'em. If they dig too deep, it could kill 'em. The person they milkin'." He scoffed again, the marauder riding beside him chuckling. "Jus' wasn't able to dig hard enough I guess."

The breath left me as I stared at the marauder, unable to form thoughts, to process what he'd said.

Several more days passed before Venyx's nose stopped bleeding. Even then, he refused to speak about it.

Word of the prisoner, and his death, spread like wildfire. From what I'd gathered, Venyx had pressed the man so hard they'd both collapsed, the prisoner rendered unconscious. It was Aidra who'd taken a knife to the soldier's throat. His body had been left in the snow—a gift to the Northerlands, someone said. Though others had far more colorful theories about what happened to the prisoner's body.

At camp, I sat between Miran and Nik, picking at my food. The Amasians made their way to the bottoms of their bowls, throwing insults back and forth, every other one punctuated by a peal of riotous laughter. I barely paid them any mind as I nibbled, staring at the deymon as he lounged before the fire, whittling knife in hand.

"You know." The marauder's voice pulled me from my thoughts and I glanced up, firelight glimmering around his towering form. He leaned down, beard hanging to his chest, the braids in his hair sweeping to either side of his broad neck. "They say the night the prisoner died, the deymon went an' feasted on his body. Why no one can find it."

My mouth dropped open, the spoon falling with a wooden *clack* into the bowl as I gawked at the man. Both Amasians fell silent before Nik gulped his food.

Suddenly, the marauder stood to his full height, threw his head back and laughed as he trudged away, chortles following him until he was clear out of sight.

"D-do deymons ... eat their enemies?" I choked out.

Miran met my gaze, mouth gaping. "I'm not-" He swallowed thickly, looking to Nik. The other Amasian shook his head, brown curls flying, shoulders raised in question, and shoveled another bite into his mouth, chewing awkwardly around it.

At rustling, my attention shifted to Venyx, my heart dropping as he rose. "I only eat the women," he said, meeting my gaze.

Nik choked on his food, leaning forward to hack up what had been in his mouth.

Heat flooded my face down to my collar, every bit of me suddenly hot and tingly as the deymon walked away.

Soft hills gave way to foothills, growing deeper and steeper as we went. A few more days, Venyx said, and we'd reach The City. My heart hammered, Cleya's words echoing in my head. The closer we drew to our destination, the more those words stung.

Bitter tears clung to my eyes, the back of my throat.

I had come to rely upon the simple familiarity of the tribe, of their wanderings and their life. On the way they viewed the world and their place in it.

We set up camp at dusk, the last vestiges of daylight flung across the horizon as night descended. As the children of the tribe ran around the bonfire, laughing and playing, I imagined what life would be like if I stayed. Would Miran stay with me? Or would he return to Amasius to be shipped off to some distant corner of the world?

If he left, would I fall in love with one of the men here? Have children? What would they look like? Would they have my lilac hair? Would their eyes be as blue as the ocean roiling in mine?

With the flames of the bonfire stripping back the grip of night, I stretched out my palm. I ran my fingernail along the center line as it stretched from one side to the other. Even as a child, Briahna had said I was special. I'd assumed she meant in that way all mothers and guardians view their children.

Over the years I'd begged Aurorian to see she'd made a mistake. I wasn't special. Couldn't be. Certainly not *that* special. How could my divine blood be proven anyway? After a while, I gave up.

Tracing the lines etched into my skin, they said nothing of my destiny. At least as far as I could tell. I would live a long life. Or so my palm said. Long for who? For an ordinary woman? Or for the Child destined to die to end the Queen Faerie's reign?

I stopped once I reached the lines indicating the children I'd have. Scoffing, I dropped my hand and stared up into the fire as it danced and curled around itself. Eventually, those flames would burn themselves out. Just like me.

Shoving my thoughts aside, I watched as a group of children snuck toward Venyx, hunched over his whittling. They hid behind the legs of warriors huddled beside the fire, spying the deymon where he sat, snickering without a clue he could hear them. A smile tugged on my lips.

Nearly too fast to see, Venyx jumped up, disappearing and reappearing before the group. The children screamed in delight and ran off in a fit of laughter as the deymon retook his seat.

So very carefully, one of the little girls crept back toward him, her words lost in the chorus of the camp. Venyx sat up and opened his mouth. With one finger, the girl reached out and pressed on a bottom fang, squealed, and ran after the others. A corner of his mouth tipped up, just for a moment, before his stoic face returned and he looked at me. I bit back my smile, sucked in my chuckling, and turned away.

"Seraph?"

I swung my gaze to Miran. "What?"

He took my hand, kissing my knuckles. "Let's go look at your stitches. It's time to take them out." He stood and pulled me with him and we wandered, hand in hand, back to our tent.

Inside, with my layers off, I eyed my side as best I could, noting the bruising had faded to almost nothing.

"It looks much better," Miran said, nodding, as he delicately cut the threads, pulling them out one by one.

"It's not so uncomfortable to ride anymore."

He looked up from beneath his lashes, tendrils of fiery curls hanging about his face. "I'll keep that in mind," he purred. I bit back my smile, heat flooding my stomach.

Miran's smile widened as he pulled the last stitch out. Rising, he pressed his lips to mine. I breathed him in, relishing the nearness of his body, the taste of his mouth. His smell. With nothing but my bra on, Miran's hands wandered across my skin, tickling the tender spot below my ribs. The heat in my stomach dropped, flourishing between my thighs and I let him push me back, opening my legs for him. Even through his breeches, his desire pressed against me. A soft moan fell from my lips, dissipating between our shared breaths.

"You do share this tent, you know." Nik's unamused voice filled the air as he stepped inside. Groaning, I dropped my head back on the pillows as Miran sat up.

"Jealous?" I asked as I sat, pulling on my shirts. Nik scoffed, glancing between Miran and me.

"I might be, but Miran's not really my type."

Miran shot up. "Out," he snapped. Nik broke into a fit of laughter as Miran shoved him toward the exit.

"I'm sorry, Miran, I'm just not attracted to red heads. You're very pretty, though."

A laugh fell from my lips and I slapped a hand over my mouth.

"Get. Out," Miran said, pushing Nik through the flaps.

"I'd love to see you kick Venyx out," he shot just before tumbling outside. Someone cried out. "Shit! Sorry!"

EIGHTEEN

THE ECHO OF A scream reverberated through my dream, jolting me awake. I sat up, chest heaving, and looked around the darkened tent, at Miran beside me. Across the small space to Nik, shoulders rising and falling in slumber.

The scream sounded again.

My gaze shot to the floor and my heart skipped. Venyx was gone.

"Miran," I said, shaking him. "Wake up!" His breath hitched and he groaned, rolling over to blink hazily before he rubbed his eyes. Someone screamed again. Then several someones. Miran's eyes went wide as he bolted upright and faced me, sober and awake.

Swallowing the rising thunder in my chest, I launched myself onto Nik. At once, his gray eyes shot open and he flipped me on my back, pinning me beneath him on his cot, a knife at my throat.

"Nik," Miran said, climbing to his feet.

Nik's eyes cleared with recognition and he sat back, flipping the knife into his palm. "Sorry," he grumbled.

Outside, something crashed. A burst of fiery light ignited the canvas wall and I jumped, breath hitching as I tried to peer into the night outside. Nik squeezed my arms before climbing to his feet. Both Amasians dressed, moving with hurried precision. Trembling, I followed suit.

"We have to go," Venyx called as he burst through the entrance. "Now."

"What's happening?" I asked, fearing the answer even as the words rolled off my tongue.

"The camp is under attack."

All the air fled my lungs at once, leaving me desperate for breath. The edges of my vision darkened, spots pinging before my eyes while my hands grew cold, clammy, and the world swam before me.

"Seraph, hey, look at me."

Chest heaving, I tipped my head back, meeting Miran's gaze as he towered over me, hands on my cheeks. He thumbed away a stray tear before kissing my forehead.

"It'll be okay," he whispered.

"It won't be if we don't leave now," Venyx growled before vanishing again.

Slipping my hand into Miran's, sliding a glance to Nik, we trailed the deymon.

Outside, the little world of the marauders was aglow. Half the tents blazed furiously. A sickening scream gurgled as someone crawled from a burning tent before collapsing into the snow, skin eaten by flames. Tears raced down my cheeks before Miran tugged me behind him.

Miran drew his sword as he looked left and right, picking his way through the trodden snow. Venyx was partially illuminated by the blazes as he led us, his cloak whipping about.

"Where are we going?" I asked, unable to think.

"Probably the corral," Nik said behind me. Miran's head bobbed in confirmation, his red curls bright in the firelight.

Somewhere to the right, another scream sounded, then another—horrid, ear-splitting things that left my gut twisted in knots. At those screams, Venyx stopped in his tracks.

"What are we doing?" Miran hissed.

Venyx gazed at us over his shoulder, the silver in his eyes flickering. Thoughts churned along his face in the same instant it occurred to me—the children.

As if reading my mind, Miran turned and pulled me to him. "The best thing to do is get you out of here," he said.

My head shook back and forth, long before I registered it, and I slipped my hand from Miran's grasp.

"Seraph, don't."

I ran.

Begging my feet to find the way, I navigated the crisscrossing pathways, dodged burning tents and people lunging toward me, jumped over a smoldering corpse, forcing myself to push the thought away. I could do nothing for the dead. But the living...

Cleya's tent was slowly being eaten by flames as I skid to a halt before it. Eyes wide, a bud of hope flickered that I wasn't too late. I didn't know what I could do, but I wouldn't leave them to the fate I'd wrought upon them.

At a groan, my gaze dropped. The old woman lay face down, clawing at the snow as if she would punish it in place of the White Army. I fell to my knees beside her and slowly rolled her over, my gaze roving her. A cut rest above her right eye, another along her throat. Her weathered hands were sliced open, none deep enough to be fatal.

"Cleya," I begged, "tell me what to do."

"Stupid girl," she seethed, eyes glittering with moisture. "I told you. You would bring death upon us like a blizzard."

"Please," I said, biting back my tears.

"Save them," she commanded, pointing a trembling finger to the tent.

Jumping to my feet, I plunged into the tent as flames curled down the sides. Part of the ceiling collapsed, burying the room where I'd had tea with the old woman. My hands rose to cover my face as I fell back, my gaze scanning the rest of the tent. The flap into the children's quarter whipped furiously in the draft created by the flames, smoke pouring out. I shimmied my scarf up around my nose, tucked it over my ears, and burst into the room.

My eyes popped open as a vise grip grabbed me and slammed me to the floor. The breath fled my lungs as my gaze slid from the claws aimed at my throat into Venyx's face, a snarl ripping across his features. Eyes blazing red.

I held my trembling hands to either side of my head. "I'm here to help," I choked out. The red faded to brown and he stood, lifting me with him. For a moment, we regarded each other. I found his gaze, the constellation of tears gathered in his lashes, the worry etched around his mouth, in the curve of his hands.

He licked his lips, gaze flicking to the room, and we turned to the task at hand.

Smoke and tears stung my eyes as I took in the sight. So many of them lay in their cots. A few coughed. Most did not.

"No," I whispered.

"Take that side," Venyx ordered, pointing. I nodded and set to work.

I sprinted to the first one, fingers desperately dancing over her little throat, relief flooding me at the pulse there. Searching for a faster way out, I spied the back of the tent as it whipped open. I wasn't sure how many I could carry, but I would get as many out as I could.

Shouldering the little girl, I went to the next cot, found a pulse, and hoisted the boy against my side, straining under their weight. Still, I forced myself on, to the other side of the room, out into the snow, and dropped to my knees, laying the little bodies down before bolting back inside.

The flames crept further down the sides.

Venyx worked silently, brows creased as he went from one cot to the next. Plucking children from their beds like flowers, he hefted two over his shoulders and another two in his arms before he bolted out.

"Seraph!" Miran burst into the tent, Nik on his heels. "We have to..." He choked on his words, face frozen in horror.

"Help!" I screeched. Neither needed further prompting as both Amasians ran to opposite sides of the room.

Under the weight of another two children, I fell to my knees in the snow, hiccupping with suppressed tears, as Miran and Nik lowered their own cargo to the ground.

Miran's hair hung about his face in sooty, sweaty clumps as he sat. He sucked in a breath and glowered at me. "I tell you to stay by my side, you stay by my fucking side," he ordered, panting. "If you want to help these people, the best thing we can do is draw the White Army away."

Tears prickling my eyes, I nodded, licking soot from my trembling lips.

Miran glanced up and he was suddenly on his feet, drawing his sword. I flipped over as a White soldier lunged toward me with a roar. Throwing my body over the children, a scream ripped from me as Miran blocked the blow, steel crashing together.

Nik jumped up, his own blade drawn as more soldiers in white surrounded us. My eyes widened as I flung my gaze around. Venyx jumped into the fray, blades swinging, the steel reflecting flames from the tent as if they, too, were on fire.

Taking in the little bodies below me, I flipped back over and gazed in horror as a section of tent collapsed. There were still children inside.

Gritting my teeth, I shoved up and ran to the tent, bursting through the flap. Smoke saturated the air, blinding me. Coughing, I waved a hand before my face and stumbled toward the nearest bed. Without checking if they were breathing, I heaved up two more children and trudged outside, dropping them into the snow. My lungs heaved in the cold air, coughs ripping through my chest.

At a glint of metal, I turned as Miran ran a soldier through, the body dropping to the ground in a heap. No sooner than he downed one another sprang forth. Nik and Venyx were locked in battles of their own.

Refusing to leave the others behind, I ran back to the tent. Mere steps away, a solid form barreled into me and we crashed to the ground. I flipped over as a soldier crawled up me, fighting for his knife. With a roar, I threw my fist into his face, kicked up with both knees, shoving away. His face went slack as he was hoisted by his collar and slammed to the snow before being run through by Venyx.

Scrambling up without a backward glance, I dove into the tent, grabbed another child, and hauled them out, collapsing atop them in a coughing fit. Through tear-filled eyes, I glanced up, finding marauders had joined the fray. With them came more White soldiers.

A crack split the night. I whipped around as one side of the tent dove into the snow, ripping the ceiling down. With an animal roar, I jumped up and ran back, only to be tackled again.

I shoved them away, kicking and screaming, not caring who it was. Deaf to the voice calling my name. Fixated on the flames as they ate through canvas walls, the bracings holding the whole thing up. Clawing at the arms holding me, I thrust my body up, a horrid cry wrenched from my throat.

My eyes went wide as the rest of the tent collapsed.

I stilled, tears falling down my face in raging rivers. A scream hurtled through me. My body doubled over, trembling against the arms that held me. My legs curled beneath me and I buried my face into a chest.

From some place just beyond me, people screamed. Cried. Knees crunched to the snow. I cried for them. With them.

My fingers dug into the cloak beneath me, into the shirt. A head rest against mine, the coarse hair of a beard scratching my face. Miran's voice whispered as he rocked me back and forth.

There was no further time to mourn.

Miran's arms fell from around me and he jumped to his feet as a White soldier lunged toward us. In a fit of rage, I hurled myself at the soldier, tackling him to the ground. I threw my fists into him. Into his face and chest, a blinding flurry of tears streaking my cheeks as he tried to protect himself from my assault. Suddenly, he threw me backward into the snow.

The soldier was on his feet in a blink, drawing his blade. From nowhere, Miran swung, forcing the man back a step, and they clashed with a resounding twang. The soldier snarled as Miran met his blows, the two on equal footing. Miran caught his blade and, twisting the two together, swatted the opposing one aside. He snarled as he jumped forward and brought the blade crashing down into the soldier's skull.

The two went down together.

Heaving, Miran pushed himself up and wrenched his blade free, kicking the body back. Vision cleared, I watched him stalk toward me, sapphire eyes burning with rage. My bottom lip trembled as I picked myself up. Instead of screaming, instead of berating me, he threw his arms around my shoulders and pulled me to his chest, burying his face in my hair.

It was only through sheer will I held back the barrage of tears, the surging emotions bubbling inside me. Miran yanked me away from him, kissed my forehead, and took my hand, following Nik and Venyx as they headed toward the corral.

Miran was right. The only way to help now was to lead the army away.

"You."

I stopped, Miran halting at my side.

Aidra stalked toward us, tears streaking his sooty, blood-spattered face. "You did this to us," he sobbed, pointing his sword at me. "You brought this upon us."

"I'm sorry," I breathed, one tear sliding free, then another. My throat constricted around the words, emotions threatening to strangle me. "I'm so sorry."

Aidra's mouth fell open, a roar just there, in the back of his throat.

"No, mate," Miran growled. "You were told this would happen."

"Go fuck yourself, Amasian cunt," Aidra spat.

Scoffing, Miran took my hand and pulled me along behind him, leaving Aidra to drop to his knees, sobbing.

"Come on, come on," Nik said, waving us over.

Mindful of the panging in my gut, I hoisted myself onto my mount and glanced around as the others saddled up.

"Ride east. Swing south," Venyx said. Miran and Nik nodded. "We should catch their attention enough to draw them out of the village."

Snapping our reins, we bolted from the corral, galloping full pace toward the battlefield. The frightening realization of our plan's success settled over me as a smattering of silver eyes shifted toward us in the dark, a thick ball of fear forming in my stomach at the sight. We turned our horses south, and I prayed the White Army followed, that hope intermingled with the terror that they would.

It took only moments to find out.

My horse's churning hooves and heaving lungs were drowned out by the ferocious stampede rising behind me, clenching my heart with all the fear I'd known it would. Chancing a glance, that fear turned icy at the horde trailing us, illuminated by the first rays of sunlight stabbing the sky to the left.

"Keep going!" Venyx screamed just over my shoulder.

Snapping my reins, I urged my horse a little faster, a little harder, begging it to maintain pace, as a hill rose before us. Another glance back and Venyx steered his mount to the horde as he drew one of his twins.

"He's fucking crazy!" Nik screamed. I glanced at the brown-haired Amasian, my every thought screaming the same thing.

Another moment and we crested the hill. I had only an instant to survey the landscape before we were hurtling downward. My horse whinnied, shaking its head back and forth in protest as fresh, soft powder loosed before us, the ground giving way in our path. I yanked on the reins, icy wind biting my eyes, loosing my gathered tears.

Beside me, Miran angled his horse to the side, galloping diagonally toward me. He reached out, grasping for my reins as I tried to toss them to him, begging myself to stay calm, even as wild fear tore at every fiber of my being.

Inches from Miran taking control of my mount, a boulder-sized force barreled into my back, sending me and my horse into a roll. The snow reached up, grabbing me as the world spun. The sky whipped by in a frenzy until I could no longer tell up from down, save for the icy press of snow slamming into my face over and over again.

Somewhere to my right, the horse screamed.

Finally, I slid to a stop. Thick, viscous nausea boiled in my gut. My head swam. Limbs shaken. I pressed my face to the ground, pulling in short, sharp breaths, begging my heart to slow, the world to stop spinning.

Breath trembling, I opened my eyes and took in the slick surface of a frozen lake, and a whole new fear clutched my breast. My gaze shifted toward the horse, mere feet from where I lay, scrabbling to gain its footing.

"Shit," I breathed. "Shit, shit, shit."

Tears prickled my eyes, grappled at my throat as the nausea fled, replaced by something far worse—paralyzing terror.

The horse shook its head, tried and failed to rise to its hooves before it landed on the ice, a sharp crack racing toward me.

Breath shaking, I rose to my hands and knees, slow as possible. The crack shot further across the surface, snaking between my hands. Spider-webbing between them.

"Fuck," I whispered, blinking away tears. The horse again tried pushing itself up. With every failed attempt, the beast became more frantic, more panicked, its breath erupting in great, foggy gasps as it desperately pawed the ice.

Licking my lips, I glanced up, around. With so much snow covering the ground, I couldn't decipher ice from embankment. Couldn't tell how far to safety. I glanced back to the frightened animal, its eyes wide and terror-stricken. Another fissure split the lake's surface.

Me or the horse.

Gritting my teeth, I lowered myself to the ice and crawled. Slid across the surface, away from the flopping animal. With another drop of its body, another fracture sounded and fresh tears blinded me.

"Please, no," I begged. The beast threw back its head and slammed once again into the frozen surface. The ice shifted, ruptured. It split open, great yawning gasps of cold water jumping out to claim us as we plunged beneath the churning waves. A horrifying whinny and the sound of my own scream carried me under as I was enveloped by cold.

NINETEEN

I LOST TRACK OF up and down. All I knew was cold. The horse continued thrashing, throwing its great head back and forth, strong legs kicking, churning the water. Finally, the thrashing stopped. The horse stilled, and slowly sank. Fighting the mind-numbing terror, I kicked in the opposite direction as the body fell, pulling against the cold, the exhaustion.

A form appeared, swimming toward me with fervor. *Miran*, I thought. Maybe Nik. But as the figure drew closer, I realized they wore white. A sob tore from my throat as I kicked backward, changing direction, fighting my body to swim from the approaching soldier.

He dredged a furious streak of white as he moved toward me, my own thrashing making no difference. The soldier reached out, narrowly missing my wrist. Floating backward, I curled my legs and kicked, catching the soldier in the chest before I rolled and swam away.

Suddenly, he was on me, hand in my hair, yanking back. I screamed, shoved against him, kicked my knees up, my legs out, making as much contact as I could. He growled against my thrashing, his free hand batting mine away, the other still locked in my hair.

Spotting a knife on his belt, I yanked it free and sank it into his chest over and over, wailing all the while, before sinking the blade into his throat. Finally, he released me and followed the horse to his grave.

Only after the soldier sank to the icy depths, it hit me that I'd breathed throughout the fight. I'd been breathing the whole time. I was breathing. Under water.

Apparently, my mother had given me more than just pretty eyes.

Hesitantly drawing a deep breath, I propelled myself through the water, in the opposite direction from the sinking soldier, toward the pink-tinged sky above.

But wait...

Where was the hole?

The cracked ice I'd fallen through. The one the soldier had come through.

No.

Shoving down the prickling panic in my chest, I kicked furiously toward the surface, hands outstretched, hoping, praying, they were swallowed by frigid air. Frightening realization rose in my gullet as I hit ice.

My chest hiccupped, blooming with a new fear. Though tears stung my eyes, I could scarcely tell them apart from the water surrounding me, and so pretended they didn't exist as I floated toward the surface of the lake, hands outstretched, tapping the ice with my stolen blade.

Furiously, I began stabbing the underside, hacking away with the knife. Accomplishing nothing save for expending precious energy I needed to keep warm.

I hiccupped again, gazing around at the frozen waters. I might have been able to breathe, but I wouldn't survive the cold.

I was going to die.

With that realization, I slammed my other hand against the smooth underside, screaming, begging someone to hear me, to see me.

"Help!" To my own ears, my voice was muffled, drowned by the water, regardless of my ability to breathe.

A shadowy form sprang to life on the surface of the lake, running across the ice before dropping to their knees and sliding toward me.

Miran's face hovered above me, eyes wide with a kind of fright I'd never seen.

"Miran!" I screamed. "Help!"

He mouthed something and pulled the knife from his boot, ramming it into the icy surface. Panic lined his face as spittle flew across his beard. Still, the stabbing and hacking scarcely made a dent.

I closed my eyes, imagining I was pressed against him. When I opened them, my heart jumped into my throat as a soldier in white ran up behind my Amasian, sword raised.

"Miran!" I screamed, pointing behind him. He swung around, jumped to his feet, and drew his sword in one swift motion, blocking the blade with precision. The two traded blows back and forth, slipping every other swing, though neither lost their balance.

I watched, helpless, as if I were the one fighting the battle.

Then again, I was fighting one of my own. Already, the tingling bite of cold seeped into my skin, crawling toward my bones. I wasn't sure what it would feel like to freeze to death, but it wasn't an experience I wanted.

Nik darted across the ice and tackled the soldier, both flying to the solid surface. Nik scrambled up as the White soldier jumped, landing deftly on his feet.

Mouth open in a silent scream, Miran raised his sword and swung toward the soldier as the man whipped around, narrowly dodging the blade. Behind him, Nik jumped, sunk his feet into the soldier's back, and propelled him into Miran, who caught the man, spun him around, and sliced his throat before dumping the body to the side.

From where he lay, Nik rolled over and pulled out a knife, furiously stabbing the lake's surface before Miran dropped to his knees beside the younger man, both hacking away, ice flying about their faces.

Behind them, another slew of soldiers descended upon the ice. I stabbed up, desperate to make them see, knowing they couldn't hear me. While Miran continued gouging the lake's surface, Nik sprang to his feet, sword in hand, and went to work against the first soldier.

My vision jumped back and forth from Miran to Nik, not sure which to follow. Anything to keep my mind off the creeping sensation climbing my legs, my arms. Swallowing my head in a thick cloud.

Nik became surrounded, fending off a group of soldiers while Miran continued working through the ice little by little.

"Where the fuck is Venyx?" I screamed, a sob bursting from my chest at the deymon's name.

One of the soldiers landed a blow to Nik's face, throwing the Amasian back before he dove toward Miran. The fiery-haired Amasian looked up and sprang to his feet, slipped, and landed on his back as the soldier pounced him.

A black streak punched through the lightening sky and I screamed as Venyx hurtled across the ice with the soldier.

Nik jumped back to his feet, slammed his head into one of the soldier's, sliced open another's neck, and shoved his blade into a third's chest, roaring as he drove the soldier back before they both tumbled to the lake's surface.

I pawed at the ice, desperate to help, more invisible tears burning the backs of my eyes as all three were locked in battles I was useless against.

Venyx climbed to his feet, face splattered with blood, before being tackled by countless soldiers. Miran was kicked back, fell, and slid backward, the deymon in white stalking toward him.

Nik felled the last of the soldiers around him. He ran toward me, dropped to his knees and continued cleaving the ice. The tingling in my limbs grew higher. I glanced at my feet, at my hands, back up to Nik, realization dawning on his face before his stabbing increased tenfold, grey eyes filling with tears. Spittle and snot coated his beard as he hacked away.

So focused on Nik, I didn't spot the deymon until it was too late.

He rose like a white cloud over Nik's shoulder. It was all I could do to scream, pounding on the ice with everything in me. The world slowed as Nik raised his head, turned around, and faced the deymon as the blade came down, impaling him.

The vibrations of my scream rang through the water as I pounded on the ice, furious, blinding tears filling my eyes.

The deymon drew back the sword and Nik collapsed to the frozen surface. He stared at me, tears freezing on his lashes. I placed my hand against the ice, beneath his, moaning as he began crawling. Scarlet trailing in his wake.

"Miran!" I screamed. "Venyx! Help!" I pounded on the ice as Nik crawled from the deymon, one hand uselessly covering his stomach. I swam beneath the surface, staying in his sight, hands held against his, as if it might help. My breath hitched as the deymon sauntered around him. "No." I shook my head, tears flooding my eyes. "Miran!" My voice cracked.

The deymon stopped at Nik's shoulders, raised one boot, and placed it upon the spy's back.

"Help!" I shrieked again, pounding on the ice.

As if accepting his fate, Nik laid his head against the ice, eyes closed, hands splayed over mine. His body relaxed.

"Nik!" I screamed, slamming my fists into the ice. "Nik! No! Nik!"

The deymon raised his sword and swung down, the blade biting through flesh and bone, severing Nik's head from his body. Blood squirted every which way, coating the frozen surface, blurring my vision. All except Nik's face, pressed against the ice.

The tip of the blade bit into the surface and was jerked away, ripped from the ice with a sickening crack.

I reeled back, hands flying to my mouth, the blade falling from my grasp, though it no longer mattered. My stomach churned, nausea filling me as hot blood seeped across the lake's surface, turning the sky scarlet as it froze in the frigid air.

Something solid hit the lake's surface, a high-pitched scream reverberating through the ice. Feet scrambled above me. Another scream.

I sank further from the surface and closed my eyes, the image of Nik playing over and over in my head. Nausea filled my gut.

The edges of my vision darkened, spots swimming before my eyes. I felt none of it. Nothing. My body no longer responded to me. Whether from cold or shock, I didn't know. And didn't care.

Somewhere behind me came a great shattering, like glass. Vision hazy, I turned toward it, a dark shape swimming toward me before I was pulled into a strong, warm embrace.

The surface rose before I could process it, and everything went cold.

I blinked. Spots swam in my eyes, though I swore Miran's face hovered above mine. Not through the ice, but there. Before me.

"Seraph!" he screamed, his voice far away. He looked up, curls flying, and he vanished.

Another moment and Venyx appeared. My hazy vision raked over him, across his moving lips, his voice lost to me, before I was cradled against him, and the world lifted away. Then blacked out.

Part Two

OF THE FINDING

THREE MILLENNIA BEFORE

FOR WEEKS SHE'D NOTICED.

Chill clung like the last vestiges of frost just before dawn. Trails of snow followed in her wake. Something akin to handprints spanned the glass windows of her private chambers, wraith-like claws holding on for dear life.

Faei had, of course, heard of the Sprites. The beings who carried Lorralei's seasons across the world. Had even sworn she'd seen Spring—a delicate thing made of flower petals and soft winds, smelling of roses and fresh grass. So it was not surprising there would also be a Winter Sprite.

Rarely was the Sprite spoken of, and so she'd dismissed the idea. Until late.

The first day of spring came and went, and still a chill lingered in the air. Ice touched her wooden floors, hugged the towering tree she called home. Crops were frostbitten, her people complained. Rivers crossing the valley floor icy to the touch.

The seasons had moved on, and yet Winter had not.

The Faire Queen tried to put this from her mind as she meandered through the garden, stopping to smell the flowers in bloom. Watch the birds flutter and sing in their pursuit of mates. It drew a smile to her lips to see such things.

And yet, she could not turn from the trouble of winter. The lingering season hovering over her valley, her home, and nowhere else.

Sighing, the Queen Faerie stroked the silky petals of a calla lily, bending to inhale the scent. Smiling, her jade eyes fluttered open, flicked up, and her body went rigid.

There, hovering behind a tree, shielded from view—save flurrying snow speckling the emerald grass—was the fabled Winter Sprite.

As if terrified, he ducked behind the trunk, pulling the swirls of his season with him.

And Faei knew.

She knew why the season did not leave. Why chill clung to the air. Rivers remained icy and crops did not take.

Her smile pulled higher as she returned to the lily. With a wave of her hand, a duplicate appeared between two fingers, frozen in time, never to die, or wilt, or fade. Holding the plant to her breast, Faei sauntered toward the tree, white gown flowing with every step. Snowy curls bouncing and swaying.

Stopping at the tree, Faei tipped her head to the side as the Winter Sprite leaned the other direction. His skirts of ice and snow fluttered, falling to the grass around him. The queen's gaze dropped to the ground, browned and decayed where he stood. Her eyes trailed back up.

"Hello," she said, voice soft as a song.

The Winter spun, flinging bits of ice every which way, the twisting vortex of his face widening in alarm.

"I brought this for you," Faei said, and held the flower toward the Sprite. The darkened pits of his eyes trailed the length of her arm to the flower. "In case you would like to take a lily when you leave Kaival."

He opened the gaping maw of his mouth, similar to his eyes, and tried to speak, though only groaning winds escaped. If the Winter Sprite could blush, Faei thought he did as his billowy, icy form fell backward.

"I cannot touch life," he finally said, though it was not with a proper voice, but the echo of one. What she imagined darkness would sound like if it could speak. "I can only take life."

"That's not true at all," she said, stepping closer. "You bring life every year. With your snows and rains."

The voids of his eyes glanced about before meeting hers again. Slowly, one spiraling limb reached out, plucking the flower from the Faire Queen's hand. And the Winter smiled. Or what looked like a smile on a being with no true face, and no true mouth.

"Do you have a name?" Faei asked, drawing his gaze back up.

He glanced back at the flower, still alive in his grasp.

"Wynnix," he said. And met her gaze again. "My name is Wynnix."

"Wynnix," Faei repeated. "What a lovely name. I'm Faei."

"Beautiful as the woman who wields it," he whispered.

"Would you like to walk through the garden with me, Wynnix?" Faei asked. For a moment, hesitancy crawled across his features. Until he looked again at the flower.

"Very much, Faei."

Faei smiled, gesturing for him to join her. They walked side by side along the grass.

Where he touched, it remained green.

TWENTY

WARMTH WAS THE FIRST thing I became aware of—deep and bone-settling, making me sweat. The second was a voice. Two voices, hissing and strained, snapping back and forth. Inhaling, the scent of a fire filled my nose too quickly and I coughed, hacking bordering on pain. The voices fell silent.

My eyes fluttered open, glimpsing my surroundings. I lay in a cave. The last thing I remembered was Nik's face, swimming in a pool of blood. The calm, soft expression he wore.

I groaned and rolled to my stomach. Nausea filled my gut, strong and sudden, at the memory replaying in my mind. Tears sprang to my eyes.

Boots shuffled over dirt and rocks before a presence was beside me, a hand on my back.

"Seraph." Sniffling, I rolled over and took in Miran hovering above me. Dark circles rest beneath his eyes. His lips were chapped, skin gaunt. As if he hadn't been eating, or sleeping. Probably both. "Are you alright?"

Somewhere behind him, Venyx scoffed. "She nearly froze to death."

"I was just asking," Miran snapped.

"We're lucky she's alive," Venyx retorted.

"Both of you, shut up," I groaned.

To their credit, they did.

I rolled onto my back and stared at the cavern wall before draping an arm over my face. Blocking out the firelight. The smell. The sounds. The men. I wanted none of it. I certainly didn't want the memories dancing behind my eyelids. Those least of all.

"What happened?" I asked. I didn't want to know, but I needed to.

"We're in an Amasian cache," Miran stated, groaning as he sat beside me. I resisted the urge to shrink away from him, to tell him to leave me alone. Grief was speaking through me, using my thoughts and voice, like a parasite. Telling Miran to not touch me would only alienate him. Then again, maybe it was better that way.

Miran continued. "We happened to be close to one at the lake so—"

"Rather convenient, don't you think?" Venyx asked.

I scowled, ran my hands down my face and shoved up to sit, glaring at the men from my bundle of blankets, giving only a moment's thought to my lack of aches and pains.

"I don't want to hear another fucking word from either of you," I growled. For a long moment, silence filled the space, occupied only by the happy grumbles of the blazing fire.

Miran scratched his beard. "We wanted to wait a few days. Before leaving. Since we still have to make it to The City and...." His voice trailed off, but I heard the implication. Not even Venyx spoke.

My gaze dropped to the floor, just below the fire as Nik's face flashed in my mind again. A sob ripped from my throat and my hands flew to my mouth. When Miran leaned into me, wrapped me in his arms, I didn't push him away. Instead, I sank into him.

I wrapped myself around him, buried my face in his chest, and wailed. Within moments, my tears soaked through his shirt, but he held me tighter. It was a long moment before my sobs subsided, leaving me hiccupping, gasping for breath. Miran's head leaned against mine, his fingers digging softly into my back, running circles through the blanket.

Once even the hiccups tapered off, I leaned away from Miran and wiped my cheeks. I drew my knees to my chest, rested my chin on them, and looked between the two left to escort me all the way to Pensen.

At one time, it had seemed like enough.

Now, I wasn't sure how we'd make it alive. I didn't even know how we'd make it out of the Northerlands. It then occurred to me. "How are we getting to The City?" I asked. Miran and Venyx traded a glance, as if it were something they'd already spent half the day arguing about. They probably had.

"We have to walk," Venyx said, the words falling like stones to the cave floor. I couldn't help the burst of laughter that dove from my throat. The deymon's silver-flecked eyes darkened, his stoic face dropping into unamusement.

"I'm sorry," I whispered. "I just-" Another chuckle tore through me, filled with all the despair and hopelessness those words wrought. "You can't seriously expect us to walk across the Northerlands."

He sighed, rubbed his face, and shoved his hood back, running his fingers through his black locks. He steepled his hands over his mouth. "I searched for any remaining horses, and they all fled." His voice rose incrementally as he spoke, as if his words weren't just for me. "We can't stay here."

I sighed, letting my shoulders sag, my back relax. I swept my hair over my shoulder and began combing the tangles from the long locks with my fingers.

"How far are we from The City?" I asked, staring across at the deymon.

"A couple days at most."

Beside me, Miran's face tightened, brows furrowing. "Seraph," he began, but stopped when I shot a look at him.

"We can't stay here," I said.

"No," Venyx said. "I suggest we travel by night—"

"Night?" Miran asked. "Are you out of your fucking mind? We can't travel *on foot* across the Northerlands *at night.*"

"And you have a better idea?" Venyx asked.

"Shut it!" I screamed, my voice echoing throughout the cavern. They both fell silent as I let my face fall into my hands. "You made sure to check if no horses have wandered back?"

"Several times," the deymon replied. "I'll check again tomorrow." I nodded absently. "We should stay another day, maybe. But we need to leave before the White Army can regroup."

I nodded again, my gaze drifting from the deymon to Miran. The spy scoffed, licked his lips, and a cold, distant smile pressed into his mouth.

"You're fucking deranged," he growled. Miran turned to me. "How can you agree with him?"

"What choice do we have? He's right. We can't stay here. And we're only a couple days from The City."

Miran ran a hand down his beard. "Fine." He threw up his hands in defeat. "Fine. But if she dies, I'll drag you back to Amasius and see you hanged," he shot toward Venyx.

The deymon glared back. "I'd pay to see you try."

The rest of the day was spent in silence. Miran tossed pebbles into the fire, the flames bursting and crackling with each stone. Venyx vanished into the shadows, hiding in some dark corner. Occasionally, the silver pinpoints of his eyes shone, but nothing else.

I lay in my nest of blankets, regaining strength in my legs from my near freeze. Apparently, it took a lot of energy to almost die. While recovering, I either drew in the dirt or braided my hair, having finally combed all the tangles from it.

After a while, my stomach started grumbling. Loud enough that Miran rose and disappeared into the back of our hideaway, returning with a sack. He eased himself beside me and placed the bag in his lap.

"We aren't able to keep a lot of food in these caches, since we don't know when it'll be used," he said, rolling down the top. The inside was coated with a sort of wax. He pulled out a chunk of hard cheese, followed by jerky. "It's been thawing."

The first bite was heavenly in my mouth, on my tongue. I wasn't sure the last time I'd eaten. Maybe that last night around the bonfire.

The bonfire.

The camp.

"What happened to the tribe?" I asked, almost afraid of the answer. Miran sighed, shook his head.

"I don't know. He went back to find them," he nodded toward the shadows, "but all he found were remains. Whatever was left of their people just ... vanished."

The food turned sour in my stomach and I set it aside, laying back down. Tears stung my eyes and I rolled over, back facing Miran. As if knowing I needed to be alone, he simply lay a hand on my hip before the heat from his body left altogether.

It was my fault. All of it.

A single tear rolled down the bridge of my nose and onto my hand, tucked beneath me. I sniffled. Closing my eyes, I dragged the blankets over my head and swathed myself in darkness. How long it took, I didn't know, but eventually, I fell back asleep.

Briahna stood before me.

"Run!" she screamed, though I couldn't force my feet to move.

My heart pounded in the base of my throat as she was hoisted off the ground before being slammed into the sand. Standing over her was a deymon, eyes bright red. Fangs dripping blood.

"Seraph," Briahna whispered, dragging my gaze to her.

Suddenly, a wall of ice separated us. It coated my feet, freezing me in place. Gasping, tears running down my face, I wriggled and writhed, trying to free myself.

"Seraph," Briahna said again.

I glanced back toward her, but it was no longer Briahna.
"Run," Nik breathed. The deymon stood above him, sword in hand.
"No," I begged, tears filling my eyes.
The sword came down.

I jolted awake at once, a smattering of tears freckling my lashes. Whispers of the dream hung behind my eyes, wielding Nik's face. A ball of guilt, of sickening loss, tore at my throat, settled in my stomach and turned it sour.

Bright sunlight streamed through an outlet above, reflecting off what looked like a mirror, illuminating the space without the need for fire. It was larger than I'd realized. Then again, the last time I'd looked, I was freshly woken from nearly dying.

Groaning, I slowly sat up, testing my body. I wasn't eager to push myself further than I was ready for. But, after resting, I felt stronger.

Miran huddled over the remnants of the flames, hands held against the embers. His sapphire eyes flickered up, a smile tugging at his lips, showing off that one dimple. I couldn't help smiling back. Just behind him sat a small cluster of bags, packed and ready for our trek across the Northerlands. It still felt foolish, though there was no point in arguing. There was no other way.

"Where's Venyx?" I asked, a light huskiness to my voice, the last vestiges of sleep clinging to me. The deymon was gone, though I knew by now he wouldn't just leave. Or at least, he wouldn't leave me. Not without collecting his payment.

"He went to check for horses," Miran said, dropping his gaze to the smoldering remnants.

I nodded absently, pulling my legs to my chest. "You still think this is a bad idea."

Miran scoffed, staring into the fire. "Because it is." He gestured toward the mouth of the cave. "The deymon has no use for either of us after we reach Pensen. He doesn't need *me* at all. What does *he* care if we die? Nik…" He inhaled sharply, eyes closed, and started again. "He's already proven that once."

"The marauders were his friends," I countered, emotions constricting my throat. Venyx's face flashed through my mind, his expression upon hearing the cries throughout the camp.

"No, Seraph," Miran said. "Cleya was his friend, and she's on death's doorstep as it is."

He sighed, ribs expanding with the breath before he settled back on his haunches and ran a hand through his hair.

Miran was right. Venyx had hardly spoken to most of the marauders. And he certainly had no use for the Amasians. What did it matter if they died? I opened my mouth, words poised on my tongue, when bootsteps echoed through the cavern, and I swallowed them.

"I spotted horse tracks," the deymon said, rounding the corner into the belly of the cave. Miran perked up. I did, too. But when Venyx came into view, he was alone. "Followed them back into the forest. Looks like a wolf pack caught them."

My pulse skipped, a spear of dread diving into my gut. "Will they be a problem? For us?" I asked, failing to keep the nerves from my voice.

"No," Venyx stated.

Miran smiled. "How? There's only three of us now."

"Wolves won't come near me. They're too clever."

Miran scoffed, folded his arms over his chest as he slowly sat on the floor. "And why is that?"

The deymon turned, facing Miran as he said, "Predators sense predators."

Miran's smile grew, his dimple digging into his cheek. "Well then, I guess we're lucky to have you." He plucked a bit of jerky from the bag beside him and took a bite, chewing as Venyx walked around him.

TWENTY-ONE

WE LEFT AT DUSK. The twin moons shone bright as we set out, casting the miles of snow in glittering silver. Millions of stars hovered above, shimmering between rolls of fat gray clouds. Streaks of what looked like faerie dust were scattered amongst them, the sky seeming so much larger than it ever had. It was breathtaking.

And freezing.

I huddled in my coats, following Venyx's tracks, pacing myself between the two men as Miran trailed behind. Marching through the snow proved to be slow and arduous, made all the harder by driving, frigid winds. How Venyx knew which direction we went was a mystery, guided only by the rising hills.

We broke with the rising sun in a small rock formation. It did little against the cold, but kept us from the snow and wind. Miran and I made a nest on the floor with blankets taken from the cache, huddling for warmth.

Just outside our temporary shelter, the wind howled, groaning and yawning against the rocks. As I lay tucked against Miran's side, it reminded me of the dying. I didn't want to fall asleep. I didn't want to invite the dreams again.

The further south we traveled, the higher the hills grew. By the time the moons reached zenith, a thin film of sweat, chilled by icy winds, had formed on my brow.

My legs ached. My back was aflame. Every bit of me exhausted. So it was a welcome wash of relief when we crested the hills and found a sprawling mass of twinkling lights strewn in a hidden valley. I'd never seen a settlement so massive. The people weren't even visible.

"Is that The City?" I asked, peering from Miran to Venyx. The deymon nodded.

"Yes. It's grown a bit since I was here last." He pulled his hood up, brightening the silver of his eyes, and stepped carefully down the side of the hill.

"It might make the safehouse a bit more difficult to find," Miran said with a sigh.

Venyx cleared his throat. "We're not going to the safehouse."

Both Miran and I turned to him.

"Yes we are," Miran shot.

"I suppose you're free to do what you want, but I'm taking Seraph somewhere else," the deymon said.

"What?" I asked. In the same instant, Miran said, "No, you're not."

Venyx faced the Amasian, his expression devoured by shadows. "It is a big place, yes, but there is also a high probability the White Army is here. Whatever soldiers fled the lake are fully aware of what you and Seraph look like, and have most likely set up watches."

"I said *no*," Miran growled, stepping closer to the deymon. Tension spread thick between them.

Everything in me screamed to stay with Miran.

But...

Aurorian had assured me I could trust Venyx with my life. "Miran," I started, stepping toward him, but the Amasian held up a hand, silencing me.

"She is under the protection of Amasius and will not be leaving my sight," Miran shot.

"This isn't up for discussion," Venyx said, turning to the sprawling city. "Seraph, now."

"Fuck you, deymon," Miran spat, holding out an arm to stop me moving. "I am in charge of this fucking mission and you'll do as I say. She stays with me."

Venyx wheeled around, coming nose to nose with Miran, silvery eyes glimmering in the shadows of his hood.

"Do you feel in charge?" Venyx asked, deep voice low, menacing. Miran's throat bobbed, but he said nothing. The deymon turned from Miran to me. "I can get us in and around without being spotted. And I know where we're going."

"Where is that?" Miran seethed.

"The Braided Beard. An old friend works there. We'll be able to get some rooms for a couple nights."

"We have Amasian agents waiting to debrief us," Miran spat.

Venyx ignored him. Instead, he looked to me. "Are you coming?"

"It'll be alright," I said, pressing myself into Miran's side. I took his hands and kissed his knuckles, stood on my tiptoes, and planted another on his lips. "We can go to the safehouse tomorrow. I'll see you inside."

He stared into the distance, saying nothing. A pang of rejection jolted through my heart; I reminded myself he was just upset. We'd traveled this far together and had never been apart, aside from his venture with the marauders. I glanced over my shoulder as I followed Venyx's footsteps, though Miran had already fallen out of sight.

A massive wall surrounded The City, reaching to the sky, its bricks thrashed by ice and wind and snow. Sections were frost eaten, crumbling and rotten. As we approached the gates, Venyx slowed enough for me to stay on his heels, for which I was grateful. Already I was tired of huffing and puffing after him. He was tall and fast, two things I wasn't.

Standing before the great wooden doors into The City, I had to tip my head to look all the way up, and still couldn't find the top. I did spot glowing lights as they flickered from the ground. More were fastened to either side of the entrance, illuminating the iron belts stretched across the wood-planked doors. My brows furrowed upon closer examination. There was no flame. On either of them.

Just before we were ushered through the gates, I started as Venyx pulled my hood up over my head. Within moments, we were on the sprawling streets beyond.

"Come here," Venyx said, placing a hand on my shoulders. He pulled me close, his warmth barreling into me. Still, I had to fight the urge to pull away. "You'll get lost if you don't stay close." I nodded before casting my gaze around.

It was the middle of the night and the streets were full. People of every kind bustled past, carrying baskets and bags, hauling carts. The pathways were bursting with life.

Lining the way were more of those strange, flameless lights.

"It's called electricity," Venyx said, leaning into me. I turned from him back to the lamps. "They're powered by wind," he explained as we shuffled through the throng. "There are turbines south of The City, attached to underground cables run to warehouses, where the power is made."

I stared up at one in awe. "How?" I asked.

He shrugged. "No clue. I never asked."

The further we went, the more people I spotted from every corner of the globe. Dwarves and elves walked side by side, wrapped in fur coats. Several people strode past, taller than Miran, than even Ni—

"Are those dragons?" I asked, ripping the thought from my mind before it could finish forming. Venyx looked over me, glancing up as the dark skinned beings walked past.

"They are. It's rude to stare at other people, too," he jabbed.

I ignored his quip. But it was still too late. The unfinished thought dashed away any of my awe. Guilt gnawed at my gut all over again.

I wasn't sure how long we'd been walking before the tall buildings nearest the wall vanished, replaced by shorter, wider, longer ones. Great glass windows peered inside, blacked out with some kind of drapery, blocking sight within.

Less people were in this part of The City, those there hustling between buildings, noses in books and across sheets of parchment. Here, the lamp posts were taller, brighter, more elaborate. The flickering and buzzing wasn't so pronounced as the outer streets.

Eventually, that portion of The City was overtaken by another section filled with the tallest buildings I'd seen thus far. Many had signs hanging above their doors, stating they were inns or taverns. This was easily the busiest section.

People stumbled down the street, seemingly unaware of the biting cold, gazing with hazy eyes and a slurred smile on their faces, giving tell as to where they'd been.

As we passed more people, I noticed none of them approached us. They barely even glanced our way. It occurred to me it might have something to do with the deymon at my side. It appeared coming into The City with him had been a good idea after all.

Venyx's stride slowed as we approached the tallest building in the district. It rose at least ten stories, every level's glass windows glittering under the silvery touch of the moons. More of those strange electric lights hung on the outside walls. On the ground floor was a large door, warped and ice eaten at the edges. Above hung the sign *Braided Beard Tavern & Inn*.

Just before reaching the door, Venyx turned to me, pressing uncomfortably close. His breath fanned my face.

"We go in together. You do not leave my sight. Stay before me at all times."

"If you don't trust this place, why bring me here?" I asked.

"It has nothing to do with not trusting th-" He stopped, sighed in exasperation, shoulders slumping. "Please just listen."

"Okay."

He nodded in thanks before placing his hands on my shoulders. I tried not to think about him being so close, pressing into my back, as he opened the tavern door. A fog of smoke and myriad smells hit me square in the face before I realized what he'd been talking about.

The tavern was bursting with bodies, the place thrumming with a lively, jovial air. A thousand screaming voices roared between the walls.

And I realized what Venyx had meant. He was afraid I'd get swallowed by the crowd. Frankly, so was I.

Twenty-Two

T HE MOMENT WE CROSSED the threshold, we were surrounded on all sides and I found myself pressing backward, somewhere between terrified of accidently groping Venyx and being groped by those around me.

As we pushed through the crowd, I became overwhelmed; my breath stilled in my lungs, the air stifling. I stopped in the middle of the room, unsure where to go, which direction was forward. The ocean of bodies too thick. And every body was a different size, different shape. Some were towering dragons in human form, their colorful heads nearly scraping the ceiling, muscled masses taking the space of two. Others were lithe elves, dancing and shifting through the throng. In the far corner, nearest the hearth, was a shimmering head of teal curls—a Sirenian—and my heart skipped a beat.

"Just that way," Venyx said, too close to my ear. His hand rose before me, pointing. A cloud of bodies shifted, just for a moment, and I spotted the bar.

I hadn't realized I still wasn't moving until Venyx nudged me forward, pushing people out of the way. For the most part, none seemed to care. One turned to glare at us, her orcish face blanching at the sight of the deymon at my back, and she returned to her drink.

A small eternity passed before we made it to the bar. A throng of bodies pressed against it, all vying for the attention of several barkeeps on the other side. The nearest was a woman. She stood nearly as tall as Venyx, long brown curls flowing down her back, swaying with each step. When she turned, her creamy brown skin glowed with the light of the lamps on the walls, her soft, amber eyes glistening as she smiled at patrons. Seven hells, she was beautiful.

Those eyes glanced up, tiptoed across my face and landed just above, her face softening into a smirk. She gestured to the end of the bar, working her way toward the far wall as Venyx guided me in the same direction.

As she approached, I spotted elven ears poking out of her hair, and it suddenly made sense.

The woman lifted the end of the bar and wasted no time pulling Venyx into a hug. He dug his face into her hair, back rising and falling with a great breath. As they pulled away from each other, she touched his cheek before tucking his hair behind his ears.

"You look good," she said, barely containing her smile.

"You do, too. How've you been?"

The elven woman shrugged. "Working. Keeping busy."

Venyx nodded. "Same."

I couldn't help the smile tugging at my lips before I cleared my throat, bringing their attention back to me.

"And who's this?" the woman asked. Either I imagined it, or a twinge of jealousy flickered across her face.

"Why I'm here," Venyx said. "Lira, this is Seraph. Seraph, Lira."

Lira reached out, taking my hand in a limp shake before she stepped back and shoved her hands into her apron, suddenly stiff and standoffish.

"Tollok working tonight?" Venyx asked.

Lira glanced back over me as she nodded and met Venyx's gaze again. "I'll go get him. Stay here." She turned with a flourish of her long golden-brown locks and vanished behind the wall of people.

Slowly, I turned to Venyx, a grin pressing into one corner of my mouth. He scoffed and leaned against the wall, arms folded across his chest.

"Don't start," he grumbled, eyes cast to the floor.

"Start what? I didn't say anything," I said with a shrug, biting back my smile.

"Good."

"So, um..."

He growled, eyes flicking up to mine.

"How long has *that* been a thing?" I asked, crossing my arms.

"None of your business."

"Okay," I crowed, facing the wall of liquors behind the bar.

We stood far too close. An uncomfortable silence passed between us before an old dwarf, graying beard in thick, beaded plaits, ambled toward us, his bulbous gut jiggling with every step. His reddened face lit from within upon seeing us.

"Venyx fucking Ravykyn!" he cried, throwing his arms wide. Something like a grin curled Venyx's mouth as he leaned into the dwarf and embraced him, lifting him off the floor before setting him back down. "Bout fucking time you came to see me, you shit!" The dwarf chuckled with every word.

"I know," Venyx returned. "I'm sorry it's been a while."

"Where you been all this time?" the dwarf asked. "We missed ya!"

Venyx took a step back. "Licking my wounds at Ace's."

A flicker of something flashed across Venyx's face, hammering alongside the guilt in my chest.

The dwarf chuckled, his rounded belly bouncing with every breath. "Ace got too soft. I'd never let you lick nothing here." He waggled his brows. "Not wounds, anyway."

Venyx shoved the dwarf back and stepped aside. Steely blue eyes raked over me.

"Behave yourself," Venyx said.

"Behave myself? You're the bad influence!" Tollok looked over me again. "So, who's this? A new bit of flesh?" He grinned wildly.

"What the fuck did I just say?" Venyx grumbled. "I'm on a job. Tollok, this is Seraph."

"Working again? What in the seven hells made you do that? Let me guess, Aurorian?"

"Aurorian," Venyx agreed. "We're just passing through. I need my room, and one extra."

"Did Lira tells you we're havin' trouble getting shipments?" Tollok asked.

"No. What of it?" Venyx asked. Tollok reached into a pocket of his apron and pulled out a small silver key.

"I can't replace the bed so easily this time."

My face fell, mouth gaping, scarlet heat jumping into my cheeks as I glanced between them. Tollok burst out laughing. Venyx sighed, his shoulders slumping.

"I'm working, Tollok. She's my ward."

"I'm just fuckin' with ya," Tollok said, passing over the key. "I know you gots yer code'n all." He rolled his eyes as he spoke. "Like keeping your sword and your weapon separate."

Venyx sighed. "You're impossible." He gripped the bridge of his nose, sighed, and ran his hand through his hair. "How long have shipments been a problem?"

"Month'r so," Tollok said. "I'll get yer other key. Hold on."

The moment Tollok walked away, I stepped closer to Venyx, all too aware of how little space lay between us. "Why is he telling you about shipment issues?"

Venyx cleared his throat, leaned into me, and said, "The White Army is holding up shipments."

A chill rushed to my feet as Venyx pulled away, his gaze returning to Tollok as the dwarf waddled back, squeezing around a barkeep. In his hand was another silver key. Venyx took it without preamble.

"The girl looks hungry," Tollok said, pointing to me. "When's the last you fed 'er?" He didn't wait for a response before calling back to bring food to his table.

Tollok started across the room, shoving through the crowd. Without a word, Venyx grabbed my arm and pulled me in front of him, marching us after the dwarf. For a moment, I wanted to protest, to tell him to stop yanking me around. Then again, it would do no good, and I had no desire to get lost in the waves of bodies, so kept in front of him.

The warmth from his hands pressing into my shoulders was stifling in a room so full. It was a welcome relief when they slid away as we stopped at Tollok's table.

It was tucked against a broad window, overlooking the street. A giant hearth blazed at our backs, heat from the flames seeping through all my layers, melting the ice on my jackets and boots. I shivered, a deep, comforting thing, and slid into the chair on Venyx's left.

Lining the wall above were more of those strange electric lights, buzzing away. They glowed bright yellow inside their little glass globes, spaced out just so, illuminating all the spaces the fire didn't. Particularly the far corner, where the gathered people appeared more like wraiths and ghouls.

Tollok chuckled. "You never seen electricity before?"

"No," I said, dropping my gaze.

"Cost a pretty coin to get 'em installed in 'ere," he said, his gaze rolling up to the lights. "They nice, though. Heard Pensen got they own kind, now." The dwarf turned to Venyx. "She ain't staying in yer room?"

"I told you already, she's my ward," Venyx said.

A barmaid approached as Venyx finished speaking, carrying a tray laden with food and drinks. She swiftly set everything down and scurried off, picking her way carefully through the crowd.

"You good with taking the room out yer cut?" Tollok asked, pulling a tankard toward him. He peered over the rim, sipped, and smacked his lips.

"That's fine," Venyx said, grabbing a bowl.

I glanced between the two, wondering what they meant, the question building on my tongue when Miran plopped into the chair between me and Tollok, sapphire eyes ablaze.

"An' who the fuck's the pretty human?" Tollok barked over his drink.

Miran glared at him before refocusing on Venyx.

"You could have told me where in the fucking city this place was," Miran growled.

"You found it," Venyx said, sipping on his stew. "Not sure what the issue is."

"Mighty impressive ya found it," Tollok grumbled, pulling Miran's attention back to the dwarf. "You ever been 'ere before?"

"Why?"

Tollok shrugged. "Only people's knows where to look can find it. An' I prefer it that way."

The Amasian turned, peered over his shoulder at all the bodies pressed together, and faced the dwarf again. "Seems like your secret's already out."

Miran's snarl vanished as I placed a hand on his arm. He released an exasperated sigh as his fingers curled around mine and lifted my knuckles to his lips.

"Oh," Tollok said, tossing a glance to Venyx. "That's why."

"Not now," Venyx mumbled. "Tollok, this is Miran. Miran, Tollok."

Tollok nodded, grunting a hello. Miran nodded in return. He was sitting for all of a moment before his stomach grumbled. Having dragged my bowl to me, I began shoving it toward Miran when Tollok pushed his toward the Amasian instead.

"Here, have mine," the dwarf said, rising to his feet. "I got shit to tend to. V, trust I'll see you on the morrow?"

"Bright and early," Venyx mumbled around his drink. With that, Tollok downed the last of his tankard and wandered off, vanishing into the thick throng.

"What did he mean by your cut?" I asked, leaning into Venyx.

"Nothing," he grumbled.

I glanced at the deymon before turning back to my food, shoving the thick stew around the bowl. Miran dug into his without preamble, eating as if famished. Venyx sipped his own, shoulders stiff and on guard.

Trying to shove them both from my mind, I took a spoonful and bit into it, savoring the flavors, the spices. Mostly the warmth. It seeped into every crevice of me, warming me from the inside out. I groaned before digging in, joining Miran as if I, too, had been starved.

The room was small, even from the doorway. Miran stepped inside, glanced around, and waved me in. The door closed with a soft click. Dim, silver moonlight streamed through the window on the far side. I took in the small bed, big enough for two. A strange, humming warmth filled the space.

"How are we supposed to see?" Miran asked.

I'd always assumed I could see better in the dark than the Amasians, but as Miran stumbled about the room, searching for a source of light, that was confirmed.

There were no candles, no sconces or torches. The light must have been the same kind as in the tavern below, but how to make it come on?

Spotting a strange half-globe on the ceiling, I followed the line from the fixture across to the wall and down where a small, strange switch rest. Flicking it up, the room burst into light, blinding at first. After a few blinks, the brightness dissipated and I could see.

Miran strode to a door across from the bed while I took in the bookcases against the walls—two of them, both laden with books.

"Hey," Miran said. I crossed the small space, pressing into his side. Beyond the door was a washroom, a tub tucked into one corner with a spout jutting from the wall. "Did you want to get cleaned up first? Or do you want me to?"

"Go ahead." Stepping onto my tiptoes, I pressed a kiss to his mouth, smiling when he leaned into me, hands on my waist. He shoved me into the doorframe, pushing up the layers of my shirts. I tipped my head back, a moan curling from my throat as one hand roamed down, grasping my thigh. "Miran," I breathed, hot kisses trailing down my neck. "Go clean yourself."

"You saying I smell?" he grumbled into my mouth.

I smiled and kissed him again. "What if I am?"

He pulled back, lifted one arm, and sniffed, pulling a face before he walked into the washroom and let the door swing shut, remaining just ajar.

My skin singing from his touch, I wandered to the window, gazing outside. The rush of running water filled the washroom.

"Mother fucker this is hot!"

Snickering, I leaned against the wall, taking in the sights below. The glowing lights lining the way nearly made night into day, and I couldn't help marveling at the genius who had invented it.

My gaze slipped up, catching my reflection in the glass, and Nik's face sprang into my mind. Slamming my eyes shut, I turned and pressed my back into the wall, begging the image to fade.

Once it did, my eyes slid open to the washroom door. Gentle curls of steam rolled out, the spray of water soothing. I shot across the room, pulling off clothes as I went. Miran turned, eyes wide, as I pulled open the curtain and stepped inside with him.

Taking his mouth in a kiss, I shoved him against the wall. He picked me up, wrapping my legs around his waist as hot water pummeled us from the side. I grabbed handfuls of his hair, forcing his mouth to my neck, blinded by passion, sensation, as he entered me.

Nik, his sacrifice, his life, was a stark reminder of how short life was—a lesson I should have known better than anyone. And I'd be damned if I wasted another moment of whatever was left of mine.

TWENTY-THREE

B RIGHT SUNLIGHT STREAMED THROUGH the window the next morning and it took a moment to remember where I was. I drew a sharp breath and looked over my shoulder. Miran lay on his back, still deep in sleep, one hand tucked behind his head, the other between us.

Easing from bed, I padded to the washroom, thankful my clothes had dried as I slipped them on and walked back into the room. Miran's head had changed positions, but still he slept on. His flaming curls spread across the pillow, along his face, and I swore he was the most beautiful man I'd ever seen.

Smiling to myself, I slipped on my boots, and left the room.

By the time I reached the bottom floor, I was wide awake and winded, so it was a welcome relief to see the floor of the tavern. There were more tables than I'd seen the previous night. I'd barely known tables existed in the place, aside from the one we'd eaten at.

A barkeep glanced up as I wandered past, nodding, as if a Sirenian woman was the most natural thing. Then again, I supposed it was. I'd seen one the night before.

It was completely different than upon first entrance. I could walk around, move without bumping into anyone. A few people sat at the tables, at the bar, but nothing like before.

Large windows the height of the wall allowed a downpour of sunlight to stream through, warming the place without the hearths, though they still burned.

The further I moved across the tavern, the louder chatter became. Or rather, a single voice, rising above the din of clinking tankards and dishes and hushed voices scattered about the place. I'd heard him speak only a little, but I was sure it was Tollok, recalling he was meeting with Venyx early in the morning.

Following the voice, I found the two sitting at the same table, Tollok's head thrown back in a fit of laughter as he spoke.

"I'll never f'get the look on that arsehole's face," the dwarf bellowed, "having his arse saved by a ... what'd he call me?"

A deep, hearty laugh followed Tollok's, and, as I drew closer, I realized it was Venyx. Venyx laughed.

"A midget," the deymon said over the rim of his cup. His brown gaze rose to meet mine, glittering molten gold in all the sunlight.

"Tha's right!" Tollok burst into another round of laughter. "Fucker. Should'a let 'im get his head crushed." He laughed again. Finally, the dwarf took notice of me. "G'mornin. Sleep well?" He waggled his brows before another peal of laughter roared from his throat.

Heat flooded my face as I glanced between the two. "I slept fine."

"Bet you did!" Tollok roared, throwing his head back. "Whole fuckin' tavern heard ya."

My cheeks burned down to my collar bone and I stilled above the chair, no longer certain I wanted to sit.

"Tol, leave her alone," Venyx grumbled as he sipped from his cup again.

"Ah, I'm jus' messin' with 'er. Sorry, Love, just a bit of fun."

"Sit," Venyx said, gesturing to the chair.

Tollok raised a hand at a passing barmaid, then gestured to me. An empty plate lay before him, remnants of food scattered across it. Venyx had nothing but a delicate cup. He sipped again.

"So, who, um, who were you talking about?" I asked, glancing between them.

"Just a couple old men reminiscing the good days," Tollok said and drank from his cup.

"Speak for yourself, old man," Venyx grumbled.

"Fuck off! You're older'n everyone here!" Tollok roared. One corner of Venyx's mouth tipped up, a fang digging into his bottom lip.

I flinched as an arm came around me, depositing a heaping plate of food. My eyes nearly popped from my skull at the sight. "I can't finish all this," I breathed.

Venyx took Tollok's fork and stabbed a bite off my plate. He chewed and stabbed another before I pushed the plate between us. Upon the first bite, my eyes rolled back, tastebuds in heaven. The food was warm and flavorful. The potatoes crisp, the vegetables strewn throughout soft and sweet.

"Remember the time Neilia got pissed cause I talked you into that raid," Venyx said.

Another burst of laughter rolled from Tollok as he tipped his head back and slapped the table.

"She was so furious, she wouldn't let me in the tavern fer two weeks!" the dwarf roared. Tears sparkled in his eyes as he spoke, whether from laughter or memories, I couldn't tell. "I had'ta sleep in the stable!"

Venyx's mouth split into a smile as his throat bobbed with laughter. For a fleeting moment, I glimpsed all four top fangs. His face lit from within as he laughed, his eyes sparkling like gems.

"Who's Neilia?" I asked.

"My dearly departed," Tollok said, his laughter fading.

"Oh. I'm sorry."

"Oh, don't be. She's been gone longer'n you been alive."

A moment of silence passed between the two as their laughter died. Venyx licked his lips, the mask of stoicism again taking hold as he speared another potato.

"Tollok?" I asked.

The dwarf turned to me. "Yes, Love."

"What did you mean last night, when you said Venyx's cut?"

"Mother fu—" Venyx started. "Do not answer that," he said, pointing his fork at the dwarf.

Tollok burst into more laughter. "Course, Love. Happy to tell ya."

Venyx's head rolled into his hand, eyes closed in exasperation.

"Few hunnerd years ago now, there used to be more ice dragons terrorizing these parts," Tollok started.

"She doesn't need the whole story," Venyx growled.

"I'm tellin' this, ain't I?" Tollok bellowed.

With a sigh, Venyx sat back and sipped from his cup, one arm tucked beneath the other.

"Anyway," Tollok started again. "I's given this job. Kill an ice dragon and the settlements'd pay me my weight in coin. O'course, I ain't got no one to go with me, and I certainly can't kill a ice dragon alone. So I goes to Ace's. Word of the time was sellswords used to haunt it, nursing wounds and such."

"Don't let him lie to you," Venyx interrupted. "He had a crew and they tried to kill the dragon. They all died."

"That's a lie!" Tollok yelled, slamming his hand on the table, rattling the dishes. "Or, at least part lie."

I looked between them, brows furrowed, unsure what, or who, to believe. A grin played at Tollok's mouth, making me think he was lying.

"As I was saying," Tollok said, turning back to me, "I go to Ace's to dig up some muscle."

"He burst through the fucking door, screaming about needing help to kill a fucking dragon," Venyx said.

"You gonna let me tell it? Or you wanna?"

"I didn't want you to tell it in the first place," Venyx groused over his cup.

Tollok rolled his eyes. "I went in, lookin' for help, and this idiot stands up, guess *stands* is a bit generous, as he was drunk off his arse, and screams he'd *love* to help. Barely remembered who I was the next day, but he took my word fer it."

Venyx grinned into his cup, shaking his head as Tollok went on. Though he remained quiet.

From the inn, Tollok recounted tracking the dragon before deciding they needed a bigger crew. With wild hand gestures, his face turned into a puppet all its own, and he launched into how they recruited a small band of young marauders. I turned to Venyx, unable to keep the thought from my head that the young, half-elven leader was Cleya. With a nod, he confirmed it.

Through the darkest season of the Northerlands, the group of twenty marched to the caves where the ice dragon nested. It was cold and dark, with only Venyx able to see clearly. The dragon took fourteen of their crew, picking them off several at a time until only Venyx, Tollok, Cleya, and three of her tribe survived. They limped from the caverns, carting the dragon's head behind them, and drug it back to Ace's where heads from the villages were waiting. The prize they garnered was enough to split six ways, each walking away with a full purse, and then some.

"I came down 'ere after," Tollok said, "lookin' to settle down, grow roots. I's gettin' tired of livin' outta a bag on my back. So I found this place. Bought it, and still had plenty left over. Just so happened he came through town one day, lookin' fer work. We found each other again in the market."

Venyx said nothing, just stared into the depths of his cup, clasped loosely in his hands. The ghost of a grin tugging at the corners of his full lips.

"Tol' him what I's doing with the money, showed him around. Though it wasn't much to look at then." Tollok glanced around as if remembering it all those years ago. He sighed, pride glittering in his eyes. "He said it sounded like a good investment, put money into it, let me run it how I saw fit. Long as I kept him a room when he needed it. An' I ain't been able to get rid of the bastard since."

Tollok burst into a fit of laughter, his belly jiggling. Venyx shook his head, chuckling.

The dwarf's words sank in and my gaze shifted between him and the deymon, dumbfounded. "You're part owner?"

Venyx nodded.

"Well, look who decided ta join us," Tollok cooed.

Miran slid into the chair beside me, rubbing his eyes. Tollok laughed.

"Love," the dwarf said, calling to a passing barmaid. "Can we get a plate an' some coffee fer the Amasian, please?"

"Course, Tol," she said, and wandered off.

"What's coffee?" Miran asked.

"Only the greatest fucking thing ever discovered," Tollok laughed. Venyx held his cup high before draining the rest of it.

Miran leaned into me, prompting me to do the same. "If you keep wandering off while I'm sleeping, I'm liable to chain you to the bed."

My cheeks were suddenly engulfed in flames as Tollok barked out a peal of laughter and nudged Venyx's arm. The deymon shrugged him away.

"I like the Amasian, V," Tollok said, wiping the tears from his eyes. Venyx mumbled under his breath.

The barmaid returned, setting a heaping plate in front of Miran, alongside a cup identical to Venyx's. I peered into the dark brown color, as Miran did the same. He lifted it, took a sip, and reeled back, setting it down. Curious, I picked it up, sipped, and grimaced at the bitterness. Venyx shoved a pair of dishes at me.

"To sweeten it," he grumbled.

"What are the plans for today?" I asked, spooning sugar into my cup. "When are we going to the..." I stopped, glancing at Tollok. Miran looked up around a mouthful of food.

"You two are staying here," Venyx said as the barmaid placed another cup in front of him. After I was done flavoring my coffee, Venyx slid the dishes back and set to work on his own. "I'm going out to get supplies."

"We have access to supplies," Miran said.

"I'd rather go out," I started at the same time.

As Miran and I spoke, Tollok began laughing again. "You two pups are hilarious." We turned to the dwarf. "Word's spread all over the fuckin' City about the White Army lookin' fer you two. A ginger human an' purple-haired Sirenian lass. You two ain't goin' nowhere."

"You'll be safe here, so long as you don't leave," Venyx grumbled, glancing between me and Miran.

"Wait," I said, drawing Tollok and Venyx back to me. "Why aren't they looking for him, too?" I pointed my fork at Venyx, sipping his coffee.

Tollok chuckled. "Love, you may not know much 'bout deymons, so let me enlighten you. Most folks can't tell one deymon from the other, an' they don' want to. They's too afraid of 'em. Most folk'll leave him alone. Those who're smart, anyway."

With a frustrated sigh, I leaned back into my chair and stabbed a piece of potato before popping it in my mouth. Though it looked as if he wanted to object, Miran continued eating in silence.

"You got it from here, Tol?" Venyx asked.

The dwarf nodded. "Aye."

Venyx returned his nod and downed the rest of his coffee before he rose and walked away, leaving me and Miran to sit with the dwarf we'd known all of one night.

"So, what the fuck are we supposed to do all damn day while he's out shopping?" Miran asked.

Tollok sniggered, waggling his brows.

I shrank into my chair, sinking into my sweater as much as possible, though it did nothing to stop the blush seeping hot across my face.

TWENTY-FOUR

WARMTH SEEPED THROUGH THE window as we sat there, my belly as full as it had been in weeks, if not months. After he'd cleared his plate, Miran went back upstairs, since there was nothing else to do.

"How long you been travelin' with that one?" Tollok asked, pointing after the Amasian.

"Miran? We've been on the road nearly two months, I think. I've known him almost eight, though." I sipped my coffee as I finished speaking.

Tollok *hmphed* and tipped back the rest of his cup, setting it delicately on the table.

"Why?" I asked.

"Oh, no reason." He tugged at the braids in his beard, left to right and back again, like a ritual. The dwarf shrugged as if it were nothing. "Ain't my business anyhow. I don't make a habit of askin' bout Venyx's doin's with Aurorian. Most the time it's best I don't know nothin'."

For a long moment I stared at the dwarf, how the sunlight carved through the thinning spots of his beard, glistened off his balding head. Once, he may have been attractive, but time had eaten away his youth, leaving nothing behind but the kindness in his wizened eyes.

"Have you and Venyx had many adventures together?" I asked.

Tollok chuckled. "Oh, yes. Fuck yes." He bellowed a bubble of laughter. "After I's got the inn up and runnin', I made a point of takin' a couple months off every year. We'd go all round the Northerlands, stirrin' up trouble. Once hunted a rogue marauder tribe. Gone crazy, started raidin' villages and shit. Nother time we had'ta go ta Cleya fer help." He laughed. "Brutal woman. Funny as shit, but brutal."

I couldn't help the giggle that fell from my lips. "I gathered that much."

"Good with an axe, and a bow. And swords. Anything with a sharp end. An' some things without," he snickered.

A hand flew over my mouth, stifling the cackle that roared from my throat. "You and Cleya?"

"Only once," he said, bushy brows furrowed. "She couldn't handle more'n that."

I was certain that wasn't the case, but said nothing. It was a joy to watch his face light up as he spoke of his younger days, and so I leaned forward, chin in my hands, and let him talk.

And talk he did.

Tollok spoke of glaciers that shone like the sun, glittering like diamond mines, and great glacial beasts haunting them. Of men taller than dragons, twice as strong, and just as brutal.

He spoke of mines filled with precious stones. Lands south of the Boundary they weren't supposed to be in, where the oceans were bright, vivid blue. Deserts that stretched for thousands of miles.

Before I knew it, the sun had reached its zenith and the tavern around us was milling with people, buzzing with their chatter. And my moment of peace, of solitude, was over. My imprisonment reinstated.

"Best get upstairs, Love," Tollok said as he crawled from his chair. "Wouldn't want to get in trouble of your guardians."

"Thank you, Tollok."

He smiled up at me before patting my hand and wandering off, immediately falling into yelling and jeering and cajoling his customers, all of whom seemed to enjoy it.

With a great sigh, I pressed myself through the crowd to the staircase and made my way up the too-long flight to the room.

Once inside, I kicked off my boots and crawled beside Miran. I slid between his arms, barely noticing when his eyes opened.

"Hey," he whispered.

"Hey," I returned.

His eyes grazed my face, pinning me beside him. I traced the outline of his lips with a fingertip, the perfectly rounded pout at the bottom, and ran my hand through his beard, pulling him into me.

His kiss was gentle and yet hard, taking—my breath, my heartbeat, everything—as his hands slipped beneath my shirt. They crawled up, a trail of fire blazing in their wake until I gasped as he found my nipples, flicking and rubbing them.

Miran shoved my knees aside, pressing into me, his hardened desire kept at bay only by the clothes we wore. Clothes I suddenly needed off.

Tugging at his shirts, we broke the kiss long enough for me to fling his layers aside and greedily drink in the sight of him. The finely sculpted muscles of his abs, the little trail of hair winding into the waistband of his trousers. How his biceps flexed as he leaned onto his arms to take my mouth again.

His fingers wound around the bottom of my shirts and they, too, were gone, tossed aside with his. The cold stung my nipples, my stomach, every part of me alive, both hot and cold. Next went my trousers, flung across the room before Miran tore my underwear away and buried himself between my thighs.

I gasped as he feasted on me, his tongue rolling over and around, digging into me. Lapping until I was curled in on myself, quivering and trembling. Moaning his name as if he were a god and I worshipping him. Or perhaps the other way round.

A burst of sensation ruptured through my being and my back arched of its own accord. My fingers dug into the blankets, then his hair. I only just recognized myself crying out his name when he came up for air and was atop me, grinning.

"Scream my name again," he growled, and thrust into me.

My hands flew to his back, scratching and clawing at his movements. He gripped one of my legs, pressing it into my chest, growling and groaning with every slap of his skin against mine.

My eyes rolled back, blinding me. I was a vessel of sensation. Glimpses of red and skin. Another burst of pleasure erupted between my legs, ricocheting up my back, into my shoulders and down into my toes. And I did scream his name. For all the world to hear.

As suddenly as it started, Miran shuddered and collapsed atop me.

Our breaths mingled, the heat and sweat of our skin making our bodies stick. Struggling to catch my breath, I closed my eyes and tipped my head back. Allowed myself to feel my body, the unimaginable pleasure rolling through it, wave after wave. The heaviness atop me where Miran rest. His heart hammering against my breasts.

Miran pushed himself up, hovering above me. One finger hooked beneath my chin and he turned me to face him before pressing the gentlest of kisses against my lips. Smiling, I stroked his face, up into his hair, sweeping aside the scarlet curls to reveal those beautiful sapphire eyes.

A wave of fatigue washed over me. Miran pressed another kiss to my lips. He gathered me in his arms and shuffled us around, wriggling beneath the blankets. I snuggled beside him, inhaling his scent as his embrace swallowed me. It was there, beside him, I wanted to stay.

I looked down at the sand, at the scarlet slowly curling toward me, and stepped back. Briahna's hand lay limp on the ground, her sightless eyes staring off somewhere I couldn't see. A sniffle tore through me, my heart pounding in my chest.

The ground trembled. With it, Briahna's body moved.

Suddenly, she turned over, her eyes, already glazed, staring up at me, and she uttered a single word.

"Run."

I jolted awake, eyes wide as Miran hovered above me, screaming. I kicked back from him, heart thundering in my chest.

"What?" I asked, breathless. "What's wrong?"

He pointed to the window. The sky was alight with furious flames, licking the dark, as if they would catch the moons on fire. My mouth fell open, gaping, as my breath fled.

At movement, I turned, following Miran as he pulled his clothes on. He didn't need to say anything else as I jumped up and followed suit.

After we were dressed, I gazed around. The ground trembled, shaking the foundations of the inn, and the whole building groaned beneath its own weight.

"Miran," I whined.

"It's okay," he said, flying to my side, a hand on my cheek. He kissed my forehead. "It's going to be okay."

He stroked my cheek again before crossing the small room to the door and flung it open. A rush of people filled the hallway, their panicked screams sinking into my ears, their pounding footsteps mirroring the drumbeats ringing in my chest.

Miran slammed the door and went instead to the window, my gaze following. My body turned to face him of its own accord. He gave the pane an experimental tug, found the lock, flipped it, and shoved the thing up before waving me over.

"Miran, I-I can't do this," I stuttered, a burst of cold burying into my eyes, into my very soul.

"We have no choice," he said, hand again on my cheek. "If we can make it to the safehouse, the others will help get us out of The City."

I gazed out the window, back to the door. "W-what about Venyx?"

"He'll meet us there," he said, hoisting himself up into the window frame. He turned to me, holding out one hand. "Do you trust me?"

I stared up at his penetrating sapphire gaze, uttering, "Yes," without thought.

Around us, the building trembled again, dust hissing from the ceiling as a great shadow swooped low above the tavern, a set of massive wings beating frozen air into the room, into my face.

I could do this, I told myself, and forced myself to believe it.

Miran shimmied out of the way before one hand came back and gestured to me. With his help, I hoisted myself up and out, picking my way over the sill to the foothold he stepped on. Though it was frozen, on the verge of crumbling at any moment, it held beneath our weight.

"Down," Miran said. I nodded, unable to form words. Refusing to face the ground.

Miran went first. He picked his way along the building, testing the hand and footholds, one hand, one foot, then the next, and another. With each step he took, I followed, biting back my paralyzing fear the whole way.

After an eternity, Miran told me to let go, and I did, sighing in relief when my feet touched solid ground.

In the distance, a dragon roared. The air around us crackled, splitting open, as it sang with energy from a breath weapon.

"Which way do we go?" I asked. Miran licked his lips, glanced up and down the street.

"We came from that way," he said. "North. So, the safehouse would be this way." He pointed in the right direction. I slipped my hand in his and we jogged down the street, stopping in the shadows intermittently to make sure we were clear.

I stayed beside Miran as we went, ducking in and out of buildings, hiding in pools of darkness. Horrors echoed around me, singing like a fatal chorus as The City was wrought down around us. The ground trembled, buildings collapsed. Overhead, dragons swooped down, breathing fire and ice, among other breath weapons. I could scarcely tell one district from another as we went, whatever class system separating them torn down by flames and carnage.

Despite the cold, my brow was covered in a spackling of sweat by the time we finally slowed. My palm was slick with it, far too warm wrapped in Miran's oversized hand as we ran.

At a fallen building, Miran held up a hand, stopping me in my tracks before he continued around the corner. Several long moments crept by. My breath evened out, heartrate steadying as I huddled in the shadows, waiting. I rubbed my arms, itchy from the juxtaposition of hot and cold. Finally, a soft whistle came, twittering in the air, and I stepped into the street.

Rounded the corner, and my heart stopped.

Perhaps it had been a safehouse. Or a home. What lay before me, however, was a pile of rubble. Emotions welled in my throat as I looked between the wreckage and Miran, huddled on his haunches, head in his hands.

"Is this it?" I asked. He nodded.

Taking a breath, Miran stood and kicked a stray brick, the thing skipping along the frozen cobblestone.

"How do we know?" I asked. He glanced up as if I'd asked my own name, then pointed. Stepping through the ruins, crunching over snow, the tiniest symbol stared up at me, etched into the warped wooden door. The Amasian sigil.

I turned, mind reeling as I gawked, mouth gaping. "They have to be here," I said.

"Seraph..."

"Maybe they're buried inside."

"Seraph, stop."

"Or—"

"Seraph."

210

I stopped and turned to Miran.

He threw his arms open. "I've already checked."

"Well..." I turned in a circle. "When did it happen?"

He laughed. "The City is being attacked, Seraph."

I stepped into the street and turned to face the building again. A fine dusting of snow covered the rubble strewn about. The bits of charred brick and wood cooled long ago. To the left, a collapsed building still smoldered.

"Miran." I faced him as he rubbed his eyes, shoulders slumped. "This looks like it ... happened ... weeks..."

My gaze grazed the building again, sliding back to those around it, and back. There were no bodies. No blood.

The White Army had been here a month or so, Tollok said. We'd been traveling nearly two months.

But how could they have known where the safehouse was?

I turned back to Miran, now pacing up and down the street, hands in his hair.

My head spun.

How adamant he'd been about getting here.

Venyx refusing to leave me alone with him, refusing to come to the safehouse.

Back to the building, to the smokeless rubble. The frost picking at the remnants of wood.

Three attacks. Each time, no one had known where we were.

My breath hitched.

Spots flashed before my eyes.

My legs refused to work.

"Seraph?" Miran rushed toward me, arms out as if I might fall. "Are you okay?"

My gaze trailed up his face, to the features I'd seen every day for eight months. The lips I'd kissed. The hands that had held me. The heart I'd fallen asleep to. The body that...

Nausea curled in my gut, curdling my stomach. The ground swept from beneath me and it was all I could do to keep myself upright.

"Seraph, say something," Miran gasped, hands on my sides.

My eyes found his, hot tears rolling down my face. My mouth gaped, the question right there, hanging off my tongue, though I couldn't speak it. Couldn't ask.

His mouth fell open, eyes slowly closing, and he drew in a deep breath. When he opened them again, the gleaming sapphire I'd come to love was gone, replaced by such a brilliant coldness I wondered how I'd missed it. His features drew together, nearly in a snarl, the smile perpetually on his lips melting away.

My breath stuttered and I stepped back. Inside, I screamed. I wasn't sure an outward cry could ever voice the tumultuous emotions writhing within.

My heart hammered in my throat as I turned and launched myself down the street, boots pounding on the cobblestone. A hand grabbed my throat from behind and slammed me into the nearest building, stars shivering through my vision as Miran's face swam before me. My body curled away from him, blubbering tears rolling down my face. I clawed at him, desperate to beg him to let me go.

Chest heaving, he leaned into me and whispered against my cheek, "You'll be a good girl and go willingly, or I'll slit your fucking throat and carry your head to Kaival myself." Every word punctuated by a seething in his eyes I begged to reel back from.

I sobbed against him; the only thing holding me up was his hand around my throat. I shuddered, the tears refusing to stop.

This was a dream. I was dreaming.

I slammed my eyes closed.

I would wake up and we would still be in bed. His arms around me. The world would be back to normal.

Wake up, wake up. Wake up!

But when I opened my eyes, Miran's face still hovered above mine, the cruelness in his gaze unmistakable. More tears blurred my vision, twisting his face into one I barely recognized.

And I realized I had a choice. The first one I'd been given.

I could go. Willingly. And I would die.

Or.

Or I could fight. And die anyway.

Either way, this ended in my death.

So I would not go quietly.

Without warning, I thrust my knee between Miran's legs. The instant he crumbled, I launched myself off the wall and down the street.

He roared. An iron-grip tore into my hair, yanking me back against his chest. The same chest I'd fallen asleep against.

Bile rose in my throat, boiled in my gut. Another sob eked its way out of my mouth.

Throwing my foot into his knee, something cracked, his shout piercing my ear as he trembled, his grip slackening just enough. Balling my hands, I wheeled around and slammed my fists into his face, sending him sprawling to the snowy ground.

I made it two steps before he reached out, grabbed my ankle and I fell face first on the cobblestone, clawing at it. A sob-filled scream ripped from my chest as Miran yanked me back, folding his form atop me, fury wrung across his features.

He reached for my hands as I punched and hit and clawed, barely able to see through my tears. Growling, he gripped one wrist and pinned it above my head. Heart hammering, my breath coming so fast spots swam before my eyes, I slipped my free hand of his grasp and palmed his cheek, brought myself up, and kissed him.

Miran stilled atop me. A moment passed, and he leaned into the kiss, pressing me into the cobblestone. I buried my fingers in his beard, arched my back against him. He groaned into my mouth as his tongue flicked across my lips.

With a breath, he pulled back, a bit of glimmer returning to his eyes. "Once more?" he asked.

I shuddered my eyes, tipped my chin up, and nodded. "Once more."

He growled and leaned into me. I trailed my free hand down his chest, skating across his abs, and further still. One of his knees came up, then the other, propping me atop them. I fumbled with the lacing of his breeches, forcing myself to remain calm as my hand slipped inside and gripped him. He hitched his hips against me as he untied my lacings. Reaching around, I tugged at his trousers, moaning into his mouth as his fingers slipped inside me.

His knees came up further as he worked at pulling my trousers down my hips. My fingers grazed his ass, down his thigh, squeezing him encouragingly. He nipped my lip before trailing kisses down my neck.

Forcing down the pounding of my heart, I skimmed his thigh, reached into his boot, and fingered the knife there. Miran stilled atop me, coming up for air. His face fell as he glanced down.

Roaring, I gripped the knife, sat up, and rammed the blade into his left eye. With an ear-shattering shriek, he fell back, clutching both the knife and his face.

"Fucking bitch!" He rolled onto his hands and knees and ripped the blade out, blood gushing from the wound. Without thinking, I scrambled up, reared back, and kicked his face. Miran flipped over, sprawled on the ground. Unmoving.

Stepping back, I glanced down at the knife. My chest heaved as I stared at it. At him. It would take nothing to end it. To know I'd ended it.

Boots pounded on the street, ripping me from my thoughts. I glanced up into the dark, suddenly remembering where I was.

With a final glance at Miran, I turned and ran.

TWENTY-FIVE

A T THE FIRST ALLEY, I dove inside, scrambling to the back until I was swallowed by shadows. Slamming my hands over my mouth, I drew my knees to my chest and screamed. My whole being trembled. My hair stuck to my slick cheeks. Mucus seeped from my nose. Spots swam and flashed before my eyes and my lungs burned for air, despite my gasping breaths.

After my voice went hoarse, I dug my fingernails into my legs, my arms, everywhere that might hurt. That might wake me from this.

But there was no waking. This was my life.

The moments crept by as I sat there, and it occurred to me I couldn't linger. I shouldn't. Someone could wander by any moment—I was surprised no one had—and the last thing I needed was to be caught.

Wiping my cheeks, my eyes, and my nose, sucking in a series of quick, shallow breaths, I shoved to my feet and crept from hiding. The way I'd come hovered in my peripheral, and I whipped my head in the other direction. Another few, deep breaths, and I stepped from the alley.

Thankfully, the street was empty.

All around, in the distance, in every corner of The City, rang sounds of battle. Crying and clashing steel. Dragons roaring. Wiping away stray tears, I scanned the street again, ensuring it was empty, and pressed on. Maybe I could find Venyx.

But as the thought passed, my shuffling slowed.

Miran had been lying to me. The whole time.

Who was to say Venyx wasn't lying?

I chuckled as it occurred to me I wasn't even sure Nik hadn't been lying.

My breath hitched in my throat. Tears stung my eyes as I was struck by the realization there wasn't a single soul I *could* trust. A sob oozed up my throat, but I shoved it down. This was neither the time, nor the place.

And I kept moving.

My steps echoed as I jogged. My gaze jumped from the windows to the rooftops, searching for those pinpoints of silver, the forest replaying in my mind. A dragon flew overhead and I stopped, ran backward, and slammed into a building, hiding until it passed.

Taking a deep, steadying breath, I glanced around again and pressed on, hoping I was headed the right way.

At the intersection in front of Tollok's place, I stopped, my gaze swinging back and forth before being drawn upward. The top half of the *Braided Beard* had collapsed, sending jolts of biting fear through me. I longed to go inside, to make sure Tollok had survived. Guilt soured my stomach, knowing I had no time to spare, and I darted across the street into the welcoming arms of the shadows on the other side.

This street was far narrower. No other passages crossed it. The buildings on either side went on for what seemed an eternity, their brick walls wafting an icy air that leached through my layers. Shivers ran rampant up and down my spine.

Finally, the unending street gave way and I found myself in a square. Littered with bodies. On the far side lay a dragon, throat opened, thick red blood coating the cobblestone, melting into piles of snow. Most of its massive body lay atop another building, collapsed beneath its weight. The thing's eyes stared open, its jaw at a strange, unnatural angle, as if someone, or something, had tried tearing it off.

I swallowed and pressed on. Whatever had done that to a dragon wasn't something I wanted on my heels.

The street continued in a series of warehouses lining either side. The ones with curtains over the windows. Glass now lay sprawled across the cobblestone, crunching underfoot as I went. I peeked inside at the gleaming metal tubes and machinery that were supposed to turn wind into power.

As I continued, the glass vanished from underfoot and the sounds of battle again drew closer. I bit back the emotions flooding my throat as my gait slowed. I stopped, looked back, but already knew there was no way, not unless I backtracked.

Easing my way forward, I stopped and peered around the corner. Writhing forms were locked in battle across another small square. More bodies littered the cobblestone, blood strewn every which way. Across buildings and snow and the ground. A dark figure, swathed in shadows, kicked the feet from beneath a soldier in white and rammed their gleaming blade through the man's begging mouth, out the other side. The movement accompanied by a sickening gurgle. The sword was withdrawn and the body fell with a wet splat, joining the others.

Hand over my mouth, I suppressed a sob and glanced back. Then forced myself onward.

Tiptoeing across the street, I dove into the shadows and curled around the corner of a building, slinking along the wall. My body trembled the whole way, one eye focused on the being as they wiped their blade clean.

Spotting a discarded sword, I stooped and plucked it off the street. From the short moment I'd observed the figure, I knew I stood no chance, but the weight was comforting.

As I eased back against the wall, the figure stopped and turned. I stilled. Like watching a predator, I slid along the ground, clutching the weapon.

The enshrouded figure vanished and I jumped back, pressed against the icy bricks. My widened gaze darted back and forth through the darkness, panic pulsing in my vision. He reappeared in front of me, swung his sword up and slammed it down. From pure instinct, I raised my own, blades clashing together with a resounding clang that reverberated down my arms and into my legs, and I buckled beneath the sheer force.

Chest heaving, I looked up at my attacker, and a sob wrenched free at the sight of Venyx, red eyes glaring at me.

His brows furrowed, he sheathed his sword in a single fluid movement. The deymon's mouth was twisted in silent rage as he grabbed my arm and hauled me across the square. The tip of my blade dragged along the cobblestone before I hoisted it up, clutching it like a lifeline.

The dissipated panic flared to blaring life as Venyx opened the door to a partially dilapidated building and tossed me inside, closing it as he joined me. Lips trembling, I righted myself and spun around, heaving as he stalked toward me, wearing a furious mask. My backward steps matched his, desperate to put as much distance between us as possible.

Whimpering, I held the blade up, but he flicked it away, the thing skittering uselessly along the floor. Before I knew it, the wall was at my back and there was nowhere to go. No more distance to separate us. He took my chin in one hand and turned my head this way and that, looking over me. I ripped my face from his grasp, withdrawing from his touch.

It was only in the darkness of that little building when his shoulders slumped. He exhaled a great breath, and exhaustion showed clear on his face.

"Are you hurt?" he asked.

I licked my lips, shook my head, damming the cascade of emotions. I would not break, not in front of him.

"You made it out of the inn." Not a question.

My mouth got the better of me. "No thanks to you," I spat.

He pinched the bridge of his nose. "I know. I'm sorry." His hand fell away and he looked up, regret hanging on his face. "I tried to get back. I *was trying* to get back to you."

My terror seeped away, replaced by confusion, as the deymon gazed around, as if only just realizing where we were. His eyes had long faded back to brown, glimmering silver in the darkness.

"Where's Miran?"

His expression, the question, his confusion, opened the floodgates of my emotions. My hands flew to my mouth as my legs crumbled, spilling me to the floor. A new wave of tears washed through me as I trembled.

"Seraph?" he asked.

I looked up at him through the torrent of tears, mouth gaping, fighting to speak around my constricted throat.

"What?" The deymon's confused face twisted, bafflement seeping out of him.

"It was Miran," I sobbed.

A myriad of emotions wafted across Venyx's face. The fury fled him all at once, the tired lines falling as his eyes closed. His head dipped toward his chest, shoulders slumping even more. One hand raised, pinching the bridge of his nose.

All at once, sheer rage filled him. He roared, one fist jabbing the wall, cracking the stone. The whole building trembled, shuddering beneath the force of his strike.

My eyes shot open and I flinched, pulling further away from him.

"I told Aurorian we should have gone alone!"

My breath hitched at his words. "What?"

He looked up.

"You knew?" I jumped off the wall and stormed across the room, shoved him, screaming, "You knew! You knew and didn't tell me!"

The deymon glared down at me. "I didn't know for certain."

"You should have told me!" I screeched.

He wheeled on me until we were flush against each other. "How the fuck was I supposed to? You were fucking him! You wouldn't have believed a fucking word I said!"

"If you hadn't spent the last month being a dick maybe I would have!"

He opened his mouth to retort, but deflated. He shoved his hands through his hair and sank against the wall, cradling his head. For a long moment he sat there, face hidden behind his arms. His hands slipped down, balled into fists, and he dropped them, silver-flecked gaze rising to mine.

"We can sit here and blame each other," he said, voice void of anger, "or we can get out of The City."

I pulled my arms over my chest and shrank away from him. "How am I supposed to trust you? I don't know you. *You've* made sure of that."

He rose, stalking toward me with all the grace of the predator I knew he was, until the wall was again at my back and he was inches away, the warmth of his breath fanning my face. "Because you don't have a fucking choice."

TWENTY-SIX

"**T**HE FASTEST WAY ACROSS The City is by rooftop," Venyx said, tipping his head skyward.

I followed his gaze before turning to face him. "I don't understand."

Instead of explaining, he picked me up, despite my protests, and slung me along his back, gripping my wrists. He then launched into the air. I shoved my face into his cloak, crying against the thick folds, before we landed atop the building.

The moment solid ground was beneath me, I dropped and scrambled away from him, staring up as the deymon turned. He strode to me, grabbed my arm, and hoisted me to my feet.

"If we're going to survive, I need you to cooperate and stay by my side."

I nodded weakly before he again picked me up and flung me over his back as if I were weightless. With a breath, I dug my face into his shoulder and gripped my wrists as he brought my legs around his waist. A wave of exhaustion washed over me as I curled around his body. Though the fatigue was wiped away as the deymon broke into a run and launched through the air to the next building.

I slammed my eyes shut as Venyx ran from one rooftop to the next. Cold air tore across my face, through my hair. As he landed on the next building, my eyes opened to the sprawling bounds of The City.

It stretched through the mountainous bowl, buildings curving into the hills on either side.

Fire consumed it all, spreading along the massive expanse. In the distance, dragons flew overhead, some locked in battle. Their roars echoed across The City as they ripped into each other. Another drew a deep breath, the air crackling, and the beast released a volley of flames. My breath hitched at the sight.

Before I knew it, we were airborne again, slamming into the next rooftop.

The tip of a wing passed overhead, drawing my vision up. A great white dragon, underbelly gleaming in the light of the flames, turned its massive head before it began circling around.

Suddenly, my mouth refused to work. My breath gone. My voice fled.

"Shit," Venyx breathed as we jumped to the next building.

The dragon tucked its wings and dove.

A scream wrenched from my chest and Venyx's hands flew up, clutching his ears as he kicked off from the rooftop. In its nosedive, the dragon drew a breath. I wrapped myself tighter around Venyx, leaning sideways as he jumped, the air snapping and crackling around us. Bright light filled the back of the dragon's mouth before it exhaled.

Venyx ripped one of my arms from his throat, changed directions the moment we landed, and jumped just as a bolt of ice and snow blasted the building. I turned as it crumbled beneath the power of the breath weapon, and we fell on another roof with a painful jolt. Venyx rolled to his feet, tossing me from his back. The world spun in a whir of color and darkness before I came to a stop. My head swam, though there was no time to recover.

A solid grip pulled me to my feet. I screamed, hitting and clawing until Venyx pulled me into his chest, his hands clasping mine.

"It's me!" he shouted.

Gasping, I looked him over.

"You can't scream that close to my ears."

I barely heard his words; the world a raucous pot of noise, all too much to handle.

"Look at me!" Venyx cried, tugging me against him. My eyes jolted to his face, sweeping over the sharp angles, the smooth planes. "We *will* get out of this, but you need to let me do my job. Eyes on me. Focus on me."

I nodded, my hair flying. He sighed.

"Eyes on me," he said, voice softening.

I breathed out, swallowing a lungful of cool air. This time, he presented me his back, and I wrapped my arms around him, let him hoist me up around his waist.

Above, the dragon circled back, wings beating ferociously against the frigid air. Both Venyx and I glanced back before we were running, and Venyx launched us through the sky.

My eyes clenched shut as we sailed across the street. And, just as suddenly, something solid slammed into us. A cry rent itself from me as Venyx roared. My eyes flew open as I sailed right for a building. Venyx reached out and grabbed me, wrapped his body around me, and we slammed into the wall, falling limp to the cold ground.

The world spun from where I lay. A pair of white boots ran toward us. I begged my body to rise, to run, to do anything, but it refused. Beside me, Venyx jumped up, drew his swords, and kicked the deymon against the opposing wall. He flipped the twins overhand and drove the tips up into the deymon's jaw, straight through the top of his skull. The blades released with a wet *twang* before the body dropped to the cobblestone.

I sobered instantly and clambered backward as another soldier rushed down the street, sword in hand. Venyx vanished and reappeared before the man, lopping off his head in a single arch of his blades.

My gaze trained on the severed head, the bodies and blood. Nik's face swam before my eyes. At Venyx's approach, I scurried away. A thick claw of dread latched onto my heart as the deymon dropped to his haunches before me.

"Hey." My gaze flicked to him, vision hazy. "Eyes on me." He stood, sheathed his swords, and reached down. "I'm not going to hurt you, Seraph."

Licking my lips, I put my hand in his and let him pull me up. As my vision cleared, I noticed the blood running from his nose. How his chest heaved. His shoulders slumped. Venyx wiped a sleeve across his face, sniffled, and shook his head.

"Are you okay?" I asked.

"I'm fine. Let's keep going." He grabbed my arm and pulled me forward before his legs gave out, spilling him into the building to his left.

"Shit!" I hissed, dropping before him.

"I'm fine. I just ... just need a moment." The deymon tipped his head back, swallowed a breath of cold air. His forehead was slick with sweat.

"Venyx—"

"I'm fine." Another breath and he hoisted me up before he shoved off the ground. I wrapped my arms around his neck as he launched to the rooftop. And returned to hopping through The City, one building at a time.

We were slammed into again. This time, there was no deymon wrapped around me. Stars flashed before my vision as I hit a wall and fell with a wet thump to the snowy street, the breath knocked from my chest. Venyx landed on his back a few feet away.

My head swam as Venyx jumped up, unsheathed both swords, and danced through a flood of bodies surging down the street. Even through hazy vision, he moved with precision, the death he dealt an art. Even when his movements slowed. As visible signs of exhaustion set in.

The last body fell and Venyx slumped to his knees, chest heaving.

A hand grabbed my arm, pulled me against a warm body. A strange, yet all too familiar scent tingled my nose. It took a moment to remember. The faeries.

I glanced at the fae woman holding me, her eyes glowing bright yellow.

Venyx stood, sheathing his swords.

The faerie giggled as her free hand rose, holding a glowing ball of light. It compressed, turning to dust. She lifted the palmful of glitter to her lips and breathed in Venyx's direction. My entire form trembled, recalling what had happened to Nik.

Venyx whipped a knife from somewhere on his belt and threw it in one motion. The little blade thunked as it sank into the faerie's forehead, and I flinched, eyes wide, mouth gaping. The body collapsed the same instant the dust stopped, as if hitting a wall, and vanished before touching the ground.

As if drunk, the deymon stumbled and collapsed to his knees, head slumped forward. He leaned on his arms, drawing deep, slow breaths.

"You're not alright," I said, carefully approaching him.

"I will be." He sat, head tipped back, throat bobbing as his jaw worked. He blew out his cheeks and shakily stood.

"The rooftops aren't working," I said, my voice a strained whisper.

"No," he agreed. Placing a hand on my back, he urged me forward, and we hurried down the street.

Venyx kept us in the shadows. If we had to cross a street, we did so quickly and dove into the dark again. Several times, we stopped to allow White Army soldiers to pass. I lingered behind Venyx, barely able to glimpse over his shoulder. When it was again clear, he urged me forward and on we went.

The City passed at a much slower rate. I wasn't sure how close dawn was, but it seemed the sun might beat us outside the walls. Still, I wouldn't press him. The few times I glimpsed his face, blood oozed from his nose. During our rare breaks, his legs shook and wobbled, chest heaving. Though I didn't dare ask if he wanted to rest a bit more. I already knew he'd say no.

We slinked down an alley, hugging the walls, until we reached a yawning square. Before we entered, Venyx threw up an arm, stopping me. Just a few steps to the right and I saw why.

Standing in the middle was a mass of soldiers in white.

Swallowing the lump in my throat, I turned to Venyx, his mind working behind his eyes. Silently, he pointed across the way, to an alley ensconced in darkness.

An agonized scream rang out, and we both stopped. My widened gaze turned to Venyx. Tollok screamed again. Venyx's hand flew to his face, his shoulders sagging in defeat. Back and forth I glanced, from the sliver of square to Venyx.

"Deymon!" a voice called. "You can have your friend back if you give us the Child."

His eyes slid open and met mine. My hammering pulse peaked as he pushed me into the shadows and held a finger to his lips.

"I've another gift, as well."

A moment later, another, feminine, voice screamed. Venyx's eyes slammed shut, head bowed. Lira. The elf woman.

My heart drummed violently, my chest heaving, as I stared at him. He wouldn't risk his friends' lives for mine. He couldn't. He hadn't even wanted to come.

"We ain't worth it!" Tollok screamed.

"Go!" Lira cried.

Tears gathered at the edges of my vision as I stared at him. His eyes opened and he sighed, deep and slow. Cast his gaze to the ground between us. His hands rose to my shoulders. I flinched, bottom lip clutched between my teeth, expecting him to toss me over his shoulder and dump me before the White Army. Part of me thought he should. Another hoped he didn't. I wasn't sure I had a right to either thought.

After all, my life had never been mine.

What I wanted, what I thought, never mattered.

And now I found myself, my life, my borrowed existence, in the hands of a man who hadn't wanted to protect me in the first place.

Whatever Aurorian had promised him surely wasn't enough for this.

Stay here, he mouthed, pointing at the ground.

My brows furrowed, breath hitching. Before I could comprehend what was happening, he walked down the alley, turned the corner, and went toward the square.

I tiptoed after him and peered around the corner as a barrage of light illuminated the square. Enveloped by shadows, I stole across the cobblestone, Venyx firmly in my vision as he went, arms held to either side.

"There he is," the deymon in the center said. Beside him kneeled Tollok, hands at his back. To the left of the dwarf, on her knees, was Lira, similarly bound. They stared up, unblinking, as Venyx strolled across the square. Tollok's eyes remained on Venyx, but Lira's went searching. I slinked back farther, to the mouth of the alley, and peered around. My fingers gripped the stone tight enough to hurt, though I ignored the pain.

"Where's the Child?" the lead deymon asked.

"I don't know," Venyx replied, voice calm, even, as he spoke.

"Go find her, and your friends are yours," the deymon said, gesturing to his left. Tollok glanced up. Lira slid her eyes to Venyx.

"How about this," Venyx said, voice going deeper. "Release them and your deaths will be quick."

The deymon chuckled. "Even for one your age, dispatching the entire White Army would be a feat I'd love to see."

The deymon holding Tollok stretched the dwarf's neck, pressing a blade just below his long, thick beard.

"Shave it and I'll skin ya," Tollok growled, his voice strained. His deymon captor smiled and turned to his commander, who chuckled.

"Go find the Child, or your friends die," the commanding deymon said, each word slow, enunciated.

"I've already tried. The little bitch evaded me."

I flinched at his words, though I knew it was just for show.

The commander chuckled, nodding. "She does seem to be quite good at that. Nonetheless, you have your terms. The Child for your people."

Lira's neck was stretched, her hair pulled back all the way, leaving her head, her throat, at an awkward angle. Her hands dropped to either side, and her wrist flexed. The pommel of a blade caught in her fingers.

My brows furrowed.

"You'll let them go because I'm being generous," Venyx growled.

"Consider them lucky I haven't ordered them gutted already," the commander said. "Find the Child, and take them. Consider further wasting *my* generosity, and they both die. Followed by you. And the Child dies anyway."

Venyx took a deep breath, his shoulders rising and falling with the action. I wished to see his face, watch the thoughts mill about in his head.

The next moments rushed by in a blur.

Lira rolled away from her captor, taking the deymon with her, and slid her blade through the deymon's throat before she popped to her feet. Venyx drew both swords and jumped toward the crowd of soldiers, roaring, while Tollok threw his head back into his captor's face, tossing the man to the ground. The dwarf drew the man's sword and slammed the blade into the deymon's head, cleaving his skull in two.

My breath shuddered. Heart slammed wildly in my chest.

As a single unit, the three worked through the gathered deymons. Blades clashed, blood flew across snow and cobblestone alike. The three moved as if they had practiced this moment, their motions fluid, in time with each other, as they danced and jumped between soldiers, felling bodies as they went.

Visions of Tollok's tales flashed through my head, imagining this was what it had been like, back when Tollok was young.

Suddenly, the commanding deymon pounced on Lira, took her by the throat and hoisted her off the ground before slamming her into the cobblestone. I flinched. Eyes wide in horror as the deymon's left hand streaked toward her, claws extending from his fingertips, diving into her throat. With a sickening, wet squelch, he ripped her throat out and Lira's thrashing body stilled all at once.

Nausea curdled my stomach. Briahna's face flashed before my eyes. "Lira!" Tollok screamed. Venyx spun around, eyes turning red.

One of the deymons rushed Tollok and kicked the dwarf's knees from beneath him.

No, I mouthed, tears filling my eyes. Tollok clawed at the deymon's hand, thrashing and screaming as the deymon gripped the dwarf's head. And pulled. Venyx rushed across the square toward his friend, swords out. Tollok's voice became high-pitched, a wailing, horror-filled scream. I bit my bottom lip as his neck ripped. Blood seeped from the dwarf's skin.

The deymon dropped Tollok's body, head in his hand, held by the dwarf's hair.

Venyx dropped to the ground. His gaze flicked over the dwarf, to the deymon. The red in his eyes lightened as he slowly looked up. He sheathed his swords, standing stock still. Suddenly, his eyes went pure, blinding white.

The deymon holding Tollok's head dropped it, terror filling his face. He stumbled back, mouth gaping, as Venyx stalked toward him. The deymon turned and ran, but Venyx appeared before him. He kicked the man to the ground, grabbed his head, and thrust his skull into the cobblestone again and again, squeezing until finally ... the man's skull popped open. Blood and brain matter spilled across the ground, over Venyx's hand.

My stomach turned. Tears streamed down my face in twin rivers. Body trembling, unable to move. A similar scene played out in my head. Blood curling over sand toward my feet.

The commanding deymon screamed out. And the whole army descended upon Venyx in a white flurry.

Claws extended from Venyx's fingertips. Slowly, he stood, faced the first deymon to attack, and plunged his claws through the soldier's face. Another jumped on his back. Venyx ripped the man off and sank his teeth into the soldier's throat, tearing it open before he dropped the body and moved to the next.

My knuckles were white, knees trembling. Briahna's lifeless face stared at me from the cobblestone, waves crashing somewhere in the back of my mind.

Sinking into the shadows of the alley, I pressed my back against the wall. Breath flying from my lips in quaking gasps. I looked over my shoulder, swiped my eyes with my sleeve, and ran.

TWENTY-SEVEN

I T MAY HAVE BEEN the south gate. Or the east. Possibly the western one. I wasn't sure how long it had taken, but eventually I'd wended my way through the streets, somehow avoiding capture—I assumed the White Army had their hands full with the raging deymon in the square—and found a throng of people all clambering for escape.

Sinking into the crowds, hood low over my face, I slipped out among them, trailing away once the gates, and the threat of capture, had fallen behind.

What had started as adrenaline-fueled escape devolved into fatigue, driven by the desire to not fall asleep. So I trudged along, feet shuffling down the half-muddy, half-frozen road.

Eventually, the first rays of golden sunlight crept up, stabbing the sky. It peppered through the claw-fingered trees, raining upon me in spears of warmth. East. I was headed east. Into the light-flooded horizon.

The road rose and dipped and curved, following the path of the hills surrounding The City. Or whatever remained of it.

It appeared Cleya had been correct. I was a blizzard of death, descending upon wherever I went.

The thought of the marauder chief brought another.

What had Aidra said? *Deymons is dangerous creatures.*

A shiver raced down my spine.

The look on Venyx's face. The blinding white of his eyes. How he'd so easily crushed a man's skull with his bare hands. I shuddered. I could go the rest of my life without seeing that again.

My feet found a rock and I stumbled, just barely catching myself. My legs trembled as I pressed on. I didn't know how long I could keep going. Just focused on putting as much distance between myself and The City as possible.

Perhaps I'd find an inn, or a tavern. Somewhere to take refuge. Even for just a night.

A peal of laughter rose from my throat as I realized I had no money. No coin in my pockets, on my person. No supplies to get me wherever I was going. Nothing.

My feet stopped of their own accord as my laughter filled the air. I covered my face with my hands, descending into tears.

Even if I were to go to Pensen, how would I get there? Yes, the Plainsmen were waiting for me, but I didn't know the way. Had no idea how to navigate the Northerlands to get there. No food, no weapons to hunt, or defend myself.

I may as well have stayed with the blood-crazed deymon for all the good running had done.

I pressed my lips into a thin line, let the tears roll over them before I licked the moisture away.

Maybe some kind soul would take pity upon me. Then I laughed. Such an absurd idea. All I'd found since leaving the safehouse was blood and betrayal. That wasn't likely to change. To think otherwise would have proven too naïve. Even if I longed to believe it.

Pushing the thoughts aside, I kept going. I'd been taught to make a bow. All I needed was a sharpened rock to shave a branch into a useable bow shaft, to strip the bark and meat of a tree to make fibers for the string. Nodding to myself, I trudged on. One foot, then the next. Keeping the road constantly falling behind.

A distant sound pulled me to a stop. For a moment, I stood there, peering around and through the trees, finding nothing. Another moment and I decided I'd simply imagined it. With my next step, though, it came again. A peal of laughter echoing through the forest.

I darted toward the nearest tree and ducked behind it, looking this way and that amongst the icy trunks. Agitation rose in my stomach as nothing came into view. The sound died, thrusting me again into silence. I chanced a move, tiptoeing closer to where I'd thought the sound had come from, and stopped short at a whinnying horse. Then another.

I turned in a circle, taking in my surroundings. There was nothing to shelter behind save for trees, and they would make poor hiding spots. Finally, I spotted a feature of rocks jutting from the earth, covered in snow and moss, a fallen, decrepit tree laid before it, hiding it from sight.

I dove behind the rock formation, skidding into the snow, and tucked myself flat against its cool surface, my fingers searching for something to use as a weapon. The only thing I found was a rock smaller than my palm. With a sigh, I decided it would have to do, and gripped it tight in my fist.

The laughter sounded again, drawing closer, followed by a myriad of voices. All of them male. My head fell back into the rock, and I cursed in frustration.

Quiet as possible, I sank to the forest floor and crept along the dirt and snow to the fallen tree, just able to make out the road beneath. The voices grew louder, and before long I could make out their conversation.

"...see that dragon piss himself in front of Veyla?" one was saying.

"I don't care how big you is, that woman is terrifying," another said, followed by more laughter. "Fucking idiot."

"Ain't no dragons to worry about in The City no more," a third said, and they all laughed.

The dragons I'd seen walking about, in the *Braided Beard*. They'd defended The City. My mind flashed back to the carcass in the square. My breath hitched in my throat, eyes widening at the revelation.

"Think Veyla's gonna find the other one?" another asked.

"Certainly fucking hope so. He deserves to have his throat slit," the first said. "Cocky motherfucker."

From between the ground and the tree trunk, I watched the parade of hooves trotting along as the men rode by, carrying on their conversation as if discussing the most casual thing, not the slaughter of people.

I kept my breath as even as I could, hoping they didn't hear me.

"Hold up," one said. "Got a stone in a hoof."

My eyes shot open as one of the horses pulled to a stop and a pair of white boots dropped to the ground. My heart stuttered to life, sending me into a panic, which only made it pound harder, making me panic all the more. Were they deymons? Could deymons hear heartbeats? Flustered, I took breath after slow breath, begging my heart to calm itself even as tears gathered in my eyes.

The man pulled a knife from his boot and lifted the offending hoof, digging a rock out before he dropped the horse's leg and sheathed the blade.

"All good?" one of the others asked, the rest waiting just ahead.

"Yeah." He climbed back into his saddle, clicked his tongue, and the group continued down the road.

I waited until they were out of sight before I sat up against the rock, relief flooding me. My eyes opened, sliding skyward, my heart plummeting at the man in white standing before me, brown gaze burrowing into mine.

I jumped to my feet, scrambling away, but the deymon appeared before me and snatched me up, growling as he slammed me against a tree. I grit my teeth from the impact, clawing at his hands. Kicked at his legs. I yelled and screamed, thrashing against him. The deymon only smiled wider, displaying his top four fangs. He pressed himself into me, flattening my legs against the trunk with his shins.

"Clever girl," he said. "Almost got away, didn't'cha?"

Dislodging one leg from beneath his, I kicked up, thrashed my hand with the stone, aiming for his head. In retaliation, the deymon slammed me into the trunk, sending stars before my eyes while the tree trembled and shook above.

"Bit of a fighter, ain't'cha?" The deymon let out a roar of laughter before he dropped me to my feet, one massive hand clutching my nape, and led me through the trees to the road. The others, all deymons, faced us.

"This one's a lil feisty," he said, prompting the others to burst into laughter. Into my hair, he said, "Let's see how long that lasts," sending shivers down my back.

"We taking her back to The City, Nyall?" one asked.

"Naw, let's take her to camp," the one behind me said. He spun me around and pinned me against his horse, reaching into a saddlebag for a length of rope. "Veyla can meet us there. Sure she's sick of that fucking place."

My gaze flicked up to him, one last, futile hope budding in my chest.

"I'm not the Child, though," I stammered. Nyall gazed at me skeptically. I pressed on, remembering what Tollok had said. "Don't all deymons get told you look alike? How do you think us Sirenians feel?"

He smirked. "Love, I seen plenty of Sirenians to know what they look like, and you's the only one who looks nothing like the others. Aside from that, we all been given an image of you." He tapped his temple, breaking from wrapping the rope around my hands.

A trembling breath fled my lips, the lump in my throat convulsing. It occurred to me where a mental image would have come from, and something in my heart squeezed painfully. I hoped Miran was dead.

"Up you get," he said, lifting me onto his saddle, and climbed up behind me.

The deymon Nyall was massive, riddled with corded muscle. This only made riding with him uncomfortable, sandwiched between his bulk behind me and the horn in front.

The procession of horses began anew, their conversation continuing as if it had never been interrupted.

I slumped forward, biting back the useless tears gathering in the corners of my eyes. I shouldn't have run. But now, because of my own stupidity, I was far worse off than I would have been otherwise.

We traveled a good portion of the day, going off-road when the sun reached its zenith, veering in a southeastern direction.

After a while it appeared the deymons forgot my existence. They broke once for food, passing around rations as they sat in a circle while I stayed in the saddle. My stomach grumbled, but I refused to look at them. Refused to let them know how hungry I was. Like it would have done any good anyway. They were just taking me to Kaival to die.

My thoughts stopped there, stomach curdling as fear blossomed in my chest, spreading to every part of me. They were taking me to Kaival. Whatever happened between now and then, whatever they did to me, didn't matter.

Cold dread speared my insides at the thought, prickling up my spine. Gazing through the tendrils of hair covering my face, I took stock of my captors and shoved aside the terror. There would be time for that later. I hadn't made it out of The City, alone, to suffer at the hands of the men now holding me.

The chatter broke as the deymons climbed back in their saddles and the clacking and clopping of hooves continued as we picked our way through the frozen forest.

We reached their camp just before dusk. It looked fitted for several dozen soldiers, though, as far as I could tell, only a small handful, including the ones who'd captured me, were currently there. A few humans wandered about in their duties, gazes lingering on me as Nyall dropped to the ground and pulled me down after him.

Just as before, one massive hand clutched the back of my neck and he guided me toward the campfire, forcing me into a spot before taking the seat beside me.

"Any word from Veyla?" one of the humans asked as he approached.

"Yeah," Nyall said. "We're gonna carry on to the coast. You lot stay here while she wraps up business in The City. Seems our friend got away and the queen wants him dead."

I glanced sideways at the lead deymon, brows twitching, though didn't dare hope. Nyall's gaze burned into me as I turned to face the fire.

"How's The City looking," the human asked.

"Like Abaddon after the Fall," another deymon said, laughing. An echo of chuckles rang out.

"Oi," Nyall shot. "Second Veyla's family just barely 'scaped the Fall. The Commander lived through it. Don't go joking 'bout the Fall."

Just like that, the conversation was over and the soldiers fell silently into their duties.

I bit my lower lip, tugging experimentally on the rope binding my wrists. It was tight, wrapped between my hands before winding around them again.

"How far you think you're gonna get?" Nyall asked. I ignored him, tucking my hands between my legs. "There's six deymons in this camp, five humans. You try to run, they won't hesitate to shoot you dead, or cut you down where you stand. All we gotta do is bring the queen proof of your death. Bringing you alive is just her preference."

I choked down the snarl rearing in the back of my throat, blinked away the furious moisture clouding my vision. Sent my rage into my hands, balling them into fists tight enough my nails dug into my palms.

"Wouldn't it be easier to kill her and be done with it?" a man across the fire asked.

"Be a waste of good flesh," said another. I looked up, meeting the deymon's eyes. The grin he wore, bearing all eight fangs, made my skin crawl.

"We ain't killing her," Nyall said. "And no one's touching her. The queen prefers her alive, so we're gonna take her alive. If," he turned and glared at me, "she gives us trouble, we'll consider killing her."

I met his scowl head on before sliding my gaze back to the flames.

"Come on, Nyall! I ain't touched a woman in—"

"No!" Nyall roared. "Veyla's orders. You wanna contest them, take it up with her."

The deymon across from me mumbled beneath his breath, but said nothing else.

I sat in uneasy silence next to Nyall, knees to my chest, as the rest of the soldiers gathered round the campfire. A few glanced at me, their gazes fleeting, as if afraid to stare too long. Taking in Nyall's hulking form, it wasn't difficult to understand why.

Cool chatter persisted throughout the camp as daylight faded. The soldiers, both humans and deymons, milled about. So few, I couldn't help but wonder if all of them would chase me if I tried to run. Or just the deymons.

As night set in, one of the human men set a small cauldron to heat above the flames while one of the deymons butchered some kind of meat. It looked like rabbit, though I couldn't be sure. I paid as little attention as possible. When chunks were dropped in the pot, my stomach grumbled at the sizzling and popping. I wrapped myself tighter around my middle, hoping to stifle the sounds.

"Layne," Nyall said, calling over one of the deymons. A shorter, lanky deymon approached, the one who had been eyeing me since our arrival. "Set out a bedroll for our guest."

"She can share mine," he said, flashing a fanged grin.

"Not funny," Nyall chided. "Put her bedroll next to mine. In case you, or anyone else gets any ideas."

Grumbling, Layne walked away.

"Why do you care what happens to me?" I asked, unable to stop the flow of words. He tossed me a glance before eyeing his men.

"The Second in Command is a woman, as is the Commander of the White Army," he said. "Wouldn't do good on me to let my men defile you when our Commanders are both women."

"But you're taking me to Kaival. So the Queen Faerie can kill me," I countered, fighting tears.

"I'm obeying orders," he said, leaning toward me. "Nothing more. What the Faerie Queen does with you ain't my business. My concern is keeping my men in line. Unless you'd rather be ravaged by five deymons."

A wall of nausea buffeted my stomach as Nyall rose.

"Set aside a bowl for her," he said in passing. The human looked up, his bewildered gaze jumping from Nyall to me and back.

"We ain't been given orders to feed her," the human said. "It's just one more mouth. We barely got food for ourselves."

"You'll feed her, or I'll assume you're violating a order."

The human opened his mouth to retort, then slammed it again, nodding. Nyall glanced back at me before he crossed the camp toward another of the deymons.

Before long, the smell of cooking food filled my nose and the grumbling in my stomach worsened. Nyall returned as the human began serving bowls, handing two to the leader in passing. The massive deymon sank beside me, placing both bowls on the ground between us.

"I'm gonna untie you so you can eat, and you ain't gonna run off. Are you?" he asked.

I met his gaze, knowing with everything in me he'd meant every word. He would keep me safe and alive so long as I cooperated.

"No."

"Good girl." With that, he loosened the ropes, his touch far more gentle than it had been when tying them, and handed me the bowl. The rope stayed coiled on the ground at his feet as he picked up his food.

The stew was thin and bland, but it was food. I ate slowly, hoping to fill my stomach before I reached the bottom. When the bottom of the bowl came first, it was disappointing, but at least I'd eaten. I wiped my mouth and set the dish aside as Nyall took up the rope, winding it back around my wrists. He stood, pulling me with him, and led me to the bedroll I'd be using for the night, right beside his, beneath a single-sided tent.

"We set watches in pairs," he said as we both sank to the thick rolls. "If you try to run, I ain't responsible for whatever happens."

The backs of my eyes burned, stinging from moisture and cold. I nodded and laid down, facing away from him. With my wrists bound, it was clumsy pulling the blanket over my shoulders, but I managed.

For a long time, I laid there, the shadows swaying through the trees as the moons dipped and crested between the clouds until my eyes became too heavy to keep open. When sleep came, it was restless, riddled with nightmares of the beach.

This time, it wasn't just Briahna's body bleeding out in the sand. It was the entire village. I found myself standing in the middle, bathed in the blood of those who'd died.

TWENTY-EIGHT

I T WAS STILL DARK when I woke the next morning, though already there was a flurry of activity. Nyall stopped before me as I sat up, or rather, wriggled up, since my wrists were still bound.

"Gotta piss?" he asked. Such a simple question, loaded with so many intentions.

"Yes," I croaked. He hoisted me to my feet by my bindings and placed a hand on my nape, leading me around the tent.

My heart hammered wildly as we stepped out of view. The deymon turned me to face him, hands on my wrists as he unbound me. I leaned away from him, holding my terror in my chest, trembling.

"I ain't gonna touch you," he said. "I'm gonna turn around and you're gonna go. Then I'm gonna bind you back up."

I stared up at him, forcing the fear down as I glowered with everything in me, until he dropped my hands and coiled the rope around his.

"Hurry up," he growled. Stepping back, I turned around, though not before him, and dropped my breeches, stanching the groan of relief as my bladder emptied. I wasn't sure when the last time I went was, but it had been far too long.

When I was finished, I stood and adjusted my breeches. Nyall turned in the same instant, toying with the rope in his hand. Instead of binding my wrists, he led me to the campfire and allowed me to eat before rewrapping the rope.

We set out as the sun was touching the horizon, keeping it on our left as it rose. Around its zenith, we found the road again and the little parade of horses flowed from the embankment of the forest down the middle in a neat line, stomping along existing tracks.

Nyall kept our horse in the center of the procession. Two rode before us, three behind.

The deymons chatted casually as we went, of things I hadn't expected. One of them, Bayitt, had a sister in Kaival who was due to give birth any day. He'd only just heard from his family the previous night. The conversation made me wonder how far away deymons could communicate, and if that was how Miran had kept in contact with whoever he'd been talking to.

Around dusk, we broke for camp. It was a small clearing, just off the road, big enough for seven bedrolls and a campfire and little else. The horses were tethered to a tree at the edge. Nyall pulled me down and untied my hands long enough for me to eat and empty my bladder.

As I sat on the bedroll, Layne's brownish-black eyes landed on me. He'd been staring a good portion of the day, though I'd tried to ignore it. I couldn't now.

"Nyall," Layne said. The commanding deymon sighed, as if knowing what Layne was going to say. "We're all stressed from battle, and now more travel. Can't we just—"

"Layne, ask once more," Nyall said, "and I swear to all seven hells I'll—"

"Okay," Layne groaned.

I curled up on my bedroll, laid down, and pulled the blankets as tight as I could, putting my back to the fire. Even still, Layne's gaze seared through me like heat from the flames.

The following day was much the same. I was unbound long enough to tend to my bodily functions and we were back in the saddle, traveling southeast.

The road curved more eastward, toward the distant coast, as the day passed. Before dusk, the sun was almost directly behind us. With so many miles passing between me and The City, a seed of fear planted itself in my gut. I was being taken to Kaival.

That night, as I lay in my bedroll, I wondered what the Faerie Queen would look like. Every story said she was the most beautiful woman to ever exist, so much so that the Winter Sprite had fallen in love with her at first sight. I supposed I'd find out soon enough.

The next morning, I woke to grumbling.

"Layne," Nyall said in warning.

"All I'm saying is, she's eating our food, using our bedroll," Layne said. A couple others muttered agreements. "Kaival ain't sending us more food. You ain't letting us kill her, so put her to use. She's gonna die anyway!"

My blood ran cold as agreements rang out among the men. I stifled the tears that sprang to my eyes, slamming them shut as boots crunched toward me.

"You ain't fucking her," Nyall growled. "No one is. Veyla's o—"

"Veyla ain't fucking here, Nyall," one of the deymons said to a chorus of agreements. "What's she gonna do?"

"And if she finds out?" Nyall asked. "What then? She'll kill you lot for disobeying her orders."

"That ain't your problem," another said. "Besides, there won't be another chance like this. She's the Child of Sky and Sea! You honestly think that other deymon didn't fuck her when he had the chance?"

"We already know one of the Amasians was fucking her," someone added. My breath halted at the words, heart stalling in my chest. Tears stung the backs of my eyes as some twisted amalgamation of hatred and heartbreak clawed at my gut.

Nyall grumbled. "My answer's still no. No one touches her." A boot struck my foot. "Wake up."

I sat up, blinking as if I'd just woken. Taking in the gathered men, I felt like a bit of meat in the midst of starving beasts, sending shivers throughout my entire being.

Nyall pulled me up and led me just out of camp, lingering closer as he waited, and as he led me back. After a quick, silent breakfast, we set off again.

The whole day, multiple sets of eyes seared into my skin. My shoulders hunched, as if I might deflect those gazes. Terror, heartbreak, and betrayal danced in my stomach. As the road churned beneath us, I tugged experimentally on the bonds around my wrists, biting back frustration when there was no give to be had. Whatever time I'd had was dwindling.

I needed a knife, or an arrowhead. Something sharp to saw through the rope. I wasn't the strongest rider, but I rode well enough. I had to get out of their grasp, and every day I was with them was a day too late.

It was becoming increasingly clear that Nyall was losing control of his men as desperation set in. The food supply grew smaller, the game scarcer the further east we went. And it was still a great distance from the coast.

I turned and glanced over my shoulder at Nyall, and beyond to Layne. My gaze locked with his hungry one, a series of trembles running up and down my spine before I turned back around. I wasn't sure how much longer Nyall would be able to keep control, and once he lost it, I'd lose the only protection I had.

Tonight. It had to be tonight.

TWENTY-NINE

D USK SETTLED HEAVY AS we broke for camp. As became routine, Nyall took me just out of range of the clearing, untying my hands so I could empty my bladder, before leading me to the firepit.

Over the past days, during my constant surveys, I'd noticed Nyall wore a knife in each boot. Neither looked like much. A pocketknife, at best. But I didn't need much to cut the rope. Just a sharp blade.

As he approached, bowls and spoons in each hand, an idea struck. It was stupid—sure to cost me if I was caught—but I was running out of both time and options.

Nyall took his seat beside me, knees flared out, one grazing my leg. Anxiously, I swallowed my first bite of stew, cringing past the bitterness. The moment would have to be perfect. And so I waited. Chewing slowly.

Two men fed the horses as another two set up camp. The fifth began cleaning the cooking pot. Leaving only Nyall. He turned away, talking to one of the men hitching tents.

Swallowing my nerves alongside the last bite of food, breathing slow and steady to keep my heartrate down, I fumbled my spoon. It landed, thankfully, between my boot and Nyall's, in a small patch of dirt and snow. I glanced up. The one cleaning the pot glanced up at the movement and turned away just as quickly. Only a dropped spoon, nothing to see.

Squeezing my hands to keep them from trembling, I leaned down, plucked the spoon up and reached into the narrow space between Nyall's boot and his leg.

One of the horses suddenly whinnied and bucked, throwing the deymon tending it back. I stilled as Nyall jumped to his feet and began barking orders. Seizing the opportunity, I grasped the little knife between my fore and middle fingers and slid the thing out, flipped it in my hand, and slipped it up my sleeve, the blade warm against my skin.

I sat up, spoon thunking in the wooden bowl just as Nyall turned and sat back down.

"What're you doing?" he asked.

"I dropped my spoon," I said, holding the offending thing up. He looked toward the cook, who nodded and shrugged.

When he bound my wrists again, the knots were tighter, cutting into my skin. Thankfully, the layers I wore were so thick he didn't notice the knife beneath the cloth. I wasn't sure how I would get to the little blade, but I would find a way.

Nyall collected our bowls and delivered them across camp, another of the deymons gaining his attention. While he was gone, Layne approached, near enough that his body heat pummeled me. He got on his haunches behind me, fidgeting with something on the ground. The curious part of me longed to know what he was doing, but the cautious part begged me to face forward, to ignore his presence entirely. Letting him know he bothered me would only encourage him.

So it took everything in me to not burst into tears when he leaned into me, breath fanning my ear, and whispered, "I've never had an angel before." Just as Nyall returned, Layne walked away. I refused to let the tears fall. I wouldn't give him the satisfaction, despite how badly I wanted to scream.

Shoving my hands between my thighs, I feigned keeping them warm while pulling at the knife's hilt until it sat just inside my cuff. After the blade was in position, I worked the rope back and forth, hoping that, eventually, it would slacken enough to let me grip my tiny weapon.

So far, the men had traded watch, with Nyall taking every other night. As I sat on my bedroll, though, something strange happened. Layne volunteered to take Nyall's place, and every fiber of my insides froze. If I was correct, tomorrow night would have been Layne's turn anyway. Something I *could not* stay for. I wouldn't survive.

"You don't got to," Nyall said.

"I insist," Layne offered. "You been doing it long enough."

Please, don't let him, I begged, knowing Nyall couldn't hear my thoughts.

"You got watch tomorrow," Nyall said, and it took everything in me to not outwardly sigh in relief.

"I'll do it," another of the men, Bayitt, said.

To this, Nyall nodded his consent. "Don't get us killed." He spoke with a playful chuckle, Bayitt laughing in return. The moment Nyall turned away, Bayitt traded a glance with Layne.

Shit. Shit, shit, shit.

To keep calm, I drew in a long, deep breath. If I was going to get out of this, I had to stay levelheaded. Panicking wouldn't help.

While Nyall laid down, I knew I couldn't stay seated. Not without making him more suspicious. So I settled into my bedroll and faced away from the flames, eyes wide and focused. I wasn't sure if I stood a chance running, but I would rather take death than what Layne had planned. Of course, that was assuming they didn't kill me afterward.

Their voices filled the cold air, rattling in my ears long after Nyall's soft snores rose beside me.

As gently as possible, I rocked my hands back and forth, working the blade from my sleeve until it butted against my bindings, rendering my wrists raw and tender. I grit my teeth as I twisted my hands, straining against the ropes, digging them further into my already bruised and shredded skin. My right arm flared to life at the pressure, burning into my palm, as I stretched my fingers, farther than should have been possible. And shoved the blade further into my sleeve.

Biting back a curse, I set to shimmying the blade against my bindings. I pressed my forearms together, holding the fucking thing still, and reached again. Frustration contracted my throat as it moved again, and I closed my eyes, praying it would stay still. And it did. I swallowed the gasp of relief when my fore and middle fingers clasped the pommel and slid it across the ropes into my awaiting palms.

Trembling, I held the thing like a damned godsend. It took everything in me to not kiss it as I settled back into my bedroll and waited. Waited for silence to fill the camp. For the fire to die down.

Waited for my one chance to get out of this.

Because one was all I would get.

Exhaustion tore at my eyes as I lay staring into open darkness. Snow drifted toward the ground, a heavy chill in the air as camp slowly quieted.

I forced myself to relax, to lay perfectly still, my mind going soft as if asleep. One by one, the voices around the campfire died until only two remained. Bayitt. And Layne. I couldn't be sure if Nyall was asleep. Several times he'd risen, walked around camp and given orders, before climbing back into his bedroll.

A while longer and Layne announced, rather loudly, he was going to sleep. His boots crunched along the snow as he crossed the small space to his roll. It shifted as he sat. Then there was only Bayitt. Accompanied by the crackling of the withering flames.

Unfurling my hands, tongue between my teeth, I flipped my stolen knife upside down, holding it as securely as possible between two fingers, and went to work.

The rope wasn't thick. If anything, it was used for corralling horses, maybe snaring small animals. It wasn't the width of it, but the sheer amount. So much was coiled around my wrists, I could scarcely move them, which only made my task more difficult. And so when the two sides finally snapped apart, it was all I could do to keep from screaming out in joy.

The next task was unraveling it.

At boots crunching through the snow, I stilled. Slammed my eyes shut. The steps drew closer—far closer than they should have as one of Nyall's snores broke the quiet.

I swallowed my pulse as those steps halted behind me. Fabric shifted. A blade was drawn. My heart stilled, my breath frozen in my lungs. Bottom lip quivering, every ounce of energy went into keeping perfectly still. I stifled a squeak as the blade punched through flesh, followed by gurgling. A hand jumped up, scrabbling at skin, at clothing.

I forced my hands to remain still, refusing to let them jump toward my mouth. I stifled a cry, eyes squeezed shut as tears seeped out and over my nose. Slowly, the scratching and clawing faded, as did the gurgling. Something thumped to the bedroll.

Unable to keep my eyes closed, I slowly opened them, a flood of tears rolling down my face.

Moments remained before the figure behind me left Nyall's bedroll for mine. The time for subtlety had passed.

I wriggled my wrists loose, chafing the raw skin, the knife still gripped in my hand. Shucking the rope aside, I jumped to my feet, and ran.

Fresh snow crunched underfoot, crisp air burned my lungs. I clutched the knife so tightly, my fingernails dug into my palm, but I didn't care. Didn't look back. Just kept running.

A single blink and Bayitt stood before me, his face twisted into a fanged smile. With no time to stop, I slammed into his chest and drove the knife straight into his throat. Roaring, the deymon reeled and threw me to the ground. Blood spurted from the wound, coating his white uniform, trailing all down his side. He fell forward into a tree, one hand holding him aloft, until his legs gave out and he crashed to his knees.

Shoving off the ground, I ran, nearly tripping over a branch. The farther from camp I got, the darker it became. The quieter it grew.

Another body appeared before me, silver eyes glinting in the dark.

My knife. I'd dropped it.

Cursing myself, I darted around Layne, a cry ripped from my gut as a powerful arm grabbed my waist and hoisted me off the ground. My body slammed into a hard chest. I writhed against him, throwing my weight into him over and over again, thrashing and kicking, clawing, a sobbing scream pouring from me in gasps. To my own ears, I sounded like a dying animal.

Layne took a fistful of my hair and ripped back, stretching my neck as the hand that held me snaked up, cupping my breast. In a mad fury, I screamed and threw my head into his face. Layne roared before yanking on my scalp. Trembles tore through me as I tried to double over, to squirm from his arms as he carried me back to camp.

Like a sack, he tossed me down. Immediately, I jumped onto all fours and tried scurrying away. A pair of hands grabbed my ankles, dragging me along snow and branches, tearing at my layers. I rolled over and kicked, yanking one leg free and smashed my boot into the face of the one who held me.

"Fucking bitch!" he screamed.

"Tie her legs," Layne ordered as he reached for my arms. Thrusting my hands up, I grabbed his face and dragged my fingernails down his skin, biting as hard and deep as I could. The deymon jumped back, roaring, "And her fucking hands!"

As another deymon leaned close to take my hands, I took the deepest breath I could muster and screamed. Those around me pitched over, hands to their ears, howling in pain.

Another deymon appeared before me. Balling my fists together, I swung them around and connected with the side of his face. The deymon grunted, the sound rolling into laughter as he reached up and grabbed my wrists while another pulled on my legs. I arched my back, braced on my shoulders, and yanked my hands free as a length of rope was tied around them.

"Bind the fucking bitch!" Layne shouted.

I kicked both feet again, loosening the rope when another pair of hands descended, pinning me. Taking hold of his hair, I yanked him down and latched onto whatever my teeth could find, sinking in until I tasted blood. He yanked away, leaving a chunk of himself in my mouth as he howled. Those around me jumped back. Flipping over, I crawled to my hands and knees and shoved up, trees whipping around me.

An arm in white appeared from thin air and swung, slamming into my chest. I barely felt the impact as I hit the ground. Stars swam in my vision, the air knocked from my lungs.

Chest heaving, Layne kneeled over me, pointing a finger as if scolding a child.

"Nyall was right. You got fight in you," he said with a smile. With what little energy I could muster, I inhaled, balled my blood-tinged saliva, and spat in his face. He only smiled wider, wiping it away. "If you gave it a chance, you might enjoy it. Seeing how you enjoyed all that Amasian dick."

Tears welled in my eyes as I stared up at him. Searing rage burst from me and I jumped up, tackling him. I clawed and scratched, roaring. My vision blinded by tears, I scarcely saw what I hit. The deymon, though, was laughing.

A hand struck my jaw, and I went sprawling to the ground. Gaping, my fingers grasped the snow as I rolled to my side before Layne dragged me to my feet by my hair.

I was shoved toward the remaining deymons, all of them with starved glints in their eyes.

"We mighta let you live a little longer," Layne said, before kicking my knees from beneath me. "You just too much trouble now."

251

Pain shot through my legs as I hit the frozen earth. A sob wrenched itself from me as one of the deymons dropped to his haunches before me.

"Oi, Layne," one of the others started. "Which is gonna kill her?"

"What?" Layne asked.

"Ain't we gonna die if we kill her?"

"She ain't a fucking unicorn," another said.

The one crouched before me looked up. "Ain't unicorns born from angels?" He took hold of my shirt and tore. One layer, then the next, and the next, until I lay bare for the cold to nip at, for their prying eyes to gaze upon. He made an approving noise before he reached out and thumbed one of my nipples. Another sob tore through me as I flinched backward, curling away from him.

"Whoever's got the smallest dick'll kill her," Layne said with a chuckle. "Just in case."

The one before me laughed in return. "Ain't got nearly so much fight now," he said, looking up at Layne.

"I still wouldn't trust her to not bite nothing off," Layne replied. "Bind her."

My chest heaved as I was forced forward, my face pressed against the cold ground. I drew in a breath and screamed, choked off by a writhing mass of tears while my hands were pulled behind my back and bound.

"Don't worry," Layne said. "All of Lorralei will remember your sacrifice." He laughed.

My hair covered my face, rendering me blind as a desperate scream ripped through me, the knots around my hands growing tighter. Further down I was forced, my legs pulled straight out. A pair of hands held them as I was bound at the ankles.

I screamed again, cut off by my sobs.

"Ain't no one to scream to," one of them called, laughter just beneath his words. My hips were pulled off the ground, greedy fingers digging into them. A rush of cold air washed over me as my breeches were torn open.

A frantic sob tore through me, my entire being trembling. Behind me, someone groaned. The boots in front of me wandered behind me. Shame filled me as those gazes plundered my body.

Warmth suddenly replaced the cold, a rock-solid bulge digging into me, separated by mere layers of cloth. My sobs increased, tears rolling rampant down my face as I pulled and tugged at the ropes, tried kicking myself flat to the ground, though I was held aloft by those hands.

"Stop fucking around!" someone shouted.

"Just savoring it," Layne said, voice husky with desire. In one last desperate plea, I screamed until I ran out of breath, until there was nothing left in me, the sound bleeding into laughter as the deymons mocked me.

Layne's body suddenly went rigid as something crashed through the forest. The deymons cried out, their roars accompanied by steel being drawn. Layne shoved me flat to the ground, pinning me beneath him.

The clang of metal filled the night. Someone screamed, a bloody, sickening sound, before their cries gurgled into silence. Blades crashed against each other. Snow crunched frantically around me.

My panic gave way to something else, though I wasn't sure what. Before I had a chance to process it, Layne jumped off me. The moment his weight was gone, I flattened myself to the ground. Freezing snow bit me, dirt and rocks and twigs digging into my breasts, my stomach. Clenching my teeth, I tried rolling over. Tried inching clear of the battle behind me, but I was stuck. Immobilized by the bindings around my wrists and ankles.

A shriek morphed into wails. A tree rustled, as if something were being shoved against it. Next came cries. Desperate pleas for mercy. A solid claw of fear clutched my heart, bringing tears to my eyes, as those pleas were ignored, and they withered into choking, then gagging, then gurgling. A blade withdrew from flesh. Something solid crunched to the ground.

Then there was silence.

Heart hammering in my throat, my breath wheezing, I blinked away my torrential tears as icy panic rose from my feet. I was blinded by my hair, tangled with bramble and snow. Couldn't move for the ropes tying me. A voice spoke, though I couldn't make myself hear it. When a hand fell on my arm I screamed, kicking and thrashing with my bound legs. Still, the voice persisted, becoming shouts. It was a single word, but my pounding blood overpowered it.

The rope binding my hands fell away. I flipped over, balled my fists and struck. The figure lunged back, shouting. Fingernails as claws, I lashed out, punching, thrashing, scratching, my wails and shrieks filling my ears. They continued shouting, but my screams drowned their voice, my flurried tears blinding me to all but my fright.

A pair of hands jumped out, took hold of mine, and pulled me toward them, a faraway voice screaming one word.

"Seraph!" My thrashing stopped, my screams dying in my throat, as a gentle hand brushed the hair from my eyes. "It's Venyx." I blinked away my tears, blinked again, and took in the sight of Venyx crouched before me, his eyes shimmering silver in the moonlight. "It's me," he said. "You're safe."

He moved down to my feet and, keeping his eyes focused on me, cut the rope binding me, pulling it gently away. I licked my lips as more tears filled my eyes before I scooted away from him. My gaze shifted to the camp. The bodies now littering it. Layne was the nearest, slumped beneath a tree, head to his chest. A river of scarlet plunged down the front of his white uniform. To the left was another body, the head removed by all but a strip of flesh.

Nausea curled my stomach as a whole new terror clutched my chest.

I looked back to Venyx.

Slowly, he sheathed his small blade and raised his hands, taking one crouching step, then another, toward me.

"It's okay," he said. "You're okay. I won't hurt you. I promise, I won't hurt you."

I sniffled and backed away again, moisture glistening along the bottom of my vision. My body trembled as my eyes swept the camp again. Another body to the far side, breeches around his ankles. Red coated the deymon's thighs. Beside him lay a little lump of bloodied flesh.

Venyx crept closer, hands to either side.

"I won't hurt you," he said.

A clipped, gurgling sob choked up from my chest as he settled beside me.

Slowly, he reached out, picking at my ripped breeches, now all but useless. I flinched away from him, backing up again. Knees curled to my chest.

"Can we take these off?" he asked, his voice holding a foreign softness. His expression gentle, a stark contrast to the carnage at his back. "I don't want you to trip. Do you know what happened to your other boot?"

Licking salty tears from my lips, my gaze jumped down. Only one boot remained. I looked around, not sure when I'd lost it.

"Okay, that's okay," Venyx said, and pulled off the remaining shoe. New, hot tears rolled down my face, slicing through the iciness as my adrenaline faded. I scurried back more, and his hands jumped to either side again. "I won't leave you here. You'll freeze to death. It's going to be much easier to move if you don't have all these ripped things on. I'll trade you."

He reached up slowly, to the buckles of his cloak, and slipped the thing off, holding it out like a gift.

When he inched closer again, I forced myself to remain still, anticipating the warmth of the cloak as snowflakes danced along my skin, parts of me it shouldn't have been able to touch. That idea only spurned more tears.

I trembled as he reached out, from terror, from cold. From dissipating adrenaline fueling my body to survive. A thick wail flew from my mouth as he pulled the ruined breeches down my legs and tossed them away. He reached for the layers of shirts and sweaters hanging around me in tatters. I sobbed, a horrid, wraith-like thing, clutching my arms to my chest, at the first tug.

"Seraph, please let me help you."

I slackened my arms, shrugged them out of the ruined things. The cold swarmed me, diving against my skin like a thousand hands all at once.

"I'm just going to put this on you," Venyx said, raising his hands, the cloak held between them. His fingers sticking up, in clear view. He leaned across me and wrapped the cloak around my shoulders. The warmth of it, his warmth, settled over me all at once. He adjusted it until it draped across me, covering my upper half, and clasped it in place. A shiver raced down my back as my eyes grazed him.

"Are you okay if I pick you up?" he asked, hands still in view. My gaze jumped between them and his face. "Just to a horse." He pointed to where the horses were clustered together, strangely calm.

Sniffling, I didn't move as he inched closer. One arm wrapped around my back and he rubbed my shoulder, pulling me into his chest.

The forest around me was swallowed by the swath of black covering him. The chill from the snow fell away. The blood strewn across the campsite like paint vanished. The surging need for survival fled all at once, and I suddenly couldn't tell up from down. Could barely feel my own skin, aside from the prickling cold dancing up and down my legs. Even that dissipated as Venyx shifted the cloak around me, bundling its black mass about my stomach and legs, down to my feet.

He shifted, one knee raised to stand. The pounding in my head stilled. And I was left with the beating of his heart in my ear.

As if beyond my control, a deep, scalding sob ripped through my trembling form as my hands dug into his shirt, holding onto him as if he alone held me aloft. My voice sounded foreign as I cried against him, barely registering as he settled against the earth and scooped me into his lap, wrapping himself around me.

"You're safe," he whispered, his voice coating my hair, which only made me sob harder.

For a long time we stayed in the snow as I cried. Everything I had ended up drenched into his shirt, though he never pulled away. He only held me, letting me cry until long after my voice turned hoarse, my throat raw from wailing, and no more tears fell.

My hands relaxed against him and fell into the folds of the cloak. Still, I remained pressed against Venyx's chest, sat in his lap like a child. He breathed softly, his cheek resting against my hair, his arms hugging me as if he would never let me go. For just a moment, it felt good to be held, to be hugged. To be comforted in a way I'd never experienced before.

I sniffled and pulled away, wiping the tears from my cheeks. Still, I was afraid to look up, to face him. I'd run from him. I'd been terrified of him. I'd be lying if I said I wasn't still. The bodies strewn around us were proof enough of why I should be. But when he brushed the hair from my face, the fear melted away, leaving behind only a man.

I settled against his chest, his shirt damp, cold, from my tears. His embrace tightened around me once again. His cheek pressed into my hair before one arm curled beneath my knees, the other against my back, and he stood.

As we passed through the camp, I shut my eyes. Refused to look at the bodies again. A part of me knew whatever he'd done had been well and fully deserved, cruel as it was. Another part simply wanted to pretend it had never happened.

More gentle than I'd known him to be, he placed me in the saddle of one of the horses and worked his way through the others, untying them one by one. The beasts, for all the fear they should have shown, butted against his hand, chuffing as if he were their friend. Not a stranger who had just massacred their riders.

When all the horses were loosed, he walked back to me, one of them following close behind.

"This is Omma," he said, gesturing to the horse. "She's going to follow behind us, cover our tracks."

I sniffled and nodded, trying to not flinch as he grabbed hold of the horn and hauled himself up behind me.

"What's this one's name?" I asked, my voice hoarse, as he pulled me into his lap, adjusting me so I sat across him.

"His name is Aures," he said, smiling down at me. A reluctant smile grew on my lips, and I buried my face in his chest.

"Who names a horse Aures?" I asked.

"Don't know, but that's his name."

As if in laughter, both horses threw their heads to-and-fro, whinnying. With one arm wrapped around me, Venyx picked up the reins and guided Aures the horse from the camp, Omma trotting close behind.

THIRTY

W E RODE THROUGH THE night and long into the next day, stopping long enough for me to insist we continue. Even if I'd been able to rest, I didn't want to. Every time I closed my eyes, I was back in the camp. The deymons surrounding me. Prodding. Laughing. Their hands on me all over again.

Sometime during dusk, Venyx led our horse, Aures, up the snowy embankment, further hiding our tracks, Omma trailing behind. It wouldn't stop other deymons from following our scent, he said, but it would slow them down.

As night fell, realization crept in that I'd been awake for over a day. My eyes burned; my body ached. Cuts and scrapes ran along my arms, hands, and legs. Across my breasts and stomach. Even on my ass. And every single one stung as cold crept through the edges of Venyx's cloak, still wrapped tight around me.

Aures's head sagged, his trots slowing to a dull walk. Even Omma trailed farther back. I spied Venyx in the failing light. And noticed, for the first time, he wasn't clean shaven. Days' worth of black scruff covered his jaw. Dark circles hung beneath his eyes.

His mouth opened into a gaping yawn, displaying all eight fangs. At the sight of those horrid teeth, an image flashed through my mind of him tearing out a throat. Blood gushing down his face.

"What?" he asked, half-yawning.

"I've never seen you with…" I gestured to my chin.

"Oh." He reached up, scratching along his jaw. "I prefer being clean shaven."

In those words lay the implication—if he hadn't spent the last week hunting me down, he would have had time to shave. And sleep. Heart heavy with guilt, I laid my head against his chest and sighed, snuggling further into the cloak.

During the night, we stopped long enough for Aures and Omma to rest. The poor horses heaved as they came to a stop, shaking their heads back and forth. Venyx fed them from a feed bag in one of the saddlebags and the animals promptly fell asleep where they stood, heads hanging heavy. It wouldn't be for long, Venyx said. He wasn't sure if one of the soldiers had called for help during the fight, but it was a possibility.

And so we backtracked, going west. Heading further into the foothills surrounding the mountains separating the Northerlands from the Plains. Our goal forgotten, at least for the moment.

More hills rose around us, teasing into the growing mountains. Over the next couple days we didn't stop, though several times Venyx slumped against me, his head hanging, swaying back and forth. Black hair falling in inky rivulets around his face. Aures veered off the road before I took the reins and snapped them, startling the deymon back to consciousness.

My own exhaustion left me reeling, my body trembling with hot flashes. Dreams tugged at my mind, though none were of the beach. The one place I dreaded going when I slept became my salvation—an escape from the dark figures standing above me, waiting for me to slip into slumber.

When it seemed we were unable to continue, the road opened and a small inn rose into view, its sloping roof covered in a thick frosting of white powder, the bottom windows illuminated against the black night.

A stable hand ran out to meet us as Venyx dropped to the ground, his boots crunching along the snow.

"Where are we?" I asked, looking up.

"Somewhere safe," Venyx said, fatigue filling every crevice of his words. He barely kept himself upright.

"But—"

"Seraph," he said, frustration seeping in, "I'm exhausted. I'm starving. And I want to bathe. Aures is exhausted. He can barely stand. Omma is on the verge of collapsing. You haven't slept, or eaten, in days. Get off the fucking horse. Now."

Without further protest, I clambered down and picked my way across the snow behind him, moisture seeping into my woolen socks. Venyx opened the door to an empty common room blazing with the warmth of an enthusiastic hearth and ushered me inside.

A series of tables dotted the room. Along the far wall sat a bar, behind which was a counter laden with colorful bottles and glasses framing a window looking into a kitchen. The smell of cooking food wafted through the air, making my stomach grumble.

From behind the bar a woman rose, a bottle in her hands. Her mouth opened to greet us before she stopped, her eyes lighting with recognition. A tired smile curled Venyx's features as the woman rushed across the room, wrapping her arms around him. Venyx returned the embrace, rocking them back and forth.

"You smell like shit," she said, stepping back. When she smiled, the points of fangs glinted in her mouth. Sticking out from her light brown curls was a pair of pointed elven ears adorned with a series of silver hoops.

"I wouldn't expect anything less," he said with a smile. The woman chuckled, brushing a hand along his cheek.

"I'd ask how you are, but your appearance speaks for itself." Her gaze finally landed on me, her thin brows pulling together. "And who's this?"

"Delthia, this is Seraph," Venyx said. "Seraph, Delthia is a very old friend."

"Nice to meet you, Seraph," Delthia said, her gaze turning skeptical.

"You, too," I responded, as realization set in her eyes.

She turned back to Venyx, her face falling, becoming rigid. "You're working again, aren't you?"

"Not by choice," he said with a sigh.

Delthia's brows pulled together, her lips pursing.

"We need someplace to stay."

"No."

"Just for a couple nights."

"Absolutely not," Delthia said, stepping closer, straining to keep her voice low.

"Del—"

"You think because I'm way out here I don't know what's happening?" she asked. "Ace's is gone, V. Ace ... Ace is fucking *dead*."

Venyx sighed in defeat, shoulders sagging. He nodded. "I know."

"The City has been wiped off the fucking map!"

"That—"

"Not to mention Cleya's tribe has been..." There, she stopped, hand going to her mouth.

Venyx pressed his thumb and forefinger to the bridge of his nose. I glanced between them, my heart sinking. As much as I hadn't wanted to stop, the idea of warmth, of rest and food, was an unimaginable kindness being dashed away before my eyes.

"I worked hard for my place, V!" Delthia seethed. "I can't have it destroyed because Rori convinced you to do one last job!"

"I swear to you, Del, that won't happen. I just need some place to rest," Venyx said. Delthia sighed, a twisted smile stretching across her mouth.

"The White Army, that bitch Faerie Queen, doesn't care what happens to those they cross," she said. "You should know better than anyone."

A low growl rumbled in Venyx's throat. He took her shoulders and shoved her back, despite Delthia's curse-laden protests, far enough away I couldn't hear the whispered words snapping and hissing between them. Several times, they stabbed accusing fingers back and forth, Delthia's mouth snarling in barely contained shouts. Then her face fell. Her eyes flicked to me, pity blooming there, and I knew he told her what happened.

Venyx stepped back from the elf, her face stretched thin with horror, a hand to her mouth. Shame filled me from head to toe, spilling from every crevice, every pore, as tears threatened to erupt from my eyes.

"Seven fucking hells," she whispered, stepping closer to me. "I'm so sorry."

My shoulders hitched, and everything in me broke at once. My first tears in days fell as a sob ripped through me. Delthia rushed across the room, pulling me into an embrace I'd been wholly unprepared for.

Digging my face into the crook of her shoulder, I relaxed in her arms. And Delthia, a stranger—on the verge of turning us away—held me. And let me cry.

When I had no more tears to shed, she pulled away, a thin smile on her beautiful face, righting my hair as it piled up around the cloak's collar.

"Suppose you'll need some clothes," she whispered, pulling the cloak tight around me. "And food, both of you." She threw a glance at Venyx. "One night."

"Thank you," Venyx sighed.

Delthia returned her gaze to me. "Luckily, some of the girls who work here are about your size, I think."

I swiped my cheeks, shifting uncomfortably. Delthia stalked across the room, leaned over the bar, and came back, a single key between her fingertips. "I mean it, Venyx. One night."

"One night," he said, plucking the key from her grasp.

"I'll send up food and clothes." She tipped her head to the floor, all those glorious golden curls falling around her angular face.

With a gentle hand on my back, Venyx guided me toward the stair-case.

THIRTY-ONE

VENYX LINGERED AT THE threshold while I slunk to the opposite side
of the room, my back against the wall. As the door closed, I
realized we'd never been alone—the forest notwithstanding.

Suddenly, the room felt too small.

My gaze stayed trained on him as he removed his sword holster,
fingers moving deftly over the silver buckle strapped across his chest.
He slid the thing off and tossed it casually on the bed. The single bed.
Just one. The only other furniture were a writing desk and chair, a chest
of drawers, and a too small armchair.

He pointed to the door on his right. "The washroom is there. I think
Delthia's had boilers installed since last time I was here."

My gaze shot from him to the door and back. My entire being fixed
to the floor. Every shadow hiding some danger I couldn't see. Or maybe
I just didn't recognize it.

As if sensing my apprehension, he gestured to the too small armchair.
"I'll sleep there. You take the bed. Get cleaned up first. Delthia will be
pissed if you dirty her white sheets." He nodded toward the washroom,
as if it had been decided.

I didn't have the strength to argue.

The moment the washroom door closed, leaving me alone for the
first time since Tollok's, my skin felt filthy. Every bit of me crawled.

Frantically, I ripped Venyx's cloak away, tossed it aside, and rushed to the tub.

I cranked the hot water until steam clouded the room, stifling my lungs. The basin filled quickly and I sank in, sucking in short breaths as the searing liquid poured around me. Set into the cuts and blossoming bruises. I tried not to cry at the mottled skin covering my breasts and stomach. Finding a rock-like bar of soap, I set to work, scrubbing every inch of flesh until it was red and raw. I only just noticed the tub was full before turning off the tap and continued my work, desperate tears streaming down my cheeks.

When I finally reached my breasts, I could scarcely touch my own body without thinking about the hands on me, and a chorus of painful sobs choked me. The soap fell from my hands, tumbling to the bottom of the tub. As it sank, I decided that's what I wanted.

I laid back, knees bent as I straightened, and allowed my hair to fall in. I tipped my shoulders, the warmth caressing my scalp, my ears, up my cheeks and finally my eyes. Through the wavering surface of the bathwater, I stared at the ceiling and released every bit of air in my lungs. Then inhaled.

The water burned, but it was the best I'd ever felt. Beneath the surface, I could scream, and so I did. I roared my pain and anger and frustration at a world that showed no love for me. The same world that asked so very much of me. I screamed and cried at Miran's betrayal, at my own stupidity for not seeing it. I screamed for Nik. And I screamed for myself. For the years of isolation. The torment of not knowing what awaited me once I left the safehouses. For the torture of never knowing who and what I was. For truth of the divinity I'd been told ran through my blood.

After I could scream no more, I relaxed. I closed my eyes as warmth seeped into my skin. The bath provided a comfort no person or place ever would, or could. I rolled over, enveloping myself completely in the tub, and pulled my arms close to my chest, let the water soothe away the memories of the hands and the blood and the beach. Fully submerged, I fell asleep, and, for the first time ever, didn't dream at all.

I was ripped from the water, from sleep, all at once. My eyes burst open, though I found nothing but black as I collided with the floor. Something warm and heavy landed atop me. Mouth gaping, I blinked and the black—Venyx's shirt—drew away, the deymon's awe-struck face sitting atop it.

Water dripped from his hair, clung to his shirt, as he hovered over me. I pulled my arms to my chest and shoved away from him.

"*What the fuck are you doing!*" I screamed, my voice reaching hysteria.

"What—" His mouth opened, closed, and opened again. "What are *you* doing?"

My brows creased as I drew my knees up, shielding my nakedness from him. "What?"

"You looked dead!" he bellowed.

Anger flooded me, red brimming my vision. "I can breathe underwater, asshole!"

He fell back on his bottom, shock spreading across his face. He cupped his hands over his mouth and ran them up into his hair.

"Yes. Yes, you can," he said, the panic gone from his voice, his face, as a light scarlet spread across his cheeks.

A laugh jumped from my throat. "You think I tried to drown myself, don't you?"

His gaze flicked to mine, one hand falling into his lap.

Venyx shook his head as he pushed himself up, stepping carefully around the water on the floor. He pulled a towel from the shelf against the far wall and handed it to me. I ripped it from him and wrapped myself as I stood, glaring with all the anger I could muster.

"And what if I did?" I asked. My grief for myself, everyone's pity for me, boiled over into rage, spilling from every crevice of my body until I trembled from it.

All traces of embarrassment were gone as Venyx's gaze met mine.

"What if I had tried to kill myself?" I asked again. My hair ran in soaking rivulets down my back and arms, chilling my skin in the cold room, but I paid it no mind as I closed the distance between us, staring up at him. "What if I had? It's my life. I can do whatever the *fuck I want with it*!"

"Do you honestly think killing yourself will fix anything?" he asked, his voice straddling a whisper.

"*I don't care!*" I shrieked. Hot tears poured down my face. "But I guess you do, don't you?"

His brows pulled together, body going rigid beneath my glare.

"If I die, you don't get paid. Do you?" The towel fell as I shoved him, then again, until the wall was at his back. He shifted, though made no move to stop me. "That's all I am to you. A payday. To the Amasians and the White soldiers, I'm a warm body. Something pretty to fuck."

I shoved him again, anger and pain mixing in my voice until I scarcely recognized it, so twisted it became.

"To the Faerie Queen, I'm an obstacle! The Pensians, I'm a pawn! What about what I want from my own fucking life!" I screamed. "Everyone is only concerned with what I give them, how I benefit them! *What my life is worth to them*!"

Venyx remained where he was, staring down at me.

"*What is my life worth to you!*" I shrieked.

He said nothing, just continued staring. His silence only enraged me further, made the tears come harder, hotter, as a sob wracked through me.

"Say something!" I screamed, shoving him again. "*Say something!*"

Unable to stop myself, I threw a fist at him, then the other, battering every part of him. Blinded by tears and fury, I wailed into him, and still he didn't move. The floor slipped beneath me and Venyx reached out, grabbed my hands and spun me around, pressing my back into his chest. I thrashed against him. I threw my head back and kicked my feet, my arms straining against his iron grip as tears poured unabashedly from me, my screams becoming wails.

Suddenly we were on the floor, Venyx's arms wrapped around my body, his legs pressed to mine. I leaned forward as far as his grip allowed and screamed. The wail died halfway out, morphing into a choking, hacking sob, and I sucked in a desperate breath. His cheek pressed into my temple, his stubble itchy against my face, and he rocked me back and forth. His grip on my wrists loosened as my sobs quieted, becoming strained hiccups against my tears. After even those died, I leaned into him, resting my sopping head on his arm, accepting the warmth and strength of his embrace as ribbons of moisture rolled down my splotchy cheeks.

All the while, Venyx said nothing. He just sat with me. Not seeming to mind his clothes being soaked through, or my naked form in his arms.

When even my tears dissipated, I let him pull me tighter to his chest, let him pick me up and carry me to the bed. He sat me down, pulled the blankets from beneath me, and tucked them up around my shoulders.

"The food came," he said, pointing to the bowl sitting on the table beside me. "You should eat."

Venyx vanished into the washroom, closing the door behind him. Running water surged to life a moment later.

More stupid, useless tears blurred my vision as I pulled the blankets above my head and laid in the darkened warmth, feeling every single drop rolling down my face and onto my arms, into my hair, across the pillow beneath me. My lips curled as I embraced my blanketed solitude. My shoulders trembled. I covered my face with my hands and silently sobbed into them, pulling my legs to my chest. Before long, there were no more tears. I drew in a shaky breath, and listened to the running water just beyond the door.

Sniffling, I pushed up and tucked the blankets around me, shoving the mess of sopping hair behind my shoulders. I turned to the bowl. On the desk across the room sat another, though it looked empty. No wonder he'd gone into the washroom after me. He'd waited long enough to eat and I still hadn't come out.

I picked up the bowl and gave an experimental taste, deciding quickly it was good, and wolfed it down. As I set the empty dish aside, the water turned off. Another moment and Venyx stepped out, shirtless. Water clung to his chiseled form, rolling down his soft brown skin, dripping from his silky black hair. He stopped.

Ducking beneath the blankets to hide my blush, I listened to his feet pad across the floor. A drawer opened, closed, and he stepped back in the opposite direction before something in the corner squeaked. I slid the blanket down as he settled into the armchair.

In his hands was the little book of poetry, eyes trained on the pages.

Cheeks still hot from blush, I shoved the blankets aside and licked my lips, ignoring the stray tears rolling down my skin. "C-can you read me one?" I stammered.

His brown gaze flicked up. But he said nothing. Fresh tears welled in my eyes. I couldn't blame him for not wanting to speak to me. Another moment passed before he stood and walked to the bed, the book stretched between us like a peace offering.

"How about you read me one."

Glancing between him and the book, I took it and let the pages fall open. A thin smile tugged at my lips at the script not of the common tongue. "I can't read elven," I said, holding it out.

"Oh." Disappointment was heavy in his voice as he took the book back. "Aurorian taught me. I assumed she'd taught you."

"She taught you to read elven?"

He nodded as he sat on the edge of the bed.

"How long have you known her?"

"Too long," he said. His tone was light. But something told me it was less of a joke than he'd made it sound.

I lay back against the pillows as Venyx carefully turned around, a dry quill in one hand, the book in the other.

"It wasn't useful," I provided. Venyx stopped, looked at me. "Elven. It added nothing of value to my education. So I was never taught."

"Did she tell you that?"

I shrugged. She hadn't needed to.

"Is it okay if I sit here?" he asked, leaning back ever so slightly.

"It's your bed."

"It's yours tonight," he offered, one brow raised.

I stared at him, curiosity niggling in the back of my mind. Had this version of him always been there? Or had it been carefully hidden beneath layers of self-preservation. Armor erected around people he hadn't trusted.

I nodded. "It's okay."

He settled further onto the bed, one long leg stretched along the blankets beside me. He opened the book, flattening the pages strewn with long, elegant script, and pointed the quill at the first line.

"This is the elven *O*," he said, tracing the letter with the quill nib. "That's an *n*." He traced the one beside the *O*.

Brows creased, I glanced up at him, then back to the page. Curiosity gave way to the smallest pique of excitement and I pulled myself across the bed, closer to him. Heat from his body wafted along my shoulder.

Letter by letter, he guided the quill down the page, slowly naming the common version of each letter to the end of the poem. He went back to the top, and pointed to the first letter in the first line.

Pushing past my embarrassment, I said the first letter, then the next, stumbling over my memory of what each one was. When I couldn't remember, he traced back over them, silently, until I picked it up and carried on. Until we reached the bottom of the page. We went back to the top, and I read each word, slowly and clumsily, but I read them.

The smile pushing through my cheeks was barely contained as I looked up at Venyx and squealed. Actually squealed. I'd never made that sound before. "I read elven."

"You did," he said, smiling in return. One fang poked out, pressing into his bottom lip before his face relaxed and he closed the book. "I think that's enough for tonight. We both need rest." He set the book aside and pushed off the bed.

"Could you stay with me?" The words flew from my mouth, shoving through the thrum of my pulse. He turned, brows drawn, shoulders tense.

I wanted to sink inside the mattress, crawl into the floor and never come out. The moments slipped by as he stared at me and eased himself back onto the bed, saying not a word. I couldn't help studying his profile as he propped himself against the headboard, half-sitting, half-laying, hands behind his head.

With a sigh, I rolled over, back facing him, and snuggled into the blankets and pillows. The bed shifted as he moved closer, the heat from his body seeping through the layers separating us. A small comfort, but one I graciously accepted.

I wasn't sure how long I lay there, fighting as sleep tapped on my brain, not wanting to submit. To find what might be waiting on the other side. Eventually, I lost that battle, and fell asleep anyway.

What the dream was, I couldn't recall. Only the grasping hands on me. As a child, or as a woman, I didn't know. I only knew that I woke screaming, my cries filling the room, tears streaking my face. My eyes darted around, unable to remember where I was or how I'd gotten there.

Arms drew around me.

"It's okay." Venyx's voice found my ears through the panic. His hands rubbed up and down my bare arms. "You're safe," he whispered into my hair, drawing me against him. "You're safe. I've got you."

I fell against his chest, clutching his shirt as he adjusted the blankets around me, tugging them back up. He squeezed my arm and pulled me closer to his side.

Licking my lips, I stared into the black fabric covering him, flipping the folds between my fingers, counting, back and forth, until my eyes again grew heavy and the beating of Venyx's heart lulled me back to sleep.

THIRTY-TWO

RICH, GOLDEN SUNLIGHT STREAMED through the window when my eyes slid open. A slight chill hung in the air, but I was warm. Tucked against something solid.

Taking stock, I realized I lay beside Venyx, wrapped in his arms. My cheek pressed against his shirt while his chest rose and fell, still in the throes of sleep. I barely remembered how I'd ended up beside him, but he was comforting. So I lingered.

Gazing up at him, I noticed he was clean shaven, his dried hair splayed around his face. It hit me how beautiful he truly was. How peaceful. I snuggled against him, relishing his arms tightening around me while he slept.

Venyx took a deep breath, flexing against me as he nuzzled my hair. His fingers ran along my bare back, sending shivers down my spine and into my toes. My hands lay curled between us, splayed against his stomach. I kept as still as possible. Perhaps he didn't remember I was in his arms. Risking a glance, whatever doubts I'd had were dashed away when my gaze met his sleepy one, and my face burst into scarlet heat.

"Good morning," he grumbled.

Unable to find my voice, I merely smiled and dropped my chin, resting against his chest. Yesterday flooded back as I realized I lay nude beside him, only the blankets separating us. Curdling, horrid embarrassment filled every crevice of my mind at how I'd acted. How I'd stood before him, unabashedly naked, screaming. I curled my fingers into fists and drew my knees as close to my chest as possible.

Why he stayed, I didn't know. How he'd stayed with a hysterical naked woman, and hadn't been tempted, eluded me. In the state I'd been in, I didn't know if I would have pushed back, fought him off, or encouraged him. But it hadn't mattered.

"Are you feeling better today?" he asked, his voice low against my hair.

I drew in a trembling breath, unsure how to answer. Did I feel like screaming at him again? No. But regret for my behavior hung like a noose around my neck—heavy and sickening.

"Seraph?" he asked, brushing my hair behind my ear.

I snuggled closer to his chest, fighting the tears brimming my eyes.

"Okay," he finally said, as if my silence was answer enough. His arms tightened around me, drawing me closer, and I breathed in his scent, eyes closed against his shirt. I couldn't remember the last time I'd been held like this. No expectations, nothing owed. Just comfort. The simple intimacy of a chaste embrace.

The smallest sob leaked from my throat, bubbling against Venyx before bursting into the silence of the room.

Something in my chest hurt. Something I couldn't touch or see. Like a weight pressing into me, threatening to crush my heart beneath its force. I'd always known my life had never truly been mine, that it was owed to the world, but having such convicting confirmation of my own ... meaninglessness. It was humbling in a way I wasn't sure I ever wanted to feel again.

Venyx stroked my hair with one hand while the fingers of the other dug into my back, holding me to him as if he knew, in that moment, he was my anchor. The comfort of his silence was a thing I couldn't identify. That he didn't ask what I was feeling, but rather let me feel it, in my own way, was invaluable.

"Venyx?" My voice was muffled, small, against the expanse of his chest, the warmth from my breath fanning my face. He pulled back, shifted on the pillow to meet my gaze as I tipped my chin up. "I'm sorry."

"For what?" he asked, smoothing the hair back from my face.

"For running."

His brows pulled together, as if he didn't know what I was talking about, but I pressed on.

"If I hadn't run, this wouldn't have happened." Before I knew it, my entire being was trembling, tears running hot and fast down my face. My words sloshed together, shaking along with my body. "We wouldn't have lost so much time and sleep and—" A sob choked my voice, but still I tried to press on, the words refusing to silence themselves.

"Hey." He pulled me back to his chest, both arms wrapped around my shoulders. "No, no, no." He nuzzled his cheek against my hair as he crushed me to him. I pushed the blankets down, fingers digging into his shirt as I buried my face in him and let the tears come. "This is my fault," he whispered. "I didn't give you a reason to trust me. I'm sorry, Seraph."

I sniffled and another sob choked out of me. His hands dug into me so tightly I felt he might absorb me, save for the blankets wedged between us.

"I'm sorry," he whispered again. "None of this is your fault. None of it."

The longer he held me, the more I relaxed into his embrace, melting into him. My tears dried, his shirt remaining damp against my cheek. But his arms were warm. His chest was solid. In that moment, wrapped up in him, nothing expected of me, he became the closest thing to a real friend I'd ever had, and a strange bittersweet joy washed through me.

"Seraph."

I looked up, blinking away the lingering tears as his brown gaze met mine.

"Do you still want to go to Pensen?" he asked, his voice calm.

My brows furrowed as I took in the serenity painting his face. "I don't understand."

"Do you *want* to go to Pensen?" he repeated.

My mouth gaped. I reeled back, not sure what to think. What to feel. "You'd be giving up your payment."

"That's my problem, not yours. Do you *want* to go?"

Tears gathered on my lashes, my breath catching in my throat. "I don't have anywhere else to go," I choked out.

"That's not what I asked."

Bottom lip trembling, I cast my gaze over his face, then to the wall behind him. My mouth opened, closed. Opened again. "Y-yes," I stammered and cleared my throat. "Yes."

He appeared unconvinced, but nodded once. "Okay."

Suddenly, Venyx tensed against me, the muscles in his arms, his chest, going taut. He turned, staring at the door.

"What's wrong?" I wiped the lingering tears from my cheeks. "Is Delthia coming?"

"No," he said, and all the warmth, all the comfort he'd spoken with was gone. In an instant, he became the same man I'd been traveling with—hard, cold, unfeeling—as he unwrapped himself from me and rose from the bed.

I sat up, clutching the blankets as he walked to the window, staying out of sight while peering below. An iron hand rose from my gut and grasped my heart, squeezing, as the air fled my lungs. Spots danced in the edges of my vision, my hazy gaze following him as he crossed from the window to the door, leaning against it.

"Venyx?" I choked out, silenced as a single finger flew to his lips. I jumped as a caressing whisper tapped against my mental walls. I looked frantically around, then found Venyx again as his eyes slid to mine.

As a child, I'd learned to shield my thoughts, to always keep my guard up. As the White Army was commanded mostly by deymons, it had been imperative to have my mind protected. But now, meeting Venyx's probing gaze, knowing it was *his* mind tapping, I had no idea how to lower that defense anymore.

He crossed to the bed and sat down, taking my face in his hands.

"I need in," he whispered. The tapping in my head stopped.

"I ... I don't know how," I whispered.

His eyes slammed shut, chin dipping to his chest as if stamping down frustration, and looked back up. He began stroking my temples. His eyes burst open, locking onto mine. Without a word, I knew to maintain that connection, to keep staring at him.

Once again, the caressing voice floated into my mind, tapping against the barricades. Falling into those pools of dark, velvety brown, softening against his thumbs on my temples, his fingers in my hair, they began to fall. One by one. And suddenly, his voice was in my head—loud, clear, and soft.

They followed the horses, his mind whispered. Panic flared in my chest, gripping me like a vise. *Delthia is keeping them occupied, but we have to go.*

I nodded, warmth trickling down my cheeks.

As if on cue, someone knocked on the door. Venyx jumped up, rushing to it. When he turned back around, door closing behind him, a stack of clothes was in his hands, topped with boots.

Get dressed. He handed me the clothes before walking around the bed to the desk.

Every inch of me trembled as I climbed from the bed and unfurled the neatly folded clothes. My hands shook as I dressed. The lacings of the bra fell twice before I finally grasped the damned things and fastened it. Next, the shirt and trousers, woolen sweater, heavy woolen coat, and finally the boots. They were slightly too big, but Delthia had, luckily, included a second pair of wool socks, filling out the difference.

When I stood, Venyx met me, swords strapped on, cloak fastened at his throat.

"How—"

His finger came up to his lips and I closed my mouth, wondering how I was supposed to talk to him. I couldn't project my thoughts.

Just think them, he whispered. *I'll hear you.*

How are we supposed to get out? I thought.

Follow me. He turned to the entrance, his steps whisper quiet. I reached out and grabbed his cloak, shoving myself into his back as he eased the door open and peered into the hallway before opening it a bit more.

As we slipped out, Venyx turned to me, finger on his lips. I nodded. We made the short journey down the corridor, tiptoeing along the wooden floor. I followed his feet, stepping where he did. Mere moments seemed to stretch for an eternity before Venyx opened another door and we stepped inside.

Whose room is this? I took in the fine paintings on the walls. The magnificent bed made with a rich, red comforter.

Del's. He gestured to me as he opened the closet and stepped inside. Without having a choice, I followed behind, stamping down the rising surge of panic as he closed the door, swamping us in darkness.

Somewhere in the back came a soft click. Venyx's hand filled my back and he ushered me into what could only be described as a void. There was even less light here. It smelled of dust, musty, with thick drafts of cold whipping through, stinging my cheeks and hands. The click came again and Venyx's tall, warm presence stepped before me, wafting into me.

This passage goes through the walls of the inn. A staircase leads down to the cellar and into the forest. That's where we're going.

I nodded, knowing he could see me. My gaze searched for those pinpoints of silver. They were there, barely, flickering as he blinked.

I can't see. How am I going to go down the stairs when I can't see?

You're not, Venyx replied. The air before me shifted. He took one of my hands, leading it up to what I assumed was his shoulder, placing it there. *I'm going to carry you.*

Swallowing, I nodded again and stepped closer, the hem of his cloak brushing my legs. I reached the other hand, following the soft, familiar fabric covering his back, the sword hidden beneath, and up to his muscular shoulder, over and around, pressing into him.

He leaned down and grabbed my thighs, hoisting me up. I linked myself around his waist and tightened my grip, holding onto him. His hair tickled me, so I faced the wall.

We then began the arduous descent down the void-laden staircase.

It hugged the top floor in a long stretch, passing rooms along the way. Inside each one was movement. Talking. Mumbles. One was just sounds, and blush rose to my cheeks as I tried shoving the noises away, considering my position on Venyx's back, so very close to him.

Finally, he rounded a corner and began descending, taking the steps one at a time, as if reacquainting himself with where the loose boards, the squeaks and trembles, were. My palms filled with sweat as I held onto him, his body heat melting into me. He ran far hotter than I did. Than anyone I'd met. Being so close to him, for such a long time, in an enclosed space, was stifling.

Almost there, his mind whispered. We finally reached another landing and he reeled around, carefully setting me down. His hands slid against my thighs as he released me. He was simply ensuring I didn't make noise, I knew, but the action still sent a flurry of red hot blush to my cheeks.

For a moment, I stood there, back against the cool wooden wall, taking in the chill air surrounding us. Venyx shifted before me. A flicker of silver glinting in the dark was all I saw, but all I needed.

We're on the ground floor, he said.

So why are we stopping?

To give us both a break, and because there are White Army soldiers on the other side of this wall.

My heart hammered to life at his words. Licking my lips, I moved toward the glimmer of silver, hands up, and found the wall. Leaning into it, voices filtered in from the other side.

"And if I refuse?" Delthia's voice shouted, louder than needed, but somehow I doubted it was accidental. "You and your bitch queen have no authority here."

Someone chuckled, a deep, condescending thing, and said, "We may not have authority, but there ain't no one stopping us from burning this place to the ground."

"A refusal to cooperate is as good as announcing being in league with the blood traitor and his cargo."

I winced. Then again, the soldiers who'd had me before had thought even less of me. Swallowing the lump in my throat, I shoved those thoughts away and focused on the conversation.

"His *cargo?*" Delthia spat. "His *cargo*, last I heard, was a fucking woman. Not a piece of luggage." Rage seethed in her voice.

"Regardless, she is a fugitive from Kaival," the first said. "He is smuggling her across an ungoverned land. We are merely trying to intercept her before they reach governed lands to prevent her from starting a war."

Fury boiled inside my gut. *Me? How am I going to start a war?*

"Sure you are," Delthia sneered. "Come on, then. The sooner you have your *inspection*, the sooner you fuckers get out of my place."

Boots sounded across the wooden floor before fading away.

I started at Venyx's hand on my shoulder before wrapping my arms around his neck as he grabbed my legs, and we carried on.

I've never even been to Kaival, I thought, trying, and failing, to stamp down my anger.

They're just spreading propaganda. Trying to scare people, Venyx said. *It'll also make negotiations with the World Council easier for Kaival if you've been branded a fugitive.*

There's no reason to call the World Council, though. I hadn't done anything. And, as the White soldiers had said, the Northerlands were ungoverned. Unprotected by the laws of the Boundary. The White Army had no authority here, but neither did Pensen.

No, there's not, Venyx answered, though the words he left unsaid—*not yet*—sent a chill through me.

THIRTY-THREE

C OLD CREPT FROM THE stone floor into the soles of my boots as Venyx set me down. It stung through my layers, kissed my cheeks, and sent goosebumps up and down my arms. Venyx's touch on my thighs only increased the rampant tingling as he dropped me.

Darkness still enveloped us. I couldn't see him, though I was acutely aware of his presence, his scent—iron and earth. His hands. His gentle caress within my mind.

He stepped away, just for a moment. Another soft click, like in Delthia's room, and light flooded the space, forcing me back, blinking against the sudden shift. A hand flew up, shielding my eyes. When I was finally able to see, Venyx stood before me, gesturing me forward. I took his hand and followed him into the room beyond the stairwell.

The walls were earthen—packed dirt smoothed between stone, same as the floor. To the right stood three large copper tanks, gas lanterns beneath them. Like giant tea kettles set to boil. Oh. Boilers. Each one had a large pipe sticking out the top, and more funneling in through the side at the bottom.

To the left were shelves—lots and lots of them—laden with jars and sacks and crates filled with all manner of food items.

Directly ahead was a stairwell leading up. Above rang muffled voices and the dull thud of footsteps. Both were drawing closer.

Venyx flew across the room to the shelves and began pushing on the wall, making his way from one end to the other. Rushing to his side, though I didn't know what he was looking for, I followed suit.

There's a trip door, he said. *It leads up and out.*

I nodded my understanding before rushing to the other end and began working back toward him. We stopped as the door to the staircase opened, Delthia's voice rushing down to fill the cellar. "Last room," she called. "Then you can get the fuck out."

Her boots thumped on the steps as she descended. I speared Venyx with a tear-filled gaze. Hissing, he glanced over his shoulder, back to me, vanished and reappeared before me, gathered me in his arms, and jumped. To quell my desperate yelp, I shoved my face into the crook of his neck.

When I opened my eyes, I was swathed in darkness, laid across his body. His cloak was wrapped around his waist, tucked between us, preventing it from hanging. His arms and legs were spread out, fixing us in the corner of the room, the floor hanging at least twelve feet below. All the power in his body channeled through his fingertips and into his feet, fastening us in the embrace of shadows.

Closing my eyes, I dug my fingers into his shirt, into the corded muscles of his stomach, swallowing my rising panic.

My eyes slid open as Delthia took the final step into the cellar, followed by three soldiers in pristine white armor.

"Well, gents, have a look," Delthia said, turning to face them, arms spread to either side. "This is it."

My gaze slipped from the soldiers below to Venyx as he peered over his shoulder. The only thing obscuring us from their prying eyes were the shelves along the floor, casting their shadows onto the wall and the corner where we hung.

One of the soldiers ran a hand down his bearded face as the others strode to either side of the room.

"What're these?" one asked, pointing to the copper tanks.

"They boil water," Delthia said. "You can have a look inside if ya like, but you won't survive."

The soldier chuckled.

The other strolled through the rows of shelves, inspecting around and between them. He opened a lid to one of the crates and pulled out a potato.

"I can assure you, no one's hiding in my produce," Delthia spat. "Get your hands out of my food, lest you wanna pay for the whole batch."

He dropped the potato, then the lid, and sauntered to his companion, standing beside Delthia.

I dug my face in Venyx's chest, shoving the drumming of my heart back down. Beneath me, Venyx started to tremble. I tipped my face up, eyes widening. He grimaced, licked his lips. My gaze slid back to Delthia. She turned in a circle, her eyes flicking over us before addressing the soldier by the water heaters.

"You satisfied?" she snapped. "I ain't hiding anyone. Why the fuck would I risk my business on some piece o' shit blood traitor, anyhow?"

"You certainly seemed concerned about the fugitive he's smuggling," the soldier beside her said.

"I don't gotta care for him to be concerned over a fellow woman, do I? But I still wouldn't risk my life and livelihood for either. If you're done you need to leave."

The soldier scoffed, ran a hand through his black hair. He nodded and whistled to his companions. "You hear anything from either of them—"

"I'll be sure to send you a greeting," she spat. "Get the fuck out."

The soldiers filed up the stairwell. Delthia flicked us another glance before sending an obscene hand gesture, and followed behind them. Venyx scoffed, a grin curling his lips. The door slammed shut and every muscle in his body relaxed at once. He gathered me in one arm and dropped soundlessly to the floor before collapsing against the wall.

He sighed, grimacing as he rubbed his legs.

Are you alright? I asked, hunching beside him.

Yes, just ... give me a moment.

Tossing a glance over my shoulder, I sat beside him, arms wrapped around my legs, and faced him. He tipped his head against the wall, throat bobbing while he drew in breath after breath. His mouth twisted up as he moved from rubbing his legs to his shoulders.

Do you wanna see if you can find the door? he asked, glancing at me. I nodded and jumped up, stepping carefully over him.

A small smile pulled against my lips as, in the opposite corner, the door clicked and swung softly open, revealing a darkened stairwell. I turned back to him, grinning.

Yeah, yeah. Don't get cocky, he said, easing himself to his feet. *I haven't been here in years.*

I've never *been here*, I chided, smirking. Venyx scoffed, stalking toward me, my backward steps matching his, until we stood in the hidden stairwell, the wall flat against my back. He towered over me, the silver of his eyes piercing through the dark. I returned his gaze, the heat from his body wafting into me.

What'd I just say, he growled inside my head, the caress of his voice curling between my thoughts. I bit back my grin as his own ticked at a corner of his mouth.

He closed the door, darkness once again enveloping us.

This staircase was stone. The steps cold. The walls seemed to shiver from the frigid air. But the further we climbed, the earthen, musty smell fell away while crisp freshness sank around us. Holding onto Venyx's cloak, I slowed when the fabric sagged, one hand flying to the wall to steady myself. At the top of the stairs a sliver of light sliced the darkness, sending a ray of gold across the deymon as he stepped into it.

He eased the door open and peered out. A bolt of light filled the room, made me shudder against it. This wasn't the flickering flames of the cellar lanterns. It was the full weight of the morning sun, bursting upon me all at once. Venyx's hand shot out, keeping me from tumbling back down the stairs.

We had only a moment to adjust before he guided me out into the cold, a fresh slew of snow falling.

I glanced up at the trees, at the puffy white clouds rolling across the sky. Then beside me to Venyx, standing like a pit of shadows in so much white.

He closed the door with a barely audible click. Voices trickled faintly from around the front of the inn. A collage of them, most likely the White Army. Punctuated by the whinnying and chuffing of horses, counting in the dirt and snow.

What about Aures and Omma? I asked, drawing his attention back to me. His face fell, and I knew.

I'm sorry, but they have to stay. They'll be okay. If the soldiers don't take them, Del will take care of them.

How are we going to get to the Plains then?

On foot. Over the mountains.

My gaze trailed up. And up. And up further. I hadn't realized how high we'd climbed, but we'd found ourselves in the thick of the mountains. Great evergreens jutted from the frozen ground, their boughs and branches decorated in puffs of white. Icicles hung from the twigs, sparkling in the sunshine. Rocks and boulders dotted the landscape, emerging like jagged teeth from the earth.

I gulped, realizing the odyssey set before us, and turned back to my deymon protector. He gestured me to him, and I obeyed. Sunlight shone through his black hair, creating a fiery visage around his head.

Remember the forest right before the marauders?

I nodded.

We're going to take to the trees. It'll be faster, but a bit jarring your first time. Hold on tight.

I nodded again, swallowing as he presented his back. I wrapped myself around his shoulders, locked my legs around his waist, and dug my face into his neck, staring up between his cloak and hair.

Ready? he asked, glancing over his shoulder.

No.

He smiled. Then jumped.

I slammed my eyes shut as he flew past the roof of the inn, landing like a cat on a branch, feet perfectly poised, despite the snow and ice coating the limb. Still, it displaced the weight. The tree trembled, and a moment later snow plopped to the ground.

A collage of faces turned all at once, hands going to their swords, though we were already in the thick of the tree, swathed in shadows. Venyx shifted his cloak, dousing me in the same darkness that armored him. For a long moment, we perched there, waiting until the army settled.

The three soldiers trailed outside, stopping to talk with the others before they saddled up and moved down the road, Omma and Aures trailing behind.

They better treat them kindly, I grumbled. Venyx chuckled in my head.

After they were out of sight, we began jumping from tree to tree, moving southwest. As Venyx had said, it was jarring, though not as bad as I'd expected.

We're gonna have to cross the road, Venyx whispered. The soldiers rode beneath the green and white canopy, chatting amongst themselves, completely unaware of how close we were.

Will it lead them back to Delthia's? I asked.

We're far enough away, there's no reason for them to backtrack.

Sighing, I nodded. I couldn't allow Delthia to be punished for harboring me. *Okay.*

Venyx nodded in return. He coiled his legs and jumped, clearing the road in a single bound before landing with a crash in a tree on the opposite side.

A burst of activity sounded on the ground, shouts ringing through the trees. An arrow flew past, digging into the trunk before us. Venyx deftly avoided another one, jumping nimbly between branches, picking up speed as he went.

"Hold on," he said, his voice strange outside my head.

I tightened my legs around his waist and buried my face against his back. A yelp ripped from me as he leapt higher, limbs creaking and groaning beneath our combined weight. Behind us, soldiers shouted back and forth. Branches snapped as deymons jumped into the trees to give chase and another arrow flew past, narrowly missing us. Venyx's entire body tensed. The muscles of his back and hips bunched as they coiled against one another. We were suddenly airborne.

A scream I barely recognized tore from my lungs as frigid wind ripped against my face, tearing through my hair, before Venyx landed on a branch clear across the forest. Even still, I made out the voices of those chasing us.

Another arrow lodged itself in a nearby tree, making me wonder how much of the White Army had buried itself in the mountains.

We stayed on the branch for only a moment before Venyx leapt to another, then another, hopping nimbly between trees. Below, soldiers called out to each other as arrows filled the canopy. Venyx dodged them all, weaving through the groaning, frozen forest as if he'd been made for it.

After a while, I slammed my eyes shut at the rapid movement, the blurring trees, and held on with everything in me. The bouncing from branch to branch filled my gut with a sour churning that made sweat bead on my forehead, filled my palms with hot moisture. Every moment I prayed it was almost over, though I had no choice but to trust Venyx would make it out safely.

When I finally opened my eyes again, we'd stopped. Venyx perched on a branch, head bowed as he drew in breath after sharp breath. His heart pounded through his back. His legs trembled.

My ears strained against the forest, listening for calls of the White soldiers. Thankfully, the wood had gone quiet.

"I just ... I need to rest. Just a moment," Venyx heaved, one hand braced against the trunk. I nodded against him. As if remembering I was strung across his back, he turned. As careful as I could, I lowered one foot, then the other, to the branch while Venyx kept hold of my hands. I moved backward until I was against the tree and slowly lowered myself as he fought to regain his breath.

"What now?" I asked.

He turned to face me, his balance, even while out of breath, filling me with wonder, and he lowered himself, one leg hanging while his arm rest atop the other knee. He licked his lips, head tipped back as his throat bobbed, drawing in another deep gulp of air.

"We keep going until dusk. Then we'll need to find shelter for the night," he said after a long moment. "They'll likely continue the search until dawn."

"Are you going to be able to make it much farther?"

He nodded, heaving another breath, one brow raised as if doubting himself. Thankfully, he wasn't bleeding. No twin trails from his nose.

"Just another moment," he breathed, his eyes drifting shut.

"Where are we going to find shelter in the middle of the forest?" I asked.

Venyx drew in another breath, head lowered against his knee. Silence filled the space between us as he steadied himself.

Finally, he said, "Since we're so far ahead"—he stopped for a breath—"we can rest in the trees."

"In the trees?" I asked incredulously. He nodded, his hair falling around his face. He brushed a hand through it, shoving the dark locks back. He reached into some hidden pocket and pulled out a leather thong to tie the tendrils back. A few strands fell loose again.

"Just for a bit."

I studied him. Even in The City, running and jumping across the rooftops had greatly winded him. Paired with the falls we'd taken, he'd been weakened a great deal. And almost immediately after, he'd fought back dozens of White soldiers in the square before chasing me after I'd been captured. As much as sleeping in the trees made me queasy, I couldn't get passed the notion that I owed him.

I nodded my agreement. The appreciation that flashed across his face was not lost on me.

"Ready to keep going?" he asked after a moment. With a sigh, I nodded again, even if I doubted *he* was ready. But said nothing. Didn't even think it.

Another deep breath and he shoved himself to his feet, then offered me a hand. I took it and let him pull me up, carefully closing the distance until I stood before him.

Once again, I clambered onto his back, securing myself to him, and off we went.

Just as he'd promised, it was dusk by the time we stopped, the White Army far behind. We were safe. For now.

As he gently set me on the branch we occupied, I looked around, taking in all I could despite the shadows. The tree was tall, yes, but the limbs jutting from it were not thick. They barely felt sturdy enough to hold my weight, let alone his.

"How are we going to sleep up here?" I asked. I didn't dare tell him, but I was terrified to move, simply for the sake of being so high off the ground, with nothing but frozen tree branches to break my fall, and probably several bones.

Groaning, Venyx hopped one branch over before he turned, gesturing me toward him. Every muscle in my body bunched with anxiety as I reached out and took his hands, carefully stepping toward him while he moved with all the grace of a feline. With a great deal of concentration, I stepped across to where he stood, my eyes constantly flitting to my feet, and the ground below.

"Hey," he said. "Eyes on me."

I nodded, locking my gaze on his.

"There's a branch here," he said, pointing behind him. "We'll lean against that one," gesturing to the one we stood on, "and sit on this one."

"I don't trust myself to not fall," I said, forcing a weak laugh as I spoke.

"If you're comfortable, I can worry about that for both of us," he said. I took a deep breath as he lowered himself, leaning back while keeping hold of my hands.

Thankful it was dark, I stepped one foot over his legs and lowered myself until I sat across his thighs, my feet dangling to either side, and leaned against his chest. He let go of my hands and wrapped his arms around me, holding me to him. The steady thrum of his heart filled me with comfort as I breathed out my nerves and allowed myself to relax.

"It's just for a bit," he whispered against my hair. I nodded, clutching my hands in the folds of his cloak.

For a long time, I lay there, listening to the rhythm of his heart, knowing it would be a while before the first strings of slumber tugged at my brain.

Just as I'd known, sleep did not come easy. Being in the canopy afforded me all the nighttime sounds of the forest without being able to see anything. And so I lay there, listening.

In an effort to distract myself, I tipped my head up and examined Venyx, his eyes glinting silver in the descending night. "How are you able to move so easily through the trees?"

He closed his eyes and took a deep breath. "My kind have an incredible sense of balance. I've always been good at moving through the trees. Even as a boy."

I smiled, trying to imagine Venyx as a child. I laid my head back against his chest.

"What were you like as a child?" I asked.

He sighed as if in thought. "I imagine I was trouble," he said. "So not much has changed."

An involuntary chuckle bubbled up my throat. "Trouble? That doesn't sound like you at all."

He laughed. I glanced up as he smiled. Really smiled.

"How were you trouble?"

He took a breath, as if considering the question. Then said, "Unicorns don't eat meat. They frown upon it, aggressively. My kind do. I was maybe ... eleven years old, mortal years"—I chuckled at the distinction—"and I wanted to try meat. So I went to the river and caught a fish. Aurorian found me like that, raw fish hanging from my mouth." He laughed at the memory, dragging a smile to my face. "She scolded me. One of her guilt-ridden ones."

"I know the kind," I said, sniggering. How many times during my own childhood had I brought that wrath upon myself.

"I wasn't allowed near the river alone for ... two hundred years, I think."

I laughed, playing with the folds of his cloak, counting them back and forth between my fingers.

"What were *you* like as a child?" he asked, throwing me off guard.

"I was..." I stopped, unsure how to answer. Much of my childhood before Aurorian was lost, forgotten in the sands of my memory. After Aurorian, I longed to go home, to not be lonely. I cried myself to sleep so many nights, begging for Briahna to come for me, though I knew she couldn't. Her death had racked me with guilt, a heaviness no child should have to live with, particularly not one so young. "I was..." I licked my lips and tried again. "I suppose I was lonely. Very quiet. The opposite of trouble."

A beat of silence passed between us and he made a sound in his throat.

"I'm sorry," he said. I shrugged as if it were of no importance. I hadn't known anything different. It never occurred to me other children didn't live like that. Not until the marauders.

"Where did you grow up?" I asked, desperate to shift the topic away from myself. "Where's home?"

"Home," he said, a heaviness behind the word I recognized in my soul. As if such a concept were foreign. "I was born in Abaddon," he said. "Though I was raised in the Lost Forest."

I looked back up at him, all other thoughts thrust from my mind. "The Lost Forest?"

He nodded.

Aurorian's home. Where the unicorns lived.

As a girl, I'd asked endlessly for her to take me there. Always, she told me she couldn't. Outsiders weren't permitted. But, if outsiders weren't allowed inside the Forest...

"How did you end up being raised there?" I asked.

Venyx sighed, tipped his head back, fingers drumming against my shoulder. A shudder ran through me at his touch. "It's a long story."

"Oh," I said, lowering my head back to his chest.

"I was born just before the Fall," he said, surprising me. "I'm not sure what you know about the Fall."

"Not much," I confessed. "Just that it was a very long time ago." Which made me wonder how old he was, though I didn't ask.

"It was brought on by a selfish bastard of a king. He spread his army too far, too wide, racked up debts he couldn't pay. Eventually, his army, and his people, turned on him, on the entire royal family, slaughtering them." His voice took on a dark tone as he spoke. "My mother only just got us out before the worst of it happened. She was killed during our escape, and I was left in the Northerlands."

"I'm so sorry," I whispered.

"It was a long time ago," he whispered in return. "Anyway, the next day, Aurorian found me. She took pity on me, took me to the Forest, and raised me."

My brows drew together as the pieces clicked into place. "You were raised by Aurorian?"

"I was." He wiped a palm across his face and up through his hair, cleared his throat, and placed his hand on my back.

"That's how you know her," I said. He sighed, shrugged beneath me.

"It was a *very* long time ago," he said, his voice so cavalier it was painful. "You should try to get some sleep."

Knowing nothing more would be said on the subject, I closed my eyes and drifted off into a restless slumber. Thankfully, tonight, there were no dreams.

THIRTY-FOUR

V OICES IN THE DISTANCE drew me from the shallow recess of sleep. My eyes drifted open, blinking away the soft aura of early morning light as it filtered through the canopy. My gaze fell to the forest floor, starting the last vestiges of slumber from my mind. Venyx's arms tightened, reminding me he was there. Reminding me he wouldn't let me fall.

Pushing myself up, I looked around, catching his profile as he stared into the distance, his expression one of focus. As I sat atop him, I took stock of myself. My legs were numb where they hung over his thighs, my feet tingling as they dangled. Then there was my bladder.

"You ready?" Venyx asked, facing me. I nodded. Though as I took in our precarious situation, I wasn't sure how I was going to get up.

"Venyx?" I asked. "Um ... I'm not sure ... how do I stand?"

"I'm going to help you," he said, his face void of emotion.

Heat rose to my cheeks. I wasn't sure what he meant, but, as I had little choice, I had to trust he knew what he was doing. At his instruction, I wrapped my arms around his neck, tucked my head beneath his, and locked my ankles around his waist. Thankfully he couldn't see my face, crimson steeped as it was, as he took my hips and positioned me in his lap. He placed his arms on the branch at his back, pushed off with his feet, and dropped to the one below, the tree groaning from our sudden weight. From there, he hopped from limb to limb to the ground.

I scrambled out of his arms, swearing every part of me had erupted in a flaming red blush. Venyx's jaw worked back and forth as he adjusted his cloak around himself and turned away, facing the other direction.

"If we go that way, we should be able to see the Plains from the mountain peak," he said, pointing up.

Hands clasped before me, all I found myself able to do was nod. Behind us came the voices of White soldiers, drawing ever closer, snapping me back to the present.

"How long will it take to reach the peak and climb over?" I asked, daring a glance at him despite the red still spread from ear to ear.

"Long enough to worry," he said. Somehow, I wasn't sure he would be able to pull off another run like the previous night. One had taken so much out of him.

"So what do we do?"

He sighed, ran his fingers through his hair, and looked around before finding my eyes. "Our best."

Anxiously, I followed him up the mountain side.

Climbing the mountain in the snow, on an empty stomach, was painfully slow. Venyx made next to no sound as he moved. I, on the other hand, crawled compared to his speed, while being clumsy, loud, breathless, and still had to pee by the time we slid behind a rockface for a break. At our current rate, solely because of me, it would take forever to get over the mountain. If we didn't get caught first.

I turned around and placed my head against the cool rock, breathing slowly through my nose and out my mouth, begging my heart to stop thundering. Every part of me, from my head to my toes and fingers pulsed and throbbed from the sheer effort of the climb. I silently cursed myself for not doing more training when still drifting between safehouses.

A thin sheen of sweat gathered on my brow, droplets rolling over my spine despite the frigid air, which only grew colder the higher we climbed. I wiped the moisture from my face and opened my eyes, gazing into the mouth of what appeared to be a mineshaft. I prodded Venyx, pointing when he turned. He met my inquiring look.

"Could we go through there?" I asked between gasps. "Or at least maybe hide for a while?"

He stood, peering into the darkness of the shaft as he pondered it.

From where we'd been moments before, the mineshaft hadn't been visible behind the rocks, so it stood to reason the White soldiers would pass right by. We had, after all, left the snow behind and scaled up the rocks, leaving no footprints. Nothing to trace at all.

"It looks abandoned," he said, stepping back. "Maybe for a reason."

"But it would cut through the mountain," I argued.

Venyx sighed. "Not necessarily." He walked around it further, the wheels of his mind turning plain on his face as the morning sun.

The calls of the White Army drew closer, pulling both our attentions away from the yawning cavern. I jumped to Venyx's side while he shifted over the snowy landscape, deciding, I was sure, which was the greater risk: the mine, or the forest.

Another moment passed and he looked down at me, his hands gripping my shoulders. His brown eyes stared fiercely into mine.

"Stay beside me at all times," he said. "Do what I tell you, when I tell you to do it. If I tell you to run, you run. If I tell you to stop, you stop. If I tell you to stand behind me and don't make a sound, you stand behind me and don't make a fucking sound. Do you understand?"

"Yes," I said, nodding for emphasis.

"It might take a few days to get through, and there's no telling what we'll encounter in there. There might not be an exit. We might have to come back. So you will do exactly what I say without arguing."

"I know," I said. "I understand."

His lips pressed into a thin line. I glanced back as another cry rent through the trees before we headed into the mineshaft.

The ground near the entrance was level with the outside, descending into the earth as heavy shadows seized the air around us. The cries from the White Army dissipated the further we went, a small comfort as we left the surface behind.

Venyx walked ahead, his footing solid and sure along the declining ground. Loose rocks skittered beneath my feet, forcing me to keep hold of Venyx's outstretched hand as we went. After a while the path leveled out and we found ourselves in an antechamber.

Faded glimmers of sunlight reached the room around us, allowing me to see, albeit poorly. I blinked several times, forcing my eyes to adjust. When they finally did, my breath caught in my throat.

Ribbons of light stretched along the rocks to either side, illuminating the chamber in a soft blue glow. More glowing rocks lay scattered about the floor, some gathered in neat piles.

"Wow," I breathed, a smile stretching across my face. Even the ceiling was riddled with the strange light.

Venyx walked to one side of the cavern, running a hand along the wall. Following his example, I crunched along the dirt to the other side, kicking through a pile of stones. The resulting echo dove headlong into my ears, vanishing down the darkened hallway stretched before us. Kneeling, I picked up a few to roll around in my palm. They were slick, cool to the touch, and crystalline upon closer inspection. Deciding they might come in handy, I picked up a few more and shoved them in my pockets before joining Venyx.

Side by side, we ventured from the antechamber into the hallway. As there were no glowing crystals, I pulled two from my pocket and held them up, illuminating the dark with their thin, bluish light.

The corridor stretched on before opening into another chamber, far wider than the last. More glowing ribbons littered the walls, the floor, the ceiling. Loose crystals lay scattered along the floor, little pools of them lying about.

"Have you heard of these crystals?" I asked as Venyx bent to pick one up.

"No," he said, turning the stone over in his hand. "I've never even heard of this mine before." He let the rock fall to the floor and we moved on.

On the far side of the chamber were several tunnels, all leading in different directions. Venyx's gaze flickered between them. Another moment and he pointed to the one on the far left. Clinging to his arm, I followed close behind.

At the end of the hall was an old bunk room. Several rows of beds, all in various states of disrepair, lined the floor, a gaping hallway at the far end. Crystals were fastened to the walls at regular intervals, casting a soft light. A few had fallen, leaving patches of darkness in their wake.

"If you want to rest, here seems like a good place to do it," Venyx said as he walked further ahead. I glanced around, took in the beds and the crystals. Between the bunks were chests, most likely used for personal belongings. A couple were rusted so horribly it was difficult to tell what they were. One had been broken open, the wood cracked and splintered, its contents emptied long ago.

A great huff of breath filled the room as Venyx returned to my side, his head turning this way and that. He glanced into the ceiling, the silver in his eyes mirroring the glowing lights. Pitching my head back, I found nothing but thick black, even with the crystals scattered about.

"Is it dwarven?" I asked.

"This is human. It's too simple to be dwarven." He pointed to the rough chiseling of the stone walls. "If it were dwarven, this would be smooth. Far more grand. Dwarves are too prideful for this kind of work."

I walked to the nearest chest and pulled the top open, heaving under the sheer weight. Old cobwebs snapped and ripped apart, making me jump back, cringing at the thought of spiders. Inside, it was still full of clothes—old and threadbare, as if eaten by moths. A couple books lay to one side. On the other was a silver flask.

"Look," I said, pointing. Brows knit together, Venyx leaned over my shoulder and peered inside. "Why would someone leave their things behind?"

He reached into the chest and pulled out the flask. Liquid sloshed inside. Dropping it back on the clothes, he picked up one of the books, the pages falling open in his hand. It was written in a language I'd never seen. Judging by how Venyx viewed it, it was possible he didn't know it, either. He flipped the pages back and forth, then through the whole thing before he snapped it closed and dropped it beside the flask.

"Possible they never left," he grumbled and flicked the top closed. A shiver ran through me. "Let's only rest a bit. We shouldn't linger in this place."

I nodded as he turned and walked to another chest across the room. It took some searching, but after going from bed to bed, nearly all the ones still intact crumbling at the lightest touch, I finally found one that supported my weight. Not daring to crawl beneath the old, musty blankets, I stretched out atop it, back against the wall, and took a deep breath as Venyx's boots echoed across the floor.

"I don't know if it will hold both of us," I said.

"It won't," he replied. He sat experimentally on the bed beside mine. It took a moment, but he decided it would hold him. Leaning back, he threw his hands behind his head and sighed, his eyes sliding closed.

Gazing into the ceiling, at the stagnant darkness above, I began to wonder if, maybe, it had been a bad idea to come down here.

We rested long enough that my stomach started to grumble, though we'd brought no supplies from the inn, and so had nothing to eat. But it was enough incentive to keep moving.

From the bunk, we traveled into the darkened hallway beyond. Relief flooded me at the sight of more crystals strapped to the walls, the intervals closer. It still wasn't much, but it punched through the thick shadows slithering between every crevice, behind every rock formation.

The hallway broke into another chamber. As we approached the middle, Venyx pulled me to a stop, his body tensing.

"What is it?" I asked.

His eyes rose to the ceiling, far higher than the ones in the previous chambers. My gaze followed, running along the ribbons of crystals embedded in the rock above, searching for whatever he'd found. Then I saw it.

A lump of white hung between the stalactites of the ceiling. For a moment, I thought it was a strange rock formation. Then it moved, the glowing blue light shifting across it.

"I know why the miners' things were still in their chests," he whispered, his tone sending barbs of fear through my body.

"Why?" I asked, despite not wanting to know.

"We're in a vampyre nest."

THIRTY-FIVE

G ROWING UP IN THE Northerlands, I'd heard of vampyres, though I'd never seen one, and had never met anyone who had. Mostly, I'd attributed them to myths meant to scare children, just as they had me when the spies told me of them.

Since there were no histories written about them—those who encountered them didn't live to tell about it—I knew little of their kind, except they were rumored to have been spawned from the seven hells.

Never in my wildest dreams did I think I'd see one. Certainly not so close.

Venyx kept an arm in front of me as the creature shifted and moved between the calcium growths on the cavernous ceiling. A loud sniffling echoed through the chamber and I realized it was smelling. Us, most likely.

The vampyre crawled across the rocks, every movement followed by a distinct clicking and scraping. Upon reaching the wall, it dropped to the ground, making me jump. A sharp metallic twang sounded as Venyx drew a sword, stepping us back from the vampyre as it continued to sniff the air.

From its crouched position, the creature stood, gangly arms falling to either side. Its long, bony fingers were tipped with razor-sharp claws, its feet much the same. Its toes were spread out, similar to its hands, as if made for gripping.

In the light of the crystals, I gazed at the beast's eyeless face. The mouth looked carved from its flesh—jagged and ripped open. Inside that gaping maw hung two elongated fangs standing solitary along its gums. Its skin was pale, luminous, almost glowing, and it became easier to understand how I'd mistaken it for rock.

Much as I tried to remain calm, my breath came in huffing gasps as the vampyre moved toward us in ragged, clumsy steps. Its wraith-like face tipped back as its lumpy nose contracted and flared rapidly, its thin, ribbed chest rising and falling in a similar pace. The thing dropped to its haunches and crawled toward us, continuing to sniff. The closer it drew, the thinner and more transparent its skin became, appearing more like the crystals illuminating the cavern.

Once mere feet separated us from the creature, it rose to its feet again, hands clenching and unclenching. It stilled abruptly.

Venyx stepped us back once more, raising his sword in anticipation.

The vampyre crept forward. Then stopped. It stood to its full height, just shorter than Venyx. A strange, pointed tongue lolled from its mouth, dripping with saliva, and it licked its fangs, moistening them. Then it hissed.

My hands dove into Venyx's sleeve, my every muscle freezing. Venyx dropped his sword arm, drew himself up, and hissed in return, baring all eight fangs as his eyes flashed red. With a whimper, the vampyre jumped back, dropped to its haunches, and skittered back into the shadows, the clacking of claws fading.

Trembling, I fell into Venyx's shoulder, gasping for breath. He placed his free hand on my back, guiding me forward as we moved further into the chamber, steering clear of where the vampyre had disappeared to.

When you said nest, I thought.

There's likely more than one, he answered. *Far more.*

I nodded. From there, we made a silent agreement to only speak mentally.

The next chamber was just beyond a short hallway, the scene inside chilling.

Skeletons lay scattered across the floor, their skulls open in ghastly screams. Various weapons were clutched in their skeletal hands or strewn about in a futile battle. Bags and belongings at their sides, the leather worn and cracked. A peek inside showed what they'd hoped to gain—precious stones and gems, likely fruits of the mine—but instead had sacrificed their lives in their vain pursuit.

The least amount of time we spend here, the better, Venyx whispered, coming to stand silently behind me. I nodded in muted assent.

The tunnel beyond curved downward, taking us further into the earth. With fewer of the glowing crystals lining the walls, it was more difficult to see, forcing me to keep rigid hold of Venyx as we went. Loose rocks rolled beneath my feet, putting me on edge the whole way, in fear of slipping and falling.

When the tunnel finally leveled out again, we were surrounded by a burst of light from a cache of crystals. They were embedded in the walls and floor, glittering across the vast ceiling like stars. More were hung, like in the bunk, while dozens more lay scattered along the floor and gathered in piles.

Beside me, Venyx sniffed. *I can smell fresh air*, he said. *It's faint, but I smell it.* I glanced at him as his silvery eyes cast about the chamber. *This way.*

Cautiously, we crept toward a tunnel to the far left, the direction Venyx indicated, as my gaze leapt about the room, searching for any signs of movement. If anything was in the chamber with us, I couldn't see it. If Venyx did, he said nothing. I wasn't sure I wanted him to.

Just as we neared the corridor, a faint clacking echoed around the cavern, making us stop. My heart skipped as I whipped my head about. With the echoing, I couldn't tell which direction it came from. Venyx raised his sword again and turned, putting our backs to the wall.

Another clacking joined the first, then another, the scraping of claws on rocks growing louder as more joined the chorus, my blood running cold. The first lump of transparent flesh appeared between a collection of stalactites. It dropped to the ground with an echoing thump and clawed its way toward us, remaining doubled over on its haunches.

I shoved myself into Venyx's side, my lungs shuddering with every breath. At another lump of white flesh crawling down the wall, tears sprang to my eyes. Then another appeared. And another. Each of them sniffed the air, crawling and ambling toward us in what had to be the most frightening scene I'd ever witnessed.

With the slightest of trembles, Venyx pushed me behind him and backed into the wall, placing himself between me and the approaching vampyres before he drew his second blade. One of the vampyres licked its fangs and hissed, followed by another, and another. Venyx adjusted his grip on his swords, widened his stance, and waited. Somehow I doubted hissing back would work this time.

The first two attacked as one. Venyx quickly cut through them, pinning the second to the stone floor with a growl before he ripped his swords away and retook his stance. In response, the remaining vampyres widened around us, clicking the claws on their feet in an organized symphony. They were speaking to each other.

"Shit," Venyx whispered. The muscles in his back tensed against me as he flipped his swords, readying himself for the next round.

Five vampyres remained, surrounding us in a half-circle. The clicking of claws continued, only dying when they moved forward as a single unit, closing the distance between us. I peered around Venyx's shoulder, moisture clouding my vision as I gazed between him and them.

The vampyres jumped toward us, attacking as one, and a scream dove into my ears, taking a moment to register as my own.

With a roar, Venyx thrust both blades up, slicing through the first vampyre before running the second through. The next vampyre dropped before us and grabbed Venyx's feet, ripping them from beneath him. A loud, echoing thud rang out as he fell and the vampyres scrambled atop him.

Breathless, I pressed myself to the wall, unsure what to do. They largely seemed to ignore my presence, and I wasn't sure if they simply wanted to get rid of the bigger threat, or they didn't realize I was there.

Two vampyres crouched atop Venyx. One he barely held off, his hands around its throat while it snapped its jaws over and over again, its whole weight pushing atop Venyx.

Licking my lips, I fought the terror boiling in my gut and lunged toward one of Venyx's swords. Picking it up, I thrust at the vampyre trying to gnaw through Venyx's boot. Its head popped up and it hissed, saliva dripping from its fangs. I stumbled back, breath catching in my throat, as it jumped toward me. With a howl, I swung up, reverberations rolling down my arms as the blade dug into flesh. The vampyre whimpered as I ripped the steel free. It snarled and pounced. This time, I swung wide and even, lodging the sword in the creature's throat.

Blood spurted and bubbled from the wound, coating both its flesh and the blade before I yanked the sword free and stumbled back. It collapsed in a spreading pool of scarlet, writhing and screeching as it died.

Gasping, I looked to Venyx as he thrust a handful of claws through the throat of the vampyre atop him and shoved it off. The remaining creatures stopped, their faces lifting to the air, and they jumped toward the bodies of their dying kin. Fangs sank into flesh followed by a sickening sucking. Nausea filled my stomach at the sight, at the sound, as they cannibalized their own kind.

I jumped at Venyx's touch, drawing my widened gaze to his face. My grip on the sword loosened, letting him take it before he fetched the second one. As he approached, I found myself transfixed, unable to look away from the feasting vampyres. Two growled at each other as they fought for possession of one body while the third suckled at the one I'd killed.

"Seraph," Venyx said, drawing me from the grisly sight. "We have to go. The smell will attract more."

Wiping my eyes, I turned and followed him to the darkened corridor as more clacking and scraping filled the chamber behind us. A roar echoed, followed by scuffling and a chorus of snarls. We shuffled down the hall, my eyes desperately searching the dark. When the growls and scrapes came louder, the echo more pronounced, our shuffle became a hurried gait. At a howl racing down the tunnel, we ran.

Venyx hoisted me in his arms. I shoved my face against his chest as the blackened walls rushed by, the scraping and howling refusing to diminish. If anything, they grew louder.

The tunnel burst opened to a great room filled with more crystals, the pathway taking a sharp downward turn. In his haste, Venyx slipped to the ground, sliding until the path met the floor. We scrambled to our feet as movement from the tunnel caught my eye. One vampyre, then a second, crawled onto the wall, mouths open, chests contracting as they sniffed.

I looked toward Venyx, his hands coated in blood. His clothes were saturated in it. "Fuck," he growled. Mine were likewise painted red. Our eyes locked. The vampyres on the wall began howling, the claws on their feet clicking and tapping.

All around, surrounding the chamber, came the echo of more howls, of more clicks and clacks and taps. In the glowing light of the crystals, more fleshy lumps shifted as they emerged from hiding, drawn by the smell of blood, and by the call of their brethren.

"Venyx," I cried, gazing up at him. He turned to me, thumbed the tears from my cheeks.

"It's going to be okay." He nodded as he spoke. I wanted to believe him, needed to, so nodded in return. "We're gonna have to move fast," he said, pulling me back into his arms.

I locked my arms and legs around him and buried my face in his shoulder. Then he was moving. I looked up from the folds of his cloak as vampyres moved about the cavern, gathering closer. It was only a moment before the whole lot moved as one, like a tidal wave, across the walls and floor, their claws scraping against the rock in a terrifying symphony.

Venyx grunted as he jumped, landing rough on the ledge of the path across the room and sprinted down the following corridor. Though I couldn't see, save for the sparse crystals tacked to the walls, I trusted he could, that he would find the way out, and we would make it through the mountain alive. To believe anything else was a betrayal. To myself, and to him.

The next cavern opened in a flurry of crystallized light. Similar to the previous chamber, the ground fell far beneath us as a steep, carved pathway hugged the rough-cut wall. Instead of following it, Venyx launched through the air to the tip of a stalagmite, hopping nimbly from one to the other, crossing the room without touching the floor. My limbs tightened around him as he went, my heart thundering in time with his.

Behind us, another series of howls rang out. The clacking chased us down the tunnel as a flood of vampyres skittered across the walls toward the opposite corridor. I swung my gaze over Venyx's shoulder and prayed we made it in time. His feet skimmed the angled pathway and we flew down the next hall as the creatures jumped to meet us, right on our heels.

The tunnel ended abruptly, following around the wall instead of curving downward. Without hesitation, Venyx launched through the air to the next stalagmite, then the next. I clutched him tighter, slamming my eyes shut against the black fabric of his cloak, and released a gust of relieved air when his feet touched solid ground.

I dropped before him, both of us breathless, leaning against the other for support, as, behind us, the vampyres howled and clicked. The vast chamber we found ourselves in offered no clear path to us. We were safe. We'd made it.

A stuttering breath flew from my lips as I glanced up at Venyx, at the sweat gathered on his brow, and I reached up to brush it away. The ground below us suddenly shifted. Confusion, and a flicker of fear, blossomed in my chest, the emotions mirrored across Venyx's face, as the rock beneath our feet crumbled. He gathered me in his arms, crushing me to him. Before I knew what was happening, we were falling.

My voice echoed around me. Scrabbling and scraping as Venyx tried to latch on to something; an inaudible curse as the wall fell away and the ground vanished.

His body tightened around mine as he turned us, placing himself below me. I clenched my eyes shut, contemplating him, myself, my short years, as we fell through the endless void. The ground reached up, catching us in a violent crash. A loud smack resounded below me, and the world blacked out.

THIRTY-SIX

H OW LONG I LAY there, I didn't know. As I hacked up dust and debris, I took stock of myself. Venyx lay beneath me. One arm was splayed to the side. His other fell limply away as I sat atop him, every part of me flaring to aching life as I did.

My hands pressed against his chest, searching for a pulse. Waiting for him to draw a breath.

He lay perfectly still beneath me.

"Venyx?" I whispered, tapping his cheek. His head lolled to the side. "Venyx." Panic crept into my voice as I called to him, knowing he couldn't hear me. I tapped his other cheek from sheer desperation, needing him to be okay, to wake up. "Venyx," I croaked, shoving the hair from his face.

A mumbled whimper rose from me as I lay my ear against his chest, pressing into him, straining to hear one single precious beat of life. But when still there was nothing, I fell away from him, braced my elbows on my knees, and shoved my hands in my hair while thick, curdling guilt feasted on my gut.

With a trembling breath, my eyes slid open, and soft light glowed around me. My gaze was drawn to the crystals adorning the walls, the trickles of water running down them, and I slowly sat up. Pools formed in small recesses, carved into the ground from the eons. More rivulets crisscrossed the floor in jagged streams. The chamber was far bigger than it seemed, stretching into dark corners from every angle.

Shoving my aching body off the craggy floor, I went to the nearest recess. Leaning over, I gazed into the pool illuminated by more crystals. The water fed into another rivulet, which ran into each subsequent pool, racing toward some unseen source. Running water was safe water. One of the many lessons I'd been given as a child.

Cupping my palms, I drew a handful and sucked it down, sighing at the refreshing, clean taste. I drank my fill, working around the painful grumble of my empty stomach. The water wouldn't replace food, but it would keep me alive.

Dipping my hands back in, I scooped up a handful and carefully lifted it to Venyx, dripping it slowly over his parted mouth. And watched with a sinking stomach as it ran over his lips and into the hair splayed beneath him.

I tapped his cheek again, each strike becoming more frantic as he refused to wake. In a sudden panic-inducing realization, I pulled the crystals from my pocket and placed them in a small glowing pile beside his head and set about inspecting him. It took a moment, but when I found the pool of blood spreading beneath him, matting his dark locks to the ground, I choked before forcing myself to investigate further.

Lifting his head, I prodded his scalp, working through the slick, sticky blood, until I found the source. His skin had cracked open, leaving a large gushing gash almost the length of my middle finger. Taking one of the crystals, I parted his hair and peered closer, the bluish light glistening on bone.

Defeated, I sat back, hands hanging off my knees.

Breath after ragged breath, I forced myself to calm down. Then I made myself stand. I went to another pool, the one I hadn't drank from, and washed the blood away. Splashed my face. The cool water sent chills down my spine, grounding me back to reality. There was a very real chance he wasn't waking. I needed to prepare for that.

Glancing at Venyx, I gathered my crystals and set about searching for an exit. Or anything resembling an exit. Just in case.

Palm flat against the nearest wall, I traced the perimeter of the room, a pair of crystals held high to cut through the thick pooling shadows that clung to the deepest crevices of the cavern. As I went, my steps echoed about. Distant howls and clicks made me stop, heart fluttering, before they vanished.

Occasionally, my gaze slid back to the unconscious deymon before I forced myself to return to the task at hand. He had yet to move, to make a single sound. I didn't know of any being that could survive such a fall, especially with the wound he'd sustained. The longer he lay there, unmoving, the more reality set in that I was likely on my own.

The wall on the far side was riddled with tiny rivulets carving through rock. More crystals were embedded in the surface, giving the running water a near-metallic glow. Sticking out of the cracks was something green, fuzzy, and fibrous. Pulling off a piece, my heart leapt. Moss.

My mind whooshed back to the many lessons I'd taken as a girl. Though his face was a vague memory, his name was lost to time. He'd told me if I were to find myself without food, but there was running water, look for moss. It was edible.

I ripped it from the wall in chunks, depositing my crystals in my pockets so I could carry more of the fibrous stuff, and returned to where Venyx lay, sitting beside him. Using the underside of his cloak—uttering a whispered apology—I set about washing every scrap of it, running it through the stream beside where the deymon lay. I'd never eaten it, but remembered it would be tough to chew. It would also keep me full a long time.

The first bite I wanted to spit out. It was thick on my tongue. A dirt-like aftertaste paired with its gritty texture made it difficult to chew. Swallowing the stuff was weird, foreign. But my stomach gobbled it up. So I ate another bite. Then another. Before long, my stomach was full. To wash the taste from my mouth, I sucked down more water and sat back, taking in my surroundings.

After my stomach settled, I pushed up and returned to where I'd left off and began anew, working my way around the walls.

Halfway through the room, the echo of a howl shot through the cavern, ringing off the stone from somewhere high above. My feet stopped in their tracks. My stomach ran cold, shivers racing down my spine, along my legs and up, tickling my scalp.

Biting my trembling lower lip, I pushed on, peeling back layers of rock with my searching eyes, until I finally found a crack in the wall. Licking my lips, I pulled my crystals from my pocket and held them high, stepping cautiously into the void. After a while, I was forced to shimmy sideways as the path narrowed, but I was thin enough to make it. The passageway cut off abruptly, climbing vertically. With a dejected sigh, I dropped to the ground, crystals clattering along the rock beside me. I drew another breath, head tipped against the cool stone.

My breath halted in my lungs.

My eyes flew open as I breathed in, then again. Thus far, the air had been musty, laden with rock and time. Here, it smelled ... clean.

Gathering the crystals in my pocket, I stood, braced my hands against either side of the chasm, and jumped. My feet caught and I shuffled up, one hand, one foot, then the other hand, and the other foot. A bit of wall crumbled beneath me, sending me back to the floor with a cry and a thud, pain shooting from my ass as I landed sharply.

Growling, I stood and tried again, with the same result.

Wiping bits of rock from my scuffed palms, I worked my way back into the cavern and spotted a ledge. It was too high a jump. Instead, I inspected the wall. Though there were handholds, they were few and far between, and I doubted my short stature would make it between each.

Frustration boiled in my gut as I stomped back to Venyx and plopped down, head in my hands. Through strands of my hair, I gazed at him.

Guilt gnawed at me. Taking the mines had been my suggestion. We hadn't had much choice, but the decision still sat heavy in my stomach.

Shoving my hair over my shoulders, I wished for something to tie it back with. I then tore off a piece of my shirt. Gaze lingering over Venyx's form, I brushed my hair with my fingers and set to work braiding it before tying the plait off with the ribbon of ripped cloth. I slung it over my shoulder and leaned forward, deciding to try the climb once more.

How long I tried, I didn't know. When I fell for the final time, my hands were riddled with scrapes and cuts. Sweat dribbled down my face, between my breasts, and along my spine. Every part of me cried out, exhausted.

For a long time, I sat there, on the cavern floor, water cascading around me from some unseen source above. It was cool, crisp. Snow runoff. Its frigid kiss was heaven against my heated skin. Cupping my hands, I gathered a palmful of it and sucked it down, took a piece of moss from my pocket and popped it in my mouth, chewing endlessly as I stared up.

I could go back to Venyx. Or I could try one last time.

My arms ached. My back screamed. My legs begged to never hold my weight again. I didn't want to climb anymore. I wanted to sit down, to wait for Venyx to wake.

Head against the wet stone wall, I closed my eyes and breathed. Sweet air drifted in from outside, filling my lungs.

There was no guarantee he would wake. If I waited for him, I could be stuck down here, and we would both die.

But I wanted him to wake. My best chance of getting to the Plains was by his side. I wasn't fool enough to think I could attempt that again. But I wasn't naïve enough to think a fall like that hadn't damaged something irreparably. Even if he did wake, there was a chance he'd never be whole again. Some part of his mind lost, broken.

And still I would be stuck here.

And die.

A peal of laughter rose from my throat, bubbling into the void around me, echoing in the silence.

"Why do all my paths lead to death?" I asked the silence. Licking my lips, I pushed myself back to my feet. Ran my hands under the cool water, rinsed my face, set one foot against the wall, then the opposite hand, and hoisted myself up.

It took every ounce of strength to heave myself to the next handhold. Thrusting one foot back, I caught myself on the opposite wall, turned, and dug my fingers into a small outlet before pulling up, sighing in a small victory when I moved up another step.

The water made the climb difficult, turning the wall slippery. I shimmied back just so, out of its path, and continued. Hand. Foot. Step. Pull.

At any moment, I expected the rock to crumble beneath my fingers. For my foot to jar something loose. To tumble back to the earth in a sore bundle, once again swathed in frustration. And so, when my right hand fell against flat, solid ground, my eyes widened in awe.

Chest heaving, I stepped again, then again, pulled with my other hand, and released a strained gasp as my head popped over the ledge and a cool draft of frozen mountain air slid against my cheeks.

Lips trembling, I shoved my feet against the wall and hoisted myself up, groaning against my weight, my arms quaking. And landed with a wet slap on the rocky surface.

For a long moment I lay there. Staring up at the wall rising above me, strung with more glowing blue crystals that turned the cave into the night sky. After my heart finally stopped drumming, I clambered achingly to my feet and peered around. More moss clung to the floor, following a small stream flowing in from outside. I plucked a few more handfuls and shoved them in my pockets. Then looked up.

The tunnel before me was mostly dark. Mostly. At the far end was a small dot of sunlight. Collapsing to my knees, I stared at it, taking it in. It was right there. Freedom. Yes, it meant getting around the White Army. But I was free.

I stood, took a step, then another. And stopped.

I turned back to the cavern below, spying the deymon lying amongst all those glittering crystals, his prone form as peaceful as I'd ever seen him.

As if they heard my movement from so far above, the vampyres howled again, drawing my gaze up. It shifted back down as the echoes died, back to Venyx. Head lolled to the side. Hair splayed around his face. Completely helpless. Just as I'd been.

He hadn't needed to come for me. Hadn't needed to save me. He hadn't wanted the job in the first place.

And yet...

He'd come for me. Cared for me. Treated me with more empathy and kindness than I'd ever been afforded, even if only recently. And asked for nothing in return.

My gaze drifted to the tunnel. To the wafting air. The running water at my feet. My boots. Up to my trousers, and my shirt and coat. Gifted by his friend. The friend who'd taken us in. Who had defended me, despite not knowing me. Despite the dangers my being there presented.

Tears prickled the backs of my eyes as I looked one last time at the tunnel stretching before me.

"I climbed it once," I mumbled. "I can do it again." And climbed to the floor, descending slowly, hoping with everything in me I wasn't being naïve. Or stupid.

He would wake, I told myself. He had to.

Shuffling back to where Venyx lay, I plopped back down and washed another piece of moss, giving it only a single glance before popping the fibrous thing in my mouth. Gnashing it between my teeth, I stared at the deymon.

"You know, you better wake up soon, or all this yummy moss will be gone," I mumbled. "I'm not saving you any." Emotion laced my voice, made it difficult to chew, to swallow. I leaned over the stream, downing more water to wash away the taste.

From the corner of my eyes, one of Venyx's hands twitched. I sat up, perplexed. He couldn't have survived, could he?

As time dragged on and he didn't move, I began to think it had been my mind. A trick of the dim, glowing light. Maybe I was seeing what I wanted to.

Then his hand twitched again, his fingers brushing the rock as if grasping for it.

I jumped up, throwing myself over his body as I pulled the crystals from my pocket and piled them beside his head. I dug into his hair, probing his scalp for the gash. The pool of blood had stopped growing. When I found the wound, it was smaller. I poked around the drying edges. Straining my eyes, I parted his hair and peered at the skin, picked up a pair of crystals and held them almost directly against him.

My heart skipped a beat.

The ends of the wound were slowly stitching themselves together, leaving behind a faint pink mark. At the very end, where I could have sworn the gash had been, was a white line. Like an aged scar.

My breath caught in my throat as I stared at him. He was alive.

"How?" I whispered.

I placed my ear against his chest and closed my eyes, pouring all my energy into listening. His heartbeat was faint, a slow offbeat rhythm, but it was there. I sat up, disbelief flooding me.

My moment of hope was cut short at a distant clicking against stone.

Another howl sounded, drawing my eyes into the yawning void above, and the vampyres beyond. Undoubtedly, they were searching for a way down. Which meant they probably smelled blood. His blood.

Shit.

Jumping back toward his head, I scooped water from the rivulet, washing the ground as quickly, as thoroughly, as I could. Blood was matted in his hair, thick and drying in places, and it took longer to wash. But I did it. Taking a handful of moss, I waded it up and shoved it along his wound, pressing it there. I stripped off my coat, then my sweater, balled up the woolen thing, and placed it beneath him, holding the fibrous stuff in place.

My eyes strained against the darkness above, though spotted no movement. But there it was again. The clacking drew closer and it dawned on me—I hadn't covered up the smell in time. Even with water saturating his hair, the stone beneath him. Blood still lingered in his clothes.

Another series of clicks sounded, echoing off the cavern walls, closing in. Then another.

When the first vampyre appeared in the glow of the crystals, my heart dropped. It crawled down the wall, the clicking and clacking of its claws digging into my brain. The sniffling as its head swiveled around on its bony shoulders.

Panic crept into my chest, fluttering through my limbs. There was still time to go back to the chasm. To climb back up.

But no.

I couldn't leave him. Wouldn't. Even as terror tore through me, screaming I'd made a mistake. I should have left. Run when I had the chance.

Trembling, I drew one of Venyx's swords. Climbed shakily to my feet. Placed myself between him, my guardian, and the creature crawling toward us.

And chose to protect him.

THIRTY-SEVEN

CLICKING ECHOED OFF THE rocks behind me, and I spun as another vampyre crawled down the wall, its nostrils flaring wildly. The claws of its toes tapped and clacked as it went, head swinging every which way, as if deducing where we were.

Another set of clicks sounded and I spun again, hefting the sword, blade pointed toward the vampyre as if it might be threatened by it. Though I was certain my holding it was far less threatening than when Venyx had.

I swallowed the lump in my throat as my entire body trembled. Feet slapped against the rock floor, and I turned again. The vampyre crept closer, nose tipped up. A cluster of fleshy white lumps crawled down the walls in staggered lines, sniffing the air, tinged with the blood lingering in Venyx's hair, on his clothes, on mine. Above, more clicks floated down, settling on the ground as the whole nest seemed to descend.

Drawing a ragged breath, I faced the ones directly before me, gritting my teeth in anticipation. The first one jumped clear across the room, tackling me to the ground with a lung-crushing thump. Only barely gripping the sword, I swung up, thankful for its light weight, and sliced through the creature's side. It released a howl and jumped back, its bony, clawed hand clapping to the wound before it raised its head and hissed.

I scrambled back to my feet, readjusted my grip on the sword, and roared.

It lunged again. I stabbed up. It swatted my blow away, knocking the sword from my grip on our way back to the floor, grabbed my head, and slammed me against the stone. Stars danced in my vision as pain ricocheted through me. My pulse thundered as panic flooded me. Putting all my strength behind my fist, I struck up, beating the thing's face, then the open wound on its side, wrenching another shriek from it.

I pulled my knees to my chest and kicked, throwing the creature off, rolled over, and jumped to my weapon. The vampyre lunged as I swung, burying the sword in its chest, sliding it easily between its ribs and out its back. With a roar, I ripped the blade free before piercing its head.

Heaving, I stepped back and wiped the blood from my cheeks, looking for the next one. From behind, another vampyre jumped on my back, wrapped its clawed hands around my chest, and sank its fangs into my shoulder. My scream echoed up the chamber, digging into my ears, followed by the vampyre's own.

The thing threw itself off me, hunched on all fours. I backed away in confusion, my fear coiling as it retched up my blood in frantic hacks. Its stomach heaved, spine jutting up and down while its feet clawed the floor. The coughs turned to a sickening whine as it sucked in a ragged breath and dropped to its stomach.

The other vampyres stopped their advance, a flurry of clacks and taps filling the cavern.

With my free hand, I reached up, pawing at my shoulder. My fingers came away red, slick with saliva and blood. Trembling, I approached the fallen form, prodding with the sword, waiting for it to jump up and rip my throat out. It remained still. Not even its chest moved.

I glanced at my red-slicked hand and swung my gaze to the vampyre's body, laying in a pool of regurgitated blood. At the next set of clicks, I stepped back and swung toward the vampyre as it cautiously approached. It growled, exposing the length of its fangs.

Thinking quickly, I ran back to Venyx, gently pulled my sweater from beneath him, soaked through with his blood, and tossed it toward the vampyre. The thing tore into it, snarling and growling, ripping the fabric to shreds.

I licked my lips, my mind spinning.

With a snarl, the vampyre tossed the sweater aside and crawled closer to me, its face vibrating with a growl. My chest heaving in terror, I dropped my sword arm and stepped forward. The creature needed no further invitation. It jumped at once, shoving me to the ground as its fangs sank into the opposite side of my throat. I bit back my tears at the sucking sensation before the vampyre jumped up, screaming.

Scrambling back, I stared as it desperately wiped my blood from its face. It began hacking, its body heaving, just as the previous vampyre, until it, too, collapsed.

I rose as the other vampyres drew near, nostrils flaring wildly, their clicks and taps a frantic wave.

When, as a child, Aurorian had told me of my divine blood, I had been reticent to believe her. Angels descended to the mortal plain once every thousand years, and one had impregnated my mother with me? It had seemed unlikely.

I'd always believed I wasn't truly the Child of Sky and Sea. That Aurorian made a mistake. The Faerie Queen made a mistake. There were hundreds, thousands, of other Sirenians roaming Lorralei. How was *I* the prophesized one?

Looking at the dead vampyres before me, lying in my blood, it was difficult to deny any longer. Maybe stories of vampyres being products of the seven hells weren't true. They weren't cursed, as people said. But dying on angel blood seemed more than just a coincidence.

Then again, they hadn't ingested Venyx's blood, just touched it.

I looked down at my hand, then up at the vampyre crawling closer to me. Steeling myself, I sucked in a deep breath and drew the edge of Venyx's sword across my skin, jumping as the metal bit my flesh. A thin line of scarlet welled in my palm.

The vampyre's nose went wild, flaring and contracting at the fresh smell. Still, its head swung away, and it crawled around me. Toward Venyx. My brows knit together in confusion. Jumping on it, I wrapped my arm around its head and pressed my hand into its face. The vampyre immediately flung itself onto its back, wailing. It ripped itself from me, clawing where I had touched before it, too, dropped to its stomach, limbs splayed out. A seared mark stretched across its skin. Its mouth contorted in a silent scream.

Chest heaving, I looked at my palm, then back at the dead thing before me.

Up on the walls, tapping echoed far into the cavern's ceiling. A symphony of clicks and clacks as they spread the word amongst themselves, the chorus deafening. Frightening.

My gaze swung back to my hand, then to Venyx.

They could touch Venyx's blood, which meant they could drink it. They could kill him.

They couldn't kill me, and now they knew it.

I raised my sliced palm to gaze at it, more blood pooling in its center, and nodded, the truth of my divinity embedding itself into my brain. Then spun around as more vampyres gathered.

Spying the remnants of my sweater, I held my hand out and the vampyres jumped back, nostrils flaring at the scent. Their claws tapped and scratched the floor, their maws vibrating with growls. Grabbing the lump of fabric, I coated Venyx's blood in mine, and tossed it forward. Like insects, the creatures scattered, jumping back from the thing holding proof of my divinity.

A small welling of victory rose in my chest.

Running back to Venyx, I dropped beside him, the sword at my side, and squeezed the edges of the cut. Once a decent amount of blood was in my palm, I tipped my hand and let the droplets fall into Venyx's hair. Spread myself through his black locks, along his cheeks and forehead. His chest, hands, arms, and stomach. Making sure he smelled of me.

I crawled over him, kneeling as a vampyre edged closer. Reaching the deymon's hair, it stopped, sniffed, and hissed before stepping back, the claws of its toes clacking wildly. As if it knew of my treachery, though not sure what it was, the thing's face tilted toward me, and it hissed. Even though I was void of fangs, I returned the hiss and crawled in front of Venyx.

The vampyre jumped back, gathering with the others on the far side of the cave. Their clicking and clacking filled the air as they communicated back and forth.

I knew my blood wouldn't protect him forever. Just as I knew it wouldn't stop the vampyres from killing either of us. But I refused to believe he wouldn't wake. Just as I refused to die. Not here.

Taking another of my crystals, I leaned over Venyx and prodded the back of his head, marveling at how much more the wound had closed. How little blood now flowed. His heart beat slightly faster, keeping a better rhythm. His breath was healthier, stronger. I brushed aside the hair strewn across his face and leaned back.

His sword lain across my lap, I took up sentry and waited for him to wake.

THIRTY-EIGHT

I STARTED AWAKE AT an echoing howl and slumped forward, one hand on my lap, the other propping my chin.

The gathered vampyres seemed to sense something wasn't right. Venyx was slathered in my blood, yes. But also coated in his own. Unable to solve my riddle, they sent forth a scout to investigate.

It crept closer, nostrils flaring wildly. The claws of its feet tapped the ground in quick succession, as if relaying what it found. The thing skirted around me, around my blood. Another few drops on Venyx's hair, and the creature jumped back, maw vibrating in a growl.

"We can do this as long as you like," I grumbled. Its head swiveled toward my voice. "You can't have him." I dipped a finger in my welling blood, and flicked a droplet at the thing. It yelped and jumped back, hissed, and scurried to rejoin the others.

Time slowed to a crawl. The world beyond the mines faded and, for a moment, I forgot the mountains were crawling with White soldiers hunting me.

It seemed ethereal, having confirmation of my destiny in the very place I might die. I'd never felt so mortal as I did sitting in that cavern, surrounded by vampyres, waiting for them to piece together what I'd done. How I'd tricked them.

Perhaps they couldn't kill me. Then again, maybe one would sacrifice itself for the trouble I'd caused. I was, after all, the only thing between them and their meal.

But I wouldn't leave Venyx to die. To do so would be killing him to save myself. No better than the world demanding my life in exchange for everyone else. And the cycle would continue.

I refused to be a part of it.

Thankfully, I'd taken moss from the ledge, though eventually it would run out. The rest, of course, was on the wall behind the vampyres. After a while, water would cease to keep me alive and I would starve. Unless Venyx woke.

Twice during my watch I reapplied my blood to Venyx's face, hair, and clothes. It was so moist in the cavern, there was no danger of it drying anytime soon. The vampyres sniffed wildly, the sound as grating as it was frightening. They growled as I smeared myself across the deymon. They had no eyes, but they made it known they could smell. And I knew with everything in me it infuriated them.

One crept eerily close as I dripped the scarlet fluid along the deymon's forehead, sniffing as I ran my hands through his hair, now more red than black. The thing stretched its neck out, growling, and licked at Venyx's blood-washed locks before it jumped back, yelping.

"Serves you right," I grumbled, focused on my work.

Setting the blade to rest on the unconscious deymon, I took up my last piece of moss, thankful I'd harvested so much. Another of the vampyres limped forward, nose to the air, as I washed the bit of fuzzy green plant in the tiny stream beside me. I plucked off a corner and tossed it to the thing.

"Eat that," I mumbled before popping the last of it in my mouth. The vampyre hissed and ambled off.

I leaned back against Venyx as I chewed, gaze shifting between him and the vampyres. Then up and around, at all the twinkling crystals, glowing their ethereal blue. If not for the vampyres, the unconscious deymon behind me, this place would be beautiful. Still, I longed to be out. For sunshine to warm my skin, to inhale fresh air.

I longed to return to the darkened crevice, to smell the sweet draft from outside. My gaze drifted toward it often, but I couldn't leave Venyx's side. And with each passing moment, my confidence in him waking shrank.

The second time I washed Venyx, my hand hurt. The cut throbbed, the open flesh burning. It couldn't be helped, I told myself. I was keeping us alive. Eventually, though, it wouldn't be enough. I'd run out of blood at some point.

Afterward, I crawled atop Venyx and parted the matted locks of his hair to examine his wound. The ends, where there had been scarring, were now clean, untouched scalp. The very center was still open, but only just. And it no longer bled. His heartbeat was strong, his chest rising and falling in a soft rhythm. Still, far too much time had passed.

With a sigh, I sat at Venyx's side and replaced the sword across my lap, fingers tapping along the blade, and watched.

Maybe Cleya was right. Maybe I was a stupid girl.

A few vampyres wandered off, the clacking of their claws across the craggy floor echoing throughout the chamber before vanishing completely. Many stayed. They licked their fangs. Clicked back and forth in their strange communication.

And they waited. For me to leave his side. To fall asleep. To have the courtesy of dying so they could enjoy their meal.

Out of sheer stubbornness, I refused to do any of those things.

Finally, my patience was rewarded.

Beside me, Venyx groaned.

All at once, my heart thrummed to life and I jumped atop him as the vampyres perked up. At first, I thought I'd heard something; it was the earth groaning. The vampyres had misheard, also. Then he groaned again, his long, dark lashes fluttering against his cheeks.

"Venyx?" I whispered, my voice strained, both from disuse and from the well of emotions roiling in my throat.

I patted his cheek, brushed the crusty hair from his face. His brows pulled together, eyelids fluttering. His tongue darted out, wet his lips, and he groaned again.

Around us, the clacking started anew. Bodies shuffled around the chamber.

Venyx shifted his feet, his boots scraping the rock.

"Venyx, please say something," I begged, my uninjured palm against his cheek. His hand rose and covered mine, his touch soft. He coughed, a hollow, weak sound, as if breathing for the first time.

"What happened?" he asked, his deep voice rough.

I reached into the pool beside us and gathered a handful of water, delivering it slowly to his mouth.

"Drink," I said before spilling it between his lips. The first few drops he coughed up in sputtering gasps before it went down smoothly. The next handful he drank with ease. "We fell. You've been passed out. I don't know how long."

"Are you hurt?" he asked, eyes still closed.

I looked down at my sliced palm, answering, "No. I'm fine. You took the worst of it."

"Good."

A thin smile curled my lips.

One of his hands touched my thigh and slid toward my hip, sending a flurry of red-hot blush across my face. His eyes slid carefully open, the silver glistening up at me—a sight I never thought I'd be so grateful to see. He must have realized where his hand was because it fell away, thumping to the cavern floor. He pushed himself up on his elbows. I scurried off him as he sat, hunching beside him.

"Whoa," I said, hands on his chest. "Go easy."

He put a hand to his head, squeezed the bridge of his nose, and drew a deep breath.

"How do you feel?" I asked, eyes flitting across his face.

"Like shit," he groaned.

"That's understandable. You cracked your skull open. For a while, I wasn't sure if you'd make it."

His eyes opened and his gaze bore into mine. "Then why are you still here?"

My brows pulled together, mouth gaping. "Wh- I-I couldn't."

"You should have."

My gaze shifted up, toward the ledge, then back to the deymon.

I sat back as he drew his knees to his chest and crossed his ankles, taking long, deep breaths, one after the other. His gaze went distant, the color draining from his face. He rolled to his side, onto his knees, and tucked his chin to his chest, forehead pressed to the ground.

"Venyx?"

"I'm fine," he grumbled.

I scoffed. "No, you're not. You almost died."

"I *will* be fine," he said.

"You can stop the overprotective bodyguard bullshit," I snapped. "I've been sitting here beside you for who knows how long, watching over you. It's okay to not be okay. Even for a deymon."

Hesitantly, I placed a hand on his shoulder, expecting him to shrug me off, to draw back from my touch. It came as a shock when he did neither of those. Instead, he leaned into it. After a while, he sat up and turned to face me, his eyes moving to the sword laying between us, then the blood coating his hands. Realization blossomed across his face as his gaze shifted past me to the vampyres, his brows creased in confusion.

"What happened?" he repeated, his voice grave.

My gaze flicked away from his intense expression. "I couldn't leave you," I said, shrugging. He hooked a finger beneath my chin, raising my eyes to his, then leaned forward, pressing his forehead to mine.

"You are incredible," he whispered. Thick blush spread across my cheeks, though I was unable to pull away. His warm breath fanned my face as his thumb traced gentle circles along my jaw, sending tremors down my back, though I'd have been lying if I said I wanted him to stop.

Low growling from behind jerked us from our moment, settling us back in the cavern of vampyres.

With a groan, Venyx picked himself up. I stayed beside him, hands on his shoulders in case he toppled. The last thing I needed was him falling into the gathered vampyres. When I was sure he was steady, I picked up his sword and resheathed it for him, unsure if he could. He didn't argue.

"That ledge is the way out," I said, pointing. He took a breath, looked around, and nodded.

"I can jump that."

"From here?" I asked. "Venyx, you just woke from—"

He took my chin in his hand, tipped my head to face him, and my words fell uselessly to the ground between us. "I said I can jump it," he repeated.

"Okay," I whispered.

As if they understood, a couple vampyres leaned forward, sniffing the air. One growled as another clicked its claws.

Venyx gestured to me. He still looked too weak to make the jump, but I didn't argue. When his arms wrapped around me, a slight tremor ran through them, a great sigh in his chest, followed by a growl.

"We can wait a little longer," I whispered.

"We don't have longer," he argued. He was right. I knew he was.

The vampyres crept closer, their claws clacking and clicking across the stone in a frantic wave as our time quickly dwindled.

"There's a tunnel that leads outside," I told him.

He nodded. "I can smell it from here."

Behind us came a low, rumbling growl. We looked in the same instant, as the nearest vampyre stuck its tongue hesitantly out and panted, as if tasting the air. Its nostrils flared and it stepped closer to Venyx's leg. He kicked at the thing, making it yelp, before it stepped back and growled. The furious clacking of its claws along the rock became hurried, violent.

The vampyre coiled its legs and jumped toward Venyx. Without thought, I threw myself between them, screaming when the thing's fangs sank into my shoulder. My cry mixed with the tang of steel as Venyx drew a sword. The vampyre wailed as it jumped off me, flinging itself across the cavern.

"Seven fucking hells," Venyx breathed, eyes wide as the vampyre thrashed and writhed, screaming in agony as it retched up my blood before collapsing. Stanching the flow from my shoulder with my hand, I ran to Venyx as he resheathed his sword and pulled me into his arms.

The surrounding vampyres lunged as Venyx pushed off the ground and launched into the air. I curled against him as the wall rushed toward us before he threw me, my body landing in a rolling heap on the ledge overlooking the cavern. Scrambling to my hands and knees, I crawled to the edge and took hold of Venyx's hand as he struggled to hoist himself up. Heaving against his weight, I hauled backward as he pushed up, colliding into me before we were up and running. A cacophony of scratching and scrabbling gave chase.

The scent of fresh air grew more potent the further we ran until, finally, up ahead, sunlight glimmered from the end of the tunnel. My heart hammered loud, though I didn't want to hope too soon. I hadn't explored it. Hadn't checked to make sure the way was large enough. But it had to be. There was no other choice.

The way shrank as we went, compressing around us, a small stream cutting through the rock at our feet. A sob cracked through my chest as the speck of daylight grew. The only thing between us and freedom was a narrowing tunnel. Far too close behind were the snarling vampyres as they clawed after us.

"Go!" Venyx screamed, pushing me forward.

Tears running in wild rivers, I dropped to my hands and knees, moving as fast as I could toward the glimmer of light. I spared a single glance back to make sure Venyx followed.

Sharp rocks scraped and cut my hands. The narrowing ceiling snagged my coat, ripping it as it pulled my hair. Further on, I was forced to my belly, slithering along the tunnel floor.

A burst of fresh air stung my face, flooded my nose, and more tears bubbled over my eyes, cascading down my cheeks.

"Venyx!" I cried. Turning once more, horror flooded me as he was yanked back, his fingers scratching for purchase. He cried out, kicking before being ripped backward again. I stared uselessly as he whipped around, eyes frantic.

"Go!" he screamed. "Get out!"

The vampyre on his ankle yelped as Venyx kicked again.

With a growl, I ran my injured palm along the craggy ground and crawled back down the tunnel.

"Seraph, no!" Venyx cried, both hands scrambling for me. I narrowly dodged him, squeezing past his cramped body just enough to shove my bloody hand in the vampyre's face. The creature jumped back with a snarling scream, whining as it clawed itself.

A strong arm grabbed my waist, hoisting me up. The world spun as Venyx turned me around and shoved me forward. Gasping in terror, throbbing with pain, I crawled, blinking away the bright light assaulting my eyes. The tunnel fell away and I tumbled into something soft before a heavy mass landed atop me.

I was yanked to my feet and jerked from the tunnel as the world came into focus. A vampyre launched itself into the sunlight, the quiet filled with a shrieking wail as the creature's white, nearly transparent skin began burning until it fell with a thump to the ground.

A soft growl emanated from the tunnel, though nothing else came after us.

I stumbled before collapsing in a heap. My chest heaved, my heart thundered. Every bit of me ached and screamed as more tears rolled heavy down my face.

His entire body trembling, Venyx dropped beside me, falling backward, one arm resting on his knee, head hanging loose on his shoulders. Crawling toward him, I pressed against his side, surprised when he pulled me to his chest. I returned his embrace before sinking into his lap and pulled his head to my shoulder.

For a long moment we sat there, draped over each other, as terror and adrenaline coursed through our bodies, flesh singing and buzzing. My breath trembling, I rested my cheek against Venyx's forehead and stroked his hair as his arms tightened around my middle.

After the shock of our narrow escape wore off, I blinked away my lingering tears and gazed around.

We sat in a small patch of grass in a clearing hugging the mountain. High above glistened patches of snow, sparkling like gems in the sunlight. The trees standing sentry around us were lively and green. Chirps and whistles filled the air.

We'd reached the edge of the Northerlands.

THIRTY-NINE

GREENERY EXISTED IN FEW places across the known lands of Lor-ralei—the Lost Forest, where legend said it was always spring, and the Great Green, a strip of land between the Northerlands and the surrounding countries where water from melting snow flowed into the parched earth. As it was still part of the Northerlands, no one country laid claim to it. And so became a refuge for animals with nowhere else to go.

So few traversed the surrounding nations to go north, the beasts who called the Great Green home had no concept of people. It was with this in mind I gazed at the deer dotting the landscape, staring unabashedly at our crossing. After assuring themselves we weren't a threat, the deer resumed grazing.

The forest of the Great Green hummed with life, void of the shouts and cries of the White Army. In our mad dash through the mines, we appeared to have evaded them. Hopefully, they would stay blissfully unaware of where we were.

Tiny rivulets flowed downhill, over the mouth of our escape route, gathering in a pond a mile south. The water was pristine and clear, and I stared in awe at so much in one place. On trembling legs, Venyx stripped and dropped into the lapping waves, drinking his fill before scrubbing the mines from his skin. Blushing wildly, I turned and faced the opposite direction to undress before joining him.

The water was cold. It shouldn't have been surprising, since it was snow runoff, but I still released a small gasp as it climbed up my hips and stomach to my breasts, cradling my heated flesh in its chilly embrace. After the initial shock wore off, I noticed how sore I was.

Dark bruises dotted my legs, running the length of both sides. The vampyre bites stung as water licked them, becoming itchy and tender the further I sank. A few moments later, as I washed the blood from my skin, my hands ran over unblemished flesh, sending me into awe. There was still so much to learn about my own body.

Behind came a loud splash and I whipped around, flinging my hair over my shoulders. Venyx raised water to his head, scrubbing voraciously, before he gathered another handful of the pond. Red rivulets ran down his back, evidence of how much blood he'd lost, and how much of my own I'd painted him with.

As water ran through his dark hair, it shoved the strands aside, and I caught my breath. Laid across his spine, directly in the middle of his shoulders, was a brand. It was small and difficult to see, but I couldn't look away. An ornate capital R with delicate embellishments surrounding it.

Venyx looked up, following some noise I couldn't hear, and his gaze met mine. I whipped around, continuing to wash the dirt from my skin. Shortly after came the sloshing of water, and I spotted Venyx wading toward the pond's rocky embankment. My cheeks once again flared with heat at the sight of so much of him before I turned back around.

I sloshed to the shore after him, covering myself with my hands, pointless as it was. Now dressed, Venyx lay sprawled at the far end of the pond, hands behind his head.

After dressing, I plodded toward him, quiet, in case he was sleeping. I couldn't imagine being unconscious for however long was any kinds of restful.

Still, as if he'd breached my mental barriers, he said, "Just resting my eyes."

I sighed and eased beside him, absently plucking blades of grass. My gaze flicked to him, wondering what he was thinking. If he'd been scared in the mines. It seemed impossible to think he would have been. All the power and strengths he possessed. But perhaps that was simply my impression of him.

Curiosity getting the better of me, I asked, "Were you afraid?"

I hoped I didn't need to elaborate. Though I also expected some snarky reply. Some insult thrown as he would have done to Miran.

Miran.

Just the thought stung. My heart ached, tears burning the backs of my eyes, though I refused to cry for him. Over him. He deserved many things. My tears were not one of them.

"Yes," he finally said, cutting through the silence. My gaze drifted up as he turned to me, just for a moment, before returning his eyes to the sky. "I was afraid. I'd have been an idiot otherwise."

"How did you heal from ... from the... How?" I asked. He licked his lips, the tips of his fangs glinting in the bright sunlight.

"My kind are able to live a very long time." He reached a hand up, turning it this way and that, as if testing the tendons in his wrist, his arm. Or maybe making sure he was still alive. "The older we grow, the slower we age. With slower aging comes faster healing. Tougher skin, denser bones. If I'd been much younger, we wouldn't be having this conversation." He turned back to me, a damp lock of black hair falling across his face.

This close to him, with nothing trying to kill us, I saw it. The tiredness in his eyes. The fine lines at the corners, as if he'd spent many years laughing, however long those years were.

With a sigh, I scooted down and laid across the grass next to him, staring up at the expanse of vibrant green canopy, endless blue sky just beyond.

"What happened down there?" he asked.

I faced him. And I told him. Of waking after the fall, exploring the cavern. Pushing aside the guilt, I relayed my attempts to escape, and my decision to stay. Finally, I told him of my scuffle with the vampyres, and my grim discovery about my divinity. After I fell silent, he picked up my hand and ran his fingers across my now healed palm.

"You found out they can't kill you, and you used your blood to save me," he said, his voice just above a whisper.

"I couldn't leave you," I whispered in return. Brows furrowing, he wrapped my hand in his and kissed my knuckles, as if in thanks, before releasing it.

Blinking away the gathering moisture, I turned back toward the sky.

"I'm told Sirenians live a long time," I said, his gaze warming my face. "They live for hundreds of years. But angels ... I don't know." I found myself unable to voice the rest of those words—I didn't expect to learn if I could grow old—and so let them vanish on my tongue.

"Everything I've heard would suggest angels don't die," he said. "Half-bloods ... I'm not sure. You're the first I've met."

I raised my hand, following the lines etched into my skin. Growing up, I'd read the palms of the spies. Told them how long they would live, if they would settle down. Though they all laughed, they stared more intently at their hands afterward. Some even traced those lines, when they thought I wasn't looking. But mine, I told myself, always spoke lies.

I dropped my hand, staring at the canopy, all too aware of the deymon lying next to me as his brown eyes drifted closed. His words echoing in my head.

We laid on the shore of the tiny pond a little longer. Just until my stomach rumbled and growled, protesting its emptiness. In response, Venyx waded back into the water, trouser legs pulled up. Faster than I could see, he flung his hand out and came up with a fish, wriggling and squirming in his grip before he took a knife to it.

We made a fire, just big enough to cook with, and immediately snuffed it. Though we weren't sure where the White Army was, it was still unwise to lead them directly to us, regardless of how long it might take.

By the time we'd eaten, the sun was beginning to set. We still had a few days until we reached the border, though our trip through the mines had hurried our path. So we walked a bit further, until the horizon swallowed the light, before Venyx mentioned finding somewhere to rest. My shoulders slumped, eyes trailing up one of the forest's massive trees. He only chuckled.

"Yes, I'm sorry, but it's wise to sleep in the trees until we reach the Plains," he said. "Once we get there, we'll have nothing to hide in."

"I really wish we didn't have to," I groaned, stepping toward him. He chuckled again, one fang pressing into his bottom lip.

Getting far too close to him, I wrapped my arms around his neck, his breath fanning my shoulder as he embraced me. Without my bulky sweater, the hard planes of his body were more acute, and I blushed furiously. He lifted my legs around his waist and I locked my ankles at his back, the movement too intimate. I made sure to hide those thoughts, tucking them somewhere he couldn't see, or hear, however it worked. Instead, I closed my eyes, focusing on his muscles as they coiled just before he leapt, his free hand grasping a branch, then the next.

He nimbly hopped through the limbs, high enough that, when I opened my eyes, the ground was far below. To fall from such a height might not kill me, but I wouldn't walk away from it. And so I clung to Venyx as he placed one foot on the branch, then the other, steadying himself as the whole tree swayed and creaked in the breeze.

I didn't dare meet his gaze as I slid from his body, feet planted precariously on the branch beneath me. The heat spreading across my face was bad enough. His hands, solid and warm on my sides, sent ripples through me.

"We can rest here," he said. The branches were in a position to create a cradle of sorts. Leaving me, again, to rest on his lap. As there were no other options, I simply nodded, eyes on my feet, as he eased himself down. He gestured me closer.

With a deep breath, I placed my hands in his and lowered myself atop him, furious blush digging into my cheeks, until I was settled in his lap. There was no chance he didn't hear the thundering of my heart, but he said nothing.

Hands on his chest, I lowered myself across him, his heartbeat drumming against my ear. His arms wrapped around me, joining at my back. The weight of them pulled me into him, holding me steady. I tried not to think about falling as I lay there, Venyx my own living bed of sorts. The stability he displayed, regardless of being sprawled between two branches, was fascinating.

"Thank you," he said, his deep voice cutting through my thoughts.

My head snapped up, and I gazed through the lilac locks hanging like a curtain between us. I tucked my hair behind my ears.

"For what?" I asked, my voice strained from the angle.

"For saving my life. For coming back for me." His hands adjusted at my back. "Thank you."

I sat up, staring at him, and his hands fell to either side, grazing my thighs before they rested on his stomach.

"You've saved my life plenty of times." I fiddled with a lock of hair, twirling it round and round my finger, my gaze shifting between my hands and his face. "Anyone else would have done the same."

"You overestimate the value of life," he said with a sigh, adjusting his hands. He reached up, plucking a hanging leaf before he flicked it away. "Besides, I was hired to protect you. Your life is far more valuable than mine. I wouldn't have blamed you for leaving. You should have."

"So you said," I grumbled.

"So, thank you," he repeated, tugging at the end of my hair.

A girlish grinned pulled at my lips as his fingers fell away from me. "You're welcome."

A chill breeze ran through the treetops, snaking through my hair to kiss my nape, and I shivered against it. He ran his hands up and down my arms, sending warmth through me.

"How's your head feeling?" I asked. He reached back, wincing slightly as his fingers dug through his hair.

"Still tender."

"Is it okay if I check?" I asked, hands open, waiting for consent. He nodded once, and I scooted further into his lap, stretching to reach around the back of his head, probing gently. My hands were warmed by all his hair, by the heat from his scalp. Beneath me, his body tensed. His grip dug into my waist, legs coiling as if preparing to jump. All too aware of how close my breasts were to him, I glanced at his shut eyes. His clenched jaw working back and forth.

"Does that hurt?" I asked, gaze flicking to the taut expression stretched across his face.

"A bit," he groaned.

"It's still swollen, but it's healing nicely," I said, sliding back down him. His hands relaxed, his body uncoiling. He sighed as his jaw slackened and his eyes opened, the silver in them flaring to life with the setting sun.

"I should be fine in another day," he said, relaxing against the branch.

As his arms settled back around me, I splayed my hand open, spying the lines on my palm in the dark, and traced a fingernail over the lifeline.

"What's on your hand?" he asked. I looked up, self-consciously curling my fingers.

"Um..." I smiled. "Nothing."

"Did the cut reopen?" he asked, taking my hand in his. I splayed my palm for him, showing there was no cut, no scar. Just unblemished skin. His eyes flicked to mine.

"I-" I stopped, cleared my throat, and started again. "The woman who raised me taught me to read palm lines."

"Oh."

I suppressed a shudder as his thumb traced my lifeline.

"Do you remember anything else from before Aurorian?" he asked.

I shrugged. "No. Not really." He released my hand. "I used to... I used to read the palms of the spies. When I was a girl. To help pass time between lessons and training. I think that's the only reason I retained it."

I expected him to ask why I stopped. When I stopped.

After I turned fifteen, with my first bleeding, the spies no longer saw me as a girl. Once, I had taken that attention as something to be cherished. The only affection I was afforded. But with the revelation of Miran, I found myself viewing those years differently, cringing at how I'd allowed myself to be treated. Used. If I hadn't, maybe Miran wouldn't have gotten so close to me. The backs of my eyes stung at the thought.

Thankfully, he didn't ask. Didn't pry. Didn't creep into my head to glimpse those thoughts I wanted to lock up and forget.

Instead, he held his palm out and said, "What does mine tell you?"

Smiling, I pulled his hand closer, my eyes burrowing through the growing dark as I traced the fine lines along his skin. His hands were softer than expected after a lifetime of fighting. Wielding a blade for coin. I marveled at the lack of callouses. The absence of scars. Only a couple freckles dotted the creases of his fingers.

I traced a fingernail over his lifeline, the crease one solid line from side to side. "You're going to live a long life."

"A long life?" he asked, snickering. I glanced up, spying the tip of one fang.

"What's so funny?"

He licked his lips, turned away, and looked back at me, eyes glinting silver in the moonlight filtering through the treetops. "I'm ten thousand years old, Seraph. A long life is an understatement."

My heart dropped into my stomach, the smile falling from my face. "Te-ten ... thousand..." I swallowed and looked at his palm, flicking my gaze back to him.

"Go on," he said, jutting his chin toward me. "What else?" His other arm curled behind his head, his eyes intent upon me as I shifted my focus back to his hand.

I cleared my throat, forcing my attention away from the lifeline to his spirit line. "This one says you have a kind heart, but you hide it behind a wall of iron and steel." I glanced up, his smile creeping back into hiding. "You haven't always had reason to be kind, but you try anyway."

"Being kind is a fool's errand in this world," he growled. "Some people deserve only the kindness of a swift death."

I shivered at his words, at the coldness of them, but couldn't disagree. Not after the horrors I'd witnessed, few as they were. I said nothing, continuing to the group of lines along the upper side of his hand and ran my fingernail down them, smiling as he reflexively tugged back.

"Ticklish, are we?" I asked.

"Tickle me at your own risk," he grumbled. Still, I spied the grin hiding in the corner of his mouth.

"These are your love lines," I said, tapping my nail against the side of his hand.

"What does that mean?"

"It means you will have three great loves in your ridiculously long life," I said, smirking. He chuckled. "And these ones," I said, moving to the lines at the bottom side of his hand, "mean you will have two children."

He suddenly went very still. His face shifted, expression turning icy, and I let his hand fall.

"I'm sorry," I whispered, curling my hands into my chest. "I didn't mean-"

"You didn't do anything." He sighed, rubbed his face, and shoved his hand through his hair. Slowly, I laid down, whatever moment between us having passed, and focused on the steady thrum in the chest of my living pillow. His arms wrapped around me, fingers threading together across my back. "I had my chance."

I tipped my head back, looking up at him.

"At being a father." He sighed, eyes going to the canopy.

For a long moment, I let the silence hang between us. Let his words settle in the cool air.

"What happened?" I finally asked. "If you don't want to tell me, it's okay."

His gaze flicked down, then back up. An uneasy silence settled between us. I nuzzled against him, accepting his answer. I'd long ago made peace with never having a family. So understood the grief of being forced into the same acceptance.

"My first child," he began, "was lost in childbirth with-" His throat bobbed, as if thinking of it, of forcing himself to relive it, was too painful. "With the mother."

"Oh." My gaze drifted into the void of blackness covering him. "Your wife?" I asked, looking up as he nodded. "I'm sorry."

"The second was lost in the womb," he said, gaze somewhere far off. Moisture glinted in his eyes.

"The mother?"

"She lived. We didn't last."

I raised my hand, gazing at my palm as I envisioned his. Two children he was supposed to have. Two he'd lost.

"I'm sorry," I repeated, simply for lack of anything else to say.

He sighed, growled deep in his throat, and thumbed his eyes before settling back into the cradle of the branches.

"Don't be," he said. "Get some sleep. We need to move early in the morning."

I said nothing as I curled my hand between our chests and let my eyes drift closed. His heartbeat lulled me into a dreamless sleep.

FORTY

W E SPENT THE NEXT morning searching the surrounding forest for signs of the White Army. I wanted to believe we'd left them on the other side of the mountains, but didn't object when Venyx suggested it. We'd barely escaped the mines with our lives. Falling back into danger would have been cruel. When it became clear they were nowhere near, we carried on, following a small creek from the pond, traveling south toward the Plains.

Between being on foot, both of us exhausted and aching, and cautiously picking our way through the forest, travel was slow. At the slightest sound, an odd smell, the hint of motion, Venyx gathered me in his arms and jumped into the trees, hiding us in shadows. Sometimes, we waded through the creek, sploshing through the cold water in intervals before retreating up the embankment to make our tracks harder to find.

The second night, we slept in another tree. Or, rather, tried to sleep. The first night, we'd simply been thankful to be alive. But as night descended again, slumber became elusive. All of my aches and pains played on my nerves, making it difficult to become comfortable.

In the middle of the night, I sat up, trying not to disturb Venyx until I realized he was still awake. His hand fell from his head and he leaned back, blinking away the moisture lining his silvery eyes.

"Are you okay?" I asked, my voice soft.

"Yes," he said as his eyes slid closed.

"Venyx," I warned.

He sighed, a tired, frustrated sound. "I'll be fine in another day."

"You said that last night." Without waiting for a response, I stretched across him, prodding the skin around the wound. The welt was still there, though smaller than the previous night. Still, it was hard, like a stone wedged beneath his scalp. My gaze drifted to his jaw as it worked back and forth, his body tense, as I eased myself into his lap, smoothing his hair.

I ran my fingers through it, combing the locks back, stilling when his hands jumped up, grabbing my wrists. For a moment, we sat in silence, our gazes locked, until he cleared his throat. I sat back.

"Is it taking longer to heal than it should?"

"Slightly." He grumbled, running a hand over his face. "I'll be fine."

Wordlessly, I nodded and laid against him.

Our pace fared no better the next day. We caught a fish from the creek, roasted and ate it before carrying on, slowly leaving behind the chill of the Northerlands with each step until every trace of snow was all but gone.

At the top of a small hill, peering between a cluster of trees, I spied my first glimpse of the vastness of the Plains. Much of it was flat, covered in wispy brown grass as far as I could see. At least from that vantage, anyway.

Staring out at a different country only a handful of miles away, it occurred to me how real it all was. While still in the Northerlands, it hadn't felt as if it were truly happening. I'd spent the last twenty years in a single country, surrounded by snow and exactly three or four people at any given time. But as the miles passed, the days vanishing one by one, that familiarity was stripped away and I was faced with a new reality—everything in my life was about to change. Nothing made that more clear than being perched on the hill, staring out at my future. Or whatever was left of it.

Venyx walked up, picking leaves from a handful of berries in his palm. He popped one in his mouth before holding them out.

"How long will it take to reach Pensen?" I asked. He sighed, tossed another berry in his mouth.

"A few weeks. Maybe a couple months, depending on our pace." He shoved his palm closer. "You should eat."

I took a handful of the offered berries and poured them in my mouth at once, barely tasting them as I turned back to the view.

"Can we rest here for the night?" I asked.

His brows pulled together as his eyes shifted toward the stark line between the Plains and the Northerlands. We'd reach it by nightfall, certainly, and there was plenty of daylight left. But tonight would be my last night in the land that raised me.

Venyx ate the rest of the berries, chewing slowly as he took in our surroundings, his gaze climbing up and down the trees. "If you want to," he finally said. I was thankful he didn't ask why. It felt silly, childish, to want to spend one more night here.

"I would," I said. From the corner of my eyes, he nodded. He didn't say anything, just placed a reassuring hand on my shoulder.

As the sun began its descent, I bathed in the creek, washing myself in cold Northerlands water a final time. After dressing, I returned to the hill and watched the light retreat. The twin moons continued their eternal dance against their inky backdrop filled with glittering gems winking down in an endless parade. When the sky finally finished its ritual, we climbed into a tree, though it was a long time before I slept.

Waiting for sleep to claim me, I tipped my head back, the last vestiges of cool winter air kissing my skin, and gazed into the night sky.

For all I complained about it, for all the trouble it had put me through. For all the loathed isolation. These lands had protected me. The vast, wild borders had sheltered me. The frozen landscape had kept me safe and hidden.

In the Northerlands, I'd fallen in love for the first time. Shared a man's bed for the first time. Learned to hold a sword, and a bow. Had been taught to read and write within its borders. Learned about my heritage. Taken a life for the first time, and saved one. Met my first deymon, I thought, peering at Venyx's sleeping face. I'd also learned it wasn't just me people judged because of what I looked like.

Taking a shuddering, nerve-filled breath, I laid across Venyx's chest and closed my eyes. Exhaustion filled every part of me, and I floated into sleep's embrace like a feather falling from the sky—slowly, and then all at once.

The next morning, we rose with the dawn and climbed carefully to the ground. Standing on the hilltop, I turned and gazed upon the Northerlands one last time before following Venyx forward. By zenith, we'd reached the edge of two lands, where the Great Green fell away to an endless bound of rolling grasses.

I'd never been more grateful as Venyx waited for me to take my final breath of Northerlands air before I stretched one leg across the border and planted my boot in Plains soil.

With that step, I halted. Glancing between my foot and him. Maybe I didn't want to go. Maybe I didn't want to die.

Then my own words came back to haunt me. I had nowhere else to go. No home. Nothing else to turn to. If I didn't go, there was every chance I would be hunted for the rest of my life. Until the moment I died. All roads, it seemed, led to my death. So the only way forward was south.

When I placed my other foot beside the first, I left behind my childhood, my home, everything I'd ever known. And walked to Venyx's side.

We lounged beside the creek, eating roasted fish as the sky shifted into a brilliant collage of colors. I took a breath and peered around. The last time I'd seen so much open land void of snow, I'd been a child.

The tall grasses bent and rolled beneath the slightest breath of wind, like a series of waves shifting sporadically.

"Seraph?"

I whipped around and faced Venyx, realizing he'd been speaking. "What?"

"Siila lays directly south, so we're going to need to go that way," he said, pointing behind me.

"What about the creek? Won't we need water?"

He nodded around a bite of fish. "It looks like it'll travel alongside us for a while. There's a lot of runoff from the mountains."

He reached into his back pocket, pulling out a small bundle. From inside, he removed the book of poetry. I'd forgotten he had it.

"We can use this to carry water," he said, holding up the pouch as he replaced the book in his pocket.

"When should we get going?"

He sighed and licked his lips, then rinsed his hands in the creek. "We can leave tomorrow morning. It's already getting late."

I looked into the sky. The twin moons shone bright, though they were mere slivers.

"Do you think we'll run into the White Army?"

Venyx shrugged. "I don't know. I assume they were told which way we were heading." My stomach dropped at the mention of Miran, of his betrayal. "I haven't felt them since before the mines, but-"

"Your head still hurts," I finished for him. He nodded.

I swallowed my last bite of fish and gazed into the softly flowing creek, shoving my thoughts aside.

A single day in the Plains had already told me one thing—it was far hotter than what I'd grown up in. Even with night settling around us, a prickling of sweat gathered on my brow and at my nape. I wasn't sure how I would sleep in the lingering heat. Cold had always put me to bed. Cold had always been there when I'd woken. At least in the heat, I reasoned, I wouldn't miss not having a blanket.

With that in mind, I pulled off my boots and coat, torn and ruined as it was, and waded into the creek, clothes and all, scrubbing away the dirt and sweat. Dripping, I pulled myself out and laid on the grassy embankment. Venyx stared at me, a grin pulling at his lips.

"What?" I asked.

"Nothing," he said, looking away. "Just an interesting way of cleaning your clothes."

"Have you smelled me lately?"

He chuckled. "I have, yes. You smell awful."

In mock horror, I picked up the nearest thing, my bundled coat, and threw it at him. Venyx, of course, caught it, laughing, and tossed it aside.

"As if you smell any better," I shot.

"I'm aware," he said, his laugh trickling into a chuckle. He laid next to me, both of us gazing into the darkening sky.

Sometime in the night, I woke without realizing I'd fallen asleep. My clothes were dry and stiff. The whistling grass plagued my senses, reminding me where I was. At my feet the creek babbled, along with a myriad of other noises I didn't know what to make of. A subtle chirping very much not a bird.

Trying to force myself back to sleep, I rolled over, facing the other direction, and squeezed my eyes shut. Between the creek, the chirping, and the wind, I couldn't get my mind to shut off, to tune out the surrounding burst of noises. Living in the snow meant almost complete silence. I didn't know how to exist in a world of sound.

Behind me, something shuffled. I flipped over, heart stuttering, to find Venyx sitting closer, nose in his book. It was strange, sleeping by myself, when I'd spent the last few nights curled upon his chest. I wanted to sleep alone, to not have another being against me, if only for the sake of not needing to, and yet I missed the comforting presence of his weight, the heat of his body. I wouldn't say it out loud, though.

Instead, I said, "What poem are you reading this time?"

He looked up, silver eyes glinting in the dark, and moved closer, laying the book on the ground, his fingers holding the pages open. "You ready for another lesson?"

I smiled despite myself and nodded.

He grabbed a long blade of grass, snapping it down until it was short, sturdy in his large hands, and pointed at the letters. One by one, he went down the page, tracing and stating each character and its common tongue equivalent until we reached the bottom. He tapped the first word, tracing each one again. Biting back my smile, I recited it, traveling down the page as I stumbled over the words.

The inn felt like a lifetime ago, though no more than a couple weeks had to have passed. Still, the letters he'd already taught me were difficult to grasp. But I read them.

Once the poem was finished, we started again, each subsequent pass easier than the last, my memory finding what I'd already learned. Between reads, I found myself giggling, a childish smile stretched across my face before I dove back in.

After I was done reading the poem a final time, I asked, "Can we read another one?"

Venyx chuckled. "I think maybe that's enough for tonight. You should get some more sleep."

Still smiling, I settled back down and gazed at him as he picked up the book and let it fall closed.

"Thank you," I said, cradling my head on my hands.

He smiled, one fang digging into his bottom lip. "You're welcome."

By mid-morning the next day, I had removed my coat and outer shirt, tying them around my waist. My brow was already slick with sweat. How Venyx could carry on in his heavy cloak, I had no idea, but just the thought made me hotter.

The first day was hot enough the idea of food barely crossed my mind. Not that I spotted anything edible as we went.

Traveling through the open Plains meant the sun beat directly on our faces. Being unused to so much harsh sunlight, I found myself wearing out quickly, needing several breaks. By zenith, I was dripping sweat, my freshly washed clothes soaked in it. It made my skin sticky and slick, a wholly unfamiliar experience. When I said as much, Venyx laughed, telling me it was something I'd have to get used to. Pensen would be even hotter.

As our first whole day in the Plains drew to a close, Venyx found a rabbit to cook. When we stopped for the night, we found the creek had followed us, wending through the grassy Plains to refill our water skin. I took no time diving into the coolness, rinsing the sweat from my skin and clothes.

While Venyx skinned and cleaned the game he'd caught, I stripped off my wet things and laid them carefully on the embankment, washing all the parts of myself I'd been unable to while clothed. Afterward, I swam back and forth across the narrow creek, enjoying the water on my heated flesh. Once I was cooled, I pulled myself from the stream and hurriedly dressed.

Already, the smell of meat made my stomach grumble and groan, reminding me I hadn't eaten in over a day. A small portion was cut into thin strips, set aside for jerky. I slowly nibbled the rest, savoring warm food in my belly.

Behind me, Venyx splashed through the creek. I fought the urge to turn, to catch a glimpse of him. He'd been more than respectful of me, I told myself, and went back to my food.

After dinner, once the fire had been doused, I laid down to sleep, but found it just as difficult as the previous night. For a long while, I tossed and turned, unable to find comfort against the bed of grasses beneath me.

Once again, Venyx shifted closer and pulled out the book. Though we worked on a different poem, it proved easier as the language became familiar. As before, he patiently traced each letter before stating its common equivalent. Throughout our lesson, I found myself stealing glances at him, smiling despite myself as I read and reread the poem until it came as naturally as the common tongue. When I became so exhausted the words blurred together, my eyes so heavy they could scarcely stay open, Venyx closed the book and settled beside me.

FORTY-ONE

A FTER THE FIRST COUPLE nights, the days began blurring together. We walked just as color kissed the sky until the final lingering moments of sunlight. Nights were spent resting beneath an endless canopy of stars dancing around the moons.

The creek came and went, seeming to wave playfully at us every so often. Sometimes it winked at us in the distance. Other times it flowed beside us, offering a cooling comfort along with refilling our waterskin.

Unwilling to acclimate to the heat, my body refused to give me adequate sleep, and so my elvish lessons continued, not that I minded. The language came far easier with so much repetition, though I was sure it was also due to Venyx being such a skilled tutor. Thinking back to when I'd first met him, I couldn't imagine him being so patient, or so kind.

There was still no sign of the White Army. I thought it would have made our journey easier, but all it did was make me nervous. Clearly we'd lost them in the mountains, though I doubted they had remained behind looking for us. It was far more logical they lay somewhere ahead, ready to spring on us the instant they were able.

Venyx improved greatly as the mine fell further behind, the lump on his head gone after only a few days. Still, he couldn't sense the White Army. He agreed—they were somewhere ahead of us, lying in wait.

With nothing else to do as the miles passed, we talked. His swords, it turned out, were older than the war, having been crafted in the elven land of Denpendae nearly five hundred years before I'd been born. He didn't say it, but the soft smile curling his mouth told me they'd either been gifted to him, or made for him, by his wife—the one who'd died in childbirth.

Though he'd been raised in the Lost Forest, after maturing at three thousand years old, he'd left. Searching for his place in the world. It was through Aurorian he'd taken up as a sword for hire. Protecting lords and diplomats. Kings and queens. Royalty and nobility of all sorts. When the topic arose of how he'd ended up at Ace's, he went stiff. And the conversation died.

As we stopped for the night, once again finding the creek, I gazed at him over the flames of our tiny fire. Ten thousand years seemed impossible to comprehend, and yet there he sat. Appearing a meager ten years older.

"Staring is rude, remember?" he said, gaze flicking up. A grin bit into his features, that one fang poking out.

"Do the handles on your swords wear out?" I asked. He chuckled, prodding the flames with one of the blades.

"Yes, the leather and wood degrade," he said. "Last I was in Denpendae, the hilts were replaced and rewrapped. The sheaths, too." I glanced at the holster beside him.

"Why is it upside down?"

His eyes snapped up, smile returning. "So full of questions."

I shrugged, grinning.

He sighed, settling against the grass. "People have many assumptions about me and my kind as it is. To most, we are nothing but living weapons. So I keep mine hidden, to put their minds more at ease." He ran a hand through his hair. "It also gives me an advantage in a fight. My opponent will often make the mistake of thinking I'm without a weapon aside from these." He held up his hands, his claws protruding from his fingertips before retracting.

"Does it hurt?"

He shrugged, shook his head. "No. Though it was strange when I was first learning to use them." Venyx glanced up. "What about you? You know nearly my entire life story."

I scoffed, one brow ticking up. "I severely doubt that."

He smiled, showing his fangs. "How long have you been in Aurorian's care?"

"I was five when I was taken," I said. "So, twenty years. She won't tell me why or how we ended up in the Northerlands, only that it was the safest place for me."

Venyx nodded. "That sounds like Aurorian." He sighed. "And the spies?"

"What about them?" I snapped, immediately recoiling at my defensive tone.

He glanced up beneath his lashes, and I swallowed thickly. "How long have you been in their care?"

I looked into the flames, mulling over my thoughts before answering. "The same time. Aurorian brokered some kind of deal with the Amasian king, though I don't know the details."

"Twenty years is a long time to be cut off from the world," he said. I glanced up, meeting his eyes.

"You're ten thousand years old. What's twenty years?"

He sighed, dropping his gaze to the flames. "I know from experience. Even for one as old as me, twenty years is a long time to be alone."

I forced a smile. "I wasn't, though."

"There's more than one type of lonesome."

I turned to Venyx as we trudged alongside the creek, keeping it on our right as the day's heat intensified. "Have you ever been to Pensen?" I asked.

He turned, one brow raised, and sighed, his pace slowing. A flicker of pain flashed across his features before his eyes slid shut and he breathed in the warmth surrounding us. "Only a couple times," he said after a moment. His eyes opened again, meeting mine. "The last time..." He sucked his bottom lip before exhaling sharply. "Wasn't on good terms."

"What happened?"

"Curious today, are we?" He flicked another glance at me, a hint of a smile tugging at his mouth. That same stupid fang poking out, taunting me as always.

I shrugged as I walked, content with the murmur of the creek, the crunch of our footsteps over dried grass.

His shoulders rose and fell with a heavy breath, his head tipping forward. Black locks fell across his face, blocking him from view. "It's something I've tried very hard to forget," he muttered, voice strained, as if withholding a cascade of emotion. He tucked his hair behind his ear, his expression the most vulnerable since I'd read his palm.

"That's why you were in the Northerlands." It wasn't a question, but he nodded anyway. "It wasn't willing, was it?"

"No." And he offered nothing else.

I didn't press him.

"Do you remember where you come from?" he asked, trudging along.

I sighed, pulling on those distant memories, most of which existed only in my dreams. The obscured, twisted remembrances of a child. Each one tainted, stained in blood.

"I remember the ocean," I told him. His gaze bore into the side of my face. "Not well. Mostly from my dreams. But I remember playing in the surf. The white sand. The water was warm. I haven't been to the ocean since I was a child. It ... pulls on me, like a part of me is missing."

I turned, those pits of velvety brown staring at me, through me, into my soul. "I'm all too familiar with that feeling," he mumbled, facing the grass sprawled before us.

"I remember the woman who raised me," I continued. "Before Aurorian. Only bits and pieces. She was kind. And so beautiful." I smiled at the memory, or the fragment of memory. "Briahna." With the utterance of her name came my last memory of her. "She died protecting me." The first life, after my mother, stolen because of me.

My throat swelled, tears stinging the backs of my eyes.

"I understand that, also," he grumbled. With a deep breath, he stopped, stretching into the air, hands falling behind his head before he ambled on at my side.

The story he'd told, of his mother fleeing the Fall, popped into my head.

"Do you remember her?" I asked. He glanced at me. "Your mother."

"I do." He swallowed thickly. "My kind have ... very good memories. We remember many things. Some things we have no business remembering." He drew a breath through his nose, and the silence stretched between us. Until he spoke again. "I recall the last days of her life. The last day in our home ... before the Fall." A strange calm wafted off him. "She would come to my nursery and take me from my bassinet. Carry me to the rocking chair and rock until I fell asleep. I would drift off to her singing."

Jealousy stung my gut at the longing to remember my own mother. Shoving it aside, I asked, "What was it? The song she sang?"

His next breath shuddered; his eyes sparkled as they filled with tears.

"You don't have to if it's too painful," I amended.

Without responding, he stilled, a smile curling his mouth. He blinked, soft and slow, and gazed up at the curls of light sliding across the sky as the sun sank.

And he began to sing.

It was a tongue I'd never heard, soft and clipped, yet lilting and poetic all at once, bringing tears to my eyes. The melody was slow—a lullaby. I didn't need to understand the words to recognize it.

And Venyx's voice was ... surprising. Deep, melodic. Soft.

I found myself drowning in his voice, the tune lingering long after silence again settled between us. Images of Briahna, the few, fleeting remnants, whispered through my head with the echo of his lullaby. A tear rolled down my face, and I let it fall.

Days passed in a sweltering haze. It became so hot, my sole focus was putting one foot before the other. And so when the creek came into view as the sun began its descent, I said nothing as I pulled off my boots and waded into the waters, submerging myself in its cool embrace. Beneath the surface, I sucked down my fill until my belly was full, lingering until a chill set into my flesh and all the sweat was gone. For a moment, at least.

As I surfaced, there came a great splash and my hands jumped up to shield myself. When I was able to see, I glimpsed Venyx shoving his hair back, a smile on his face.

"No splashing," I grimaced, flicking water at him. He chuckled and splashed again. Mouth screwed up, I cupped my palms and threw a handful at him. To which he jumped forward, sending a cascade into me, knocking me backward. With a shrieking laugh, I jumped up and splashed again.

Like children, we laughed and screamed, tossing handfuls back and forth. Lost in the moment, I jumped on him, sending us both beneath the babbling waves. Venyx popped up, gasping, eyes and mouth gaping.

"*You* can breathe underwater!" he spat, a smile splitting his face. Biting my lower lip, I turned and made for the shore, a laugh bursting from me as he waded after me. One arm lashed around me, pulling me to him. I fell into his chest, wrapping my arms around his neck as he encircled my waist.

Biting back my smile, I gazed up at him. How the sunlight turned his brown eyes molten gold. He reached up, brushing my soaked locks behind my ears, his touch gentle. In return, I swiped the hair from his forehead and back over his shoulders.

His arms wrapped around my shoulders, pulling me closer. I sank into his embrace, my ear against his chest. Listening to the thrum of his heart.

"I think it's too hot for a fire tonight," he whispered into my hair. I nodded my agreement.

After a while, we pulled ourselves from the water and laid out on the grass. With a sigh, far deeper than intended, I watched as the sun painted the sky a vibrant collage of colors, the light kissing the world good night. Already a few stars were visible on the eastern horizon, the above treasure trove winking amidst the twin moons the darker it grew.

Though it never cooled, even after our romp in the creek, the warmth from his body washed over me in a comforting wave, reminding me of his presence.

"Do you know anything about the constellations?" Venyx asked. I turned to face him, taking in his profile, the glimmer of silver in his eyes. And faced up again.

"I know a bit about navigating with them," I confessed, "but nothing else. The skies were never clear enough in the Northerlands to actually look."

He made a sound, shifting closer so our shoulders brushed, and raised his hand to the heavens.

"That one," he said, tracing some invisible shape in the stars, "is Brofon."

Smiling, I turned to him as a grin pulled at his lips, displaying the tips of his fangs.

"You're not even looking."

I chuckled. And followed his hand to the sky. He outlined it again.

"I don't see it."

Nudging closer, our heads touching, he took my hand and traced the constellation, going over it again and again until the vaguest shape of a dragon emerged.

"Brofon," he said, and let our entwined hands fall, separating between us.

"The first dragon," I muttered. He nodded against me, the back of his hand warm against mine. The tiny hairs on his forearm tickled my wrist.

"The first mortal," he breathed. "He was so beloved that, once he died, the gods plucked his soul from his body and placed him in the heavens, so he might always be near them."

I smiled. His hand shifted against me, the heat of his skin seeping into my bones. My cheeks burned, though I made no move to pull away. Instead, I nudged closer, something like butterfly wings flapping in my stomach when he moved his fingers to brush mine. Goosebumps rose up my arm, spreading through me at the contact.

"And that one," he said excitedly, tracing another, "is Evelya. The greatest Abaddonian swordsmith. Her swords were works of art, able to slice the air itself."

"You made that up," I said, chuckling. Venyx turned to face me, a grin splitting his face.

"I didn't, I swear." He turned back to the constellation. "Her work was so famed, the gods wanted her for themselves."

I leaned my head closer to him. He returned the touch.

"And ... that one," he said, tracing another, "is the god, Tabeto. So beloved by mortals, it angered the other gods, and so they trapped him in the sky."

"Is that why the Amasians say the gods abandoned us?" I whispered, as if afraid we were being overheard.

"Who knows," he answered.

"Are there any others you know?" I asked, turning to face him. He met my gaze, eyes glittering in the night.

"Many others."

In that moment, his face bathed in silvery light from the stars and the moons, he was the most beautiful being I'd ever seen. And all I wanted was for this peace between us to stay. To never leave this field.

PART THREE

❄

OF THE FOUND

FOUR CENTURIES BEFORE

THEIR WORDS HUNG LIKE ice in the air, biting her skin, making the room colder. And yet, there he slept. Remnants of flesh lingered about his form, while the swirling vortex of his true self returned, bit by bit, as the heat from her body, her touch, left him.

Despite the cold, she'd opened the balcony doors. Let the winter breeze slice along her heated flesh, raising her nipples against her soft lace gown.

Golden sunlight rose on the horizon, and Faei knew today he would leave.

She did not know if he would come back. Not this time.

Tears prickled her eyes at the thought—that he wouldn't return. She wasn't sure she wanted him to. And yet, she didn't want him to leave. The previous night, that very argument had spiraled into love making so intense, it rivaled the heat of Summer.

The Faerie Queen padded across the chilled wooden floor to the bed. To where Wynnix lay. In this fleeting form, long white hair flowed across his pale back, mimicking the snowy tendrils of his true self. His long legs and arms were slung across the bed, wrapped in silk sheets. His delicate face, all sharp, chiseled edges, like ice, was relaxed. She longed to see those sleet blue eyes one last time.

She wanted him to stay, to forgo his ancient duties, to curse the world so intent upon keeping them apart. Tears tore through her eyes, the swirling frigid air turning the droplets into miniscule glaciers cutting along her cheeks.

Her hands trembled as she called forth her fae magic, balling it between her palms. Jade, like her eyes. Hot and searing against her skin. The glowing light warmed some inner part of her; she didn't have to choose between him and her people, her duties. Not with the power she held.

Yes, he would be angry at first, but he would come to see.

She would go before the World Council, and they would grant her wish, let her rule from afar. Let her be with him, always. And there would be no more arguments. No more tears. No more sleepless nights wondering if, next year, he would not return.

She plucked a long strand of white hair from his head, just as the ends faded back into ice and snow, dropped it in the glowing ball, let the magic absorb it, and shoved the glimmering jade into her chest, into her heart.

He would understand. One day. And he would love her again.

Wynnix took a deep breath in his still-mortal lungs and raised himself on his arms, gazing at her. And there they were—those beautiful sleet eyes. The blue so pale, so pure, they appeared almost white.

"Faei," he said, voice still sleep-addled. "What are you doing?"

"Nothing, my love," she said and lay back down, shedding the lace gown. She touched his cheek, reigniting his corporeal form. Delaying the inevitable. The moment he discovered what she'd done. "I wanted to look upon you."

He sighed, pulled her closer, and pressed his lips against hers, his skin warm, whole. She ran a hand through his hair, her feet along his legs, eliciting the Spritely magic once again, as Wynnix rose and shifted, lowering himself between her waiting thighs.

"I'm sorry, my love," he whispered into her ear, trailing those words in his kisses along her cheek and back to her lips. "I don't want to argue. I just want to be here, with you."

"I know," she sighed against him. "I'm sorry, too. For everything."

He nuzzled her cheek. "All is forgiven," he said, taking her hands.

Faei tipped her head back, moaning as he entered her. He was slow, passionate, unlike the violent, raging winds that drove into her the night before. They took their time, savoring each other. Driving each other over the precipice of pleasure again and again. And with each subsequent wave, his words throbbed in Faei's head.

He forgave her.

And so he would.

One day.

FORTY-TWO

I WOKE TO SEVERAL voices. At first, I thought I'd become stuck in a dream—that strange limbo between wakefulness and sleep. Upon listening, it became impossible to believe because, thus far, all the characters in my dreams used the common tongue, and the language being spoken was anything but.

My eyes drifted open, settling on a back swathed in black, his hair playing in the breeze shifting through the grasses around us. Sitting just beyond him was a circle of men, their gazes straying from my guardian to me. Their faces, of course, were filled with awe. I started, jolting up all at once.

Venyx turned, gesturing me forward. "Good morning," he said as I settled beside him. I grumbled it back, leaning into him as the bouquet of eyes grazed over me. His presence was comforting before so many men I didn't know. I forced back the memories of my last encounter with a group of strange men as Venyx continued speaking in the same tongue I'd woken to.

"Child of Sky and Sea," one of them said. He bowed his head, dark eyes glancing down. He was easily one of the largest men I'd ever seen, larger even than those around him. One side of his skull was shaved to the scalp, the other dripping with silky black locks to his chest. Every inch of him was pure muscle, his body radiating power. "I am Mato," he said, his gaze meeting mine. "We have been sent by Queen Geaith to escort you to Siila. You and your guardian. We were expecting more of you."

I nodded, keeping Venyx in my peripheral as I looked over each of them. There were six, all of them warriors—in their stature, in their build. In the expressions they wore, the weapons strapped to their bodies. They donned fighting leathers, their corded arms left exposed.

"It's Seraph. Please," I said in return.

I don't think Aurorian warned them of the change of plans, Venyx whispered in my head. I forced a smile, unsure what to say.

One by one, Mato went around the circle of men and introduced them.

Each spoke the common tongue, albeit in varying degrees. Two of them, Calian and Nuka, approached me eagerly as we rose. Aside from Mato, they spoke the common tongue most fluently. Calian appeared a few years younger than me; Nuka about my age.

They strode beside me, flanking me, as they guided us to the group of horses drinking from the nearby creek. I eyed them warily, shrinking between them as much as possible.

"Did the gods give you your hair color?" Calian asked, fingering a strand as he turned, walking backward through the grass. Hot blush spread across my cheeks as his dark eyes feasted on me. With a tight smile, I pulled the lock away. He ran a hand through his thick, black hair, shoving it away from his face, flexing the rigid muscles in his bicep.

Nuka skipped forward and shoved the younger man aside, spitting something in their tongue.

"My mother gave it to me," I mumbled, pulling my hair over my shoulders, winding it between my hands.

"Calian," Mato called. He walked at the forefront of the group, alongside Venyx. "Leave the Child alone. She is not for you."

"Nuka," one of the others, Kishil, said. Nuka hung his head, his long black hair hanging over his face as he slumped to the older man. Kishil wrapped an arm around Nuka, hugging him to his side, muttering something.

Calian fell back in step beside me, smirking.

Once we reached the horses, the others swung gracefully into their saddles, making mounting more of an artform than a simple action.

"We brought an extra horse for you and the Child," Mato said, gaze fixed on Venyx. "We didn't know if you would have your own or not."

"We were expecting the unicorn," another of the men, Makya, said from atop his mount. "The queen will be curious." His horse stamped back and forth, clearly eager to start moving.

I glanced at Venyx, unsure what to say, what to tell them. What I was allowed to.

"That she will be," Mato agreed from his saddle.

"Business *Seraph* and I will happily explain to your queen once we reach Siila," Venyx said. Mato nodded and shouted something at his men. My gaze wandered between them, unable to miss the wink Calian sent me.

Venyx stepped between me and the Plainsman. "Will you be comfortable riding in the same saddle?"

I shrugged, whispering, "I'm not sure what choice we have."

"That's not what I asked," he grumbled, stepping closer. The Plainsmen gathered together, muttering in their tongue.

"Yes," I finally said. I'd already ridden with him. Wearing nothing but his cloak, no less. Had used his body as a makeshift bed more than once. A week or so sharing a saddle would be fine, I told myself. He nodded and gestured for me to mount up.

I climbed into the saddle, forcing my legs to cooperate, and braced myself as Venyx swung up. Any lingering blush from Calian's flirtations was reawakened as Venyx nestled behind me. I tried to ignore the looks of the younger Plainsmen as Venyx draped his arms to either side, taking our horse's reins.

"We ride until dusk," Mato said. "The quicker, the better."

"That's fine," Venyx said. "We've moved at the same pace."

The Plainsman nodded and snapped his reins, spurring his mount forward.

The six of them rode in an irregular circle around us with Mato directly ahead. As we went, I often found Calian and Nuka tossing glances at me, though the younger of the two was more aggressive with his gazes.

They spoke little as we rode. Occasionally, Mato shouted an order in their tongue, the men quickly responding. They kept their weapons within reach, always on guard. As if expecting an attack at any moment.

Do you trust them? I thought, unsure if Venyx was listening. He shifted against me. I tossed a glance over my shoulder as his eyes grazed the surrounding men.

I make a point of never trusting anyone, his mind grumbled in response. *Like any other nation, the Plains people will have their own agenda. Their own reasons for wanting you.*

What did Aurorian tell you? I asked.

He sighed, the heavy breath ruffling my hair. *Only that she brokered some kind of deal with Amasius allowing us passage through the Plains.*

Will that be affected by her not being here? Anxiety stung my gut at the thought. She'd said nothing of the sort, had given no indication her presence would be required, though I supposed I should have expected it. I knew little of Aurorian's dealings, of her relationships with other countries around the world. I did know she was important. Royals of every nation treated her as such. It made me wonder what she'd promised them in return.

I don't know. Venyx's voice rang loud in my head. *I suspect they would want some kind of credit for turning you over to Pensen.*

What would that mean, though? Would I no longer be under Amasius' protection? Would the Amasian diplomat take me instead? The more I thought of it, the less I realized I knew. Yes, Aurorian had taught me politics, the dealings and goings-on of the world. She'd taught me the royal sigils, the royal houses. What the World Council was—a member

369

of each royal court across the known world acting as representative for their nation.

Aurorian had told me nothing of the deal brokered for my protection. Or what would happen once I was in Pensen, aside from … aside from my fate. Maybe the rest didn't matter. In that moment, though, traveling with warriors surrounding us, armed to the teeth, leading us to their queen for permission to cross her lands, I felt ill-equipped. And it was becoming more obvious how little she'd told Venyx.

As Mato promised, we broke for camp at dusk. The creek was nowhere in sight, but the horses each carried several water bladders in their saddle bags, along with sacks of dried meats and berries. Still, Nuka and Kishil wandered off hunting.

"Make quick of it!" Calian shouted after them. "I'm hungry." He winked at me.

With a sigh, Venyx stepped in front of me, drawing his swords. He spun them over his hands, then under, before flipping one flush against his arm, handing it to me, grip-first. Calian's face dropped, his throat bobbing before the Plains warrior wandered to the firepit.

"What's this for?" I asked.

"For fighting," he said flatly.

"Very funny." I took the offered weapon, wrapping my hand around the leather gripping. I swung it a few times, testing the balance. Somehow, it had been lighter in the mines. Maybe it had been my adrenaline.

"We're gonna start training," he said, stepping further away from camp.

My brows flicked together, eyes grazing over the Plains warriors as they glanced up, attention piqued.

"I know how to fight," I said, turning to face him.

"You know how to not die," he retorted. "I've seen you fight. I'm not sure what Aurorian taught you all those years, but it wasn't proper swordplay."

He flipped and spun the sword a few more times, stepping backward as he did. To create more space, I was sure. Not to show off to the Plainsmen whose gazes burned into my back.

With his free hand, he waved me forward. I obeyed, standing before him, sword limp at my side. Our first encounter flashed through my mind, the pain a single, softened, blow had caused, and I winced. ·

It's just training, his voice, soft and caressing, whispered in my head. "Tonight we'll focus on stance."

"My stance is fine," I grumbled.

He nodded, flipped his blade so the flat lay across his shoulders, and gripped it at both ends like a staff. He then prowled around me. His gaze became a physical touch as he assessed every part of me. I wasn't sure I'd ever felt so vulnerable before him, not even when we'd been curled up on the inn floor, me dressed in nothing but water and tears.

Why don't we work on keeping that guard up? his voice whispered.

You *insisted I drop it in the first place, remember?*

His chuckle floated in my mind as he stopped in front of me, dropping the sword, tip first, into the ground. His hands rested on the pommel, one atop the other.

"Yes, well, if I can access your mind so easily, others will be able to. Unless you learn to recognize friendly and unfriendly presences, and can choose who you let in." He gave no time to respond before the blade jumped out, swatting my left ankle.

"Ow! Dick!" My foot jumped up, and I shook out the sting.

He smiled, one fang pressing into his lip. "Widen your stance. Bring that foot forward. Makes it harder to knock you on your ass."

With a sigh already laced with frustration, I did as he said, planting my left foot forward.

He made another round, eyes sweeping across me. "Back straighter," he said, tapping my shoulder blades with the back of his hand. "Shoulders back, relaxed. They need to move on a moment's notice. If one shoulder is tensed, you reveal which direction you'll move. Same with your legs." He tapped my thigh with the sword. "Relax."

"It's hard to relax when you keep hitting me," I snapped, looking to the ground.

Again, he stood before me, grinning, that stupid fang pressing down. He wet his lips, ran a hand through his hair, and stepped closer. Then closer still. I stared up at him, heart pounding. Aware of how close his hands were to my stomach where they rest atop his sword.

"The best way for me to protect you is to teach you to protect yourself," he said. "So do as I say. Understand?"

I swallowed hard and nodded once. "Yes."

"Good." He stepped back. "Now that nothing is actively trying to kill us, this is the best time."

I sucked on my bottom lip and dropped my gaze to my feet, focusing on the sword I held. Then peered up at Venyx through my lashes; he seemed so casual, so calm. The sword in his hand the least deadly it had ever been, and yet there was nothing more lethal.

He waved me forward. "Attack me."

"You said we're working on stance," I countered.

"We are. I want to see how you attack, if you have any tells we need to work on." He waved me forward again.

With a sigh, trying to ignore the attention behind me, I charged, my arm as relaxed as possible until just before I struck. Venyx danced to the side, tapped his blade against my ribs, and I slumped at once.

"Raising your sword above your head is an excellent way to die quickly," he mocked. "It's a wonder you've lasted this long."

"Go fuck yourself," I mumbled. Behind me, he chuckled.

"I can hear you," he said. I spun around and swung my sword at his relaxed stance. He flicked my blade away, effectively disarming me before nodding toward the discarded weapon. I trudged through the grasses, plucked it up, and shuffled back. Already tired, hot.

Nuka and Kishil walked back to camp, several rabbits in hand. Though their words were inaudible as they approached the others, a delighted glee glimmered in Nuka's eyes as he and Kishil glanced over.

"Forget them," Venyx said, pulling my attention back. "You and me. That's it. That's all that exists."

I took a deep breath.

Well after the sun sank into the grassy horizon, until the writhing flames alone illuminated us, we trained. Or rather, Venyx danced around me, disarming me at every turn. I was certain I would be covered in welts and bruises the next day, from all his *corrections*.

Sweat stuck to my brow, slid down my cheeks. Ran in rivulets down my spine and between my breasts. My trousers clung to my legs as if holding me together.

Exhausted and hungry, I plopped to the grasses, the sword dropping before me, and fell backward with a great huff. My chest heaved, heart pounding furiously. I groaned when he came to stand over me.

"We aren't done."

"I am," I huffed. I wiped my brow. He nodded and sank to his haunches beside me, the leather of his boots creaking with the movement.

"We're done when I say we are."

"Venyx," I whined, closing my eyes. "We still have a long way to go. If this is some kind of torture for the last few weeks, can we resume tomorrow? I'm starving and thirsty and tired."

"Fine. Tomorrow."

My eyes slid open as he rose to his full height. My heart danced, skipping several beats, as he reached between my thighs and plucked the sword from where I'd dropped it.

At the sound of voices, I turned. The Plainsmen chatted wildly before Calian stood, a wide smile on his handsome face.

"I would like to-" he stopped, as if thinking of the right word, "spar." He nodded enthusiastically. Poor bastard.

With a groan, I shoved myself up to sit, gawking at the hand Venyx offered me, and felt weightless as he pulled me to my feet.

Venyx's eyes were fixed on the young Plainsman, as if he were a predator sizing up his next meal. "Do you have a sword?"

"Venyx, I don—" I started. He raised a hand. I groaned, my words dying on the hot wind blowing through the grasses.

"I have this," Calian said, drawing the curved blade hanging from his waist. It was long, wide toward the tip, more suited for cleaving skulls than training. Venyx nodded, his face a mask of complete neutrality.

"Venyx," I grumbled, stepping closer to him. His brown eyes flicked to mine. "Please don't kill him."

He only smirked. There was that stupid fang again.

I dragged my feet to the campfire, plopping between the warriors seated there, and plucked a chunk of meat from over the flames. My stomach growled at the sight, at the smell. With the first bite, my eyes rolled back, and it was all I could do to suppress a moan at the warm food passing into my belly.

When my eyes fell open again, Calian was pacing back and forth before Venyx, sizing the deymon up.

"Deymons fight good, yeah?" one of the men, Aluk, asked over the fire.

Over the last several weeks, I'd seen various kinds of fighting from deymons. Sometimes they were truly skilled, making it into an artform, like Venyx. Other times, it was pure carnage. Death personified.

"Not all of them," I finally said. "But him? Yes."

Aluk nodded, the short spikes of black hair running center down his scalp bobbing with the motion.

"Calian is one of our best," Makya said. "He was allowed to come with us because of his skills with a blade."

Mato nodded as he chewed his food.

Great.

Calian was the first to move. His speed was something otherworldly, especially for his height. He rushed across the short distance and swung up. Still, a single flick of Venyx's smaller, shorter blade clanged in the silence and Calian jumped back.

Beside me, the Plainsmen pointed, their hushed voices commentating what was happening, or I assumed, since they spoke in their tongue.

The Plains warrior jumped forward, blade crashing down, but was again blocked. And again.

Venyx, for all the world, looked bored. As if he were merely entertaining the warrior.

"Come on, Calian!" Nuka shouted.

The sniggers from the Plainsmen, mostly Nuka and Aluk, grew, as the men watched. Mato and Kishil sat with bowed heads, pointing, talking excitedly. Their excitement only grew with every move Venyx made, as if they were carefully assessing him. He was an outsider. A ten-thousand-year-old deymon warrior. How could they not find him fascinating?

The Plainsmen hooped and hollered, laughing uproariously, when Venyx jumped, far higher than the Plainsmen had, and arched his sword through the air. Calian rolled out of the way as the blade sank greedily into the hardened ground.

"I think he pissed himself," Kishil said, a thin smile lighting his ethereally handsome face. The men around him roared with laughter.

"Be grateful he's not *trying* to kill you!" Nuka shouted into his cupped hands.

Makya and Aluk both nearly fell forward from laughter.

Venyx ripped his blade from the earth and stalked to where Calian lay flat on his ass, chest heaving as he stared up at the approaching deymon. But took Venyx's offered hand, allowing himself to be hoisted up, and they walked to the bonfire.

"I don't want to spar with you anymore," Calian groused, flicking a sour look toward Venyx as the deymon lowered himself beside me. I didn't bother biting back my smile, glancing between him and Venyx.

Aluk smiled at the youngest warrior and slapped him on the back. "Now we all know not to fight him. Thank you."

And the Plainsmen burst into laughter. Mato handed Venyx the last of the rabbit, his face softening. "Perhaps one day I will be brave enough to spar with you."

Venyx smiled around the water skin he drank from, baring all eight fangs.

"How did you become so skilled with a blade?" the older Plainsman asked.

Venyx shrugged. "Time. One of the few things I've had in abundance. Being raised by unicorns helped."

Several of the Plainsmen's faces fell open in awe.

"You were raised by unicorns?" Nuka asked. "Are they as beautiful as is said?"

"They are very beautiful, yes," Venyx answered before biting into his food.

"They are warriors, yes?" Aluk asked.

"Yes," Venyx said. "The most powerful warriors in the world."

"Then why not they kill the Faerie Queen?" Aluk asked.

The Plains warriors turned to Venyx. So did I. A question I'd been asking myself a very long time.

Venyx shrugged. "Their reasonings are their own. I can't speak for them." He sighed and took another bite. "I was only raised by them."

Mato nodded, accepting his response. Aluk seemed less convinced, but said nothing else.

"And what of the Child?" Calian asked.

"What about her?" Venyx asked, tensing.

"How did you come to protect her?"

"Why should an angel need such a fierce guardian?" Makya added.

I looked to Venyx, unsure what to say, how to respond. He took a breath, swallowed his bite, and threw the bone into the flames, the remaining fat snapping and crackling.

"We have a mutual friend," Venyx said. "She asked me to watch over her, take her to Pensen on her behalf."

"The unicorn." Mato's voice was hard. It was a statement, not a question, as he sat up straighter, his bulk appearing larger.

"Yes."

"Have any of you met Aurorian?" I asked.

Several of them laughed, shaking their heads.

"She has been to Siila several times to visit the queen," Mato offered, "but no. None of us have met her."

"How recently?" I asked.

Venyx's gaze bore into me for a flicker of a moment before he turned to Mato. The Plains warrior shifted.

"Enough time has passed she does not know Aurorian is not escorting you," Mato explained. "Unless she came after we departed Siila."

Somehow I doubted she would have, but said nothing. I hadn't been instructed to not tell the Plainsmen about her dealings, but I knew the power of information. She was in Amasius. Or said she would be. Warning them of a possible coup in Dracon. That wasn't information I needed to hand to the Plains.

"We should get some sleep," Mato said. "We will begin with the sun. There is a bedroll on the saddle." He pointed to our horse.

Venyx rose to fetch it while I stayed behind, watching the flurry of activity as the Plainsmen made up their own beds.

I knew Venyx would give me the bedroll without having to ask, so it came as no surprise when he laid in the grass alongside it, using his cloak as a pillow. I curled up on the roll beside him, knowing sleep would be a long way off, and gazed up at the millions upon millions of stars stretching in every direction overhead. I wasn't sure I would ever get used to that sight.

Long after the soft breaths of the Plainsmen rang around us, I turned to Venyx, still awake, and found him lying back, book stretched out above him.

"Which one tonight?" I asked.

He turned to me, lowering the book to his chest. Silver flickered in his eyes. He rolled over, placed the book between us, and we picked up where we'd left off, going over another poem until sleep pulled at my eyelids. Until I could no longer keep my head aloft, and every part of me screamed for rest.

Finally, I fell back on the bedroll and succumbed to the crushing waves of my dreams. Relieved when I wasn't greeted by a sea of red, but rather a lilac-haired girl running after a flock of birds in the surf. And the face of a woman I hadn't seen in over twenty years.

FORTY-THREE

AYS SLID UNEVENTFULLY BY as the Plains passed beneath us. To the south, the creek followed our trail, winking and blinking under the pressing heat of the sun's furious golden rays. I asked what season it was, or which it might be, but the Plainsmen didn't know.

"Spring, summer, autumn. There is no difference," Aluk said, cantering alongside me.

"The seasons are tired," Makya said. I glanced back as his horse trotted behind ours. "From centuries of no winter. Each bleed into the other. Soon, it will be only summer. Endless, burning days and nights. Even the Northerlands will melt. They do already."

He pointed back to the creek, to the winding waters cutting through the Plains, toward the mountains separating their land from the Northerlands, and I shivered at the thought. The monsters lurking within those tombs, beneath the rock and snowcaps.

"Word come from the last meet," Aluk said. "The South is little better. Their peoples die in numbers as big as the mountains. From no water, no food."

Guilt stabbed my gut ruthlessly at his words, reminding me of my grim duty. The world would not be righted until my task was done.

I slumped against Venyx as we rode, my core and back stiff from training. Venyx only chuckled, telling me at every turn, every grumble and complaint, that he'd gone easy on me. Calian, he said, had suffered worse. Which did nothing to ease the pain from the welts along my legs and sides and back.

By zenith, a thin film of sticky sweat coated my brow, ran rampant down my spine. Made all the worse by the stifling heat of Venyx behind me. He'd taken off his cloak, the thing slung over our saddlebags. Even still, his shirt clung to him, highlighting the hard lines of his body. Reminding me that, though he kept himself fully covered, every inch of him was chiseled to perfection.

A fact brought more to attention that evening when we finally stopped and I found myself having to peel my eyes from him as he rolled up the sleeves of his black shirt, exposing the length of his corded forearms. I dropped my gaze, forcing myself to look away.

He waved me forward, circling me, tapping whichever part of me was out of alignment, off stance, until I forced my body into compliance. We then went through the paces—me trying, and failing, to attack him while he disarmed me over and over and over again.

"I don't remember Aurorian being this hard on me," I complained, tightening my grip on the sword. Venyx swung his around, then switched hands.

"Aurorian was too soft on you," he said. "She never would have allowed me to fight with such lacking skills."

My frustration growing, I recalled his sparring session with Calian—one of the best swordsmen Siila had to offer—and how the warrior hadn't stood a chance. How bored Venyx had appeared. How relaxed, at ease.

When my legs could barely support me, Venyx took my sword and dismissed me. I trudged along the grass and dropped like a rock before the fire, the heat feeling wonderful against my sore, sweaty body.

"If you keep training like this, you will be able to kill the Faerie Queen alone," Nuka said, laughing around a mouthful of food.

I forced a smile at his joke, though found no humor in it. I didn't know if the Plainsmen knew the grim fate I'd been appointed, and I didn't care. The most powerful people in the world knew, and that seemed to be the only thing that mattered.

Venyx groaned as he eased himself beside me and shoved both hands through his sweat-dampened locks. He dropped his hands between his knees, leaning forward on his elbows, and gazed at me a moment, nudging me with his shoulder. The smile he brought to my lips was genuine, and I nudged back, resting my head on him in pure exhaustion.

The Plainsmen spoke loud, joyously, in their tongue as we sat silently side by side. A few moments was all it took to become curious enough to interrupt, asking what had them so animated.

It was Nuka who said, "Aluk is telling how he almost died from a cat when he went too close to the mountains." His words were barely intelligible over the cackles pouring from him.

"Most of us have heard it," Mato said.

"I haven't," Calian replied.

"He ran up a tree," Nuka said, "until the cat climbed after him, and he jumped into a pile of antelope dung. He stank so bad the cat ran away."

The men burst into uproarious guffaws again, tears welling in their eyes at the tale. Beside me, Venyx barely contained his laughter, the sound deep and velvety and full of genuine joy. My own snickers trembled out of me and I tipped sideways into Venyx, failing to hold myself upright.

"What of you?" Makya asked, nodding toward me and Venyx. "You crossed the great white lands. What tales do you have?"

My giggles died in my throat at the question. Our path across the Northerlands had left a trail of blood in our wake, none of which I wanted to relive, let alone offer up as tribute to the men before us. So much death had followed me from that last safehouse.

So it came as a relief when Venyx answered for us both. "We got trapped by the White Army in the mountains," he said, "and had to take refuge in an abandoned mine."

A thick, writhing hush fell across camp, as if they knew what had awaited us there. What we'd found in our search for refuge. Calian swallowed his bite, bright eyes going wide.

"Did you find the..." Nuka started, then stopped, and tried again. "Were the bloodeaters there?"

"We've heard tales," Mato said after a moment. "Warriors have been sent into the mountains for food. They don't come back."

I sat up straight and turned to Venyx as he fingered the back of his head. Then launched into our tale through the mines. How we'd stumbled upon the remnants of the bunk room. The vampyre nest. How we'd run, and gotten ourselves stuck. The fall.

The men trembled when Venyx described it, smacking his hands together for emphasis. Several looked as if he shouldn't be sitting in front of them. I still barely believed it myself. There'd been so much blood. He then relayed what I'd told him, of my efforts to escape, my decision to stay, to save him. Finally, he told them of our flight from the mines. The blood I'd spilled, painted him with, to keep him alive, and to fend off the vampyres chasing us.

After the tale was over, several moments passed before anyone spoke. It was Aluk who broke the silence, uttering a single word in their tongue, his dark brown eyes shifting to me.

I shook my head. "I don't—"

"It means Death of Death," Mato said. "Long ago, the Undying were revered by our people. Before the Faerie Queen stole them. They would sometimes pass into our lands, theirs so close."

My gaze shifted to Venyx as the warrior spoke, but there was nothing to be seen. No emotions to be noted. He merely sat and listened.

"When Men were still new to this world, and the Undying already ancient, our kind revered them as children of the gods. To save the life of one was said to be a good omen. A gods' blessing," Mato said. The warriors around him nodded, their faces solemn.

Again, I looked to Venyx. He still sat, silent.

"The Amasians say the gods abandoned us," I said, though the words lost their strength as I uttered them, dying on the warm breeze serenading the crackling flames.

The Plainsmen chuckled. Then Aluk said, "It is because Amasians not listen." He pointed to his ears as he spoke, and gestured with splayed hands to the heavens. I gazed up, tipping my head back to take in the vast expanse of endless stars. And felt so very, very small.

Routine was easy to fall into on the road to Siila. I woke, packed my sparse things on our horse, and we rode. And rode. And continued riding until dusk. At which point, we disembarked for the night. Two Plainsmen set off to hunt dinner while the rest set up camp—making the fire, laying out bedrolls.

Venyx and I trained. By the end of the first week, I wasn't nearly as sore. Not so easily exhausted. It became easier to slip out of his grasp, to not be so readily disarmed. Though I still ended up on my back, chest heaving, by the end of each training session. But he no longer remarked on my stance. No longer swatted me with his sword.

His instruction became less vocal, more visual, showing me how to grip the sword. Forcing my blade into an extension of my arm rather than a separate tool. Moving to reduce anticipation of my direction, to dance through each move. And it was very much a dance. A dance of blades, of death.

I held onto Nuka's words to Calian—I was grateful he wasn't *trying* to kill me. Only instruct. Instruction that, I had no doubt, would someday pay off in ways I would never imagine. If I lived long enough.

A thought I constantly shoved from my mind.

Every day closer to Siila was another closer to Pensen. To the day of my judgement. When I would be shipped off to Kaival, never to set foot outside those cursed lands again.

I couldn't make myself want to go, regardless of the lives I would be saving. Every glance at Venyx made me wonder if he knew. If Aurorian had told him. Part of me thought perhaps he did, and this was just another job. I was merely a means to an end for whatever sum awaited him at the end of our path. Another part, however, screamed she hadn't told him. That she would have gone to great lengths to ensure he never knew of the grim responsibility she'd placed upon his shoulders.

The reaper of my soul. Unwilling or otherwise.

But as the days slid slowly by, the mountains to the north growing smaller and smaller as we trudged ahead through stifling heat and rolling, brittle grasses, those thoughts of him mingled with others.

Riding before him, I became increasingly aware of every plane of his body. The hard, rigid muscles brushing my arms, my back, and legs, as he guided our mare. The way his throat bobbed when he laughed at things the Plainsmen said or did. How gentle his hands were when he reined in a horse, or fed one of them. Brushed down their glorious, glossy coats. The deep timber of his voice when he gave an instruction, either on the training field or over poetry in the depths of night.

Then there were the moments we spent training. Those last dwindling rays of sunlight slashing through the silky strands of black hair falling just beyond his shoulders, turning them brilliant shades of red and gold. I found my gaze following his hands whenever he ran them through those locks, wondering what they might feel like in my own hair.

As he began our instruction, my gaze, of its own accord, locked onto the shirt clinging to his skin. The small triangle of bare flesh on his chest laid open for the prying eye. The tendons in his arms as he went through the motions of brandishing his sword. The power of his legs with every step, every move.

From the moment I'd met him, I'd known he was beautiful. In the months that followed, I hadn't appreciated it. Now, it seemed, that was all my mind could hold, as if the thoughts of him were a dam, keeping the waters of my death at bay.

"Seraph." His voice cut through the stillness of my thoughts as I lingered on the ghostly image of his stomach, rippling beneath the damp fabric covering him, and met his brown eyes, golden in the light of the dying sun, just as he threw up a leg and kicked.

Before I knew what happened, I found myself flat on my back, staring up at the cloudless sky, at the bright pinks and purples of the last vestiges of day. I groaned, sighed, and relaxed against the grasses. Then tensed as he hovered over me, dropping to his haunches with his elbows on his knees.

"A bit distracted today, are we?" he asked.

I opened my mouth to retort, but could think of nothing aside from his face. How he might look in a different place hanging above me. My cheeks suddenly blared red hot and I sat up, shoving those thoughts as far from my mind as possible.

I had been working on controlling my mental barriers. Testing the walls Aurorian had helped me build as a child. Feeling for friendly minds. I tested them against Venyx as we rode, speaking to him through that link without allowing access to my thoughts.

In that moment, as the image of his face above my own clawed its way to the forefront of my mind, I slapped a heavy hand over the barriers blockading him, making sure it was tight—not a single flickering image of those forbidden thoughts seeping out—and sat up, panting, from exhaustion, frustration, soreness. I rubbed my face, shoved my hands through the damp lengths of my hair, and pushed myself to my feet.

"Are you fine to continue?" he asked as I plucked my sword from where it had landed. I peered at him through my hair as I rose and let my head fall back, sighing.

"Yes." I forced the word out.

It occurred to me that, maybe, my developing fascination for him was simply a way to distract myself from the impending future lingering on the southern horizon. The one on the other side of Siila. But he was far from the only distraction I'd developed.

When in the midst of training, our swords locked together in a mock dance of death, I couldn't think of what awaited me in Siila, or in Pensen. There was no room to consider his body, or how it might feel against mine. There was only each stroke of my sword. The reverberating shudder through my arms with each blow. I was using it as a crutch, and I knew it. Had come to rely upon it over the days, weeks, since passing under the guardianship of the Plainsmen. Though I would never admit it to Venyx.

"Are you sure?" he asked, one brow raised.

Sweat slithered down my cheek, dripping onto my shirt. I wiped it away with the back of my hand, licked my lips, and said, "Yes."

He nodded, and prowled to my right, and I caught myself observing how he moved with each step. He cleared his throat, snapping me back to attention, and my cheeks again went red.

I adjusted my grip on the sword and took my stance.

Venyx crossed the space in a single bound, sword arching toward me in a glinting line of steel. Instinct taking over, I thrust my blade up, barely catching his as it raced down. Even though I knew, felt it in my arms, how much he was holding back, the force of it rushed down my torso and into my legs. I wasn't sure if I would survive a blow under the full force of his strength.

He feinted back, swung up, and I matched him, blow for blow, gritting my teeth at each connection.

I knew he was going easy on me as I strained beneath every strike. My form buckled, my body protesting, but I held my ground. And noticed, from the corner of my eyes, the Plainsmen sitting a bit straighter, their gazes turning toward us.

Eyes on me, he whispered, pulling my attention back. Back to the deymon I was very, very grateful was not trying to kill me.

I groaned beneath another blow, swung my sword up and around, only just deflecting it to step away and catch my breath in time for his weapon to slam into mine again. My back and arms protested, screaming against the abuse.

"Get him!" Calian shouted.

A flicker of movement was all it took. My attention was drawn away, flicking toward the warriors huddled around the fire.

Venyx swung up, loosening my grip on the blade. Instinct took over and I stepped forward. My left hand knocked his blade up while my right shot toward the grip. He smiled, dropped the sword at our feet and snatched both my wrists, twisted me in his arms, and slammed me back into his chest.

My breathing was labored as I sank into him. His heart thundered against my back, his pulse thrumming where he gripped my wrists, holding my hands against my chest.

"Any faster and you might have had me," he whispered, breathless, against my ear.

"Maybe you're just a good teacher," I panted. He chuckled, the movement vibrating into me.

"And you're a good student."

I turned, glanced at him over my shoulder, suddenly aware of his body, pulsing with breath and adrenaline, slick with sweat, pressed against mine. His brown eyes found my blue ones, and stayed there.

For a moment, the world around me faded. Nothing existed save for him. His arms around me. Our heated bodies connected, fueled by sparring.

His smirk faded, hiding the points of his fangs behind his full lips. His hands slackened, thumbs rubbing circles where he held me.

My gaze flicked from his eyes, backlit with silver in the failing daylight, to his mouth, and back. Heat sizzled where I touched him, pooling in the pit of my stomach. Glowing white hot. Tingling throughout my limbs.

His head moved down a fraction of an inch, eyes fluttering closed. Mine drifted shut, head tipping to meet him. His breath wafted across

387

my face, my lips. Someone shouted from the campfire and I tore myself away. The warm breeze filled the gaping space between us as Venyx went to retrieve the sword he'd stripped from my hand.

Chest still heaving, I reached down, picked up his sword, and handed it to him, refusing to meet his gaze.

A ripple of chatter drifted across the warriors in their tongue as I took my spot. Probably for the best. I didn't want to know what they were saying, already knowing what they'd seen. Heat flared in my cheeks at the thought, as the remnants of heat from Venyx's body slowly faded.

When he sat, there was a space between us I didn't bother to fill.

After the others' snores drifted across camp, I rolled over, away from Venyx, closed my eyes, and forced myself to sleep. There were no elven lessons.

My dreams were of that moment. Stretching just a bit longer. I could almost imagine what his kiss felt like. For a moment, I thought his voice whispered in my head before vanishing.

Awkwardness, thick and palpable, followed us in the days afterward. The companionship Venyx and I had developed since peeling ourselves from the mines seemed to have vanished in a single moment and I found myself mourning it. The only friend I'd ever had, regardless of the job he was tasked with.

I wished with everything in me I could turn back time just a few days, a week, and force myself to stop glancing at him. Stop admiring him. Then maybe I'd have my friend back.

If the Plainsmen noticed, they said nothing. They talked and jabbed and chatted amongst themselves, laughing and chuckling as if nothing had changed. Just when it seemed I might lose my mind from it all, the first glimpse of Siila rose into view on the horizon, and my heart skipped a beat.

When we made camp that night, Venyx sat next to me. His warmth pressed against me. I was afraid to meet his eyes. Afraid I might find that same hunger I'd seen in the spies' time and time again.

He nudged my shoulder, prompting me to look up. It wasn't hunger there, but a tipping of his mouth instead, a single fang pressing into his bottom lip. Then that familiar voice, surrounding my mental wall, tapping. Knocking. Asking permission to enter.

I let him in.

I'm sorry, he said. My brows pulled together. *I didn't mean to make you uncomfortable. It won't happen again.*

I'm not sure—

Yes, you do, he retorted, cutting off my thoughts as they formed. Our almost kiss flashed through my head. *I don't want to go into Siila, before the Plains Queen, with tension between us. So I apologize for my behavior.*

For a long moment, I was unable to do anything but stare at him.

I'm sorry, too, I finally said. He said nothing more, just nudged me again. I allowed myself to melt into his side, place my head on his shoulder, and smiled when he leaned against me in turn.

Simply for the sake of being unable to sleep, we continued our elven lessons before I drifted into an uneasy slumber. Dreaming of Siila, standing before the queen, wrapped in chains and dragged to Kaival. When I started awake, I inched closer to Venyx, his warmth, the scent of him, enough to ward the nightmares away.

By midmorning, the buildings of Siila rose before us. They were clay and stone and canvas, a myriad of walls and textures. Nothing like the towering buildings of The City.

As we neared, a mass of people became visible, and my heart thumped like a wild rabbit in my chest. It reminded me of when we'd first entered the marauders' camp months ago, though it seemed a lifetime ago. Somehow, I doubted those gazes would be the innocent awe of the marauders. Mere fascination.

These people knew who I was. What their warriors had gone to fetch. They lived in a land stricken by the Faerie Queen, the curse she subjected the world to. They would know what I'd been brought here for.

I scanned the faces of the warriors trotting alongside us. Mato called out orders and the men formed a line stretching before and behind. I glanced over my shoulder, catching Makya's eye as he fell into position, one corner of his mouth tipping just a bit, offering a small amount of support before he vanished from sight.

Just breathe. Venyx's voice filled my head. His warmth against my back was reassuring. The arms on either side, gently guiding our mount, kept me grounded as the walls of Siila drew closer. And all those faces came into view, every single one of the hundreds gathered, craning for even a small glimpse of me.

I wasn't sure what to expect as the crowd parted for Mato's horse. But the hushed silence, those gazes, all varying shades of blacks and browns, careening toward me, was unnerving. They did not murmur with excitement like the marauders had. Children did not light up at the sight of my hair, reaching out to touch it. It was so quiet the sound of my heartbeat hammering against my chest was surely heard by those gathered.

The whole of Siila seemed to have amassed just to watch me pass through their streets, the main thoroughfare packed. I forced my gaze forward, staring at the solid planes of Kishil's back, the prickling stubble growing along his shaved scalp.

"Child," someone called. My eyes danced over a woman, holding her baby, tears streaming unabashedly down her face. A watery smile stretched across her mouth as she held the squirming bundle in her arms. My own tipped lips were packed with nerves before I forced my gaze forward again.

By the time the crowds finally died, when a building, the largest in Siila, rose before us, its towering clay walls stretching from side to side, I was shaken. Outwardly so. Though I hadn't realized it until Venyx dropped the reins and wrapped his arms around me, drawing me into him.

I closed my eyes at his embrace, breathed in the scent of him—iron and earth—and melted in his warmth. The tremors vanished, but the sting of tears remained.

Mato cleared his throat and I slid my eyes open. Venyx's arms dropped from around me. He dismounted, going to clasp the warrior's arm as I climbed down.

"It's been an honor," Mato said, taking my hand. He delicately kissed my knuckles and bowed his head.

"Will you be escorting us to Pensen?" I asked.

A corner of his mouth curled up and he shrugged. "I do not know. That would be for the queen to decide. We would be honored of the task."

Mato's men waited to the side. When I faced them, to offer a parting wave, they bowed their heads, some donning smiles, before they fell into line behind their leader and left. Leaving me and Venyx before the towering doors of the Siilian palace.

What do you know of politics? Venyx's mind whispered. I glanced up at him as the door opened and a tall woman, black hair swaying down her back, stepped into the rich, golden sunlight.

Her face was placid as she approached and bowed her head. She was dressed in a strange fabric, soft and billowy, the length of her skirts swaying in the warm, gentle breeze.

"If you would follow me," she said, her voice deep and feminine.

Venyx fell into step behind me as we obeyed.

I'm not sure what you mean, I answered. *I've been taught court etiquette. Aurorian equated so much of it to a game, of trying to outmaneuver everyone else.*

Yes, that's the gist of it, he responded. *But when dealing with royalty and nobility, the other person has power over your life. So, while it is a game, it's a dangerous one. The Plains queen will be no different. She will be looking to use you to her advantage. The Amasian diplomat more so.*

I nodded, more to myself, and studied the arching hallways we passed through. A large chamber opened up, bustling with people. They glanced at me, though didn't stop in their duties. Then I remembered, these people had undoubtedly seen Aurorian on multiple occasions. What was a Sirenian before a unicorn?

Another hallway enclosed us, then another chamber before we reached a tall set of double doors, gilded with gold and silver swirls. The mark of the Plains was etched into the wood and clay—a rearing horse. The guards standing sentry barely glanced at either of us as they pulled the doors open and ushered us inside.

Of all the rooms we'd walked through, this was by far the largest.

A dome hung overhead. Open windows carved into the clay ceiling allowed shafts of sunlight to pour through, bathing the room in late morning air. The floor looked like packed earth, though was solid like tiles. Guards, all dressed similarly to Mato and his men, lined the walls, a spear in one hand, the other gripping their swords.

Across from us was a dais, flanked by more guards. Atop it sat a chair, a copper Plains sigil on the wall behind it. On one side stood the woman who had led us here. On the other was a tall, lanky man, blond curls shorn close to the sides, the top combed back. He was dressed in vibrant blues, the Amasian sigil pinned to his breast.

Seated in the chair was a woman. Her back rigid, face placid. Long black locks flowed over her shoulders. Her russet skin spoke of at least a decade more than my twenty-five years. Her clothes similar to those of our escort. A simple copper and gold circlet sat on her forehead.

"Bow," our guide said, "before her majesty, Geaith. Queen of these Plains lands."

FORTY-FOUR

Forcing a smile, I dipped into a curtsy—what Aurorian said was appropriate—and rose, my gaze rising to meet the queen's.

Geaith's eyes tightened around the corners as she took me in, then slid to Venyx, flanking me from a step behind.

Finally, she spoke. "Welcome, Seraph, Child of Sky and Sea, to the Plains." She took a breath, her gaze again sliding past me to my guardian, and asked, "And who might you be?"

Venyx stepped before me. He dropped into a bow I'd never seen, one far more formal than I'd been taught. One knee touched the floor, fist to his chest, before he rose to his full height. "Venyx, of the Lost Forest," he said. "I act on behalf of the Lady Aurorian, escorting the Child in her stead, as she is away on urgent business. She sends her apologies for the change in protocol and deeply regrets having not informed you beforehand."

My brow twitched at his words, the slick elegance he'd spoken with. As if used to not only addressing royalty, but commanding their attention. Then again, he had said he was a royal bodyguard.

Geaith's gaze didn't sway until he finished speaking. Lingering a little longer, as if considering him.

"And why, agent of Lady Aurorian, did she *not* inform me of this sudden change?" Geaith asked. There was no warmth in her voice. Only hard, icy grace.

"I cannot speak to her reasoning," Venyx said. "She only requested I express her deepest apologies. I do assure you, Your Highness, I have been granted permission from the Prime Minister of Pensen to travel with the Child. It is she, through the Lady, for whom I was contracted."

"Her permission," Geaith spat, like a soured piece of fruit, "not mine." She drew a deep breath, her brown eyes flicking to the Amasian at her left, then back to Venyx. "I do not appreciate a deymon being allowed to roam my lands without my permission. It would seem there are plenty of those already."

"The Lady Aurorian did not inform Amasius of this, either," the Amasian said, his tone matching the Plains Queen's. Venyx inhaled, but the diplomat spoke before he had the chance. "Perhaps it would be best to speak with the Child without her ... guardian."

My heart dropped to my stomach as my gaze jumped from the Amasian to the Plains queen, then to Venyx's shoulders, suddenly rigid.

Geaith drew a breath and leaned to one side of her seat, a hand delicately curling before her mouth. Her brown gaze flicked to the guards on the far side of the hall. "Please escort Deymon Venyx from the throne room."

Tears sprang to my eyes as Venyx shot a glance over his shoulder, meeting my gaze. I licked my lips, words dancing on my tongue, ready to beg for him to stay, but he went without argument. When the door closed behind him, it echoed through my head with finality, as if it were already decided he was being stripped from me.

"Please forgive us, Your Highness," I said, forcing the tremor from my voice, blinking away my tears, "for the sudden change in plans. I apologize you weren't informed, but I can assure you, I am in good hands."

The queen's appraising gaze shifted from me to the door Venyx stood behind, as if raking over him through the wall. "Yes, I'm certain you are."

I trembled for him beneath the weight of her gaze, heat rising to my cheeks as I kept my focus solely on her.

"Regardless of your many apologies," the diplomat spat, "none were informed of this egregious breech in our contract with the Lady Aurorian. Not to mention the absence of the Amasian agents who—"

Geaith raised a single hand, silencing the Amasian. The Plains Queen sighed, as if tired of the conversation, the interruption to her day, and flicked a finger toward the woman at her side. Her adviser stepped forward, bowing low enough to reach the queen without the older woman moving, save for a tip of her chin.

As they spoke, whispering back and forth, the Amasian eyed me, his cool gray gaze taking in every part of me, something akin to a smile and a sneer on his clean-shaven face. I glanced at the door, my heart thundering. Hoping Venyx was there, I opened a window on the barrier of my mind.

Can you hear what they're saying? I asked, unsure if he was listening. That familiar tingling whispered in my head.

It's inappropriate to listen to royalty convening with their advisors, Seraph, he teased.

I never took you for one to play by the rules, I jabbed, damming the flood of tears squeezing my chest. A chuckle rang in my thoughts, his deep voice echoing in the halls of my mind.

They're considering turning me away. Having an Amasian replace me alongside Geaith's men.

My heart dropped to my feet. Dark spots flashed in the edges of my vision at the idea that he'd be thrown from Siila, that I would be forced to continue the trek with an Amasian.

They're discussing the ramifications of defying Pensen by not allowing me across her lands, he continued. *It might also offend Aurorian. Dismissing her agent may have negative consequences, and may lose her as an ally.*

I forced a breath down my throat, into my lungs, edging back the blinding threat of panic.

Another moment and Geaith's adviser stood to her full height, long hair falling down her back as she stepped from the throne. The Plains Queen faced the guards, her expression a mask of steel. "Retrieve the deymon," she ordered. She folded her hands in her lap, eyes flitting between the two of us as Venyx was led back into the room, retaking his stance at my shoulder.

"Deymon Venyx, of the Lost Forest," Geaith said. He stepped forward, head bowed. "I grant you permission to cross my lands with the sole intent of fulfilling your contract with the Prime Minister of Pensen and the Lady Aurorian. Once you have fulfilled this task, you will leave."

"Thank you, Your Highness," he said.

"And what of Amasius?" the diplomat asked, drawing Geaith's attention. "The Child is still under Amasian custody. An Amasian should escort her. Should have *been* escorting her."

Geaith sighed, sinking back into her seat. "Whether Amasius is with her makes no difference to me. You will be free to speak with her at a time of your choosing. Discuss it then."

He bowed his head, all his curls remaining fixed in place with the motion. "Of course, Your Majesty."

"We host a feast tonight, in honor of the arrival of the Child of Sky and Sea," Geaith said. "Child, I do expect you in attendance." I nodded, afraid of speaking, of saying the wrong thing, and so remained silent. "Deymon Venyx, I extend an invitation to you. Whether you accept is your choice."

"I would be honored, Your Highness," Venyx said with a nod.

"I have set a room for you, Child," Geaith continued, "however, I was under the impression the Lady Aurorian would be joining you, and so have set her rooms to ready, as well." Her eyes lingered between us before shifting to Venyx. "I hope that is sufficient."

"It is more than generous, Your Highness," Venyx said.

To no one in particular, Geaith said, "Please show them to their rooms."

It wasn't the queen's advisor who escorted us from the hall, but a young man, black hair falling to his shoulders, like Calian's, though he appeared younger than the warrior.

Another door opened, leading into a hallway filled with light. Shafts of it streamed through cutouts in the walls, high above our heads. A warm breeze played along the passage, teasing my hair, sweat prickling my brow. Venyx's steps tapped the floor in my wake.

The young man turned a corner, down a corridor to a large chamber lined with doors. Across the hall was one flanked by guards. Their gazes were distant as we approached, as if not seeing us.

The young man first stopped to the immediate left of the guarded door. He turned and bowed his head to Venyx. "This will be your room," he said. Venyx glanced at me only a moment before slipping inside and disappearing. I swallowed my thunderous pulse as the young man went next to the guarded room and gestured me inside.

The room was nearly as large as the last safehouse I'd stayed in. Rich carpets lined the floor. A window cut into the clay wall allowed a playful breeze to dance along the tasseled curtains. A wardrobe sat on one side, wide enough to contain an entire set of clothes, though I wouldn't be here long enough to use them. I ran a hand over the soft items hanging inside. Most were the same browns others around the palace wore, though I didn't mind. It would be a reprieve from the dirty, crusty things I'd been wearing for ... I suppressed a shudder, refusing to think about how long it had been.

"Child," the boy said, pulling me from the thought of fresh things covering my body. "A bath has been prepared for you, just through there." He pointed toward a curtain at the other end of the room. It hung from the top of the archway to the floor, completely sealing the washroom from view.

"Thank you," I said with a nod. The boy bowed his head and left, closing the door in his wake.

I turned in a circle, taking in the vastness of the room. My gaze was drawn to the bed between two windows, easily big enough for several people to sleep comfortably side by side. I'd never slept in a bed so large. The ones in the safehouses had always been small, little more than bunk cots.

Reluctantly, I turned from the bed, from the soft blankets and mound of pillows, to the curtain concealing the largest washroom I'd ever seen.

A large copper tub sat in the middle, steam wafting from the surface of the basin. Groaning at the thought of warmth enveloping me, I toed off my boots and peeled away my worn, crusty clothes, leaving them in a pile of dust on the slick reddish tiles.

I dipped one toe into the warmth, curled back at the heat, and slowly lowered my foot, groaning as I submerged myself up to my chin. I wasn't sure I'd felt anything so wonderful since Delthia's inn. The memory flashed through my mind, my body, slick with water, curled on the floor, wrapped in Venyx's arms as I cried.

Tipping my head back, I relished the water creeping along my scalp, through my hair. A bar of soap sat to my right, perfumed with citrus and floral scents. Taking it up, I set to scrubbing the miles off my skin.

Geaith hadn't said when the feast would start, but I figured, since I was required to be there, they would wait. Still, she seemed volatile enough without me taking the whole day to wash myself.

I scrubbed every part of my body, the road falling off my skin in sudsy patches, before I set to work on my hair. It had grown in the months since we'd set out, falling just past my waist. Then reminded myself, since *I* had set out.

When Aurorian had come back, saying we were leaving for Pensen, I hadn't been sure what to think. What to feel. I was simply grateful I wouldn't be leaving with strangers. I'd have the same spies who had been with me the last six months. Miran and ... and Nik. And Aurorian would be with me.

Something heavy settled in my chest at the thought.

Aurorian was in Amasius, dealing with whatever crisis awaited me once I got to Pensen. Nik—tears stung my eyes at the thought, his final moments flashing before my mind. How peaceful he'd looked. How at ease with his own death. I wondered if I would look that peaceful, if acceptance would wash over me the way it had him. And I would die knowing ... knowing what? I knew nothing. Nothing of what would happen after I died. I didn't even have the luxury of knowing my death wouldn't be in vain.

Then there was Miran.

I sank below the surface of the water at the thought of him. Sickening, twisting betrayal curled my stomach. Had he gone to me knowing he would betray me? He must have. So many of the spies, they ... they'd shared me. But him...

I'd thought him different.

And the talks. All those late night conversations. The things I'd told him. Only just now realizing he'd offered nothing of himself. I'd been too at ease. Too occupied by his touches, his kisses. His adoring attention. The way he'd treated my body, as if it were a temple to be worshipped.

I swallowed the disgust. Disgust at him, at myself. How I'd thought him so different than the others, I didn't know. I'd become drunk on his touch, on his commanding presence. The way he'd made me feel, I'd never stopped to consider anything else.

Surfacing, I banished those thoughts of Miran as rivulets fell from me. Let him lie on the floor as I crawled from the tub, like the water trailing behind me, and told myself to leave him there. Just as I'd left him in the street of The City.

I should have killed him. Made sure he was dead. For what he'd done to me. How he'd used me. Then again, what right did I have to be angry at him, when I'd allowed the same thing to happen with the ones who'd come before. I'd built the road to my own destruction long before he came along.

Sniffling, I wrapped a thick cloth about myself and padded through the curtain. A shiver ran up my spine, despite the warmth, as I stood there, dripping wet and alone.

Going to the wardrobe, I chose a simple set of clothes, similar to what Geaith had been wearing. Soft and honey brown, the shirt hung off my body, allowing me room to move while still being snug. The skirt hung to my knees. It was loose and flowing, gentle as the air outside. I'd slipped on some underthings beneath, and straightened it, feeling strange in so little clothing. I'd gotten so used to layer upon layer, wearing a skirt, my legs exposed, was foreign.

I ran my fingers through my still damp hair and wove it into a gentle plait, allowing it to fall down my back. After slipping on a pair of thin leather shoes, I stepped from the room and into the corridor, finding Venyx already there. His hair, also wet, was slicked back. Our eyes met and I couldn't help as my lips curled.

"You look nice," Venyx said, smiling as he stepped closer.

"*You* look strange in something other than black," I chuckled. The soft brown shirt was more fitted than his billowing black ones, while the trousers were straight-legged, and not so distracting as his usual ones.

He threw his arms to either side, huffing, as if not sure what to do with himself. "Yes, well, I'm not leaving in these."

I chuckled.

A throat cleared and we both turned, facing our young guide, ready to take us to the feast.

The hall was packed. It appeared the whole of Siila had come to join the celebration, making my mouth suddenly dry. Every muscle in my body refused to move, my feet planted firmly on the floor.

Tables lined the room, surrounded by handfuls of people. Each of those, in turn, was laden with food. Roasted vegetables and meats. Bowls of fruits. Flat breads and loaves.

At the far end rest a table on a dais, similarly laden with mounds of food. In the center sat Geaith. At her right was her advisor, the Amasian diplomat to the right of the younger woman. Both ends were filled with people I hadn't met. Two chairs stood empty—the one directly to Geaith's left, and the one beside it. I swallowed hard, knowing which was mine. Thankfully, she'd saved the seat beside mine for Venyx.

You can do this, Venyx's voice whispered in my mind. I sent a single glance to him before stepping from the corridor and into the hall, and every person in the room took to their feet, including Geaith.

My heart hammered loud as a war drum as I walked the unending length of that room. My hands trembled at my sides. Each step was a mile long, each breath punctuated by a series of knives running up and down my legs, my back, prickling me. Blinding anxiety threatened to strangle me as I went, the table, my seat, seeming to crawl back several steps for each of my one.

Finally, the table appeared. I walked around it, taking my seat beside Geaith, thankful for the buffet between me and the people filling the room.

Geaith turned from me to the crowd. She raised her goblet, the mass of people filling the hall following suit. "To the Child!" she cried. As one, they echoed her chant before drinking.

That call resounded in my head, ringing over and over as I realized this entire city was celebrating me, but not my arrival. They saluted my sacrifice. My blood. My death.

I wasn't sure where he'd come from, but Venyx suddenly sat beside me, squeezing my hand in his. I melted into that touch, the warmth of him. His skin on mine.

Did he know? Did he also wish for my death? Worship it like some sacrificial deity? Counting down the days until my spilled blood set them all free? He had to know. How could he not?

His hand fell away as Geaith began speaking, though I didn't register what she said.

I was going to die.

I was going to die and the whole world would be watching. Waiting for the moment the Faerie Queen's blade pierced my heart.

And killed us both.

FORTY-FIVE

D URING ANY OTHER TIME in my life, I was certain I would have wolfed
down the food on my plate. I would have savored every bite. In
this hall, surrounded by people celebrating the last months of my life, it
was ash on my tongue.

I ate because Geaith scrutinized me otherwise. To turn her focus from
me to the hall. Because eating was a distraction. If I did not, Venyx
knocked incessantly on my mental barrier until I took a bite, until I
swallowed the morsel, and took another.

I couldn't think about how much he knew, what all Aurorian had told
him. What he might have known from the rumors spread about the
prophecy; what was said about me, my life, and my death. The ties to
unicorn blood, even if those rumors were little more than whispered
theories allowed to run rampant.

How could he not know? my mind murmured. How, indeed? Had he
spent so much time drowning in a bottle he hadn't heard those rumors?

Again, I shoved those theories away, pushed them into the farthest
reaches of my mind. The cruelty it would take to accept money for
escorting me to my death was insurmountable, and I couldn't consider
it. To mull it over any more than I already had.

But, like flies, they kept coming back, buzzing through my head before
I again swatted them away.

I hadn't realized how long I'd been wrapped up in those thoughts, of convincing myself to not give them any more credence, when Venyx's knee knocked into mine, and I popped my head up, swiveling my gaze toward him. He gestured to the empty hall.

Geaith rose from her seat, drawing my attention. For a moment, it seemed she might say something before she stepped down from the dais and left the room, her advisor trailing behind. Leaving the Amasian diplomat sitting in his chair, sipping from his goblet.

"Quite the celebration, wasn't it?" He set his cup next to his empty plate. Brows furrowed, I stared at him, wishing I was back in my room. His eyes flickered up before he turned back to the goblet, smirking. "I suppose not. The affairs in Amasius are far more entertaining. In Pensen even more so." He sighed. "Though, I suppose you'll find out soon enough."

"I'd like to go back to my room," I said, shoving to my feet, Venyx standing at my back.

"I think not," the diplomat said, glancing up. "He may go," he pointed to Venyx, "but you and I have things to discuss."

"I'd prefer him to stay," I grumbled. The Amasian chuckled.

"You are still under Amasian custody, Child."

"It's Seraph."

He faced me, the smirk falling from his mouth. "You are still under Amasian custody, and he is not to be privy to conversations had between Amasius and our ward."

"He'll hear anyway," I countered. "He stays. Or I go."

His grin returned. "You sound like her. Your unicorn. She's not adept at negotiations, either." He sighed, filled his goblet with more wine, and motioned for us to sit. I glanced back at Venyx before retaking my chair. "King Daryn sent me to debrief you, and the Amasians who were *supposed* to be escorting you. Instead, I find you in the company of a deymon. Do enlighten me as to how that came about."

"Aurorian hired him to take me to Pensen," I began.

The Amasian scoffed, set down his cup, and glanced up. "I heard that bit. I refer to the absence of the two Amasian agents we sent to you."

"They were killed," I stated. Nik's face flashed before my eyes. All the blood. The vision of Miran came next. Laid out in the street of The City. Regardless of whether he *was* dead, for all points and purposes, he was.

"I do believe there is more to that story than a simple blanket statement," he said, sighing, "but, for the moment, I accept it."

"I'm not sure what else you want me to say," I snapped, shrugging.

"The agents we've sent to you in the past have been among the best Amasius has to offer," he said, swirling the contents of his cup.

"They're still only human," Venyx grumbled behind me.

"Indeed." The Amasian glanced up, meeting Venyx's gaze before finding mine again. "Nonetheless, as Amasian property—"

"I'm not property," I spat, though he ignored me, barreling on as if I hadn't spoken.

"—we have the final say as to who escorts you. Regardless of whether the Pensian Prime Minister hired him or not. An Amasian will guide you the rest of the way."

"No."

He stopped, looked up from his cup, gray eyes meeting mine, and scoffed. "No?"

"You heard me."

He smiled, glanced back to his wine. "I do believe you are mistaken as to who is in charge—"

"Your *agents* spent the last ten years fucking me," I spat.

The man stilled. He set his glass down and looked up, all traces of amusement gone.

"I don't want another of those bastards near me."

A grin split his lips. He opened his mouth, closed it, and opened it again, gaze flickering between me and Venyx. "I'm sorry?"

"You heard me," I repeated.

He coughed into his fist before downing the contents of his goblet, refusing to meet my gaze. "Amasius will be required to conduct a formal inquiry, to fully investigate your allegations—"

"Allegations? I just told you what happ—"

"These are serious charges placed against some of the finest men from Amasius," he snapped, finally meeting my eyes. "Yes, there will be a formal inquiry. In the meantime, you will go—"

"I'm going with Venyx, or I'm not going at all," I spat.

He swallowed, refilled his goblet again, downed it, and met my gaze. He opened his mouth, closed it, and stood, leaving without another word.

On trembling legs, I rose, shuffling silently beside Venyx back to our rooms. In the corridor, I barely glanced at him, unable to meet his gaze. His fists clenched and unclenched, his jaw working back and forth.

"Did Nik ever—"

"No," I said. "He never touched me." I glanced up as he nodded, eyes flickering red.

"I'm sorry."

Sniffling, I shrugged before entering my room and closed the door, blocking out the world beyond. Once inside, I stripped off my clothes and went back into the washroom. I didn't care that the water was cold, dirty from my bath. I sank into the tub, submerged myself completely, and screamed.

When the water became too cold to stand, I climbed from the tub and crawled beneath the blankets in the oversized bed. Though I relished the warmth enveloping me, the softness of the mattress, sleep evaded me. I stared out the window, into the winking heavens, counting stars.

A far simpler task than facing whatever dreams awaited me on the other side of slumber.

I hadn't dreamt of the spies, those first ones, since Miran came to me. His touch, his kisses, poisonous as I now knew they were, had chased them away.

After fighting sleep a while longer, I jumped from bed, threw on a shirt and pair of trousers of the same soft fabric, the slippers I'd used, and left my room. For a moment, I wanted to knock on Venyx's door. To ask if I could crawl into bed with him and let his comforting warmth lull me to sleep. But the idea that Geaith would send someone to fetch me in the morning, only to find me in bed with Venyx, didn't bode well. So I decided against it.

The guards paid me no mind as I wandered the halls. The servants, entrenched in their nighttime duties, even less so. Eventually, I found the doors we'd entered through that very morning, though it seemed far more time had passed, and I stepped into the cool night air.

Further separating Siila from The City, the streets were quiet as I walked. There were no wandering merchants. Certainly not dragons. No bawdy dwarves in taverns, though the thought filled me with guilt.

After wandering more, I reached the edge of Siila, and an open field just beyond, lanterns flickering in the dark from where they sat in the grass. Grunts and heavy breaths made me pause, wondering if I should go back. Just as I was about to turn around, twin pinpoints of silver flashed toward me.

I meandered through the field as Venyx jogged forward, chest heaving when he finally stopped.

"What're you doing?" I asked, glancing over him, at the sweat on his brow.

"I was about to ask you that," he said. "Couldn't sleep, so I came out here. Calian, Nuka, and a couple others are playing kickball. Thought I'd join them."

"Kick ball?"

Through the shadows, Calian jogged toward us, a ball under his arm. "It's a game," the Plainsmen said.

"What's the purpose of it?" I asked, glancing between them.

Venyx shrugged, grinning. "Just to have fun."

"Would you like to play?" Calian asked.

Suppressing my smile, I nodded and followed them into the field.

The purpose was simple—kick the ball away from the opposing team and score as many points as possible. Calian and Nuka showed me how to kick and maneuver the ball across the field. After, we broke into teams. Venyx, of course, was on the opposite team. He only smirked when I complained.

Long into the night, we played. By the second round, I was covered in sweat. My hair had come loose from its braid, my legs weak and wobbly, but I didn't care. I couldn't recall the last time I'd had fun. I suddenly wasn't sure I ever had. Certainly not this much.

I learned to block an opposing team member, to steal the ball from them, which I did more than once. At one point, I collided mercilessly with another Plainsmen, who quickly jumped to his feet, horrified, until I burst into laughter.

Nuka, I learned, was quite good at the game, better than anyone else on the field, aside from Venyx. A skill I wasn't aware he'd had. One he had no qualms with showing off at every opportunity.

Fueled by adrenaline, I weaved between players and kicked the ball from between Venyx's feet, laughing as I ran from his grasp, though not fast enough. I glimpsed as Calian caught it, kicking it down to the far end, before I was yanked back into a solid chest. My head tipped back in bellowing mirth. Venyx's own chortles filled my ears, though faded as my eyes met his.

A foreign intensity filled his face, the smile slowly slipping from his mouth. Lungs heaving, every limb throbbing, I became aware of his body pressed against mine. His chest beneath my hands. Mere fabric separating us.

He reached up, brushing a lock of sweat-drenched hair behind my ear, his fingertips running down my cheek, brushing my neck, my shoulder, before his hand landed on my arm. And further down to my waist.

I wondered what that hand would feel like on other parts of me. How gentle it might be. And realized too late the whispering swirling in my head before I slammed my barriers up. Heat unlike anything I'd ever known flooded me from the tips of my toes to my face as Venyx's arms dropped. I stepped back, still fighting for air, as both teams rushed past.

FORTY-SIX

WARM SUNLIGHT SPLAYED ACROSS my face, seeping into my skin through the mound of blankets. I sucked in a breath and let my eyes flutter open, taking in the massive bed. So much room I couldn't touch the sides with my arms spread.

I yawned and sat up, stretching. I wasn't sure I'd ever slept in a bed so comfortable. Every part of me wanted to lay back down, to let the mattress again swallow me up, devour me in one gulp, and go back to sleep. To stay there.

As sleep dissipated from my mind, the previous night returned. Heat seared my cheeks at the memories. My hands on his chest. His arms around my waist. How gingerly he'd swept the sweat-dampened hair from my face.

Scooting to the edge of the bed, I swung my legs over and braced my hands there, mulling over the awkward walk back to our rooms for the second time that night. I'd glanced up at him as he'd fumbled over his tongue, words not quite forming, and let his mouth fall closed.

His mouth opened again, tips of his fangs glinting, and he licked his lips. Before he had a chance to speak, I'd forced a ghostly smile to my face and left him in the corridor.

Shaking my head to clear the memory, I pushed to my feet and went to the washroom, a neat pile of clothes already laid out. A pretty brown dress and soft leather slippers.

Stripping off my night things, I slipped into the water in the copper tub, scrubbing myself as quickly as possible. The less time I spent, the less time I had to think. About him. About me. About all the other things I forced behind a wall in my head.

Once done, I stepped out, toweled myself off, and dressed, walking into the room as a knock sounded.

I sighed, already wanting this morning to be over.

The same servant from yesterday, come to fetch me to have breakfast with the queen. Venyx was already waiting in the corridor. We exchanged a quick glance before silently following the boy.

It was a much smaller room than the vast hall we'd dined in the previous night.

A long table stretched down the middle, piles of food laid out for the taking. A collection of people, all from the feast, sat around it, talking in hushed voices. Geaith sat at the head, deep in conversation with the Amasian diplomat on her left. She didn't look up as Venyx and I were shown to the empty chairs on her right.

Swallowing, I took the one directly beside her, Venyx on my right. Though his warmth was a comforting presence amidst all the eyes on me, I didn't lean into him. Reminded myself to not reach for his hand. But kept him in my sight, to remind myself he was there.

It occurred to me to ask Venyx what the conversation was about. He could, after all, hear the whispers shared between the queen and the Amasian. But that would mean again opening my mind to him. Something I wasn't keen on doing. Not after last night. So we sat in awkward silence as a servant came up behind me, loading my plate with food.

My eyes widened as the mound before me grew. Unsure how to signal I had enough, I cleared my throat. The servant stepped back. Geaith slowly swung her eyes to me, her expression hard, cool, as if affronted I'd made such a noise.

Heat spread through my face down to my neck. I wanted to slip under the table.

"Did you sleep well, Child?" Geaith asked, popping a bit of diced fruit in her mouth.

I forced the corners of my lips up. "Yes, thank you."

"And are you enjoying the fruits of Amasian labor?" She gestured to the food laden table. My gaze flicked to the diplomat directly across from me, though he scarcely looked up.

"Y-yes," I stammered.

Her brown eyes dropped as she speared a bit of meat on her fork. "Good. You and your ... guardian will be leaving for Pensen today. After breakfast."

My brows furrowed in question and I shot a glance to my right, meeting Venyx's perplexed gaze.

"That's a bit sudden," he said, shifting in his seat.

"As if I owe either of you further hospitality than I've already given?" she asked curtly.

"N-no," I stammered.

"I received word this morning from the White Army's Second Commander. They are razing villages along the western side of my lands. Punishment, I am certain, for harboring an enemy of their crown," she said. My throat went dry, face falling as I took her in, the placid expression donning her features. Speaking as if she were referring to the weather.

"I'm sorry," I mumbled.

She ignored me. "I realize this is not your doing, precisely," Geaith said, and took a bite of food. She swallowed before continuing, her gaze again meeting mine. "But I will not allow my people to pay the price for a war that is not theirs."

My jaw dropped, the implication clear. "I never wanted war. It's no more mine than yours," I said, forcing my voice to remain steady, the stinging tears in my eyes to stay hidden. "This began … hundreds of years before I was born. So how is it *my* war?"

She took a breath around another bite of food, her back going rigid as she dropped her fork and knife. The room became deathly quiet. All those gathered peered to the end of the table, to me and to Geaith, absorbing the conversation. As if waiting for a battle to erupt.

Venyx's mind knocked on mine, and I knew what he would say. Calm down. Don't allow her to rile me. In that moment, I didn't care. I refused to be blamed for starting a war that began before I was even a thought. Before the prophecy had even been in existence.

"It is *your* war more than anyone else's," Geaith said. "Aside from the Queen Faerie, of course. She doesn't desecrate these lands because my people have leveled a grave insult against her, but for your head. Because she knows the same thing everyone at this table does. Everyone in Pensen. You, dear Child, are the only one with the power to stop this. All of it. We both know how this ends. As does she."

Biting tears threatened to spill over as I met the queen's piercing, unyielding eyes. I was aware of every sizzling gaze as Geaith picked up her fork and continued eating as if she hadn't ordered me to go throw myself onto the Faerie Queen's blade. As if my life meant so little. The grandest thing I might do would be to die.

I'd always known, always, that's what was expected of me. But to have it put so callously—

"Am I correct in assuming you'll be sending escorts with us?" Venyx asked, interrupting my thoughts, the battle of words between me and the Plains queen. She turned that cold gaze to the deymon at my side.

"My general, Mato, and his men are preparing mounts now. You will meet them once you've finished," Geaith said.

"I'm not hungry," I blurted out, the food before me unappealing, as if rotted.

"Then I suppose it's time to depart," Geaith said sharply. "Pensen awaits."

413

I shoved back from the table and jumped to my feet, unable to leave the room fast enough. Venyx tapped on my mental walls again, but I ignored him. I shoved past the guards, winding my way through the halls toward the exit, latching onto the little details from the previous day, until bright, golden sunlight rained upon me.

A stiff, warm wind washed over me as I stepped outside, forcing myself to breathe. Inhale. Exhale.

For a moment, I stood there. Hands over my eyes. Breathing. The breeze rustling my hair. The grasses playing along my legs. I hadn't changed back into my own clothes. I had no riding pants. But I wasn't going back inside. I refused.

When my hands fell from my face, Mato approached me, a smile playing on his mouth.

"Good morning," he said, far too cheerful for the weight squeezing my chest, my heart. "The horses are just this way. We have packs for you and Venyx. Clothes and such for the journey."

Willing myself to walk, I followed him. Calian looked at me, too happy, and waved. I didn't wave back.

"This one is yours," Mato said, strolling alongside a dazzling white mare as she chuffed. "Her name i—"

I didn't wait for him to finish. Instead, I rushed to the mare, gave her only a moment to sniff my hand, and jumped into the saddle, snapped the reins, and galloped off. Putting as much distance between myself and this place as possible.

Behind me, someone cried out. Then another someone. Venyx, from the sound of it.

Tears tore at me, falling freely down my face as I rode. The mare beneath me, as if sensing what I needed, galloped faster. Wind tore into my hair, across my tear-stained face. Heat blared atop me. Siila fell behind and an endless grass ocean spread out. How long until I reached the ocean? Perhaps I could swim across it, to the South. Or maybe dive beneath the waves and find the other half of myself. The one calling to the depths of the seas.

414

A black and white stallion galloped alongside me and Kishil reached out, snatching my reins away, pulling my mare to a stop.

"You do not want that way," he said roughly, pulling my horse around to face the opposite direction. "Abaddon is there. Or what is left of it."

I trembled as I was turned southwest. The way to Pensen. A great, heaving sob tore through me and I bent forward atop my horse, hands flying to my face. Kishil said nothing as I burst into tears, holding my reins, keeping me in place. Forbidding me from escaping the nightmare of my life.

Venyx's scent filled my nose as his arms encircled me, pulled me into his lap. His horse bumped against mine, my legs warm beside his, where they were trapped between our mounts.

I nuzzled into the crook of his neck, his chest absorbing the potency of my wails.

"It's okay," he whispered, rubbing soothing circles on my back. "I've got you."

Vaguely aware of the other horses circling us, I pulled away from him, willing the tears to stop. He thumbed the moisture from my face, adjusted my hair over my shoulders, and helped me back into my saddle. He said nothing before gesturing to Kishil, and took my reins, pulling my horse alongside his own as we began trotting. Heading southwest.

If he hadn't been aware of my fate before, I was certain he knew now. But still, he said nothing.

Terrified of lowering my mental walls, of reaching out, I settled in my thoughts. Waited for him to tap along the barrier, to ask permission to speak to me. But his silence was thick, resounding, as we rode within the circle of our Plains escorts. Though they were more like executioners, leading me to the gallows. And my own personal death trotted beside me, the reins of my life in his hands.

The way passed by in silence. I resumed my evening training with Venyx, but we said little to each other aside from meager conversation. Our brief stay in Siila seemed to have strained the friendship we'd built over the weeks, months, since leaving Delthia's inn, though I couldn't recall how much time had passed.

Being trapped in the vampyre mines had skewed my timeline. Ace's Tavern was a lifetime ago.

During our training, I focused on him as little as possible, choosing instead to stay in tune with my sword, with my body, how it moved, how it felt. To do otherwise would allow those thoughts of Venyx back into my mind, which only felt like a betrayal to myself.

He knew, I'd decided. He had to. And was complicit, like everyone else, that I was to die. An angry seed sprouted in my gut that I had once considered him a friend.

I wanted to ask, to demand the payment he was receiving once we reached Pensen. Whatever monies he deemed worth my life. But every time I worked up the courage, it shattered an instant later, and I once again shriveled into a ball of blissful ignorance, telling myself it was best I didn't know. And once again wrestled with myself if he was actually aware of what he was delivering me for, or if it was simply my anger and frustration, the lack of power over my own life, screaming that he knew.

Instead, I took my anger out on him during training.

It was becoming easier to slip his grip, to avoid the pitfall of allowing him to disarm me. Still, I carried the knowledge I would never best him in a fight. He was too quick, too strong. Reminding me that, if I chose to run, if I chose to leave him and my Plains jailors, I would never get far.

The deymons who'd captured me, the White soldiers he'd saved me from, flashed in my head. How much younger had they been than him, how much less powerful, and I hadn't stood a chance. It was laughable to think I could ever evade the deymon protecting me.

Sweat dribbled down my forehead, along my cheeks, as I leaned over, hands on my knees, panting. I wiped my brow and looked up at Venyx as he rolled his neck back and forth, his shoulders. A thin sheen of sweat glittered along his brow, but he wasn't nearly as winded. Didn't seem as affected by the growing heat the further south we traveled.

Since I'd insisted my training be more intense, to combat the growing sense of dread, Venyx had obliged. Ensuring I could barely stand by the end. Often times, I ended up hobbling to the campfire, surrounded by snickers and chuckles as the Plainsmen watched me dump myself in my seat, mumbling under my breath how much I hated him.

But I didn't.

As terrifying as I knew him to be. As powerful as he was, as strong, knowing he could tie me up and carry me to Pensen without breaking a sweat. I didn't hate him. Maybe I should have.

Groaning, I picked up my sword and straightened, rolling my shoulders and neck, trying, and failing, to loosen the muscles there, screaming from the never-ending exertion placed upon them.

"Ready for another round?" Venyx asked, facing me again.

My reply was a single nod as I adjusted my grip on the sword. My borrowed blade. The twin to the one in his hand. With a sigh, he returned the gesture and lifted the collar of his shirt, mopping sweat from his brow. The black fabric lifted, revealing a strip of flesh above his trousers, one side of the V traveling into his waistband. The perfectly chiseled flesh there.

My mouth went dry, throat working as I suddenly forgot what I was doing.

"Hey."

At a glint of silver, my gaze shot up, narrowly blocking his sword in its downward arch before he reared back and kicked, landing me on my ass, a blossom of pain smattering my chest. Groaning, I fell back, eyes squeezed shut.

Somewhere above me, he chuckled.

"Thought you would have learned by now to not let your guard down," he teased.

I opened my mouth to retort, but nothing came out, and so I let it fall closed again. There was no point in arguing. I had let my guard down. Had allowed myself to become distracted. By that narrow strip of skin.

I opened my eyes and met his as he leaned over me, brows raised, his lips curled upward. How rarely I'd seen him smile the last few days.

"I got distracted," I said hoarsely.

"I noticed," he replied before dropping to the grass beside me. A faint grunt whooshed from his throat as he sat. He pulled his blade across his lap, thumbing the steel, as if checking its sharpness. I had no doubt it could still sever a single hair.

With a sigh, far deeper than intended, I turned and looked up. Into the sky as the sun painted it a vibrant collage of colors, the rays of light kissing the world good night. Already a few stars were visible on the eastern horizon, barely twinkling in the fading day.

How many more nights would I get to see the sky? The stars? How many more times did I get to spy the twin moons in their eternal dance? Would I be able to see them again before I was shipped off to Kaival?

As if he were in my mind, listening to the whirlpool of my thoughts, Venyx took my hand and squeezed. I slipped my fingers between his and nuzzled closer, my head on his shoulder, breathing in his scent. Absorbed the warmth of his embrace as he rested his cheek against my hair. We gazed into the sky as day was swallowed by night and the constellations winked down.

For just a moment, the world beyond that spit of field ceased to exist. As did tomorrow.

FORTY-SEVEN

SINCE OUR NIGHT UNDER the stars, the tension lifted between us. We laughed again, talked. Resumed our mental training. Friends again.

Still, I couldn't bring myself to stop looking at him. To not observe his every move, tracing the way his body worked. I simply had more control over my mind, making sure he never found those thoughts. And, we were careful. We touched only when necessary, dancing around each other as if afraid we might singe the other's skin.

Sleep still evaded me, and so we picked up our elven lessons as if they'd never stopped. But it had been weeks since my last nightmare, the one in Delthia's inn. I sighed at the passage of time, of how much existed between the present and then. It really had been over a month since we'd fled the grasp of the White Army, since we'd plunged ourselves into the vampyre mines and very nearly did not come out.

As the days grew hotter, longer, the closer we drew to our destination, we rose earlier, mounting up before the stars and moons tucked themselves in for the day. Before the sun cast its golden fingers across the grassy lands. It seemed to wave every morning as it rose, blinking blearily, as if astounded we hadn't waited.

The cool air of the lingering night felt wonderful on my skin. Every day I dressed in sweat. My clothes clung to me. My hair forever plastered to the nape of my neck, even when I pulled the long, lilac tresses back in a braid. And so resorted to tying it in a topknot, keeping its weight off my neck, off my back as much as possible. It did little to alleviate the discomfort.

Not long after we'd set out for the day, the first rays of daylight peeked over the distant eastern horizon, the sun stretching its arms wide as it woke. I yawned along with it. My elven lessons had gone long into the previous night, sleep evading me far longer than usual, so it was a great effort to not fall asleep in the saddle.

I stretched my arms up, out, arching my back into the glorious sensation, and dropped them to my sides. And became aware of eyes on me. I turned as Venyx's gaze flicked past me, as if observing the dregs of night on the northern horizon. My breath hitched, heart stuttering. But I said nothing.

He was safety. He was comfort. He was a blade to fend off the world. At least until Pensen. Nothing more. Just as I was a payday.

And I forced my gaze away.

A little higher the sun rose, igniting the lands in golden light. Blue stretched overhead before melting into the retreating darkness in the west. Wispy white fingers spread across the azure canvas.

One billowy formation caught my attention over my shoulder, to the south, just off course. When I turned, it wasn't a cloud, but smoke. The others seemed to notice at the same time as our group stopped in the grass, horses chuffing and whinnying in an off-kilter chorus.

Aluk said something I didn't understand, his dark gaze traveling to Mato, off to my right. The Plains general nodded once and replied in their tongue.

"The queen said the lands were being razed," Venyx said, as if in reply to whatever the Plainsmen were saying. "That's structural smoke."

My breath hitched as my gaze slid from Venyx to the humans, a great, tightening vice gripping my chest.

"Yes," Mato said.

"It could be a trap," Makya added. Mato nodded. "Meant to lure us in. The White Army could be waiting."

"They could be," Mato agreed. "It would be best if we go around. Stay the course."

I shifted in the saddle, glancing between them. "What if there are survivors?" I countered, pulling the gazes of all six men toward me. Nuka and Calian exchanged a glance. "They might need help."

"Seraph." I turned to Venyx's voice.

"Bu—"

"As Makya said, they could be lying in wait," Mato said, pulling my gaze back to him. "Wandering into their grasp, even under the guise of help, would be unwise. We keep moving."

"What if they aren't there," I ground out, ignoring the sting in the backs of my eyes. "There might still be people alive." Even as the words left my lips, the marauder camp flashed through my mind.

Mato turned to Venyx. The deymon sighed, lowered his chin, and closed his eyes. He fell silent for several long moments, still atop his horse. When his eyes again opened, they were full of something like sadness. Remorse.

"I can't feel the White Army, but they could be hiding themselves from me. There are no heartbeats there. None." His eyes slid to me as he spoke.

"That's that," Mato said, and snapped his reins. The group followed him, continuing west.

My gaze swung back to the smoke, and my mind ventured to all those months ago. The torched tents. Burned bodies littering the snow. The children.

My bottom lip quivered as guilt pooled in my gut, settling heavily over me.

"Seraph," Venyx called from ahead. I didn't turn to him. I ignored them all.

Instead, I snapped my reins and spurned my horse—south.

"Seraph!"

Crouching in the saddle, I pushed my horse faster, knowing Kishil could catch up, and refused to let him. Not before reaching the village.

Smoke rose like a twisted, rotting blade into the lightening sky before one became many and my heart sank further. Before long, the last remnants of night had retreated to the far west, hugging the edge of the world, and the village lay directly ahead. The scent of smoke, of—my stomach curdled—burnt flesh, filled the air. Tears sprang to my eyes, though not simply from emotion.

Venyx trotted up beside me. When I met his gaze, he didn't appear angry. His face wasn't curled in silent fury like Mato's. Rather, he appeared sympathetic, understanding, as we ventured into the village side by side.

When the first tents passed by, only slightly damaged, and the village opened before us, even the quiet rage on Mato's face vanished.

Though many of the dwellings still stood, they were little more than charcoal remains. The grass beneath our horses' hooves was blackened, charred, making me wonder how the fire hadn't spread, consuming the Plains around it. Blood was strung across the ground, huts, like paint. My stomach churned at the first body, nearly vomiting at the next one.

When we finally came to the village center, tears sprang fully formed in my eyes.

Bodies. Parts of bodies. Belongings. Strewn across the blackened grasses like little more than rubbish. I flung my gaze up, eyes and mouth wide, as Venyx swung from his saddle and dropped to the ground. The Plainsmen followed suit.

"Search for survivors," Mato called out, turning to me. "Since we're here."

The men spread out in different directions.

"Stay here," Venyx ordered before joining them.

I clambered from my saddle, feet crunching over the charcoal grass, and drifted toward the remains of the giant bonfire, so reminiscent of the one the marauders had built every night. The village wasn't nearly as large, didn't cover as much ground. Still, I couldn't stop comparing them.

I stepped carefully over a doll, the horse-mane tuft of hair on the thing's head scarred by flames. I reached down, plucking it up to grip it tight to my chest, wondering where the child was who'd owned it. Images of the marauder's children, trapped inside the burning tent, flashed through my mind. My stomach turned again.

I walked around the firepit, glancing at the remnants of a one-sided battle. Those who'd killed these people phantoms for all the evidence of their existence. Most of the bodies littering the village center were elderly, or women. Few men among them, making me wonder where they were.

The women...

Several lay face down, skirts shoved above their hips. Sickness boiled in my stomach, churning and bubbling at the pools of blood beneath their heads and necks, as if their throats had been slit just after, their violated bodies left to die.

A similar scene flashed in my head, one where I'd been lucky, but only just.

I covered my mouth, barely containing the sickness as I continued wandering, before deciding to check the huts in the center, if only to make the search faster for the warriors.

Doll still clutched to my chest, I parted hut entrances, straw ropes and beads clacking and whispering. Some fell apart in my hand, leaving streaks of ash as they crumbled. I jumped back as another hut collapsed entirely, burying whatever, whoever, had been inside. I left the remains to its ashy tomb and moved on.

In a hut only partially scorched, I found a woman. Body rid of clothing, legs stretched painfully apart, any remaining dignity laid bare for the world to see. Her throat slit to the bone, eyes wide, mouth parted in a silent scream, begging for her life even in death. No mercy had come. Her middle had been sliced open, as if in sport. Her body desecrated in every way.

Stumbling back, I fell to my knees beside the hut and retched, gasping and gagging, forcing myself to breathe around the vomit, the tears. The doll still clutched furiously in one hand.

"You okay?" Nuka's voice sounded behind me.

I spit the last remnants of vomit into the grass and nodded, wiping my face, then my mouth, on my sleeve.

Taking long sips of air, I pushed myself onto trembling legs and moved to the neighboring hut, but Nuka was already there, so went to the next.

As I parted the beaded curtain, my face fell, mouth gaping, grasping for some kind of reason.

Dozens of children were piled inside, stacked like a rubbish pile. Their little bodies in all states of flayed. Most of their throats had been laid open, a cascade of blood painting each of their little faces. Their bodies. I stumbled back. Barely noticing as Nuka approached my side, thick brows drawn together as he took me in and turned to the hut.

His scream filled my ears. The warrior dropped to his knees, clutching his middle, and screamed again.

The village was suddenly filled with cries, steps, dust—both ash and dirt—and the others swarmed around us. Venyx looked over me, caught my eyes, and peered inside.

Mato screamed next. Then Makya. Kishil fell to his knees just outside the hut, clutching his horrified face.

A strange calm settled over me, the edges of the world blurring as I turned and stumbled away. Someone said my name, but I caught only the ghost of that voice. The doll clung to my chest, as if I might protect it from the horrors it had witnessed.

My feet carried me through the village, out the other side. To where the charred grass stopped. Stretched before me, on a bloody battlefield, I found the men.

I dropped to my knees, doll clasped in my claw-like fingers, and screamed.

FORTY-EIGHT

O VER THE REST OF the day the huts were slowly disassembled. Pieces of remaining wood were used to build pyres large enough for the several hundred dead lying throughout the village. They were built just beyond the border, near the battlefield, the only place large enough to accommodate so many. Each body placed upon those final resting beds with care.

Each of the men's faces were covered in ash by the end of the after-noon, each one lined with tears, cutting through the dust and debris. And each and every one used every ounce of strength they possessed when they carried the bodies of the children, the desecrated bodies of the women, to the pyres.

While they toiled away, working through the village, building the pyres and carefully laying the bodies across them, I did my own work.

Taking one of the only baskets left unaffected by the ravages of the White Army, their mark wiped away save for the blood, I went through the village, gathering the belongings scattered about. One for every body.

Whether they had belonged to the same person, or several people, I didn't know. Regardless, they had been objects of the people here. Tokens of their lives. Proof of their existence before the White Army. Before me.

So I gathered them, sniffling while I plucked them up. Wiping the dust and ash from each one as best I could.

Tears snaked down my face as I stooped before each token, using the bottom of my shirt to brush the ash and dust away, ignoring the drops and ribbons of dried blood.

Each time the basket became too full, my items tumbling into the dirt, I picked them up and cradled them, like the doll, and carried them to the pyres. Set them on the ground in a pile, and went back for more. Kept careful track in my head of how many there were. And how many I had left to go.

There were six pyres in all. Each laden with bodies. People. Lives snuffed out in payment for a debt not theirs to pay.

Mato lit the first one, the one in the center, chanting some prayer in the Plains tongue as he touched the torch to the wood, flames spreading with each kiss. While smoke and fire curled around their legs, their toes, I beheld their faces, their closed eyes. The other Plains warriors followed suit, kissing their own flames to the pyres, repeating the same prayer in the same tongue. Each one's massive shoulders trembling from the weight of their task.

I stood back. Standing only for Venyx's arm holding me aloft. Tears raced down my face, my neck, diving into my shirt as if they, too, were ashamed of what had happened here.

As the flames took, as the pyres were engulfed, Venyx began to sing.

Not the lullaby. Something dark, somber. Some tune meant only for the dead. In the same tongue he'd sang his mother's song.

When the final verse ended, the deep sound of Venyx's enchanting voice fading, I set to work. Took each token, each gathered item, held it to my heart and kissed each one before tossing them in the flames. Hoping the people who had died here, the ones cursed to pay the price for my breath, found peace in the next life.

We stayed until the pyres were consumed. Waited for the flames to die, for the bodies to be whisked off into the heavens, to join the stars peering down. They seemed to shine a bit dimmer than the previous night—their own silent mourning prayer.

The Plains warriors stood vigil over the pyres, then sat. Saying nothing amongst themselves. And so Venyx and I did not speak.

The flames curled and danced, waving in their own tribute as they carried the dead to the life after this one, the one that had been unjustly cruel. By the light of those flames, I glanced at my palm. Traced the lines there. The now invisible line I'd carved into my flesh to kill the vampyres, and spill proof of my divinity.

I knew little about the actual prophecy surrounding my birth, having heard it once. Long ago.

Aurorian said it meant I was to die. Die so the whole world might live. How, I asked her, innocent to such things. And she'd told me. Only once.

Once had been plenty.

When the world was being forged, before life had been placed upon it, the angels had gazed down and wept for its beauty. The beauty they had no one to share with. Those tears had sunk into the ground, into the grass. Fallen as rain upon the trees, sprouting flowers. And from those flowers, the first unicorns had been born.

Long after mortals came to be, they killed a unicorn. Such a cruel, twisted crime, to smite something so pure, so good. The angels, angered by the act, struck down the assailant. And cursed any who did the same to perish with the life they stole.

So it was reasoned, the death of the offspring of an angel carried the same weight as a unicorn. To kill the child of an angel must mean death to the one who stole such a precious life.

Too bad I was the first, and only, child born in our world from the seed of an angel.

It was a beautifully tragic theory, but a theory nonetheless. Aurorian had no proof. The world had no proof. Only an old tale.

I glanced up at the pyres, at the dimming flames, the night seeming to grow darker for it, and back at my hand. Wondering what would happen if such a thing weren't true. What if... What if once she killed me, the only thing that happened was the end of my life?

If it wasn't true, all the lives that had been lost, all those who had died protecting me, given their lives to end the Faerie Queen, had been in vain.

I glanced again at the pyres.

What if I died, and the only thing that happened was nothing?

Frost kissed my cheeks. Gnawed on my bones.

Confused, I opened my eyes. Found myself on my bedroll, in the vast emptiness of the Plains, but I was alone. I looked around, spotting the other bedrolls, but the Plainsmen, Venyx, were all gone.

"Hello?" I called, rising to my feet. No response came. No one answered. "Venyx?"

Turning for one last glance at the ghostly remnants of camp, I shuffled forward. The horses were gone. Even mine.

"Venyx?" I called again, with the same result.

Heart hammering, eyes stinging at the isolation, the abandonment, I kept walking. Maybe they had...

No.

They'd left me. They'd all left me.

The grasses swayed in the warm breeze, playing on the legs of my trousers. Tugging at the long tresses of my hair.

Ahead rumbled a white mass. It roiled in the sky, barreling toward me. My breath hitched. I stepped back, but not fast enough. I blinked, and a fierce wind struck me, howling in my ears, slamming into my body, while bits of ice, sharp like blades, cut into my skin, pierced my face, my eyes.

"Venyx!" I screamed, knowing he couldn't hear me.

As suddenly as the winds came, they vanished. When I opened my eyes, I stood calf-deep in snow. The Plains buried beneath it, swallowed by it. Smoke curled on the horizon. The pyres. Those six pyres with all those bodies.

Turning back around, I trudged forward. I blinked and found myself walking into ... the marauder's camp. As it had been that last day. It, too, was empty.

"Hello?" I called, glancing between the tents, wandering, meandering down the gaping paths between them. "Cleya? Aidra? Anyone?"

My feet found the center, as they had before. I looked up at Cleya's tent, only it wasn't Cleya's. It was a hut. From the village. Swallowing a dry breath, I stepped toward it, reached out, and shoved aside the straw and beads hanging over the entrance, stepped into the yawning darkness beyond.

Inside, it stretched far larger than it should have. Filled with beds. Cots. So many of them. All empty.

"Hello?"

No one answered.

Further into the hut I went, feet crunching over grass and snow and ... I looked down. Ash. Bone.

I jumped back, eyes filling with tears, and my gaze shot up. The beds were gone. In their places were bodies. Children.

Rivers of blood ran over them, painting their faces. Their arms. Legs. It pooled on the floor, mixing with the snow, melting it, so the two ran together. I stepped in it, like that day on the beach. My feet washed red.

My gaze jumped around, desperate to find someone alive. Tears streaming down my face, I walked through the piles of bodies, glancing over them. Checking. But no. All of them, every single one, was dead.

But they weren't just Plains children. They belonged to the marauders, as well. Their fur-lined coats soaked in blood, as it sank into the soft fabric the Plains children wore. Their little braids saturated, dripping.

"Venyx," I sobbed, eyes darting around.

A hand darted out, grabbed my leg, the palm cold as its clawed grip tightened. With a start, I looked down, part of me thankful I'd found one alive. And stared into a pair of bright blue eyes, waves roiling and crashing in their depths. Lilac hair coated, painted, soaked in the blood of the children laying atop her. Atop me.

I went rigid at her touch, at the sight of my own face. Using my leg for leverage, she pulled herself from beneath the mound of children atop her, neck stretching so her eyes never left mine. A rush of blood fell from her opened throat.

One hand jumped to my own neck, blood hot and sticky, slick against my flesh.

Panic seeped into the edges of my vision. Heart wild, pounding, drumming.

Her mouth fell open, and a cascade of rot, of more blood, rolled out. It dribbled down my chin in thick rivulets. Coated my tongue.

I screamed.

I jumped awake, vaguely aware of the bedroll beneath me. Those cold fingers latched onto my ankle. The blood at my throat, coating my chin. My own dead eyes staring up at me. A scream ripped through the night.

I kicked, thrashing against the hand, the lingering dream, scooting back, away from it. From her. From me. My death. The debt I had to pay. The price carved into the flesh of so, so many.

Hot tears streamed down my face, my throat going raw as I realized it was me screaming.

A presence barreled into me. Hands on my face.

"Seraph!" he cried. He turned me to face him, those endless brown pools glimmering silver in the dark. "You're okay, you're safe."

My gaze was again pulled down to my ankle, though there was nothing there. Only the bunched-up blanket I'd kicked aside in my desperation to be free of the wraith-me.

"Eyes on me," Venyx whispered, and I slid my eyes back to him. The scream died in my throat, devolving into choking sobs before I fell forward into his chest. "You're safe." His arms wrapped around me and he sat, pulling me into his lap. "I've got you."

My fingers gripped his shirt, and I clutched him until my hands hurt. His cheek pressed into my face as he rocked back and forth, whispering over and over that I was safe. I wanted to believe those words. Wanted to melt into the warmth of his embrace. Even while the remnants of the dream stuck to me like smoke.

Over the sounds of my wails, Mato said something. Venyx ignored him, instead continuing to rock me, whisper to me. His arms tightened, pulling me closer.

"Venyx," Mato demanded, stepping closer.

"She's fine!" the deymon roared. "Go back to sleep. She's fine."

"Should we be worried ab—"

"No! Go!" Venyx wrapped me tighter in his embrace. "You're safe," he whispered.

Eventually, the tears dried up. My throat was raw, sore from screaming, from wailing. My fingers, aching and sore from gripping him so tightly, relaxed, and I softened in his lap. His embrace remained strong.

With nothing but those little whispers in my ear, he laid us back on the bedroll, curling his legs against mine.

"You're safe."

I didn't allow my eyes to open, terrified of what I would see. Instead, I nuzzled my face further into his chest, tuning out the world, the mumbles of the Plainsmen so very near, until I was consumed by the thrum of Venyx's heartbeat. His whispered words. Pliant against him, I finally fell back asleep with a silent prayer that I never dreamt again.

The village, and all those smoldering pyres, fell behind as we continued southwest. The dream lingered in the forefront of my mind, those piercing, dead blue eyes haunting me. Bodies of all the children, every one of them drenched in their own blood, plaguing me.

I didn't sleep.

When I did, it was stolen moments here and there. Terror filled me every time I closed my eyes, waiting for the blizzard to return, to wash over me. Fill the Plains with snow. And bring back that hut.

I sat hunched in the saddle as we went, my hair falling like a curtain between me and the men, including Venyx. It was an effort to keep my barriers up, to forbid him entrance into my mind, but I did it.

Every breath became painful, as if it was a betrayal. To those who'd died, those who would die. All of it, all of them, for me. How many more lives would I claim before my own was ended?

I knew Venyx worried over me. Saw it in the glances he cast toward me. Every time he touched my elbow, or helped me dismount simply because I shook too much on my own. Those eyes begged me to sleep, but I couldn't. I couldn't bear to see those faces again. Stand in that pool of blood. Feel my own dead hand grip my ankle.

The Plainsmen watched me more closely, their gazes like a physical touch. They rode closer, encapsulating me. Even at dinner, when we all

432

huddled around the campfire, though I felt none of its warmth. Saw only its bite into the flesh of the bodies we'd burned.

Just after we broke for camp, Venyx tended the horses, leaving me alone, albeit briefly, with my captors. My jailors.

I picked at my food, the ashy taste on my tongue even more prevalent than before. The world grew hazy, swaying back and forth as I sat there. My body desperate for the sleep I couldn't, wouldn't, give it.

Mato sat beside me, his steely brown gaze glaring into me.

"You need to eat," the warrior said.

"I'm fine," I mumbled, the phrase becoming my default anytime anyone, including Venyx, asked after me. The Plainsman chuckled, a hollow, sad thing, and I turned to him.

"The bags beneath your eyes would say different," he grumbled

"I'm. Fine."

He nodded, though didn't appear convinced as he shoved up and walked across camp. As I sat there, staring at the bits of shredded meat in my hands, I couldn't help but think how much I sounded like Venyx, and laughed inwardly.

Venyx sat beside me a moment later, his warmth filling my side. Exhausted, I lay my head on his shoulder, bottom lip trembling. And sighed as he laid his head atop mine.

Across from us, I noticed the glances. Mato and his men observing us. Their eyes flickering over how close we sat. I tried to pay it no mind, but wondered if Venyx noticed, too. In that moment, I couldn't be bothered with it. Not when the only comfort I found, the only sleep, was in his arms. The heat of his body chasing away those dreams. Allowing me rare, precious moments of peace.

FORTY-NINE

S LEEP DID NOT COME the next night; my own terror kept me awake. Instead I laid there, gazing at the stars, the grasses swaying and whispering and dancing in the breeze rolling around me. The soft breaths of the others caressed my ears while they slept.

During that time, when even the shadows had no place to crawl from, I thought of running. Of jumping on my horse, taking what supplies I could carry, and leaving them, all of them, behind. But as the first rays of sunlight broke across the eastern horizon, I remembered there was nowhere to go.

Geaith would likely put a price on my head. Her whole army scouring the lands for me. How far would I truly get before they found me? Before I was wrapped in chains and dragged to Pensen?

My heart heavy with grief, with guilt, cheeks sticky from tears, I watched the sun rise. Its warmth washed over my face. And wondered how many more mornings I had left.

As we rode, my head lolled forward, body slumped in my saddle. I tried so very hard to keep myself upright. But exhaustion seeped from me, poured from me. It was all I could do to eat. To relieve myself. Several times Venyx offered to let me ride with him, so I might sleep in the day, when the nightmares might not plague me, but the growling glare from Mato struck the idea down, and I declined. I assumed it had to do with the warriors riding closer to me, edging Venyx further away.

A thick tension filled the group the further from the village we went. Something amongst us had died alongside all those people. Not even Calian flirted. He rode, silent and sullen, on my right, gaze occasionally flicking to me, and past to the deymon riding on the outside of our party.

When we stopped to make camp each night I insisted upon training. I could barely stand, scarcely hold the sword aloft, but maybe, just maybe, if I fully exhausted myself, I wouldn't dream. Even if my theory had been proven wrong on the first night, I still insisted.

When Mato argued, saying it was too unsafe to wander off just the two of us, now with proof of the White Army so close, Venyx agreed. Much to my dismay. I could barely keep on my own two legs, let alone block an attack properly.

So I spent my evenings, long into the nights, sulking as the others ate. Resting as much as I was able. Stolen moments here and there. Sips of sleep, just enough to keep going. But each day became an effort. Breathing became painful. The sun's rays stabbed my eyes, as if in punishment.

Venyx, I noticed, grew increasingly frustrated by my lack of sleep. The Plainsmen did, too, but seemed more inclined to allow it. Probably because when I finally did pass out, it would be easier to drape me across one of their saddles and ride straight for Pensen.

Nearly a week after the village, when I could scarcely stand and was nearly trampled by my own horse, I did sleep. Only to wake, screaming, at the same nightmare. The image of blood pouring from my child-face's mouth stuck behind my eyes as I cried and wailed into Venyx's chest. Not even his embrace could stop the trembling.

I did not sleep again.

The scent of dawn so close, I pushed myself up from my bedroll. Rolled the thing up and dropped it back in the grass. Determined to not fall out of my saddle again, I stomped to Venyx and nudged him with my foot. One eye popped open, glowing silver in the darkened morning.

"Get up," I ordered, my voice heavy, laced with fatigue.

"Why?" he asked as he sat.

"We're training." Without waiting for a response, I turned and walked from camp, far enough away we wouldn't wake the others while trading blows. The last thing I wanted was to be scolded by Mato.

Half expecting to end up alone, I turned around and was caught by surprise when Venyx traipsed after me, drawing his swords from their sheaths. He handed me one, grip first, and stepped back, swinging his blade hypnotically.

I stood before him, sword wobbly in my hand as the deymon flipped his blade over and over, back and forth, loosening his shoulders, his arms. My legs wavered, eyelids heavy, as if weighed down with bricks. While Venyx stretched, his gaze bored into me, grazing my face.

Venyx stalked the short distance between us, swatted my sword up into position, and flicked the flat of his blade against the backs of my legs, my shoulders. "You want to insist on training, stay in position," he growled.

Rolling my shoulders, I lifted my sword, forced my legs and back to go rigid, remaining soft, leaving movement in them, and immediately succumbed to the slump I'd held only a moment before.

Circling back around to my front, Venyx growled, eyes flashing red, and swung.

My eyes shot open, locked with his, and my sword jutted up on reflex, barely blocking his blade.

"Venyx!" I screeched, yielding a step, then another, as he rained down blow after blow. He swatted my blade as if it were a toy, pushing me further and further back, no kindness on his face. The gentleness I'd become used to gone. "Stop!" I screamed.

He pelted me with more blows, each more powerful than the last.

Next came the tapping. That gentle whisper on my brain as he asked for permission inside.

Trading blow for blow, I growled in return, and shoved his mind away as I blocked another attack.

"Let me in," he said.

"No!"

He growled again, shoved harder as a blow came down. Picking between my mind and my sword arm, I jumped back and clutched my head with my free hand as a sharp pulse stabbed me. My legs trembled, threatening to spill me to the grass.

"Seraph," he warned. I looked up, found only fury, and attacked. Shoved him back, pummeling him with blows until he was forced to yield. "If you let me in, I can take it away! Make it so you never see that dream again."

He wasn't breathless as he spoke. I, however, barely heard him over my drumming heart, the frantic pulse of my lungs as my chest heaved. Heat singed across my skin, sank bone deep, making me all the hotter despite the early morning chill.

"I don't want you poking around my head!" I said, shoving again. He yielded another step, willingly. He was letting me win. Which only stoked my rage.

"I just want to help!" he shouted. "You haven't slept in days! You barely eat!"

Tears stung my eyes as I swung and missed, nearly spinning myself to the ground. "Why do you even fucking care!" I screamed, breathless. I stepped back, staring at him as his form glittered from the moisture edging my vision. My bottom lip quivered as I stared at him, took him in. "You're going to leave anyway!"

I sucked in a breath. Something dark, some deep pain, flashed across his face as his eyes again flickered red.

"If you won't let me help, I'll have no choice but to leave!" he screamed, stepping closer, the swords we held forgotten.

"You're just going to dump me in Pensen, so why does any of this matter?" I sobbed, shaking. "Take your money, and leave. Just like everyone else."

His jaw set, going rigid, the brown swallowed by red, and he chucked his sword to the grass before closing the distance between us.

"You aren't the only one who knows what it means to be abandoned!" he roared, snatching my sword from my hand and tossing it to the ground. I flinched, stepping back, reminded of why I'd feared him. Face inches from mine, he screamed, "I do not abandon you out of choice, Seraph, but if you don't let me in, I can't help you!"

"You still chose!" I screamed, shoving him, fear be damned, "to take the fucking job!"

"I chose nothing!" He towered over me, our noses nearly touching as he roared, the red in his eyes lightening, edging closer to pure white. His fangs elongated, the tips of claws poking from his fingertips. "I didn't have a fucking choice!"

"I've never had a choice!" I wailed. "My choices were stripped from me the moment I was conceived!" I shoved him again, though it was weak, spilling me to the grass. I wrapped my arms around myself as my sobs turned to wails, screeches of pain from some place inside I couldn't see. Somewhere so deep the hurt might never go away.

I kneeled, hair spilling around me, and screamed into the grass.

Venyx knelt beside me, his arms wrapping around me, pulling me into his chest. I buried my face there and released everything into him. One hand came around, cradling my head, the other digging into my back, as if holding me together. And he rocked me. Back and forth.

This time, when his mind tapped against mine, I let him in. I didn't have the energy, the will, to push him away.

Say the word, Seraph, he whispered into my thoughts. *Say the word, and you won't step foot in Pensen. Ever.*

I didn't dare meet his eyes as my tears dried. Didn't answer. Said nothing as those words reverberated in my head.

He knew.

He knew and was offering me a way out.

I just didn't know if I could trust him.

And what of everyone else? Of the world? What if I did leave? Ran? Chose me? Who would choose them?

Shoving those thoughts aside, I nuzzled further into his chest, breathed in the scent of iron and earth. And let him hold me.

Just a moment longer.

FIFTY

V ENYX AND I DID not speak of it. That moment in the throes of morning. But a new kind of terror gripped me, held me fast, and refused to relinquish its hold.

There'd already been one spy, one traitor, in my midst, one I hadn't seen. Not until the last moment. I'd allowed myself to get too close to that danger. Shared its bed. Maybe love it. And it had nearly cost me my life.

Glancing sideways at Venyx while we rode through the grasses, I couldn't be sure it wasn't the same thing. *He* wasn't the same thing. Yes, he'd had plenty of opportunities to hand me to the White Army, but so had Miran. He'd saved my life, killed so many of them. But so had Miran. Jumped into a frozen lake. Used his body to break our fall, incapacitating himself.

How many times had Miran thrust himself between me and danger? How many times had he risked his life for mine? How many times had he told me I could trust him?

Tears tore silently through me in the depths of night at the memories. At the possibility of allowing it to happen again.

I couldn't tell. Couldn't see a difference. If I asked, he would only deny it, which Miran had. Countless times.

So we rode in silence. Ate and gathered round the campfire in silence.

The Plainsmen spoke amongst themselves, ignored both me and Venyx, as if knowing the words we'd exchanged as the stars winked out. Their voices were inaudible, but their hands and fingers moved. A silent communication. Maybe to prevent Venyx from hearing something he wasn't supposed to. I wasn't sure.

Along with the growing tension, the Plainsmen closed the gap separating me from Venyx as we rode. Calian, as usual, kept to my right. Mato trotted on my left, with Makya in front and Aluk riding behind. Kishil and Nuka at front and in the rear. Venyx said nothing. He merely looked over the men as if they were little more than insects. Perhaps, to him, they were.

That night, the seating arrangement was drastically different. The spot I typically sat in had a Plainsman on either side, leaving just enough room for me. Another spot lay open between Mato and Kishil, the largest men in the group. Wordlessly, Venyx dropped between the Plains leader and the warrior and I sat between Nuka and Makya.

Venyx didn't look at me as we ate. No one spoke.

The warm air was stiff. Harsh.

After many failed attempts, I caught Venyx's gaze. Held it for a fleeting moment, and let the barrier surrounding my mind open just enough for him. That same familiar whisper, soft and caressing, filled my head.

What's happening? I asked, allowing the terror, the worry, to spill from every word.

They think you're going to run, was all he said before his voice withdrew from my mind.

I swallowed my food in a thick bite, nearly choking, and cursed myself for not finishing before my question.

I glanced around as the men ate in silence, not even exchanging glances with one another. And felt less like precious cargo, and more like a prisoner being escorted to her death. Then again, wasn't I?

Sleep still evaded me. Every time I closed my eyes, those images, that dream, returned, frightening me back to wakefulness. But now there was a new threat to consider at night, when the men were deep in the throes of slumber.

What if they killed Venyx while he slept?

The camp I'd been captive in had shown that even an older, more powerful deymon stood no chance at having his throat slit in the middle of night.

Would they risk Geaith's wrath in breaking the alliance with Aurorian?

If it meant the difference between me running, and getting me to Pensen, I already knew the answer.

I tried not to consider those things as I lay atop my bedroll, curled in on myself. I wasn't going to run, I told myself, even as my head screamed to leave while I still had the chance. But to run would be to choose myself. One person over the entire world.

Guilt at the very idea ripped through me as I lay there, staring into a vast ocean of whispers and moonlight, into the distance where shadows met the stars. And whatever lay beyond.

Where would I go if I ran? Who would take me in? Protect me? Why would they? To do such a thing was foolish. It wouldn't be just the Plains hunting me, hunting them, but the world. There would be no running. No hiding.

We rode in hot, sticky silence the following day. The same line of men separating me from Venyx as we trotted along.

Still, he said nothing. He didn't argue. Didn't push. Whether it was to keep peace with them, or to fulfill his own motives, I didn't know. If I were being honest, I was afraid to ask, and so said nothing. Simply let myself be surrounded by them as we went along. Carrying a simultaneous fear and hope that Venyx was my undoing, or my savior.

Where would we go? I asked, wondering if he was listening. His gaze flicked toward me as a ghostly caress swarmed my thoughts. He licked his lips, tightened his grip on his reins. Throat bobbing as the silence lingered between us.

Let me think on it, he finally said. And his voice vanished.

Fear pulsed in my head, echoing Miran's voice.

Another few days of silence, of compliance, and we crested a grassy knoll overlooking a village. Thankfully, one very much alive. Within its borders people went about their lives. Even from this distance, the delighted shrieks and laughs of children floated through the air.

Just beyond the village was what appeared to be a war camp. Tents jutted up from the ground, dozens of them. If not hundreds.

As the question formed on my tongue, a small group of warriors trotted up the hill on horses, and nodded to us. Each was heavily armed, swords and bows hanging off their muscular forms. Their brown eyes flickered over me, then to the deymon, and back. No wonder or awe lay in those gazes. They scrutinized me as if a plague had entered their midst. Perhaps one had.

"Siila sent word," one of the men said, his voice clipped, restrained, as he spoke. He gestured behind to the village, to the war camp just beyond. "You cannot go that way."

"Why not?" Mato asked. I glanced between the men.

The warrior sighed, licked his lips in thought. "The White Army blocked us from Pensen weeks ago."

My brows furrowed as I peered between them, an amalgamation of relief and horror washing over me. It was a blessing and a curse to be cut off from Pensen, from my destiny. From the shrinking future stretching finitely before me.

Tears sprang to my eyes as I looked across the village again, wondering if the death following me would swallow them, too. Adding more names, more faces, more lives, to the blood coating my hands, my conscience.

Those hands appeared before me again—grabbing, clawing, touching. Then the faces. The hundreds of blood-painted children. Of myself.

Geaith's words haunted me, unfurling alongside Cleya's. *Stupid girl.*

Seraph. Venyx's voice filled my head, dragging me back to reality, to the present, and I let him cradle my mind. *Eyes on me*, he whispered. He breathed deeply, sending the exhalation into my mind. I followed suit, steadied my breathing. *You're safe*, he whispered.

His breath grounded me, the thrum of his pulse chasing away the iron fist on my heart.

One breath, exhale. Another inhale. Exhale.

Mato nodded to our hosts. "Lead the way."

We trotted as a close-knit group down the knoll toward the village, and, just like in Siila, a crowd was gathered to greet us. They parted as we rode through, their eyes wide in wonder, amazement, as they peered at me.

Hands reached up, brushing my horse, my leg, thigh. Someone touched my foot. Another reached for the end of my braid.

"Child," someone whispered. Many of them kissed their fingertips and extended their hands up, out, gifting me those kisses.

"Child," another cried. I turned to the voice and caught incredulity painted across Venyx's face.

Someone muttered something in their tongue, hands outstretched.

"They say you come to save them," Aluk said, bringing up the rear. I glanced over my shoulder at him, caught his rigid glance as he reached down, easing the crowd back.

Many of the eyes staring up at me were tear-filled, twin streams running down their cheeks, hands poised over their mouths.

Heat rose to my face as I shrank away from them, from their hands and chants and cries and tears. I didn't want to be here. I certainly didn't want to be worshipped. Not for dying. The only gift I had for these people was my life, and I wasn't sure I wanted to part with it any longer. Glancing down at their reverence, just the thought of keeping my life to myself felt like sacrificing them in my place.

I swallowed the lump in my throat as the crowd fell behind. The villagers gathered around the central bonfire so similar to the sacked village. Standing before the fire was a man—tall, broad shouldered, half his skull shaved clean. He wore the same browns Geaith had donned, little beads of copper hung about his neck, along his waist. Standing beside him was a woman little older than me, her swollen belly filled with the promise of life.

Beside me, Venyx cleared his throat. A glance at him and I dismounted, as the others did, as he did, and approached the gigantic man and the slight woman at his side.

"Welcome, Child," the man said. "I am Chief Nibowin. This is my wife, Wiconi." He gestured to the woman.

I found the swell beneath her breasts, unable to look away. I'd never seen a pregnant woman before. It was all I could do to peel my eyes from her belly and find her face, the soft, sweet smile playing across her full lips as she nodded to me. I looked to the man beside her.

And my gaze again shifted to that belly.

What had I wrought upon them by coming here?

FIFTY-ONE

THE CHIEF TOOK MY hands and tugged me closer to him. I didn't have the strength to pull away, to hold myself in place. Couldn't find my voice to beg Venyx to make him let me go, though I knew he wouldn't. I was in dangerous territory. Amongst supposed allies.

"We welcome the revered Child of Sky and Sea into our home!" the chief declared to a chorus of cheers and cries. I curled away from those voices as much as possible. "Tonight, we hold a feast in her honor! To celebrate the end of the wars, and the downfall of the Faerie Queen! With the arrival of the Child, we know the dead have not fallen in vain!"

Tears stung the backs of my eyes at those words. Thick, sickening guilt curdled my gut at the very thought of running, of abandoning these people. Abandoning the one thing I'd been born to do.

"Stay as long as you need," Chief Nibowin said, his words for me alone. The only response I could muster was a single, weak nod.

My gaze drifted again to Wiconi as the chief motioned toward her, down to her belly, how she cradled it, and I mourned. Mourned the life I would never grow inside my own body. The children I would never bare. The love I would never have.

Somewhere far away, the chief continued speaking, his words lost as my gaze fell to the ground, between the two of them.

I could run. In the night. Go west. Find the White Army and hand myself over. If I did, it all might stop. They might retreat. Go home. Leave these people alone. And maybe, just maybe, the Faerie Queen would kill me herself. And the curse she'd placed upon the winter would break. The world would be set right as we both died.

Maybe.

I barely noticed the warm breeze as it rushed along my cheeks, the tears rolling down them, through my hair, tugging strands loose from the braid.

If nothing else, once I handed myself over, once they gave me to their queen, I would no longer be concerned with what happened in this world.

Because I would be dead.

A mental knock ripped me from my thoughts. I glanced up, Nibowin staring expectantly at me, mouth poised in a question already faded on the breeze.

He asked if you would like to participate in a cleansing ceremony tomorrow, Venyx provided. His voice in my head paused, as if wanting to say something else, before it withdrew. Instead, my mind was surrounded, cradled, mental arms thrown around me, squeezing tight. How I wished the hug was real.

Licking my lips, I glanced sideways toward Mato, hands folded before him. He nodded once.

Turning back to the chief, I stammered, "Y-yes."

The gathered crowd broke into cheers, hollers, cries. Chief Nibowin bowed his head, his lips pulled into a thin line.

"C-can I keep my guardian with me?" I asked, straining to be heard over the cries. Nibowin's brown gaze flicked past me, to Venyx, before he faced Mato.

My stomach sank at the silent conversation passing between the Plainsmen, worsened when the chief turned that tight-lipped smile back toward me.

447

"You will be well-looked after," he said, squeezing my hands. "As he has the queen's blessing, he will remain close."

I forced my mouth to curl and tugged my hands free. My gaze drifted back to the chief's wife, to her belly, to her face. How would she feel if her child had been handed my fate? Would she willingly hand her baby to the world? To be gutted and sacrificed? Or would she protect that child? Hold on with everything in her?

Maybe she would do as my mother had and die, avoiding the problem all together.

Though Venyx followed behind, a legion of men separated us as I was escorted to my lodgings, only a few down from the chief's. When I stepped inside, I started, the body of a woman, degraded and desecrated, lying on the floor. Blinking, the image vanished, and I found myself alone. Save for the guards stationed outside. For my protection, I'd been told.

Where Venyx was to sleep, I didn't know.

"We'll find someplace for him," Nibowin said, his smile strained.

For a moment, I glanced around, taking in the hut. It was nearly as large as the room I'd had in Siila, sans the washroom, with a bed large enough for several people, piled high with blankets and pillows and furs. The floor was made of more skins, covering the grass beneath. The walls, made of straw and clay, were sturdy, unadorned.

Sat upon the bed was a neatly folded outfit. Fingering the cloth, I looked about again.

A bucket of water sat in one corner, a rag hung over the side. Guessing its purpose, I set about cleaning the road from my skin. Wiping until the dirt and dust were gone, until I was rubbed raw and gleaming, the heat already prickling the water away. I plaited my hair in a long braid, the tresses still damp, and threw it over my shoulder before pulling on the clean clothes, the leather slippers.

Once dressed, I sat on the edge of the bed.

I knew what would happen if the White Army discovered I was here. The last village was a testament to the carnage they left in their wake. The chief's wife flashed through my head. Her belly, pregnant and protruding. And the woman in the hut returned to my mind. Her gut laid open, and it occurred to me—it was possible she, too, had carried life.

My gaze rose toward an outlet at the top, gleaming reflections bouncing off one metal plate to another, and another—a clever trick to filter in sunlight. So unlike the flickering electrical lights of The City. Yet another casualty strung about my neck.

Mere days separated me from Pensen. So Mato said.

A tremor shuddered through me, trickling down my spine. Fear like blades clawed at my heart, my chest, at what awaited me there.

Venyx's words rang in my head. *Say the word.*

My lips trembled, shook, with the echo of those words, how it had felt to be in his arms when he whispered them in my mind.

Miran's bright, sapphire eyes filled my thoughts. The words he'd said. Promises he'd made. All the times he'd begged me to go, to run away with him. He'd keep me safe, he'd said. And the whole time, it had been a pretty ruse. A farce. He'd been lying to my face, a knife poised, ready to sink into my back.

My gaze dropped to the cool, soft pants I wore, and I picked at some invisible thing on them, forcing back the flood of emotions threatening to drown me.

The expression he'd worn the last time I'd seen him, the cruel gleam in his eyes, the absolute callousness there. The words the White soldiers had said...

A tear fell, splattered on the back of my hand.

If there were gods, if they truly hadn't abandoned us, all I needed was a sign. Something to point me in the proper direction. Let me know trusting Venyx wasn't another stupid mistake.

As we rushed toward Pensen, my remaining time was quickly dwindling, and every moment mattered. Every decision counted. I couldn't afford another blunder. I couldn't afford to trust anyone again. Not like I'd trusted Miran.

Sniffling, I stood, smoothed the clothes, and pulled my braid back over my shoulder, ran it through my hands.

I wiped my tears and parted the strands of straw and beads. The full weight of the heavy Plains sun barreled atop me as my gaze swept the village. So full of life, of sound.

Near the center, toward the large bonfire, Mato's men were gathered, huddled together. Venyx stood among them, back to me, his cloak slung over one shoulder. His hair pulled back in a half-topknot.

A girl, no more than five or six, wandered up to him, staring at the deymon as if she'd found a unicorn, her dark eyes full of wonder. The men paid her no mind, so wrapped up in their discussion. Not to be ignored, she reached a tiny hand and tugged on Venyx's cloak. He looked down, caught her beside him, and dropped to his haunches before her.

Only Aluk seemed to notice, a flicker of a smile crossing his face before he returned to the conversation.

The girl pointed to Venyx's mouth, opened her own, and tapped her teeth. I bit back my rising chuckle, suddenly reminded of a little girl in the marauders' camp who'd asked the same thing. My heart melted as he obliged and ran his tongue over the top four, then the bottom four fangs.

Nose wrinkled up, the girl shrank back with a giggle, and cautiously reached out. No sooner had the tip of a finger tapped one of those deadly points Venyx chomped down on her hand. Not enough to hurt her. The squeal of delight was testament enough as her fists curled back into her chest before she ran off.

As Venyx stood, his eyes found mine and I held his gaze for a long moment, entranced, before he turned back to the warriors.

FIFTY-TWO

T HEY BARELY NOTICED AS I slid between Venyx and Calian, both men towering over me as they parted to let me join the circle. For just a moment, my breath caught as the warriors enveloped me, until the weight of Venyx's hand wrapped around mine and I shrank into his side.

"The best way to get around it would be to head south, then west," Mato was saying.

"Without knowing how far south it extends, how practical is that?" Venyx asked.

The warrior who'd met us, guided us into the village, looked over my guardian, wary, and took a breath. "Our warriors fighting the White Army say they don't have enough men to extend across the Plains. They wait for ships from Kaival to complete the blockade. If you travel far enough south, you will get around."

"At what cost?" Nuka asked.

"We need many more than seven men to make this journey," Aluk added. Calian and Makya nodded their agreement.

"We'd just be throwing away our lives," Makya said. Mato's gaze flickered over me, and the weight of it bore me into the ground.

"We plan on joining the fight day after tomorrow," the village warrior said. "We will be taking men with you. You ride with us, we will make a blockade of our own, get you around it, and you carry on to Pensen."

My heart hitched, pulse fluttering through my limbs, my head. "You said more ships?" I asked.

"Yes. We have scouts on the shores who see sails crossing the Emerald Ocean. They will be here within ... weeks."

I bit my bottom lip, sucked in a breath to force my anxiety back, to keep myself present, even if all I wanted was to vanish. To let the panic take me, for the world to fade away. Venyx squeezed my hand, weaving our fingers together.

"Maybe I've been away too long," Venyx countered, "but an assault of that scale should trigger the World Council."

Mato nodded. "Our queen requested it be gathered. We have yet to hear back."

"Because of the Boundary," the village warrior added, "Pensen is obligated to remain neutral..."

"But their hand may be forced," Mato finished. "An invasion of this size has not been seen since—"

"Since the last war," Venyx said. Mato nodded. I gazed up at my guardian, silent memories sliding across his face, and wondered what it had been like, the wars before. All of them trying, and failing, to overthrow the Faerie Queen. To release what she'd stolen.

How was I, one person, supposed to do what the whole world could not?

"Enough of this," Mato said, turning to me. Somehow, I doubted it was due to the somber tone the conversation had taken, and more with how comfortable I was tucked beside Venyx. "It was requested I take you to Chief Nibowin to help prepare for the feast tonight."

I glanced down at my clothes, then back up to the warrior. "I thought I had."

He chuckled, dropped his hand on my shoulder, and led me from the group, dislodging my fingers from Venyx's. I glanced at Venyx over my shoulder as he was pulled in a different direction.

"You will be expected at Chief Nibowin's side tonight," Mato said, leading me through the village. "It is a great honor to be included in such a thing."

I said nothing as Mato led me toward the largest hut in the village, one surrounded by guards. Women's voices floated from inside, their laughter and banter filling me with a sense of ... something. I couldn't recall the last time I'd been around more than one woman at a time.

The guards pulled back the flaps of the hut and a large preparation space opened before me. Vegetables and grains were laid across tables, women peeling and cutting and dicing as they talked. Their voices cut off abruptly as Mato and I entered, a collection of brown eyes turning toward me.

A flicker of awe passed over their faces as each mouth turned up with a carefully placed smile before the chief's wife approached and took my hands.

"Thank you," Wiconi said to Mato, dismissing him. With a bow, he turned and left. "We are so pleased to have you here, Child."

"It's Seraph," I said coolly. Far too quietly. She nodded and smiled, as if only partially hearing me.

"The gods have blessed us on such a special occasion," she said, leading me toward the rear of the hut. "They gifted us this."

Splayed on the grass was an antelope. A single arrow punctured its eye. Clearly dead, for its chest was still, legs limp on the floor. I found myself transfixed by its gaping face.

Would I wear that same expression once I was dead?

"...the largest we have been gifted," Wiconi was saying, pulling me back to the present. My gaze flicked up to her face. "It is a sign we are to be blessed."

I swallowed, staring down at the animal, and forced my gaze up as she handed me a knife.

"It would bring good luck to have the sacred Child make the first cut," she said. "To bleed the gods' gift."

I swallowed again, forcing my hand to grip the knife.

Work around the hut ceased as bodies surrounded me, observing my every move as I kneeled before the carcass.

"Here," Wiconi said, pointing to the animal's neck. "It will bleed faster."

Licking my lips, I scanned the beast. The arrow embedded in its eye. Like the knife I'd plunged into Miran's face.

I wanted to say no. To drop the knife. To leave this hut. The village. Walk to the ocean, however far it was, and wade beneath the waves. Never surface again. Whatever that meant for me.

But the press of bodies around me, their curious faces, the tension in their hands, arms, as they stared down at me, pinned me in place. Held me there.

My lips quivered as I adjusted the knife in my hand, poised the tip of the blade above where she'd shown me, and pressed.

It was sharp, sinking into the beast's hide, into flesh and fur and veins, with ease, and a waterfall cascaded out, gushing across the grass, over my slippers, the hem of my pants, the knees where I knelt. Across my hands.

It hadn't been dead long. The scarlet washing my skin was too warm, too fast.

Blood along cobblestone streets flooded my vision. Rushing across my hands as I took a life.

My breath hitched. Heart skipping wildly.

Miran's blood. The blood of the White soldiers, the ones in the forest. Their bodies hacked apart by Venyx's blades. Ribbons of red strewn across scorched lands, painting the walls of a hut where a woman lay, bared open for all to see. Her life snuffed out. A river of scarlet running along the faces of those children. Pooling beneath them.

I couldn't breathe.

My throat closed off as the knife fell from my hands. My vision dimmed, going hazy around the edges.

I sucked in breath after desperate breath, but my lungs remained empty. Blood, thick and sticky, coated my hands, ran between my fingers. Soaking into the knees of my trousers.

"Child?" someone asked, though the voice was like a wraith, both there and not.

"Are you alright?" The gentle tone sank into my ears, but did not reach me.

My stomach curdled.

Lurching to my feet, I shoved past the bodies surrounding me, ignoring their calls, their protests. Ignored the blood dripping from my hands, prickling my legs and arms and feet.

The hut was too close, too small. I needed air.

Stumbling from the structure, I spilled into daylight, a myriad of faces gazing at me, expressions blank, lifeless.

Another breath, but still no air.

Faces blurred as I went, eyes sticking to me, to my back, as they whispered *murderer*.

Killer.

Selfish.

I sucked down another breath, stumbled through the grass, through the village. The huts were all too close. The people too close.

Their breath ran down my neck, my spine. Heartbeats drumming loud in my ears.

I turned, faced a line of homes on either side, and saw the darkened streets of The City, littered with bodies. Dragons flying overhead, toppling buildings. Children screaming, crying for parents they'd never see again.

The marauder's camp. Bodies crawling through the snow, their skin melting as they died. Their wails filled my ears, dug into my bones. A burning tent collapsing, children still inside.

I stumbled again, clawing through the gathering people, faces twisted into masks of hatred. Hands outstretched, ready to tear the flesh from me, to claim the life that was theirs. Retribution for the ones I'd stolen.

A sob ripped from my chest as I burst from them, from the final row of huts, and out. Into the field beyond. And kept going.

Breathe.

Breathe.

I sucked down another breath. Then another.

And fell to my knees.

A warm breeze swathed my face, suffocating me, as a wail tore from my gut. Eyes filled with hot tears, I dropped my gaze to my hands, still coated in blood, and saw not an animal, but all the people who'd died because of me.

Nik's face flashed through my head, hovering just above the ice, so peaceful as he accepted his death. The death I'd dealt him.

My breath hitched, heart stammered. The moment of air I'd been afforded was snatched from my lips as my lungs closed off.

My tears came harder, faster, as I clawed the grass, desperate for air that wouldn't come.

Cleya whispered in my ear, *stupid girl*, and I knew she was right.

I collapsed forward, begging my body to cooperate as my vision thrummed, darkness dancing before me, spots swimming over my eyes, across them.

All those faces. All those people. Nik. Tollok. Lira. Ace. Lives I'd stolen for merely being in their presence.

Hands suddenly gripped my arms, hauled me up, and something, someone, grabbed my chin, lifted my face. Twin pools of brown glistened before me.

His voice was there, filling my head. *Come back to me*, he whispered. One hand stroked my face, shoved the hair back. Wiped away the tears.

"Eyes on me," he said.

Like a bolt, a sob tore through my chest and I blurted his name, my breaths gasping, sodden. I clutched my hands, still blood-soaked, to my chest, as if I might cradle the lives I'd taken, plead forgiveness, knowing I had no right to it.

"Seraph," he whispered. *Seraph, come back to me.*

"Venyx," I gasped. My mouth fell open, silent, wracking wails pounding out of me while I fought for another gulp of air, and greedily drank it down. "I can't do this." My head bowed as another sob wracked through me.

"Tell me what to do," he pled, eyes full of helpless despair. All the harshness, the coldness I'd known the past months was gone, fled in the warm breeze rushing across us both. "Tell me how to help."

"Please kill me," I wailed. "I don't want to go."

I shook my head, tears cascading down my cheeks, pattering across my trousers. I glanced up, caught the look on his face, the bone-chilling expression hanging in his eyes as he took me in.

"Please kill me."

He went utterly still. His face a mask of stoicism as his grip fell from me, and I nearly collapsed without his support. Again, his hands were on me, pulling me into him.

Like a child, I curled into him, pressed my face into his chest, and let him cradle me. Let him rock me. My fingers dug into his shirt, into the skin beneath as wail after wail tore through me.

"I'm here," he whispered against my hair. "I'm here."

By the time the tears finally stopped, when I regained my breath, and I simply sat in his lap, memorizing the rhythm of his heart, I realized he hadn't told me I was safe.

We both knew I wasn't.

Not even him, with all his thousands of years, all his gifts and strengths, could protect me.

FIFTY-THREE

THERE WERE NO TOASTS. No chants or cheers. No cups raised to me, my life, my death, my sacrifice.

I sat beside the chief and his wife, their three children sitting around them, and tried to ignore them, the concerned looks Wiconi passed me throughout the night.

Apparently, my outburst had terrified her, the women in the preparation hut, the chief, and half the village. Not to mention Venyx. He was silent after Mato found us in the field, though I scarcely remembered walking so far.

After Mato insisted I climb from Venyx's embrace, I was escorted to my hut and scrubbed the blood from my hands. It had taken everything in me to not dissolve again, as all that red slid from my fingers.

Venyx had been asked to keep his distance from the festival, regardless of my protests. So, wherever he lurked, I didn't know. Occasionally, the whisper of his mind caressed my own, checking on me.

The villagers danced and sang, going in circles around the bonfire, hands and eyes raised to the heavens, mimicking the flames in their movements. Wiconi mirrored them, her thigh pressed against mine, trying to get me to join her merriment, but I didn't have the energy. It had taken every ounce of strength to come from my hut when Mato called for me.

Eventually, she stopped trying. Tension snaked through her as she turned from me, but I couldn't be bothered to care. Every glance in my direction, every whisper of my name, had me a breath away from another crack. Entertaining the people celebrating my impending death was not something I was inclined to do.

The night dragged on. Drums beat alongside foreign instruments. Voices carried on the hot breeze, crackling with the blazing fire. Children ran about, chasing each other in games I didn't know. Occasionally, one would stop, approach, and reach out to touch my hair, or gaze into the roiling oceans buried in the depths of my eyes before Wiconi hissed, sending them scurrying.

"They get so excited," she said, her mouth turned in a thin smile. I dropped my gaze to my lap, avoiding her eyes. If I looked at her, I'd be drawn to her belly again, and that viscous curl of jealousy would wrap around my insides at something I'd never get to experience.

Tugging at the hem of my trousers, the beads adorning my slippers, I sniffled back tears and glanced over the blaze, at those dancing around it, and turned to Wiconi as she and her husband rose, calling to someone.

Licking my lips, I dropped my shoulders and returned to picking at my clothes.

"How are you enjoying the feast?" Mato's voice was thick, with worry and something else. Something I didn't want to consider. He stood beside me, massive, muscled arms folded over his broad chest, and I glanced back down, my lips curling into a sneer. "I'm not finding much joy tonight, either," he confessed, dropping to his haunches. "I would rather be on the way to Pensen. Since our journey has doubled."

I let my hair fall between us, a curtain of sorts, though it didn't drown out his words, the tone of his voice. The warrior sighed, plucked a blade of grass and twirled it between his fingers before discarding it.

"I admire you."

I turned to him, my hair falling against my shoulder as I took the warrior in, the lines of his face more visible in the firelight.

"What you're doing. Even if it's not something you want, or choose. That you are still doing it..." He paused, looked up into the night sky, then back at me. And smiled.

Tears stung the backs of my eyes. I longed to snatch that smile from his face, to throw it in the flames and watch it burn. My throat swelled as his meaning set in. He'd drag me to Pensen if need be.

"Sometimes, to protect its herd, an antelope will sacrifice itself so the rest may live," Mato said. He took a breath. "It is not something to be enjoyed, but it is a thing that must be done. For the betterment of those who remain."

A bitter taste rose up my throat, coated my mouth, and the words poured from me before I could stop them. "Have you ever asked the antelope what *it* thinks of its sacrifice?"

His gaze dropped. "Sacrificing one for the many is honorable." His brown gaze again met mine. "You will live on. For years. Generations. In the stories we tell. For people all over the world. In all our memories."

I turned away, my lilac locks covering my face before he could see the tears rolling from my eyes. Tried to stifle the sobs creeping up my throat. Shrank from Mato's hand as he placed it upon my shoulder before rising and walking away.

I stared into the flames as they danced back and forth, crackling in their own song. And considered, for a moment, throwing myself into them. Their precious Child. I hiccupped and shoved the thought down, back into the deepest, darkest corners of my mind. Before Venyx could hear it. Before I could give it life.

How much time passed I wasn't sure, only vaguely aware of Chief Nibowin sinking into his seat beside me. I glanced up as he found my untouched plate of food. The one I'd felt too sick to look at for more than a moment.

"If you'll pardon me," I said, voice hoarse, pulling the chief's attention toward me. "Thank you for the festival, but I'm tired."

I glanced over his features, the pity lingering in his eyes, before I took his nod as approval and shoved to my feet.

Inside my hut, I kicked off my slippers, tugged off my trousers, and crawled under the mound of blankets, burying myself beneath them, and pulled the pillows close.

At a flash of light, I started, my vision blurry as Venyx entered, eyes glowing silver.

"The guards are still attending the feast," he muttered, standing at the side of the bed. "I wanted to make sure you were all right."

A sob choked its way up from my gut, guttering out my mouth as I crumbled at the sight of him. He toed off his boots and climbed into bed beside me, beneath the blankets, pulling me into his chest. His scent, his warmth, filled me between the gasps and cries. One hand stroked my hair while the other rubbed circles along my back.

He sighed into my hair, pulling me tighter, his smattering of stubble scratching my face.

"I thought you liked to be clean shaven," I muttered into his chest. He chuckled, rubbed his jaw.

"It doesn't seem as important right now," he replied, and hugged me tighter.

I tangled my legs in his, relishing him pressed against me. Sniffling, I closed my eyes and nuzzled closer, breathing in iron and earth, those timeless smells. And let myself drift off against him, his fingers running through my hair.

It was warm when I woke the next morning. And found myself alone. The only indication he'd been there were the pillows, still holding the impression of where he'd slept. The rumpled blankets he'd climbed from beneath.

I sat up, a sense of longing tugging at me, of missing something I'd never had, and climbed from bed. Slipping on my trousers and shoes, I padded outside, blinking away the bright sunlight.

Groups of people sat in the village center, an assembly line of arrows among them. They barely glanced up as I walked past, braiding my hair as I went. I paid them little mind as I headed for Chief Nibowin, huddled together with Mato, my stomach sinking.

They'd told him to leave. Threatened him. Something.

I shoved those thoughts aside, forced my feet to continue, to plod ahead until the two men towered over me, their voices soft, hushed. It wasn't until I cleared my throat they faced me.

"Good morning," Mato said, a stiff smile curling his lips. "Feeling better today?"

I ignored him, instead facing the chief. "Where's Venyx?"

The man cleared his throat, shot a glance to Mato, and slid his gaze back to me before speaking, *not* answering my question. "We were just discussing you," he said. "Whether you would still like to participate in the ceremony tonight, since your..." He stopped. "Since yesterday," he finished, rushing forward. "Your journey has undoubtedly been very taxing, and if you are too tired to participate, I understand. But ... our, my people would greatly appreciate your presence."

"We *are* going to war for you," Mato added, venom dripping from every word. Only then did I turn to him.

"You're not going to war *for* me," I spat. "You're going to war to decide who gets to kill me."

His eyes darkened, mouth sliding open in retort before the chief blurted out his next words, disrupting the brewing argument between me and the warrior.

"I understand this is a very difficult thing," Nibowin said. "But, you are a gift from the gods. And your sacrifice will be rewarded in the next life."

I faced him, unable to wipe the disdain from my face as I said, "I would rather rest up for the journey. Since it's doubled." Mato's head dipped, a smirk tipping one corner of his mouth.

"Of course." The chief nodded, not bothering to hide his disappointment.

"Where's Venyx?" I repeated.

"I'm afraid we haven't seen him all morning," Mato said. "Perhaps he left."

I flung a glare at him before shoving past the warrior and walked further into the village. As I stormed away, I spotted Calian, hunched before the remnants of the fire, running a whetstone down his curved blade. He looked up, a smile stretching across his mouth as I approached.

"Have you seen Venyx?"

He nodded and pointed. "He was meditating in the grass," the young warrior provided, "when we came back from sparring."

His voice followed me as I hurried past, not bothering to listen to the rest. No one stopped me as I left the village, heading east into the tall grasses, the warm wind following, as if it, too, was eager to find my guardian.

Why, I didn't know.

Maybe I just wanted to ensure he hadn't left. Not that I could blame him. I wouldn't. I didn't. I just wanted to see him, I told myself.

And, for a moment, I almost believed it.

FIFTY-FOUR

THE WINDS WHISPERED AND sang through the grasses, tugging against my trousers, loose tresses of hair hanging about my face. Warm, radiant sunshine beat upon me. A thin film of sweat already clung to my brow, and I wondered if the heat would last into the night again. At least when riding, the breeze rushed into my face, cooling me, even if only slightly.

I wasn't sure what I expected to find. Whether he would be meditating, or pacing. Perhaps weighing his options. Of leaving behind his payment, the word he'd given Aurorian. Me. So it was a surprise to find his black-swathed form sitting on a large rock in an ocean of waving grass, cross-legged, chin in his hands, his brown eyes staring at ... nothing. His focus on the distant northern horizon.

Anger wafted off him, from the tense set of his shoulders to the rigidity of his back. So I approached him like one might approach a predator.

Taking a deep breath, hands wringing together, I crept through the grass toward him, forcing a smile to my lips. One he did not return as those pools of brown flicked up before he dropped his chin and buried his hands in his hair, a curtain of black separating us.

Not sure what to say, how to begin, I said the first thing that came to mind, the only thing that might have him so upset. "I'm sorry. F-for the episode. For not telling you sooner." Another tense smile, but it was wasted. He didn't even glance up. "It's not something I go around telling people. But you shouldn't have had to find out that way. So, I'm sorry."

Silence stretched between us, punctuated by the hiss of rolling grasses.

"Aurorian never told me," he grumbled, his voice barely audible. The breeze tugged on the hair laced between his fingers. "But I knew. I've known."

My brows furrowed, something inside pinching my heart.

"I told myself she wouldn't make you do it. It was your choice," he mumbled. He took a large breath, held it for a long moment, and exhaled.

"So when you asked me..." I began, "when you asked at Delthia's..."

He sighed, a heavy, regretful thing, and let one hand fall, leaning his head into the other, as he picked some imaginary speck of dust off his trousers. Licked his lips, the tips of his fangs just visible. "She didn't tell me," he continued, "because she knew I would have rejected the job. So she offered me something she knew I couldn't turn down." He sighed again. Shook his head. "I would do what I was hired to do, if that's what *you* wanted," he grumbled. "I wouldn't force you to not go."

I nodded, absorbing his words carefully, tucking them away to examine later. My gaze dropped from the shadowy confines of his face, still drenched in his hair, to my hands, and began digging dirt from my fingernails, simply to keep from staring at him. If I did, I wasn't sure I would be able to continue standing. Not without bursting into tears.

"If it's about the money," I started, "you're still going to get paid. You haven't wasted your time on a dead girl. I'll make sure of it once we get to Pensen."

I glanced up as his gaze snapped to mine, a cold, ravenous fury filling his features. My hands stilled, spine going rigid, and I stepped back.

"Is that what you think of me?" he growled. "What you think my concern is?"

466

Tears filled my eyes, my throat swelling at the accusation. "I don't know what to think, Venyx. What else is there?" My shoulders raised in question, hands poised delicately before me. My taut body filled with fear as he stood and stepped toward me, a ferocity unlike anything I'd seen blazing in his eyes, turning them deep, fiery red.

"I don't give a shit about the fucking payment, Seraph," he hissed, his breath fanning my face, warming the tears in my eyes.

He snapped away and stalked through the grasses, hands flying through his hair as palpable fury sang from his every move, reminding me of a beast cut off from its dinner.

I licked my lips, unable to speak, to move. I needed to leave, to be away from him, but couldn't bring myself to step back. His movements transfixed me, held me in place, until words poured from me in a tear-filled babble. "I don't know what you want from me."

He stopped, went rigid, before he whipped around and crossed to me, those eyes burning red. "I want to know what *you* want!" he roared. "What does *Seraph* want? From your own fucking life! Aside from letting the world butcher you! Letting Aurorian butcher you to sate her own fucking guilt!"

My mouth fell open, gaping, as his words barreled into me. Even the tears stilled on my face until he whipped back around, continuing his rage-filled pacing.

"I don't know," was the only response I could muster, the only words I could force from my lips, though they were weak, as if my own chest, my throat, knew the lie. As if my tongue could taste it.

"That's bullshit and you know it!" he roared, wheeling around.

"What else do you expect from me!" I shouted, tears pouring, running into my mouth, the salt from them coating my tongue. "I've only ever known that I am to die! This is what I was made for! My one purpose!"

"Every bit of that is a fucking lie!" he bellowed. "All of it! And you fucking know it!" His hair flew about his face as he roared, red eyes verging on white, his fangs elongating in his rage. "One thing! You must want one fucking thing for yourself!"

I shook as I stared at him, at the utter violence in his eyes, and found I wasn't afraid, not of him, but of the sheer emotion he was displaying ... for me. And shook my head, denying all of it.

"No," I said, hair clinging to my face, to the tears. "This is my job."

He scoffed, turned away, and shoved his hands in his hair. "People are dying because of me, Venyx. What would you have me do?"

He was suddenly in front of me, pressing into me, the heat from his body wafting over me, breath fanning my face in frantic bursts. Those eyes pure white.

"After you've lived as long as I have, you get used to people dying. And they do. Every fucking day. No amount of your blood, not a single fucking drop, will ever change that. Every bit of the bullshit you've been fed is a fucking lie," he seethed. "If it's not this, it will be something else."

"I don't know what else to do," I sobbed.

"Find another way."

I hiccupped, shook my head in confusion, at the idea that something, anything else, might change my fate. "I do—"

"What do you want, Seraph?" he asked.

"I don't know!" I screamed.

"You are too strong a person to let them slaughter you like a fucking pig."

"I'm tired of being strong!" I shrieked, shoving him back. "I don't want to be strong anymore!"

Lips in a tight line, he nodded. "What do you want?"

"I can't have what I want! So it doesn't even fucking matter!"

He chuckled, licked his lips, and turned away, stormed toward the rock, past it. "And what is this elusive thing you want?" he asked, his tone mocking, seething, cold and cruel, reminding me of the man I'd met all those months ago. The one angry at the world.

I screamed my response before I thought it, before the words formed in my head, before I processed what they would mean. "I want you!"

And stopped.

My breath hitched in my throat, body going still as I traced the path of those words right as they reached him. He stopped. And turned to face me.

All at once, my head and chest caught up, and I couldn't get enough air. I gaped, unable to move beneath the weight of his gaze. Paralyzing fear gripped me. And I realized ... I was going to die anyway.

"I want you," I repeated. Those eyes, pure white, shifted back to red, though the tension didn't leave his form, his shoulders. "I want a family. I want a home. I want children. I want to feel a baby growing inside me. I want love. To be loved. To love so much it hurts." The brown reclaimed his eyes, but still he didn't move. Every moment he was silent was like another nail driven into my heart, and so I barreled on, if for no other reason than to say I'd held nothing back. "I want a life that's mine."

My gaze fluttered over him, watching for a sign, anything, of what he felt, but he gave nothing away. The apology rest on my tongue, though I refused to voice it. He'd asked. I'd answered.

His hands fell to his sides. The breeze toyed with the strands of his hair, tugged at his clothes.

My breath hitched. Terror gripped every part of me. That he'd leave. He'd leave and I'd never see him again. He'd abandon me to my fate.

Then he was moving. Rushing through the grass. My chest heaved at his gait, his speed, bracing myself for the words about to leave his lips, their icy bite cleaving into my heart. Before I could speak, before I could move, he barreled into me, the hardness of his body slamming into me. My face was in his hands, and his lips were on mine.

A single breath and I melted into it, into him. I allowed myself to fall against him. My hands reached up, clung to his shirt, pulling him closer, though no room remained between us.

His fingers dug into my hair, thumbs on my cheeks. His lips were soft. Gentle. Sweeping across mine with a subdued hunger I'd never known. I breathed him in, slid my hands up his chest, and around his neck, my fingers playing in the length of his hair, running through those silky strands.

469

One of his hands slid from my face, down, around to my back, cradling me, pulled my hips to his, nearly lifting me off the ground. My head lolled back, and I pushed forward, into him, into his kiss, silently demanding more. Parted my lips and relished his tongue dancing across mine, the taste of him.

The longer we were locked together, standing in the middle of the field, the hotter the intensity grew until I could barely stand it. I was cast into the flames of him, of myself, us, joined by our lips, our arms entwined around each other.

The hand on my face slid into my hair, cupping my head, tipped it back, allowing him more access. And I drew him further in. Ran my tongue over the tips of his fangs, traced his lips as I greedily drank him in until I was drowning in him.

It wasn't until my lungs began burning, begging for air, that I pulled back, and he did the same. We were left, arms tangled around each other, eyes locked together. The reality of what just happened sinking in.

How the world had shifted with three little words.

FIFTY-FIVE

I SUCKED IN A greedy breath, swimming in Venyx's gaze. His thumb rubbed small circles on my back, warming me, sending soothing vibrations up my spine as I stood, wrapped in his arms. His other hand woven through my hair.

Slowly, his palm slid down to cup my face, and he leaned forward, eyes closed, his long lashes kissing his cheeks. I rested my forehead against his, absorbing him. Taking in the beat of his heart as it returned to normal, same as mine. Coming down off the high.

My lips tingled from his. Every part of me burning, alive, singing from his touch, his kiss.

I was afraid to move, to slip from his grasp. If I did, I might wake and find it had been a dream, a wonderful lie crafted by my own head. So I stayed utterly still. Even though I longed to kiss him again, to taste him again.

Moving my head just so, I found his lips, in the same instant he found mine. His embrace crushed me to him, raising me off my feet as his tongue slipped inside my mouth, danced along mine. He set me back down and broke the kiss, digging his face into my hair. I rested against his shoulder, relishing his fingers on my back, my scalp.

And never wanted this moment to end.

As if waking from a reverie, that subtle, whispered knock sounded on the wall surrounding my mind.

I shuddered a breath, slid my hands from his hair to his chest, fingers digging into the fabric covering him.

He knocked again. I eased those barriers open, let him slip inside, a shallow step, before his voice filled my head. A flickering whirlpool of emotion burst through the whisper curling around my thoughts.

Please let me help you, he pled.

I clenched my eyes shut, biting my lower lip to hold back the cascade of sobs threatening to hurtle themselves from my throat. He sighed against me, warm breath caressing my cheeks, the tears trailing there.

I know how difficult trust is to come by, especially for you, he whispered, his voice like silk in my mind. *No words can bring that kind of security, and I would expect no less.*

I tightened my grip in his shirt, buried my face in his shoulder to snuff out the tears. One hand dug into my back, clutching me as if holding me together. It felt very much like he was. The other played in my hair, then slid to my shoulder, squeezing me tighter, harder, against him.

All I want, he said, *is to keep you safe. To keep you alive.*

My lips trembled as the echo of his voice washed away my thoughts. I wanted to believe him. Wanted to trust him. Every instinct told me he was, perhaps, the only safe person I'd ever met. Even while experience told me I would never have such a luxury.

There's nowhere to go, I whispered in return. *We can't go to the Northerlands. We'd never make it.*

His voice fell silent. The fingers of his mind slowly pulled back, loosening their grip on my brain.

Dread filled every part of me as his silence dragged on. And on. As his non-answer rang in my head, clutching my heart tighter, colder, than the iron grip of panic.

But then, he said, *Abaddon*, and the word flooded every part of me. *We can go to Abaddon. We can hide there. Not for long, but...* He stopped, considering, and carried on. *I have a friend I can reach out to, see if she would be willing to help. It may take time. Either way, we'd have to leave tonight.*

Trembling, I opened my eyes and pulled back, took in his face, the expression he wore. No hint of a smile. No jokes. He cupped my jaw and his thumb stroked my cheek.

It's the one place in the world no one would dare go, he said.

His home.

At a loss, I simply stared at him. Not sure whether to trust him, to believe the words in my mind.

It would not be an easy life, he said, stroking my face. *We would be hunted. By everyone. I could not guarantee you a home. Or freedom. It would not be a life for children.*

My breath hitched, tears reigniting in my eyes.

But I would protect you, keep you as safe as I can. All I wish in return is to know you still breathe.

What about Aurorian? She travels—

Let me worry about her, he said, his voice matter-of-fact. *Focus on now. We need to move quickly. The moment we leave—*

They'll be hunting us.

Yes. He sighed, as if the very thought were exhausting. If I were being honest, it was.

But.

For the first time in my life, I had hope.

I played with the folds of his shirt, counting them back and forth, before meeting his eyes. He brushed a lock of hair from my face, tucking it behind my ear.

How will you reach your friend? With your mind?

Yes. She's another of my kind. I haven't spoken to her in a long time, so I'm not sure she'd be willing to listen. He rubbed the bridge of his nose before running his hand through his hair. *But I'll try. She would be our best chance of getting out of Northern Lorralei. Not that the South would be safer.*

473

Gazing into his face, I found myself believing him. Despite myself. It was not a want to believe him, not a desperation to do so. But belief. Simple. Raw. One soul to another.

Sighing, I laid my head against his shoulder, closed my eyes as his arms wrapped tighter around me.

So, he started again. *We'll leave tonight. We'll ride hard. Carry only enough to survive. If you choose to go with me. If you choose this life.*

I let a moment of silence trickle between us, considering it. Considering him. Would I harness that seed of hope? Let it sprout within me? Or would I carry on with the course set before me long before I'd been born? The course I no longer chose to accept.

Maybe there was another way. Maybe I could find it. That certainly couldn't happen if I were dead.

We leave tonight, I whispered in return. He sighed, a relief-filled thing, and kissed my hair, hugged me tighter.

The war party would leave in the morning. The ceremony would take place tonight. Somewhere in that small space of time, that sliver of night when the world slept, I would trust the man before me.

Not because I had to. Not because I was his job. Or an oath sworn to a king he'd never met. Not to appease Aurorian, or to satisfy Pensen.

Because I chose to.

FIFTY-SIX

MATO AND CHIEF NIBOWIN were surveying the arrows already made. Piles and piles of them by the time I made it back to the village. Still, more were needed. It was clear in their tones, on their faces, when I approached, without hearing a word either of them spoke.

The warrior looked up first, catching my eyes before I turned to the chief at his side. Mato may have only been human, unable to glimpse inside another's mind, but he saw things. Things others did not. And I didn't trust myself to not wear our hastily erected plan on my features as I approached the pair.

I was to distract the villagers, the warriors, while Venyx reached out to his friend. Tonight rest upon the success of him pulling together this fool's errand. So I would do my part, anxious as it made me.

I cleared my throat, catching Nibowin's attention. It was Mato who reeled back, massive arms crossing his chest in disbelief, when I said, "I would like to attend the ceremony after all. It would be an honor to take part." I tried to ignore the warrior's sullen expression, the skeptical gaze he pierced me with, as the chief's face lit with excitement.

I forced back the prickling guilt at the lie, telling myself it wasn't. Not really. I didn't want them to be hurt. Or die. Maybe, if I left, they wouldn't go to battle. Perhaps a naïve thought, but I clung to it anyway.

"We would be honored to have you attend, Child," Nibowin said, his smile spreading thick across his face. I stifled a cringe at the use of the moniker I so hated. Despised after all these years. But returned his smile, nodding graciously.

I was not the disheartened wreck of a woman from yesterday, but one filled with hope. Even if merely a kernel. A small, glowing ember. One spark was all it took. Just one. And I intended to warm myself with it, despite the odds stacked against me. Despite all I had to fear. I wanted to believe, so chose to. Still, I could not fan the flames of my hope too brightly, for fear it would seem false.

The rest of the morning was spent going over the ceremony. What it entailed, what my role would be. How I would help them.

I would simply be a beacon. A force to rally around. I would bless the weapons, the warriors, beg the gods to show them mercy on the battlefield. Or swift deaths if mercy was in short supply.

It was only when the chief asked me to beg my father's blessing that I halted, suddenly unsure if I could carry on.

"I've never asked him for anything," I said meekly. I didn't even know his name. Didn't know what he looked like.

"That is okay," Nibowin offered, a gentle hand on my shoulder. "You need only ask his blessing, here if need be." He touched my brow.

I drew a breath and nodded. Exhaled.

"I'll try."

"After the weapons are blessed, we will request the gods spill as little blood as possible," he said.

That needed no lie to cover. I hoped for the same. No more blood spilled on my account. No more coating my hands.

"The warriors will dance, asking for the gods' blessing," the chief said, motioning to the massive firepit in the center of the village. "You are welcome to join if you like."

I nodded again.

Inhale. Exhale.

I could do this.

By early afternoon, Mato appeared slightly more convinced, though stayed by my side as I was led back to my hut. He remained outside, with the guards, while a flurry of women filled the space, washing and scrubbing until my skin felt thinner. Raw.

Though they chatted about me, to me, I could barely keep my thoughts inside the hut, on the drifting conversations.

Venyx was to hang back, stay away, until the end of the ceremony. Though I wanted to believe in him, a deep, gnawing fear clawed at my belly. While I was distracted by the prayers, the dancing, the warriors, and the blessings, he would run.

If he didn't, if we truly went through with it, how far would we get before the Plains army gave chase? Found us and forced me to Pensen. Would they kill him? Would they be able to? How many men would it take to bring him down?

As those thoughts swept through my head, more piled in. Of his friend. Would she truly help us? What if she said no?

And, of course, what Abaddon looked like. If it was truly a country of ruins, of death, as so many said it was.

Just as quickly as the women flocked, they left.

Forcing my breath to remain calm, I walked from the hut into the village, toward Chief Nibowin and his awaiting family. Wiconi held one child on her hip, the others at her side.

Plastering on the realest smile I could muster, I joined the family, planting myself at the chief's side as he announced to the village I would be participating in the ceremony. And made myself stand steady as a chorus of cries and whoops rang out.

The first part took place amongst the growing cache of weapons. Tipping his head back, hands raised to the heavens, Nibowin requested the arrows find their marks. The swords made swift work of their enemies. The aims of their wielders strong and true. After he was done, he turned to me.

Smile strained, I closed my eyes and turned inward, reaching for a link I'd never bothered to test. Never looked for. Didn't even know if it existed. And begged the man, the creature, the being, whatever he was, who had sired me, to allow the men around us to walk away unscathed. To allow me and Venyx to get away. To be allowed to live my life and find another way to kill the Faerie Queen.

When I opened my eyes, the villagers' gazes clung to me like water droplets.

Unsure of what to say, having not received an answer, I turned nervously to the chief and smiled. It seemed to be all the confirmation he needed.

The bonfire was lit as the sun began its descent, great flames licking the sky, chasing away the darkness. With the fire came the dancers. The warriors all in battle leathers. Alongside them danced their wives, if they had one. Each stamp of their feet was accentuated by a cry and a clap, while drummers played on the other side of the village center, the thrum of instruments sinking into my chest.

As I watched, I wondered if I was making the right choice. To run. The faces of those who'd already lost their lives because of me flashed in my mind. Guilt chewed through my gut, pierced it, then boiled in it.

Was I a coward for running? For choosing me? My life over the world?

Tears stung my eyes at the thought. One rolled down my cheek, splattering on my hand, drawing my gaze down. I traced a fingernail through the teardrop, right over the spot where I'd sliced my palm open. Spilling my blood, proof of my divinity.

But it wasn't enough.

It only proved what I was, not what my blood could do. The consequences of killing me.

And what if the Faerie Queen didn't? What if she had another kill me, as a precaution? What then? My life, the lives of those who'd died for me, were lost. Still forfeit. In vain. She hadn't reigned this long by being careless. Not like me.

Stupid girl, Cleya had said. Maybe I was.

But how was I to save the world, restore balance to it, if I died and nothing came of it? What did that accomplish?

Venyx was right. There had to be another way.

And I would find it.

A tug on my hand pulled me from my thoughts. When I looked up, I found Aluk's smiling face.

"Dance with me," he said. Not a question. Not a request.

"Isn't the dance only for couples?" I asked, biting back the smile trying to burst through the darkness filling my head.

"Not only. Friends, too," he said. I couldn't help but laugh, and let him pull me to my feet.

It wasn't the same dance as the others. They were all in sync. Dancing round the bonfire in tune with the drums. Their calls short bursts, followed by a resounding clap.

Aluk dragged me somewhere to the south of the village, where Mato's warriors were. Where they held their own dance. Their own tribute. Kishil and Makya remained off to the side, partially hidden by shadows. But the others—

They danced round in circles on their own, trading partners every few steps. Men and women alike, adults and children. Laughter hugged this little corner of the village.

I didn't think as I danced, observing their feet for all of a moment before getting lost in the rhythm, the cadence of their voices, singing their own song. I stomped and clapped and cried out between breathless peals of laughter, going round in circles with the warriors, with children from the village, men and women I'd never met.

We were the same in that moment. Just people. On the last night we might exist. Might share time in our world. And so I laughed. And sang, despite my inability to do so.

As the last rays of light slipped beneath the horizon, a dark figure appeared, presenting his arm to me, smiling so big all eight fangs were on display.

I took Venyx's arm and we danced. We stomped in circles before I went to the next partner and the next, round and round, until I came back to him. Chest heaving from exertion, throat sore from laughter.

And I fell into him, tipped my head back to meet his eyes, and, like all those weeks ago, found myself alone. Just him before me. All else ceased to exist beneath the weight of his gaze. His hand on my waist, another dug in my hair. The softness on his face, in his eyes, the part of his lips.

At the first mental knock, I opened the barrier to my mind, and his voice filled me.

I reached my friend, he said. My heart thumped in my chest. I didn't make a sound. Simply let him continue as we danced round and round. *She's in the South. She said she can sail up and meet us on the southern coast of Abaddon. We'd have to hide there until she reaches us. But, it's unruled, and large. People from other countries don't cross its borders for fear of those lurking within.*

I swallowed at the information, my only response a small, imperceptible nod before asking, *How long will it take to get there?*

A few weeks.

This was happening. We were really going.

All at once, the world caught up to us. Bouts of laughter rang all around as Calian yelled at Nuka, the two clearly having drank too much.

I turned back to Venyx, the expression gone, but found comfort in knowing it had existed. He'd looked at me like that. Held me so tenderly.

I just hoped with everything in me I was making the right choice.

FIFTY-SEVEN

A GENTLE WHISPER FILLED my head, mulling about my dreams in a dark form. Not dangerous. Not threatening. Comforting.

His face flashed in my mind and I drifted from slumber, like floating down a stream, and found those eyes peering down at me from the shadows. Pools of molten silver in the dead of night.

Only a handful of sentries are still awake, he said, bringing me fully to consciousness.

I trembled as I pulled myself from bed, as I removed my soft, Plains clothes and donned my worn travel things, not caring for modesty in Venyx's presence. There wasn't a part of me he hadn't already seen. Besides, by now I knew he posed no threat. Not to me. Whatever monster lurked within the depths of his mind, even that was beyond him.

I hadn't known where he'd stashed his swords until he pulled the sheath from beneath the bed and drew it over his shoulders, securing the strap across his chest. He pulled his hair back, tying half up to keep it from his eyes before he grabbed his cloak and approached me, still knelt over the side of the bed, tugging on my boots.

What for? I asked as he held it open. Still, I rose, let him drape it across my shoulders, buckling it on.

I'm hard enough to see in the dark, he offered as he plaited my hair before tying it off and stuffing it in the cloak. *You, however, stick out like a flower in the snow.*

A smile played at my lips at his gentle touch as he adjusted my hair, the cloak around me.

Somehow I don't think anyone would object to seeing me leave, either, he grumbled. I couldn't argue. There was nothing to dispute. Mato had made *his* opinion clear.

As he checked his swords again, I stared through the dark at him, my hands wringing circles around each other. My nerves working through me. Venyx's eyes flicked over me before he stepped closer. His hands cupped either side of my face as his lips found mine. I reached up, running my fingers along his jaw, into his hair, as his tongue danced along mine. I shivered at his touch, at the taste of him, the fire ignited in my belly. Far sooner than I wanted, he pulled away, leaning his forehead against mine.

"It'll be okay," he whispered against me. "I'll keep you safe."

Another sigh.

I reached up, grabbed his wrists before he could draw away, and met his gaze. He stared back, thumb stroking my cheek. He leaned into me, lips brushing mine once more. Far too quickly, he pulled away, though there was no time to question it. To protest it. Regardless of how much I wanted to.

There would be time for such things in Abaddon.

Venyx turned, presenting me his back, and I accepted it without explanation. Wrapped my arms around his neck, my legs around his waist, and clung to him. Without the cloak between us, the swords cut into my thighs, pressing uncomfortably into me. I would bare it. For however long I needed to.

Hold on very tight, he whispered. *We may need to move fast, but I'll try not to.*

I nodded against him, recalling him moving faster than I could track. How he seemed to vanish and reappear within a blink. Whether I'd suffer any effects from moving at such speeds, I wasn't sure, but didn't ask. Not as he crept toward the hut entrance, then stopped.

The question formed on my lips, curled in my head, but never got any further as footsteps crunched along the grass just outside, slowing right in front. Through the strands of grass and beads, a silhouette turned, facing us. Still cast in shadows, there was nothing to see, but it didn't stop my heart from thundering in my chest. From every nerve in my body standing on end, waiting to be caught.

Several long moments dragged by, the footsteps fading. Only once they were gone, Venyx slipped out the entrance and into the night.

His steps were feline for all the sound they made as he crossed the grass, sinking into the inky outlines of the huts. My entire being shook as I clung to him. Head tucked against his shoulder, my only view was a mere sliver between the hood and his body, my arm around his neck shielding my face.

The world seemed to understand his desire to be silent, for there was no breeze.

From shadow to shadow we drifted, using it as a cloak, a camouflage. Even the moons, the sky, seemed to be on our side as the night deepened. The light cast from those two celestial bodies dimming so I could scarcely tell the difference between structure and land.

His breath hitched and we were suddenly airborne, landing with a whisper of movement atop a hut. Below, just visible over the peak of the little home, another set of guards strolled by.

We waited until the warriors passed before Venyx dropped to the ground and resumed his shadow hopping, making our way through the circle of the village toward the corral, to the horses. The way was slow, every other step halted at the slightest sound. Halfway there, Mato's voice sliced through the night as the warrior spoke to some unseen presence.

"The queen asked that I monitor the situation," Mato was saying, "but the damned deymon is a problem. The Child is becoming too close to him."

"It is understandable," the chief responded. "Considering all the way they traveled together."

Mato made a frustrated sound. "It seems to be more complicated than simply growing close. The queen felt it might be an issue the closer we got to Pensen. I believe she saw something no one else did. Perhaps not even them."

As their voices faded, I gripped tighter around Venyx, digging my face into the crook of his neck. He reached up, one hand squeezed mine, and we were moving again.

Mercifully, the corral was vacant when we reached it, save for the horses.

Venyx hopped over the rail and I slid to the ground, following as he went to his mount, allowing the mare to sniff his hand. She butted his outstretched palm, chuffing, as if happy to see him. Rubbing her snout, he smiled, then kissed her, and crossed to where the saddles were, quickly plucking the tack off the fence.

"Do you know how to saddle a horse?" he asked as he worked through the straps and buckles.

I shook my head, holding the cloak in place so it didn't swallow my face with the motion. "No."

"Just as well," he said, not a hint of disappointment in his tone as he tightened the saddle around the horse's middle. "We can't be separated if we only have one horse." He moved to the reins. The horse, surprisingly, opened her mouth for him, let him set the bridle before closing it again. "Can you get some of those water skins?" he asked absently, throwing a pointed finger behind me. I turned to a small pile of them leaned against the corral.

"How do you know they're water?" I asked, plucking them up, one for each hand.

"I can smell it," he offered, glancing at me as I approached. "Just in the saddle bags."

I did as instructed, dropping them inside the bags before going back for another two. If it would take weeks to get to Abaddon, we'd need the extra water, though guilt gnawed at my belly for taking it from the Plainsmen.

Would they still go into battle tomorrow? Would there be reason to? Maybe they would join forces with the White Army, charging across their lands to reclaim me.

As I dropped the water bladders in the second saddlebag, I dug around, finding pouches of dried fruit and meat.

"We have food," I said, holding one up.

"Good." He finished strapping on the reins and gazed at me over the horse's back. He gestured to me and I came around, standing in front of him. He adjusted the cloak around my shoulders, made sure my hair was still tucked inside. I watched his hands, my own folded before me, unsure what to do.

Nerves boiled and bubbled in my stomach, threatening to turn my legs molten.

"I need you to listen to me," he said, his voice commanding, but soft. "Do as I say when I say it."

I nodded. He returned the gesture.

I took his shirt in my hands, pulled him closer and tipped my head back, staring into his face as his gaze roamed me like a physical touch, as if memorizing me. Another kiss. Slow. Gentle. Soft. Lingering more than the last two. His tongue ran across my lips and I parted for him, my own dancing along his before he pulled suddenly away and hoisted me into the saddle.

"Stay low," he instructed as he took the reins.

I braced my arms around the horn and leaned forward, let the cloak drape across me, becoming a shadow, as Venyx led the horse to the village outskirts. My heart hammered as I spotted someone walking toward the corral, holding in my relief when they kept going, never looking that way. Never noticing the man guiding a horse laden with their precious sacrifice.

They would hate me for this. The world would hate me for this. I wasn't entirely sure *I* wouldn't hate me.

We will find another way, Venyx's voice echoed in my mind. Through the shadows of the hood, I gazed at him. He didn't look back. Didn't turn toward the village, just kept walking. Vanishing in the night, like they'd hoped he would.

My breath didn't become even until the huts melded into shadows, until the glittering embers of the bonfire, drifting into slumber, became a small, speck of light over my shoulder. Venyx tapped my thigh and I sat up, scooting forward to allow him room.

My heart, however, kept pounding, wondering if he would, indeed, take me to Abaddon, or if I'd signed my own death warrant. If I'd handed myself over to the Faerie Queen, gifted in his strong, beautiful hands.

When he climbed into the saddle behind me, my heart still racing, I glanced up at the stars, silently counting, tracking. My body sang as I realized we were pointed east.

Venyx snapped the reins and the horse jolted into a gallop across the grasses. I glanced back as the village grew smaller and smaller, then up at the sky. Finally, I allowed myself to relax. Let the tension slip from my shoulders, my back.

"With any luck, they won't realize we're gone until morning," Venyx said. "By then, we'll have miles on them."

A strange, warm sensation settled in my chest, pooled in my gut as my gaze again flicked up, checked, and rechecked, making sure we were headed east. Toward Abaddon. Away from the coast. From Pensen. From the White Army.

With only the drumming of my heart, the horse's powerful lungs working beneath us, her hooves digging into the ground, the sudden bellow of a horn split the night.

My heart dropped at the echo piercing the shadows, digging painfully into my ears. I looked back in the same instant Venyx did, toward the village, as it bellowed again. One long blast of air ripping through the silence.

Tears filled my eyes. The sound blared through my head until I could scarcely tell the difference between the lingering ring and its next peal.

Spots and darkness edged my vision, my lungs suddenly too empty and yet too full.

Venyx wrapped an arm around my middle, tightened me against him.

"I need you, Seraph," he whispered. "I need you to remain present. I will protect you." I nodded against him, a brittle, frantic thing, and sank into him, shoving the panic away.

Venyx snapped the reins, urged the horse a little faster. A little harder.

Tugging at the edge of my hood, I looked back to the village. The bonfire burst to furious life, glimmering on the midnight horizon, casting slender blades of light along the grass. Venyx glanced, only for a moment, then did a double take in the same instant my breath hitched. Panic easing back into me as a horde of horses charged from the village.

Heading east.

FIFTY-EIGHT

ANOTHER ROAR ECHOED, RIPPING through the dark, through my ears, as we rode. Venyx pushed into my back, leaning forward as he spurned the horse harder. Lights thrummed in my eyes, in time with the horn's blare. The moons poured a silver blanket across the Plains, illuminating another legion coming round the back, from the war camp.

Over my shoulder, the first swarm thundered across the land.

"Venyx."

"I know," was all he said.

His arm flew from around my waist and he gripped the reins in both hands, guiding the horse off course, south, faster and faster, to outrun the sweep. To not be caught in it. But our horse carried two bodies—double the weight.

A sinking realization gripped me—we weren't going to make it.

Once they caught us, they would kill him.

Stinging tears clawed my eyes, tremor after tremor running the length of my spine.

Another glance at the approaching cavalry as they closed in, their horses swift, unencumbered by two bodies. The flats of their blades glinted in the moonlight, spurning their mounts faster.

Warm wind buffeted my hair, ripping across my face, my eyes. The cloak was shoved back and I pushed it down, around my neck, to keep from blinding Venyx. Our horse's lungs pumped, bursting with air as it churned through grass and dirt.

I should have taken the offer when he'd first asked. I should have acted sooner. I should have trusted him.

Stupid girl.

Stupid. Stupid girl.

A loosed arrow tore through the air, narrowly avoiding us. A scream wrenched from my throat as I curled into Venyx's chest. Another dug harmlessly into the grass.

Growling, Venyx shifted the horse again, further south, distant hills waving, taunting us.

I glanced over my right shoulder at the Plains warriors fanning out, preparing to overtake us. Some stood in their saddles, bows raised. A volley of arrows was loosed, picketing the grass. Venyx growled again. Our horse whinnied, either from fear of the arrows, or Venyx's growing frustration.

Just as the horde on the left began closing in, the one behind loosed another volley. Venyx yanked the reins to the right and we were free, riding alongside those behind us. No longer in their sweep. Though there was no time for relief.

The blaring lights of panic bleated in the edges of my vision as another arrow flew across the horse's head, whipping through her mane. For a moment, I feared she would buck us, but she kept pushing, kept running. The world around me, the noise and chaos of the approaching army, dimmed as my head pulsed and throbbed. To ground myself, I gripped Venyx's arms, dug my nails into him, expecting him to shrug me off. He only pressed his chest further into my back, his whispered voice filling my head.

I won't let you die, he hissed.

More arrows flew around us, pelting the ground with little thunks as they dug home. I clung to Venyx's words, his back pressing into me, the warmth of his skin beneath my hands.

Another volley flew from the left, whipping around us. I screamed as an arrow ripped across my hair, my panic absorbing Venyx's roar. The horse screamed. The mare's front legs gave, and the ground rushed up. The world went flying as the grass reached up to snatch me. I was aware of nothing, only darkness, both warm and cold setting in before I lay still, face first in dirt and grass.

I lifted my head as Venyx rolled to his feet and drew both swords, separating me from the surrounding army.

Breath hitching, I slowly stood. Flush against Venyx's back. His cloak sheathing me in a wall of shadow, all save for my tumble of lilac hair, loosed from its braid.

The ocean of warriors parted and Mato and Chief Nibowin trotted into the inner circle, their faces stoic, letting nothing show as they dropped to the grass.

Mato stepped forward, hands to either side. His sword still on his hip. Glanced between the twins Venyx gripped. The solid wall of deymon between himself and me.

"I don't want to kill you," Mato said, as if soothing a rabid beast.

"I'd love to see you try," Venyx growled. Mato smirked.

The warrior shook his head, his chest length black hair trembling on one side with the motion. "If you hand over the Child, we will let you live. But you will not set foot on Plains soil again."

Fingers digging into Venyx's shirt, I looked up at him, judging the planes of his face, waiting for some sign, something that gave away his thoughts.

"You let me take her, and I won't kill you," Venyx retorted.

"We both know I can't let her leave."

"Then let's see how many of you I take down with me," he growled, tightening his grip on his swords.

"No," I bellowed, the word coming out before I thought it. I went to step around him, place myself between him and the warrior, but his arm jutted up, blocking me. *Venyx.* His voice vanished from my mind.

Venyx, I seethed. A trickle swept in, curling around my thoughts, his name pinging around my head. *We're not both getting out of this alive.*

I'm not letting you be butchered, he retorted. *Your life is yours. You're not a pawn, not a sacrifice. It's yours.*

Warmth spread through my chest, down into my feet, as I gazed at him. My hands dug a little further into his shirt, to the skin beneath, the solid form of him.

Are we talking about me, I asked, *or you?*

I see no difference.

"I know you care for the Child," Mato said, stepping closer, hands moving further away from his sword. "I know you care for Seraph, I do. I love my wife, and I would gladly die for her." My brows twitched, and I flicked my gaze over Venyx's shoulder from him to the warrior and back. Still, his face betrayed nothing. "But this thing, ugly as it may be, must be done. She will set us all free. It is the price that must be paid to restore the world's life."

Venyx shook his head. "Even one life is too steep a price."

Mato scoffed. "And how many more lives would you allow the Faerie Queen to claim in searching for another way to end this? When the answer runs through the veins of the girl at your back. One life over the entire world? You've lived longer than all of us. Tell me, is it worth it?"

"Yes," Venyx growled. "For all the years I've lived, I can tell you with absolute certainty, the killing will not stop with her." He laughed. The first show of emotion since we'd fallen. "You fucking mortals. You always think killing one more person will end all the killing everywhere. Slaughtering one woman will end it all, restore balance. Give the world life again." He shook his head. "The divine are not unicorns. Killing her won't end anything. It'll just give Faei what she wants."

Mato sighed. A moment of silence, broken only by the chuffing of horses, the shuffling of bodies in saddles. The warrior nodded, looked away, and returned his gaze to Venyx, those brown eyes flicking to me. "No, we do not know for certain whether her death will end the Faerie Queen. If it will restore what was stolen. But we have no other options.

There are no more wars to fight. Kaival has proven its power. This is what we have left. And I think you will find the might of the world stronger than that of a single deymon."

The tears prickling the backs of my eyes rolled hot down my cheeks.

"You're gravely underestimating the *deymon* before you," Venyx growled. "Take one more fucking step and you die where you stand."

"If you kill me, you declare war on the entire world."

"Do you see me trembling?"

Mato's mask of impenetrable stoicism fell at Venyx's words. In the same instant, I gazed up at him.

Venyx suddenly straightened, eyes shooting to the ground. His arms dropped. Mato's brows drew together, the men around him exchanging glances. The horses stamped, shaking their heads back and forth. Some stepped backward, fighting the reins that held them.

"Venyx?" I asked. "What's wrong?"

His eyes snapped up, traveling over the heads of the Plainsmen surrounding us, beyond them, west, and the ground began quaking. The Plainsmen looked down, their own rumblings joining the horses' as a wash of alarm flooded their ranks. It wasn't much, a shift in the soil, a slight tremor, but as the silence around us thickened, the panic of horses growing steeper, it intensified.

Mato turned back to Venyx.

"You and your fucking horn alerted the White Army, you stupid bastards!" Venyx roared. A searing bolt of panic speared the length of my spine, right into my toes, the quaking growing steadily stronger.

"West!" the chief bellowed, mounting his horse. "Turn about!"

As the ranks before us shifted west, the men behind moved in a singular wave, flanking the others. There, on the horizon. Under the blanket of silver light. A mass of white crested a distant hill, rampaging down the grasses like a tidal wave.

"Protect the Child!" Mato roared, jumping back into his saddle. He and Chief Nibowin shoved to the front of the ranks.

The absurdity of it all hit me. Chuckles bubbled in my chest, even as fresh tears filled my eyes. The men forming a tight line between us and the White Army drew their weapons in a single, fluid movement, and I burst into hysterical laughter, stepping back from Venyx to double over with it.

Venyx's face contorted with confusion as he gazed at me, then over his shoulder at the swiftly approaching army.

"I fail to see what's so funny," he glowered.

A hand over my mouth, I forced the laughter back, wiped the tears from my eyes, and stood, trying not to stare across the open fields toward the wave of death that would swamp us in mere moments.

"They're going to die protecting me," I said, fighting back another surge of hysterics, one hand pointed toward the Plainsmen, "just to kill me anyway."

Our eyes locked, and my laughter soured, dissolving into tears. My face screwed up. Fear filled every part of me, every crevice, at the dire realization.

With a growl, Venyx pulled me into his arms, into his chest, and pressed a kiss to my lips. "You're not going to die," he mumbled against me.

I closed my eyes, the tremble beneath my feet deafening, drowning out the commands of Mato and Chief Nibowin.

And I knew he was wrong.

FIFTY-NINE

THE WORLD SEEMED TO crash upon us as we embraced. Venyx shifted, looked up and around. I followed his gaze to a Plains warrior mounted at the rear end of the line.

"Venyx?"

He said nothing. His eyes went dark, as if focusing far away. The warrior straightened in his saddle, backed his horse, and trotted toward us. My brows furrowed, confusion filling me, as the man dismounted and took several steps backward, staring straight ahead, eyes glassy and unseeing. Hands limp at his sides.

Thick, unfurling terror gripped me as I glanced from Venyx to the soldier and back.

"Get on," Venyx ordered.

"Venyx, what did—"

"What'd I say?" he countered. Swallowing my fear, I pulled myself into the saddle and scooted forward, making room for him as he climbed up behind me. The Plains warrior still stood, unmoving, unblinking, as Venyx guided our stolen horse around, faced east, and snapped the reins.

I glanced over my shoulder the same instant the warrior blinked dazedly, spotted us, and began shouting. The army of Plains warriors turned, gazing around in confusion. A single moment was all it took before half of them peeled off, charging after us.

I sank into Venyx's chest as we rode, closed my eyes, and prayed. Prayed to whatever gods might still linger in the heavens, maybe even to my father, that we made it out. That we escaped this. Whether my prayer would be answered, I didn't know. I did know the strength of Venyx's arms as they tightened around me. The surging, thunderous hooves pounding the ground at our rear.

"If the Plains and Kaival can get battle-locked, we'll have a chance," Venyx said, breath grazing my ear.

I hadn't wanted the Plainsmen to die for me. Hadn't wanted them to go to battle. So much for my blessing their ceremony.

Another peek at the White Army as they rushed forward, gaining ground on the Plains warriors. At the very rear of the Plains' charge, the first warriors were felled by arrows. The first horses of the Kaival cavalry intermingled with the Plains'. Gulping down the air slamming into my nose, I faced forward as the first screams of battle rang out.

The beast below us rushed on, hooves striking the ground, lungs pumping through warm night air. I gripped Venyx's arms, willing my sight to keep fixed on that promised eastern horizon, when the first White soldiers entered my peripheral, nocked bow in hand.

Venyx screamed at our horse, nudging it faster. Pushing it beyond the point of exhaustion. The arrow was loosed, flying through the air. It ripped through my hair and I hunkered down with a cry. Behind me, Venyx growled. Another arrow whistled past, digging harmlessly into the grass. I glanced up as a Plains warrior fired at the White soldier, missing.

"Take the reins," Venyx shouted. He shoved them into my hands, not waiting for a response, and I took them, hunkered down, pressed beneath his weight. When the next arrow was loosed from the White soldier's bow, Venyx snatched it from the air, reeled back, and threw it, impaling the soldier through the throat. The man toppled backward. The Plains warrior gaped between the felled soldier and Venyx, then back again, horror lining his face.

The stampede behind us raged on, punctuated by the screams and wails of both men and horses as the two forces collided on our tail. I snapped the reins, silently begging our horse to keep its momentum, to keep going, pushing on, as a Plains warrior was downed on our left.

A scream ripped from my throat and tore through my ears as an arrow whizzed by on its path to the earth. I glanced over my shoulder as Venyx pulled a knife from his boot and threw it, lodging it to the hilt in a White soldier's face. The body careened to the ground. Whipping my head the other way, a Plains warrior threw himself onto the saddle of a White soldier.

We weren't going to make it. Before, it had been a fool's hope. Now, the idea was laughable as we were swarmed from both sides, from behind, by Plains and Kaival soldiers alike. I screamed again as another arrow flew past, then another, dipping my head to keep myself as small a target as possible.

One of the White soldiers edged his horse near our own, ripped a dagger from his waist, and held it aloft. With a roar, Venyx grabbed the man by the throat and thrust the dagger into its owner's chest before tossing the body to the grass.

Our horse whinnied as a spear embedded itself in the grass. Just barely reigning the beast in, I steered around as the projectile shook and trembled from impact, and pushed on.

Screams echoed and rent the night. Hooves beat across the grass. I shook my head as disbelief tingled through me. If the gods did exist, if they hadn't abandoned this world, they would not hear me. That realization shook me as the ranks closed in. Both Plains and White armies collided, firing arrows, trying to stop us, blockade us. In mere moments it would be over, and there would be no running. No escape. My fate would be sealed. So would Venyx's.

As if that last thought had come to fruition, he jolted into me with a grunt, hissing between his teeth. I glanced back, gaping at the arrow sticking from his shoulder.

I whipped my head around as more arrows whizzed past, guiding our horse through the fray, then turned as Venyx grit his teeth, snapped the shaft in two, and ripped out the head, reached around and discarded the rest.

"I'm fine," he said, answering my unspoken question. "It's already healing."

Another spear dug into the ground. This time, Venyx leaned over, ripped it up, and threw it back, landing it square in the stomach of a White soldier.

Behind us, the Plainsmen, the horses, the very earth, seemed to shatter as a roar split the night. I looked up as a dark shape blotted out the sky, blocking the stars. My heart skipped a beat, breath hitching in my throat.

Another roar sounded, echoing across the Plains, as the giant beast dropped low, lower, wheeling around until it faced us, red wings spreading in either direction. My eyes went wide, mouth gaping, as the thing stood tall and began sucking in a breath. The air around us crackled, snapped in the wake of that massive chest, the inhale meant to send dozens to their doom at once.

Venyx's hands were suddenly on mine and he yanked back the reins, forcing the horse to skid to a stop. We wouldn't clear the path, not in time. Before I knew what was happening, his arms were around me. His legs coiled beneath us, and we were airborne as a writhing mass of flames tore through the dark, swallowing our horse, and everything behind it, whipping back and forth. Before we could clear the thing, one massive wing jutted up, crashing into us.

We landed with jarring suddenness, slamming into rock and dirt. My teeth rattled, my head swam. Every part of me throbbed. But there was no time to process, no time to think, as Venyx pulled me up, shoving me behind him before he drew his swords.

The White soldiers spotted us the same instant the Plainsmen did. I couldn't see him through the chaos, through the swarming mass of bodies, but I heard Mato cry out to those still alive. The Plainsmen began forming a rank, circling us, placing me and Venyx in the middle, as the White Army corralled us in.

I looked back and forth at the human shield forming before us, my chest heaving.

Soldiers in White tried ramming through, but were met with swift, sharp blades, the air vibrating with their horrendous cries. Some jumped, clearing the Plains warriors in a single bound. Venyx stepped forward, blades flashing beneath the light of the twin moons. Within moments, the sickly scent of blood filled my nose. The world around me vanished as I fought a wave of panic. Black dots seeped into the edges of my vision, my lungs heaving, wheezing.

One soldier fell at Venyx's blades, then another. The dance he wove marked in blood, in screams. Wiping my eyes, I willed myself to remain present, refused to forfeit my life when Venyx had worked so hard to defend me. So I plucked up a fallen sword and stood beside Venyx as the next wave broke our Plains line.

He glanced at me over his shoulder and smirked. I returned it, just a glimmer of one, before he charged the soldiers leaping over our surrounding wall of warriors.

My heart thundered as one of them rushed past him, straight for me.

I would not die. I would not go quietly.

The blade rushed down and I thrust mine up, blocking its path before I shoved back, matching blow for blow. Venyx's tutelage rang through my head with every strike, every absorbed impact. *Find an opening.* Even the smallest would do. When it came, when the soldier dropped his arm, just a fraction, I struck, slicing clean and quick. Shock coated his face before he fell. There was no time to celebrate, or mourn—I wished for both—as another came. Then another. The line of Plainsmen was breaking, bit by bit, as the warriors fell.

Within moments, mere breaths, the line shattered, and we were swarmed, both by men in white and Plains garb.

Bodies thrust this way and that, swallowing me. I lost sight of Venyx, of Mato. Could barely see the sky through the throng of carnage. I knew only the glint of my blade in the dark, reflecting the light from above. Only the tang of blood as I felled another soldier wearing white. Though it scarcely mattered.

When I found myself in a pocket, I whipped around, crying Venyx's name. Wherever he was, he'd been washed away by the swarming bodies, by the pulsing clash of armies. Even the soldiers seemed lost in their bloodlust, forgetting what they were doing as the urge for survival violently thrummed.

A soldier broke through into my clearing, my blink of peace, and rushed me. Pinning the panic back, I swung my blade up and unleashed, slicing back and forth, matching each blow, the screams of dread giving way to rage. The throbbing pulse edging my vision turned red, not for survival, but for myself. Before I knew it, the man dropped to his knees, gurgling, as blood and gore surged from his throat.

I stepped back, breathless, and looked around, baffled by myself, by what I'd done. A seed of exhaustion peppered my eyes, my gut, though every other part of me sang with a fire I'd never known, and I gazed around for the next one.

But it wasn't a soldier that stepped before me.

It was a woman. A deymoness. A touch taller, her eyes shone and glittered silver in the light of the moons, twin blades clutched in her hands. Black hair braided flush against her scalp.

I looked her over, knowing intrinsically she could cleave me in half without struggle, and I shuddered.

She raised her blades, a roar racing from her throat, as she brought them surging down.

SIXTY

I BLOCKED THE DEYMONESS' blades just in time, though the force shattered me to my feet. The very ground trembled in the wake of her blow. My body vibrated, sang, aching, though there was no time to recover. I would not survive another impact. Knew it with everything in me. All I could do was get out of the way of what had to be thousands of years of pure power, pure rage.

My eyes shot open as she reared back and struck again.

Stumbling, over my own breath and the fallen littering the ground, I scrambled up, my gaze never leaving those pools of endless silver-flecked brown. And met a wall of bodies at my back. Pulsing, thrumming, writhing in the depths of battle. They did not waver, did not give.

The deymoness smiled, stalking closer. We both knew there was nowhere to go.

Seraph! I started at the voice, taking a moment to realize it was Venyx shouting in my head.

Venyx? Where are you? I licked my lips, looked left and right, then left again, searching for a way out.

Run, now!

Where are you? I begged.

I'm trying to get to you, but I need you to run!

The deymoness' eyes shifted from silvery brown to red, grazing over me as I took her in, holding Venyx's words in my mind.

She raised one blade, pointing at me, and snarled, "I refuse to lose my head for you, little half-breed bitch. I'm done chasing you. If I have to take your corpse to Kaival, so be it."

My memory whooshed back, returning to the camp all those months ago, the White soldiers who'd taken me. They'd mentioned a dey-moness, Veyla.

Yes, Seraph. Her name is Veyla. She is nearly as old as I am! Fucking run! Now! Get away from her!

Chest heaving, his words filling my head, sinking into every fiber of my being, I darted left, jumping over corpses, but she was there before I could blink. One sword shot up and I raised my own, blocking it. The blow reverberated down my arm, into my shoulder, and I cried out. Another strike and the blade fell, useless, to the blood-soaked ground.

I stared at the sword, debating only a moment whether to dive after it. I glanced about, at the feet stamping around me. And made my choice. If I had to crawl away from her, I would.

"Let's see how true all that bullshit is," she roared, raising her twins, swinging them wide to cleave my head from my shoulders. My body went rigid and I stepped back, waiting until the last moment to drop.

I was suddenly tossed to the ground, into the muck and grass, and glanced up as the deymoness' blades swung straight through Mato's shoulders and out either side. He fell to his knees, his torso toppling sideways, plopping to the saturated earth. My stomach soured, bile rising in my throat, as I looked between the fallen warrior and the deymoness, terror clawing at my belly, at my chest. Bone sliced clean through, so quick not even a speck of blood rest on Veyla's blades as she turned those red eyes from her kill to me.

Seraph! Venyx screamed into my head. *Run! Now!*

Biting back the onslaught of tears, I rolled over onto all fours. Scrabbled through the muck, distancing myself from the mud my fingers sank into. The gore on either side. The bodies I climbed over. And crawled.

My heart was on the verge of bursting from the rate it drummed; my lungs pulsing, throbbing, choking on the smell of sweat and blood and piss and shit—the smells of death. I trembled with every fistful of earth I pushed away, weaving through the forest of feet and legs, my tears trailing behind. There was no time to stop and swipe them away, so I let them fall.

I didn't know how far I'd crawled, but a hand fisted my hair and hoisted me up. Every part of me came to screaming life at once and I kicked. Thrashed and screamed, clawing at the face of the one who held me. Barely glimpsed him before I was dropped, plopping into the mud.

Venyx stood before me, hoisting the deymon from the earth, eyes blazing red. The man squirmed, eyes alight with fear before Venyx reared back a handful of claws and thrust them into the soldier's middle over and over, traveling up his chest to his throat, before he dumped the body on the ground.

For a moment, I was only able to stare at him, trembling from fear, shaking to my very bones. But then he held out a hand, those eyes shifting from red to brown, and I knew he wouldn't hurt me. The same could not be said for the writhing mass of bodies around us. I let him haul me up and he tucked me into his side, head turning this way and that.

"We need to find a way out," he shouted, though I barely heard him over the cacophony of battle.

I wasn't sure either of us knew which direction to go, though any way was better than being stuck in what had to be a living, thriving hell. Plainsmen and White soldiers locked together in the throes of war, their eyes blank, vacant, only their own lives, their own existence visible as they fought on.

Someone rushed toward us. Venyx drew a blade, flicked it across the soldier's throat, and the body fell, another piled atop the growing mountain of carnage.

Then another rushed us. My hand still clutched in his, Venyx swung his blade. Quickly, the soldier realized his mistake, terror blossoming on his face just before Venyx cleaved his head from his shoulders. He moved forward, tugging me behind him.

I glanced around, suddenly swamped by bodies, the noise, the endless forest of death, the river of blood at my feet, squelching beneath each step. The smells, sights, sounds of it all swallowed me. Buried me in an avalanche of war. I couldn't breathe. The edges of my vision blurred, my body refusing to move. Venyx whipped around, seeming to realize he tugged at dead weight, and he was there, before me, sword sheathed, hands on my face. His breath fanning my skin.

"Eyes on me," he whispered, eyes locked on mine, though I barely heard his voice. Could scarcely see him, nothing beyond him, behind him. I reached up, clasped his hands. "Eyes on me."

I nodded, tears rolling down my face.

"I won't let you die," he said. "I've got you."

I nodded again. And he was gone.

My hands stretched before me, holding the air where he'd been. My chest heaved, panic setting in. I couldn't breathe.

"Venyx," I rasped, glancing furiously around. He'd been swallowed, by the bodies, by the war, I wasn't sure. But he was gone. "Venyx," I said again, my voice drowned in my tears.

Veyla stepped before me, her eyes no longer red, but white. I stared across the space between us as she raised her swords, those deadly arcs racing toward me, nothing to stop them. Nothing to block them.

Nik's face rushed across my vision. The moment before he died. And I let myself feel that calm. Even as hot tears streaked my face.

The world came to a screeching halt as I opened my eyes, met my death head on, while the blades carved the night.

A searing, blinding pain, shot from my shoulder, through my body, down my side. I was thrown back, narrowly missing those arcs as they raced through the air. My back slammed into the ground, jarring me.

Bright, vibrant agony raked through me, exploded inside me. Blurring into the edges of panic until they became the same thing, filling me.

I reached up to the shaft embedded in my shoulder, hot blood already oozing from the wound. And I stared up at the sky, at the stars, as they shone upon me. Hanging there, above my head, was the constellation of Tabeto.

My body relaxed, and I fell into the peace Nik must have felt. Whether it was death, or sleep, I wasn't sure. But the pain stopped. The panic subsided.

And the world around me ceased to exist.

SIXTY-ONE
VENYX

THERE WAS NO TIME to react before a body barreled into me, ripping me through the battlefield. There was scarcely time to suck in a breath before my face was shoved into the grass and muck, the tips of claws digging into my scalp.

Burying my palms in the ground, I shoved up, channeling every ounce of strength through my shoulders, roaring as I pushed against the hands holding me. Reaching back, I grabbed the fucker who'd thought they could kill me and slammed them to the ground, drew back a hand, and thrust my claws into their chest, barely glimpsing the face beneath me. Their breath guttered out, body going limp, and I jumped up, muddied hair flinging about my face.

I clawed the muck from my eyes and turned to where Seraph had been.

My heart dropped.

Veyla stood before her, swords raised. Poised to deal the death blow nothing, not even divine blood, could save her from.

Shoving through the throng, I rushed forward, roaring Seraph's name. She couldn't hear me through the din. I reached for her mind, screaming for her to run. But she lay trapped in her fear. Like a plague, panic spread through the threads of her thoughts, blocking me out.

Veyla swung with a roar, her blood-red eyes filled with rage.

Nothing left to do except jump the distance. Shove her out of the way. Take the blow myself if needed.

From nowhere, a crossbow bolt sliced through the air, punching through Seraph's shoulder, throwing her back. Bewilderment swamped her face, mirrored on Veyla's. Seraph fell. To the mud and muck, lost to my vision. Veyla's arms fell to her sides as she searched for the one who'd fired.

Jumping the distance, I landed before Veyla, narrowly clearing the space between her and Seraph, laying prone on the ground. Those beautiful ocean blue eyes closed. Panic tore through me, the worst thrumming in my head. Blocking out the writhing sounds of carnage, I focused on her. The heartbeat I'd spent the last months memorizing. She was alive.

Drawing my swords, I turned to Veyla and bared my fangs. She hissed in return and rushed forward, swords glinting in the night. I stepped back, careful of Seraph's legs, and knocked aside one blow, then the next, the clang of blades rippling through the enveloping cacophony of war.

Her eyes flicked behind me and I whipped around as a White soldier reached down, daring to claim Seraph. With a roar, I sliced through one wrist, then his throat, before wheeling back to catch one of Veyla's blades on both of mine.

Her strikes were fast and hard, burning with the rage of failure. Defeat hung in her eyes; she hadn't foreseen coming this far south. Had already been expected to claim the Child for her queen.

It was for her own life she was fighting. To go back empty-handed would mean her death.

I wasn't going to let her walk away at all.

Clutching her blades between mine, I ripped them from her and flung them to the ground. She reeled back, hissed again, and lunged forward, knocking into me.

My swords fell from my hands. The softening ground pummeled into my back as Veyla gripped a handful of my hair and slammed my head into the earth. I grabbed her braids and yanked her down, tearing into her throat, blood and flesh filling my mouth. She howled, tore herself free, and jumped up. Roared and lunged again.

Again we went down. I bashed my forehead into hers, punctured her side with my claws until she screamed, scrambling to get away. With my free hand, I clutched her throat, squeezing, despite the gushing blood. The wound already puckering and closing.

I flipped over, slammed her to the earth, placed one hand on her chest, and gripped her hair with the other. She kicked, clawed, and scratched. Her screeching roar morphed into a scream, devolving into an hysterical squeal as I twisted, skin and bone giving way. Her neck buckled beneath my rage. Her claws rammed into my sides, her knees kicking into my back. With one final furious roar, I tugged, and she went slack as her head ripped from her body, dangling free before I tossed it aside.

Plucking my swords from the mud, I sheathed them and dropped to Seraph's side.

Hissing, I probed the wound. The arrow had gone through, sticking out both sides. Already, there was so much blood. She'd bleed out either way, but if I removed it, she'd die faster. The first fingers of panic creeping in, I picked her limp body from the ground and glanced around. The writhing bodies paid me no mind. They didn't care for the woman in my arms, the entire reason they were killing each other. Once the two sides collided, all reason had fled.

I jumped. Again. And again. Beyond the reaches of the raging battle and bloodied earth. On solid ground, the grass swaying around us, I laid her out.

"Fuck!" I roared, hands diving helplessly into my hair. I then noticed—she still wore my cloak. Tearing it from her throat, I pulled it from beneath her and, gripping it with my teeth, ripped it to strips. It was filled with gore, muck, and blood, but there was nothing else to stanch her ebbing flow of life.

Wringing out as much of the mud as possible, I stuffed the cloth into the wound, damming the flow, though knew it wouldn't hold long. It'd take weeks to get to Abaddon. Time she didn't have.

I jumped as a body skid to the grass before me, claws shooting from my fingertips as I lunged across her and hissed, my vision going red.

It's just me, Aluk spoke into my mind, hands held to either side. I started, gaping. Took in the crossbow at his side. *I want to help her.*

You wanted to kill her, I growled, returning to my work. Dismissing the impossibility of his thoughts in my head. Already, my fingers were slick with her blood, carving a path through the scarlet sticking to my skin.

No, the warrior said. My gaze jumped to him in disbelief. *I want her to live.*

So many of the Plains warriors had guarded minds, but his was open, so I dove in. Peeking where he allowed me, finding the truth in his words. Pulling back, I licked my lips, coated in Veyla's blood, and spat.

"You want to help? Hold her so I can wrap this," I ordered.

The warrior nodded, scurrying up Seraph's side to hoist her shoulder off the ground. My hands trembled as I wrapped the cloth around her, tying it as tight as I dared. Too tight, and I risked cutting off circulation to her arm. Too loose, and she'd bleed out.

"She won't live to Abaddon," Aluk said, his muck-filled hair waving back and forth in the breeze.

"I know," I barked, giving no thought to him knowing where we'd been going. He didn't recoil. I sighed, bit back the surge of emotions overwhelming my senses. I sniffled, growling deep in my throat as I wrapped another length of cloth around her shoulder.

"Pensen can heal her."

My head snapped up. Caught the warrior's brown eyes.

"They can heal her."

"They want to kill her," I spat.

"If you not take her, she die anyway," he countered.

I dropped my gaze to her face. And knew he was right. There wasn't enough time to get to Abaddon. Not enough time to reach the ocean, so her blood could heal her. I wasn't even sure she'd make it to Pensen. Without another option, I nodded and met Aluk's gaze.

"I need a horse."

He nodded and jumped to his feet.

I finished wrapping her shoulder, checking the strips were as tight as they could be, then hoisted her into my arms, her body light as I jogged toward Aluk, already rushing back, a horse's reins in hand.

I shouldn't have waited for her to ask for my help. The moment I found her in the tub, thinking for one blinding moment she'd taken her own life, I should have abandoned this fucking job. Whatever guilt Aurorian had plied her with worked—she still wasn't convinced her own life was worth saving.

But I refused to watch another soul be used and discarded.

"I'm sorry, Seraph," I whispered into her hair. "I swear to the fucking gods I will get you out of this. I will get you out of Pensen. You will not die."

"She is our fastest," Aluk said, bringing the mare closer. With no time to touch the horse, I dug the fingers of my mind into the beast's thoughts, and told her to trust me. She needed to trust me. Because I needed her.

The mare whinnied and threw her head back before presenting me her flank. I climbed into the saddle, Seraph in my arms, as Aluk dropped the saddlebags and all the supplies in them. I didn't object, needing every ounce of speed the mare could offer.

SIXTY-TWO
VENYX

MERE MOMENTS AND THE cacophony of war at my back ceased. My heart stuttered in my throat as I glanced back. The first golden glimmers of morning burst on the horizon, and the two sides realized what I was doing, where I was going, and who I carried.

Cursing, I faced forward, and urged the horse faster.

Seraph's head bobbed against my chest. It was all I could do to keep her anchored against me, one arm fastened around her ribs. My free hand gripped the reins, snapping, as I begged the horse onward.

Above, streaks of gold cut through the black, obliterating the constellations.

Behind, a stampede. A chorus of cries and screams as both armies fought on the move, slaughtering each other while vying to be the first to catch me.

It would take days to get to Pensen from the village. Days. Time she still didn't have. And I cursed myself again.

The cold muck and mud coating her shoulder gave way to warmth as blood seeped from the makeshift bandage. I hissed, dragged her further up my lap and tightened my grip on her, tucking her head beneath my chin.

"Seraph," I whispered, "I need you to stay alive. I need you to live. Please forgive me for this. I will get you out. You will not die."

I shifted her again and urged the horse harder, knowing the animal gave everything she had. But it wouldn't be enough. Both Seraph and I would be dead before the glistening walls of Pensen graced my vision.

As if to pronounce that fact, giant wings flapped behind me, followed by a guttural roar. Cursing, I glanced over my shoulder as the massive red dragon rose like a beacon of death from the battlefield and shot forward. Toward me. Heartbeats separated us. Hissing, I turned back around and spurned the horse on, planting fear in its head. The beast cried out, but went faster.

The air around me crackled. The sky darken by degrees as the dragon inhaled, readying themself for when they caught up.

A great exhale, like a torrid gust of searing hot wind, burst to life behind me, filling the air with smoke and flames, charring the land. With every beat of those powerful wings, every thrum of that massive heart, they drew nearer. And there was nothing I could do.

In desperation, I yanked the reins left, out of the dragon's path, and a fiery cascade of breath descended just behind me, in my peripheral. The horse's panic bleated in my head as heat nipped its hind legs, singing its tail. To avoid it bucking me off, I dug the claws of my mind deeper and made the beast stay its course, going against every bit of my conscience by forcing it to remain in my command. And hated myself every moment.

With an earth-shattering roar, the dragon swooped through the air, diving toward me. The thrum of their heart drummed in my head. Aware of the approaching stampede at my rear, I yanked the reins back, forcing the horse into a dead stop. The dragon sped past, the massive draw of their wings carrying them faster. Though I didn't allow myself relief. Not when they pumped those nightmare limbs and pulled themselves up higher. To arc back around.

I snapped the reins and shot off again, just out of range of the arrows firing behind me. Still, far too close for comfort. Within moments, they pelted the ground on all sides, flew through my hair, zinged past my shoulders. I ducked my head to avoid being hit, knowing it would take only one. I would be down. Seraph would be lost.

Tossing a frantic glance back, the Plains warriors returned fire to the White soldiers, some finding their mark. Bodies fell to the ground, trampled by the dozens, hundreds, of hooves giving chase behind me.

Whipping my head back around, I tightened my left arm on Seraph, my right hand on the reins, and bid the horse just a little faster.

Blood coated my left wrist. Dripped onto my leg. I shifted Seraph, her head lolling back, and my heart plummeted. Her face was ghostly white, lips a shade of blue. Roaring, I shifted her back, rest her against my shoulder. And shook my head, fighting back the tears lining my eyes.

I'd waited too long.

"Fuck!"

The beat of wings caught my attention as the dragon circled back around. For a moment, I closed my eyes. Begged the gods, fates, angels, whatever it took, to let me save her. My eyes snapped open and I cursed again, spittle coating my lips.

The grasses reached on forever, going in every direction. The sun continued its ascent, taunting me. But I wouldn't surrender. I'd already sworn she wouldn't die, and I refused to break that vow.

The thrum of hearts beat against my eardrums, shattering my concentration on the dragon above. The war at my back. It'd been far too long since I'd stretched my senses so thin, though I only had myself to blame.

Figures rose ahead, dotting the horizon. Shit. The blockade. The raging battle the Plains warriors were supposed to join. I'd run right into it.

But there was no time to consider it. No space to slow down. The dragon circled back, dropping lower, the air again crackling, igniting under the draw of their massive lungs.

The battlefield drew up quickly, those fighting on either side stopping at my approach, faces gaping in fear at the horror chasing me. I ignored them all, plowing straight through their ranks as the dragon unleashed another breath, decimating everything in their path. Screams and blazing flames filled the morning. No time to consider the damage, the cost to the Plains army.

A quick glance back revealed the survivors abandoning their warfare to give chase, joining the ranks of those already tailing me. I roared my frustration, then glanced down, reminding myself what I fought for, and pushed on.

I jerked the reins to the right, narrowly missing the field of flames, and into the firing arrows. I swerved back, on the tail of that horrendous breath, kicking up ash and embers as the flames died and the dragon rose to circle around.

An arrow shot through the air, whipped up my hair, the head grazing my cheek, though the wound was healed by the time it dove into the grass.

My chest pounded in time with the beast below me. Her heart beating so much faster than natural, the claws of my mind buried in hers the only thing keeping her going. She had no pain, no exhaustion, saw only what lie ahead, heard only my command. But eventually, her body would give out. Regardless of my order.

I hugged Seraph tighter, sent a whispered prayer we were almost there. But I was fooling myself.

Another shot of crackling air rippled behind me. I shook my head, roared, and stared straight ahead.

A torrential firestorm unleashed behind me, searing my back. There was nowhere to run. No direction to change without being bombarded by arrows and spears. Even with the Plains warriors fighting back, I had nowhere to go. So when the first flickers of flame reached the horse's tail, I jumped up into the saddle, balancing long enough to gather Seraph in my arms. Planted thoughts in the horse's head that she was in a field full of green grass, free and happy, and hurtled forward through the air the instant before flames consumed the beast.

My teeth jarred as I collided with the earth. Seraph tucked into my body, I rolled and sprang to my feet. I looked back, just a moment, as the armies surged forward, the dragon rising again to circle back around. I'd given myself space, just out of range of the volley, but by nothing more than hairs.

And so jumped again. Slammed back into the ground, running with everything in me, every ounce of strength my legs possessed. My lungs pumped furiously, filled with blood and death and ash. But I kept going.

The air crackled, singing with furious life as those wings filled my ears again. I shook my head.

Heat nipped my back as flames licked the ground to my left, drawing nearer. With a grunt, I shoved my feet into the earth, changed directions, and ran back, toward the oncoming dragon. In a single bound, I cleared the distance and rammed my feet into their snout, the blow carrying the full force of my body and strength. Before the dragon collided with the ground, I jumped forward in a furious run, sparing only a single glance as the dragon rose to their feet and shot up, roaring.

The air crackled, singing with fiery life. I'd given myself only moments. Pulling Seraph up, I kissed her forehead in a silent goodbye. But kept running. If it spared us a few more precious breaths, I'd keep going.

Heat and flames licked the air, my back and legs, as the dragon drew closer, closing the gap between me and my death. I was surprised I'd lived so long.

I jumped once more, my legs buckling on impact. Exhaustion tore through me. If I jumped again, I wouldn't get back up. We'd die there, in the grass, swallowed by flames.

Up ahead, a dark form took shape, another massive heartbeat blaring in my head. There was no time to question it as I ran, every breath spent keeping ahead of the dragon at my heels. It burst into view, and my breath hitched. Suddenly, it was upon us.

A great blue dragon roared before ramming into the red at my back.

I skid to a stop, tumbling to the grass and turned as they collided, falling in an embrace of wings and claws. The blue took the red by the throat and bit down, scales cracking and splintering, teeth sinking into flesh. Fresh blood sprang to the air, followed by a roar. The red ripped themselves free, reared back, and drew in a crackling breath. The blue followed suit.

So consumed with the dragons, I barely registered the thundering earth until I turned, an army of silver surging past, rushing around me like a river before colliding with the armies at my back.

SIXTY-THREE
VENYX

A TORRENTIAL DEATH DANCE burst around me. I whipped my head around, seeking a way out, but there was none. The roar of dragons drew me back, planted me firmly on my feet, as they both drew a breath, but the blue was faster. A crackling bolt of lightning erupted into the red's mouth, the earth shuddering as the body collapsed.

I turned again. If there wasn't a way out, I'd make one.

Hoisting Seraph's limp body over my left shoulder, I drew a sword with my right hand. A faerie, yellow light blazing in her palms, landed in my path. I raised my sword to attack, but a massive blue head shot down before I had the chance, snatching the faerie in their teeth. One lingering scream was the only evidence the faerie had existed at all.

I nodded my thanks to the dragon, who barely acknowledged me, before moving on, and focused my attention on the surging battlefield.

From the thick, a White soldier charged forward, sword raised high. I batted the blade away, locked our weapons together and spun them, flicking the soldier's aside before I kicked him into the path of a charging, riderless horse. The soldier screamed before being trampled.

Chest heaving, I looked around. She couldn't hang upside down much longer. It'd only make her bleed faster.

I needed cover.

Whipping toward the red's carcass, ignored by the raging battle, I ran for it. Sword still in hand, I cut my way through the throng, downing soldiers along the way until the shadow of one wing fell across us.

I sheathed my sword and lay Seraph down as gently as possible, brushing the hair from her face. She was so pale. Blood coated her left shoulder, the mucked cloth sticking to her skin. For all points and purposes, she already appeared lost. Gritting my teeth, refusing to believe I'd failed, I leaned over her, listening for her heartbeat. Probed her neck and wrists for a pulse. It was there. Shallow. Weakening with every beat, but it was there. I nearly collapsed with relief, sending praise after muttered praise that she was still alive.

I kissed her forehead, her cheeks, her lips and went through the sodden strips of cloth, tightening them as best I could, trying to stanch the flow of blood, to keep her life in her weakening body.

At charging feet rushing toward me, I whipped around, jumped up, and drew both swords. The first White soldier went down within two strikes. The next two charged at once. Adrenaline coursing through me, I traded blows with each of them, swords bouncing and slashing from one to the other before finding home in one of their throats, then the other.

Breath ragged, I stepped back, wiped the sweat from my brow, and glanced over my shoulder, making sure she was still there. My ears strained, listening for that faint, precious pulse.

When I turned back around, a trio of horses galloped toward me. Fight still surging through me, I took my stance and hissed at them, my vision going red at the edges. As one, the three warriors slid from their horses and stepped forward, unarmed, the crest of Pensen glaring off their breastplates—a robed woman holding a scroll in one hand, a flaming torch in the other.

The one in the center, his armor edged in gold, stepped forward and removed his helmet, a mass of black curls falling around his bearded face. His free hand went up, keeping in my view. The other two lingered back, gazes flicking between me and Seraph, though they didn't dare come closer.

"Deymon Venyx?" the one before me asked. He edged across the bloodied ground. "My name is General Atani of the Pensian army. I am here to help." He pointed toward Seraph, hand still aloft. "Is she alive?"

"Yes," I croaked out, swords still clutched in my fists.

"I've come to take her to Pensen," the general said, taking another tentative step closer. "We can save her life. But you have to let me near her."

I glanced between the three, hissed through my teeth, and straightened, sheathing my swords. Glowering, I turned to Seraph and kneeled over her, my back facing them as I placed another kiss on her lips.

"Please forgive me," I whispered, touching my forehead to hers. "I *will* get you out of this."

So very gingerly, I picked her up, cradling her in my arms, and walked to the Pensian general.

Atani whipped his head around. "Call the dragon. Time is not on our side." One of the others ran off to do his bidding. He waved the other over and the soldier cautiously approached, eyeing me warily. "He will take her, just for a moment," the general said as I growled.

My gaze dropped to Seraph's face, and tears stung fresh in my eyes. I placed her in the soldier's arms and stepped back, forcing my vision toward the general as he reached into his breastplate. I knew what he was about to give me. But I didn't want it. Not anymore. Not at the price I paid to get it.

Thinking quickly, I reached into my back pocket and pulled out the book, glancing over the worn leather cover, and held it out. Atani's hand stopped.

"Give it to her when she wakes," I asked. "Please."

His eyes flicked from me to the book, wary.

"Please," I begged.

The general nodded once, took the book, and placed it in a pouch on his waist. And reached back in his breastplate for my damned payment. The thing I'd paid with Seraph's life for.

A tiny scroll.

With a trembling hand, I took it. Glanced from it to Atani to Seraph, and back to the cursed paper I now held.

"Pensen thanks you for your service," Atani said, though I didn't look up as I unwound the string binding the scroll. "By order of Prime Minister Patama, your pardon is granted. Your exile is lifted."

Blinding tears ravaged my eyes, blotting out the elegant script scrawled along the paper. Words I didn't need to read. I was free. I could go home.

My gaze flicked up as the soldier passed Seraph to Atani, and I wanted to give it back. Take her instead. But to take her was to kill her. So I crunched the page in my fist and stepped back, bowed my head, and let them carry her away. Swearing on my life I'd get her out.

No matter the cost.

Sixty-Four
Seraph

WARMTH ENVELOPED ME. CARESSED my face, swam in my hair. Softness cradled my body. My eyes fluttered open and snapped closed at the brightness above. Golden light filled my vision, percolated through my eyelids. I drew my brows together, tried again, and looked up.

As the bright, golden light faded, blue stretched above me. Soft. Like the sky.

Brows furrowing, I searched for the last thing I remembered, clung to the memory of being shot, of falling back, staring up at the stars. I had to be dead.

But as I came further into my body, pain ripped through my left side, bringing me into awareness.

Somehow I doubted being dead would hurt so much.

A groan rose from my throat, filled my ears, the room around me, as I tried, and failed, to push myself up. Somewhere to the side, someone gasped, followed by shattering glass, metal clanging to the floor.

"The Child!" a woman screamed, her voice becoming smaller and smaller, same as a pair of rushing footsteps. "The Child is awake!" In the distance, a door opened and slammed shut, sending shards of pain through my already pounding head.

Slumping against the bed, the fingers of my right hand, my good hand, found I was lying in a bed. I stared back up at the ceiling. The blue hanging above.

Not the sky, but a canopy. In the richest, softest blue imaginable. Strung with little beads and tassels swaying in the warm breeze. A breeze that smelled like...

The ocean.

The smell of salt and water lapped against the scents swirling about the room. Cinnamon, with something else. Something I couldn't place.

Leaning forward, I took stock of myself, where I lay. A rich swath of blankets covered me, the comforter atop a swirling mass of colors, vibrant and vivid. Beautiful. And soft.

Another groan and I shoved myself up, growling at the bolts of pain shooting through my left side. I grabbed my shoulder as I sat up, turning to investigate as the blankets fell away. I was dressed in a white, strapped gown, a bandage wrapped around my shoulder, down my bicep, and under my armpit.

As I sat, I took in more of the room. It was large. Larger still than the one in Siila. The floor, the walls, the ceiling, all white marble, blues and pinks and silvers swirled into its depths. Rugs covered the stone floor, similar to the blanket—vivid and vibrant. Lush with color. Tapestries hung on the walls. As did little lights. Tiny globes reminding me of the ones in the Braided Beard.

Venyx.

Shoving gingerly to my feet, every step as if I walked across glass, I glanced around. Through the massive open double doors of the bedchamber into the adjoining room beyond. A sitting room. A chaise and chair sat on one side of a low-sitting table, across from a sofa. Another door, closed, on the far wall.

Shuffling into the adjoining room, I expected to find him lounging on a piece of furniture. One of the many pieces. More chairs and tables dotted the corners. One sat beside a massive set of balcony doors, sheer curtains fluttering in the warm, oceanic breeze. Just beyond was the lulling roar of the sea.

I headed toward that sound, the smell. The call of water. And knew where I was.

Maybe he was outside. On the balcony. Reading a poem. Waiting for me to rise.

Behind me, the door opened before I got the chance to explore. I turned, regretting the motion as another jolt shot through me. My eyes widened at the woman who entered the room, her pale blue gaze meeting mine, matching my surprise.

Aurorian gaped, eyes roving me.

"You shouldn't be up," she said, breathless.

"Where's Venyx?" I asked, ignoring her.

Her gaze shifted left, then down. She opened her mouth, closed it again. And crossed to me without a word until her hands were on my good arm, leading me away from the balcony, back into the bedchamber.

"Where's Venyx?" I repeated as she ushered me back to the bed. "Where am I?"

"You're where you're supposed to be," Aurorian said matter-of-factly, as if she knew I knew. "It's not good for you to be up and moving. You've sustained a major injury. You need rest."

My gaze shot up to hers. "I've rested enough," I snapped. She reeled back, eyes going wide. "Where's Venyx?"

She sighed, her shoulders slumping. "It will be explained after you've rested."

I scoffed, whipped my head away from her, and bit my bottom lip, forcing myself to remain calm. I closed my eyes, damming the cascade of tears filling them. He was dead. It was the only explanation. He'd saved my life by giving his.

Somewhere to my left, far away, Aurorian droned on. Speaking of the war now raging across the Plains. The summoning of the World Council. Something about the Prime Minister, but I tuned it out.

My eyes slid open. Found the little table beside the massive bed. And the tiny book resting atop it.

My throat swelled.

Pushing past Aurorian, I dropped back to my feet and shuffled toward the table, the book. Venyx's book. One corner was saturated in bloodied mud, but it was whole. Intact. Swallowing the lump in my throat, I plucked it up and hugged it to my chest.

"It would be best if the Prime Minister explains about Venyx," Aurorian said, her words bringing me back. I turned around, staring at her.

"What?"

"It is a ... delicate matter, one you should hear from her." She sighed, fingering the end of the braid hanging over her shoulder. "Besides, she wishes to speak with you."

"Delicate matter?" I gaped, my fingers digging into the book. "That explains nothing, Auro—"

"I'll go let the Prime Minister know you're awake," she said, and left.

Her retreating footsteps faded. The cool stone vanished beneath my bare feet. Darkness edged my vision, spots swimming and blinking before my eyes. Inhaling, I breathed in the scent wafting from outside, absorbed the sounds. The gentle roar of water bursting against land.

When I came back to myself, I shuffled across the marble to the balcony doors, through the cascading curtains.

The stiff, ocean breeze rushed across me, through me. Tugged at my hair. Vanquishing the spots and darkness. Filled my lungs, my chest and heart. I breathed it in. Walked to the edge of the balcony, and gazed out.

Stretching endlessly in every direction, not a cloud in sight, was the sky.

Just beneath, filling the world from horizon to horizon, was the sea.

ACKNOWLEDGEMENTS

I am not entirely certain I've ever exercised as much patience and perseverance with anything as I have with the creation of this book. It was a labor of love, spanning two decades from inception to publication. And my list of people to thank is innumerable. So if I've forgotten you, it was not intentional.

My beautiful sister, Evie, for being one of my first beta readers, even when you didn't want to be. For all the times I went off on a tangent, describing some portion of the book, a quip about a character, some setting, none of which you had any idea about. For always supporting me and my dream. And always listening when I needed to get it out. For your love, even when I was impossible, and for fully accepting my world as is, and for always 'getting it.'

Mom, thank you for giving me the drive to pursue this, to stick to it, especially on the days it seemed impossible.

Chris, for launching me on the path to finishing this damn thing. You know what you did.

Aunt Brandy, for your tough love and insistence I follow my own path. For giving me somewhere to go in my toughest moment.

Joyce, for being the very first person to fall in love with Venyx, long before I ever did.

Hannah, there aren't words. But I'll do my best. For the late night (for me) conversations about plot twists and narcissists. For going over and over every line to make sure they were perfect. For reading and rereading and reading again this monster of a book and loving every moment of it. For believing in this book, the characters, and my vision, especially on the days I forgot how to. For helping me pull off Soft Miran Era, even if you thought my ambition was insane. For your guidance, your support, and your friendship. One day we will be on the same continent. At a writer's convention. Or a book signing. For all the one days ahead.

Kerri, I cannot imagine how this book would have turned out without your fierce guidance and belief in these characters. You are a force.

Rhea, for being my first alpha reader. The first one to give feedback on this monster project and helping me take that first step to perfecting it. For all the little quirks you caught that no one else did that really helped me 'see' this thing as it needed to be seen.

Rebecca, for crafting such a gorgeous cover and helping me visualize my creation. For putting such a beautiful face to my first book. Here's hoping we continue working together throughout the series!

Luan, thank you so much for bringing my world to life with your beautiful map! I look forward to the next one.

Danika—the first artist to help me visual my characters. There are no words. Except thank you. Here's to a long friendship, and partnership.

Mrs. Greico, for being my very first editor, and instilling in me the belief that someone would enjoy reading my writing.

Krystal, for believing in my worlds, and all the crazy characters in them. For being my very first fan. And for giving me my very first review.

To my extraordinary beta readers: Alyssa, Angelina, Alecia, Betty, and Marilyn. For taking the time, and taking a chance, to read my book, for letting me know how much you loved it, and all the ways it could be perfected. You were the very first people to read this thing (aside from me) so close to completion. Your love for this world, these characters, held my head up high on the darkest days leading up to publication. There are no words that will ever do justice for what you've given me.

A very special shoutout to Ariadne. For not only being on my list of amazing beta readers, but for believing so wholly in Seraph and her journey, and in Venyx, it renewed my love for them. Kept me moving forward when all I wanted was to give up. Thank you for sharing my posts on social media, for the likes and comments, for networking for me. For bringing me into Foundry, where I found my home. Thank you.

My amazing ARC readers, thank you for giving this baby author a chance. For helping me bring my book into the world with all the love and support I could ask for and more. And to my amazing Street Team, the Winged Sirens, for hyping me up and screaming to the world about this book—you cannot ever imagine how you helped me through the final months before publication.

Mark Martin, you will never know the inspiration you left me with. You brought Tollok to life, though it took me a while to realize it. May you rest in peace.

A shout out to the YouTube channel, Trailer Music Empire for powering me through draft three. Some of the most epic scenes in the book were written to the cadence of your videos.

To Margaret Weis and Tracy Hickman and the world of Dragonlance. For saving a fifteen year old girl and making her fall in love with fantasy. And for Tanis. Always for Tanis.

To Akira Toriyama, may you rest in peace. I am saddened we never got a chance to meet, but you gave me something I can never repay. The desire to use my voice.

ABOUT THE AUTHOR

Raised on a steady diet of sarcasm, fairy tales, Disney, and anime, K.M. Mohr has always been a storyteller. An avid reader of all genres, her true love is fantasy, with a dash of steampunk. When she's not reading or writing, you can find her at the movies, or sipping on a Frappuccino, regardless of the time of year. Though she grew up in Northern California, she now calls Seattle, WA home.

You can follow along with K.M. Mohr by subscribing to her newsletter, *The Daily Mohr*, on Substack for updates on her upcoming works, and for short stories and exclusive OSAS content.

Check her out on her socials—
@km.mohr.indieauthor
Instagram
Threads
TikTok